MW01034703

ENDORSEMENTS

"Mark E. Fisher soon had me immersed in the world surrounding the coming rapture of Christians as Earth's final days unfold. This realistic, edgy, and true-to-scripture drama will keep you reading and show you what your future holds."

Larry Orth, D.Min.,
Outreach Pastor and prophecy student,
Calvary Evangelical Free Church

"Every generation since Jesus left this world and gave the Holy Spirit to reside with us has wondered when the end will come and Christ will establish His full reign and all will be as God intended. Fisher presents a provocative and compelling contemporary narrative of our times alongside very thorough biblical prophecy and apocalyptic literature that makes one wonder as the disciples of Jesus asked before His ascension, "Will you now restore the Kingdom…?" The end of the book left me with great resources and in want of more of the unfolding story!"

Willie Grimm,
Interim Discipleship and Equipping Pastor,
Riverwood Community Church

"The Day the End Began is an engaging, up to date and believable account of what is coming! The portrayal of Davato as the anti-Christ was chilling, and the dynamics of the Turner family responding to the changing events kept me turning pages. But alas, the pages ran out. Now I have to wait for the next installment."

Charlie Meyer,
Pastor of Living Hope Church

THE DAY THE END BEGAN

DAYS OF THE APOCALYPSE, BOOK 1

MARK E. FISHER

Extraordinary Tales

Publishing

THE DAY THE END BEGAN: DAYS OF THE APOCALYPSE, BOOK 1 BY MARK E. FISHER

Extraordinary Tales Publishing
P.O. Box 6196
Rochester, MN 55903

First Extraordinary Tales edition March 2022

Print Book ISBN: 978-1-950235-12-4
EBook ISBN: 978-1-950235-11-7

Cover art purchased from 123rf.com
Interior Formatting and Cover Design by BookNook.biz
Editing by Deirdre Lockhart of Brilliant Cut Editing

Available in print from your local bookstore, Amazon, or https://bookshop.org/shop/ingramsparkbooks.

For more information about this and the author's other books visit: MarkFisherAuthor.com

Library of Congress Cataloging-in-Publication Data:
Fisher, Mark E.
The Day the End Began: Days of the Apocalypse, Book 1 / Mark E. Fisher 1ˢᵗ ed.

Printed in the United States of America

CONTENTS

PREFACE

The world is racing at light speed toward the end. No one knows the day or the hour, but most of the signs have been fulfilled. And after recent events, this author is convinced that God's judgment on a sinful, lawless world could come at any time—suddenly and without warning.

How many opportunities have this nation and the world been given to see the truth about God? Yet it has rejected and denied him. It has held fast to hard-hearted immorality.

The Bible tells us that, when a people refuse, again and again, to turn to God, he abandons them to their sins. As a result, the thinking of the people and their leaders becomes so twisted and insane, they declare that evil is good and good is evil. And when insanity rules, when wrong becomes right, when the spirit of the age embraces everything God abhors, all that is left for a perfectly holy God is to render judgment—in all his terrible wrath and power.

We see the proof of God's abandonment in the anarchy, moral chaos, and lawlessness now shredding the fabric of our society at breathtaking speed.

Thus, there is no more momentous story, and none more important for today's world, than the biblical account depicting the end of planet earth. Over a quarter of a century has passed since the Left Behind series went to print, and it's time for an updated vision of the end, one reflecting how recent events have set the stage for the coming of the Antichrist.

But this is a novel. And story, character, and reader interest must be paramount. So, my first goal in this writing is to bring the reader a gripping, compelling story, well told.

Yet be forewarned: If you adhere to the worldly values of the culture, worshiping at the altars of wokeism and political correctness, or if you are offended by the commands, values, and teachings given us by the God who created the universe, then this book is not for you. Do not buy or read this book.

Unless . . .

You honestly accept the challenge to consider that which opposes your worldview and, quite possibly, changes your eternal destiny.

In the process of telling my tale, I hope to take the predictions of the end-times events given us by the New Testament apostles and Old Testament prophets and bring their apocalyptic prophecies, as much as any flawed human can ever hope to achieve, to vivid, seat-gripping life. I hope to adhere to the general biblical outline, without adding to or subtracting from the basic predictions of the inspired biblical text.

Yet, by its very nature, a novel requires the author to speculate, to add fictional persons, scenes, events, and details. Some may object to the prophetic visions I've given to Margot Durand. But who's to say whether, in the end times, new revelations might not occur and to the most unlikely of recipients? The Bible tells us it may happen. Without speculations of that kind, our story might tread an all-too-familiar path.

There are, of course, different opinions on how to interpret the end-times passages. For this series, I have drawn upon my Masters of Ministry work, delved into the biblical apocalyptic literature, attended prophecy conferences, and followed the teachings of two great end-times scholars: Mark Hitchcock and John McArthur.

Proving that the Bible is true is beyond the scope of this writing. But it is my firm belief, based on science, logic, philosophy, and facts supported by physical evidence, that the Bible is, without question, true. The Christian Bible—written over some twelve hundred years by some forty different authors from many different countries, having many different occupations, ethnicities, and backgrounds, all of whom kept to a single, unwavering theme—such a work can be nothing but the revelation of an all-knowing, all-powerful, all-loving God.

I have tried not to be preachy. Yet my characters must, naturally, face the consequences of their belief or unbelief. And those who believe—some before and some after the Rapture—will at times try to convince those who do not. In this story and in our present world, the difference between believing and not believing is of eternal import.

Know also that this is a story of the supernatural and of the worlds beyond. As one character puts it: ". . . the gates of the underworld have been thrown open, and the forces of darkness have been loosed upon the world." So here you will find mortals caught in a spiritual, and sometimes physical, battle with demonic forces.

Some scenes take place in Heaven and in Hell. For these, I have relied first on the Bible, and second, on the real-life accounts of people who were pronounced dead, were taken to either place, were brought back to life, and then related what they experienced. Such incidents are called Near-Death Experiences, and I believe, when in agreement with Scripture, they were given to certain individuals as evidence of the afterlife for the purpose of convincing unbelievers and skeptics here on earth that the spiritual realms described by the Bible do, indeed, exist.

I warn the reader in advance for the chapter describing one character's journey to Hell. That chapter still haunts me. It was based on two different, first-person, near-death accounts of visits to Hell, of which there are few. Let it stand as a stark warning for God's judgment upon unbelief and apostasy.

Most hellish near-death experiences are so horrible, the participants suppress their memories of them. Note that what I have described is only one of three types of reported hellish experiences. It is *not* the second death in the lake of eternal fire—the final destination of the unredeemed after the Great White Throne Judgment.

To learn more about the biblical foundations informing this book, please see the Scripture References section at the end.

So read, enjoy, and take heed. . . .

The following events could occur suddenly, without warning, and if they happen in our lifetimes, every person on earth will face one of two destinies—

Either they will be transformed in the blink of an eye, taken up to live in the eternal, blessed presence of Christ, their souls overwhelmed with a love so great they'll have no words to describe it, their spirits overflowing with joy, happiness, and peace.

Or they will remain on earth to live through a time of terror, destruction, and judgment such as this world has never before seen.

P.S. For those who have enjoyed my historical fiction, both for the Christian and general market, I have not abandoned it. *The Sun Shines Even In Winter: A Novel Of Invasion and Espionage in World War I*, written for the general market, is coming soon.

Mark E. Fisher
Rochester, Minnesota
May 2021

THIRTY YEARS
BEFORE

CHAPTER 1
AN UNHOLY BIRTH

Naples, Italy

2 Thessalonians 2:3 (NLT): *Don't be fooled by what they say. For that day will not come until there is a great rebellion against God and the man of lawlessness is revealed—the one who brings destruction.*

When Giachetta Violante clutched the bundle to her chest and pushed through the hospital's back door, she triggered an alarm. But it wasn't the hospital authorities she feared. It was the thin-faced man with the scar on his cheek, the one calling himself Drago.

The warning clang followed as she hurried down the damp alley. A chill November breeze whipped her skirt about her legs, and she shivered. Walking quickly, she reached the street and sent a frantic glance in both directions.

Would Drago come for her today? Would he know when she took her baby home?

But of course he would know. Somehow—a shudder rippled down her spine—the League knew everything.

After merging with passersby on the avenue, she hailed a passing cab and gave the driver directions. But a block later, the Naples traffic slowed them to a crawl. Even at eight o'clock at night, Italians were still going places.

Staring through the back window, she expected to see him in a car behind. But all that stared back was the glare of headlights.

Two days after her new neighbor, Marzio, had raped her—a rape she'd never reported—thin-faced Drago forced himself into her apartment. But as she raced for the phone to call the police on the unknown intruder, he stopped her with a single sentence: "Giachetta, I know everything that's happened to you."

Stunned, she backed away, hands covering her mouth.

"The Marzio who forced himself on you was a thief." Drago's smile was smug. "He specialized in motorcycles. He sold black tar heroin and methamphetamine. He associated with Sicilian mobsters. And when he moved across the hall from you, he knew exactly who and what you were. He knew because we told him. Yes, Giachetta, and when he took you there on the floor, you treated him just like any other customer. You didn't fight him, did you? Then afterward, the Master came upon you in all his power and glory."

As he spoke, her heart beat wildly, and her eyes sought escape from her own apartment. But Drago blocked the way. "How do you know such things? There's no way anyone could know all that."

"The League knows everything. Now you bear Marzio's child, and when you bring him home from the hospital, we will come for him."

His answer crawled across her shoulders like a spider's legs across bare skin.

Then he was gone.

That's when fear took possession of her soul. For how could this Drago, coming from what he called The League, know such things? How could they know she was pregnant? And even if she was, what right did they have to take her baby?

The Master was surely the black and evil presence that had come upon her the moment Marzio had pulled away. And the shadow of his being had darkened her mind and enveloped her body in a way that still shook her with fear.

Before the Master came upon her, Marzio was standing with clothes in hand, a lustful smile curving his lips. But after the dark shadow had invaded every corner of the room, stark terror twisted Marzio's face, making his eyes wild and crazy. Naked, he fled across the hall and slammed the door shut on his apartment.

Later that night, using his own pistol, he shot himself in the head. And when the police came, she told them nothing. Then she huddled in a corner on her kitchen floor until dawn.

For the next month, she stopped receiving customers and withdrew from the world. Money appeared in envelopes, shoved under the door. She didn't question, for surely it came from the League. With it, she paid the rent, bought cigarettes, amaretto, a few grams of heroin, and even groceries.

Though she always took the pills to prevent the marks from getting her pregnant, somehow—just as Drago predicted—Marzio had given her a child, a boy she was told. Three times, she tried to destroy it, but whenever she headed for the abortionist, something happened. First, the clinic was closed. Then the taxis wouldn't stop for her. And when she finally arrived at the clinic, the line was so long, they told her to come another day. She planned to go again.

Eventually, she shook off the terror of that horrible night, and, feeling somewhat safe, she received her first customer. But the man she propositioned was a setup, and the police arrested her for possession and for violating article 5 of the Legge Merlin law for "soliciting in a scandalous manner in a hotel."

The rest of her pregnancy she spent in jail. Until a week ago when someone—they had to be from the League—arranged for her release. Last week, she returned home.

Two days ago, a taxi rushed her to the hospital. Then came birth pains so terrible, screams so intense, she thought she was dying. The doctors were worried, and after the birth, they sedated her and kept her overnight.

This morning, she'd parted the cloth, had a good look at her kid, and gasped. Never had she seen such a beautiful baby. That such a wondrous creature had come from her body, a body she'd abused so often and so long, was amazing. Then the child—her child!—had opened his eyes. He'd been born only yesterday, and already he opened his eyes! And when Davato's glance caught hers—for that most unusual name just popped into her head, unbidden—she'd been so mesmerized, so struck with wonder at the beauty and intelligence behind those blue orbs, she knew she could never give him up.

Now the taxi dropped her off in the busy street below her building, a three-story ancient structure with crumbling bricks long in need of repair. She paid the man, hugged her bundle close, and hurried past the graffiti, the discarded needles, the urine smell, and up the stone steps, dark with age and mold. Once inside, she locked the door.

She'd had only a week to prepare for her baby's arrival, and now she looked around for somewhere to put him. Her place had only two rooms—a kitchen with a table, and a room doubling as bedroom and living room. The bed would do, and there she laid him.

As she did, his little eyes opened again, fixing hers with a stare so uncanny and hinting of intellect, it unnerved her.

"Still, you are a cute little baby, Davato." She ran a hand across his cheek. "And I'm going to keep you. But tomorrow, we'll have to move. I'm not going to let anyone take you."

Glad to be home again, she breathed deeply, threw off her coat, and went to the kitchen. Grabbing a bottle of amaretto, she poured a glass.

She was taking her first swallow when the door slammed open, a door she'd just locked. Sloshing yellow-brown liquid, she dropped the glass on the counter then ran into the next room.

A grinning Drago stood between her and the bed, and her breath caught. Two figures wearing hoods entered the room behind him.

The first threw off a cowl, revealing a man of about forty, clean-shaven, with thinning white hair, pockmarked cheeks, and gaunt, hollow eyes that bored into hers.

"Y–you have no right to be here." Her voice wavered. "And y–you can't take my baby."

"Don't be difficult, Giachetta." Drago reached down to lift Davato from the bed. "Your child has a great future in store for him. But not with you."

Tears streamed down her cheeks. "You can't do this."

"We can, and we must, Signorina Violante." The older man spoke with words as smooth as honey. "We'll give him nothing but the best. Wealth and comfort. The best education in the best schools. When he's older, he'll drink the best wines, eat at the best restaurants, stay at the best hotels. We'll introduce him to men of power and influence, guiding him every step of the way. He will lack for nothing."

The woman threw off her hood, revealing mousy brown hair and a narrow nose. Ignoring Giachetta, she spoke to the man. "If the time is right, he could be the greatest leader the world has ever known. We've waited so long for this. Over two thousand years. The signs are all there. Could he really be the one?"

Scowling, the man raised a hand for silence.

Chastened, the woman faced Giachetta. "Your job is done, signorina. Don't stand in the way of your child's destiny."

Drago laid the baby in the woman's arms, and the smile that stranger rained upon little Davato sent a shiver down Giachetta's back. She took a defiant step toward them. "No. He's mine. You can't do this."

"But it's already done," said Drago. "And before we go, I have something for you." From his jacket pocket, he removed a black pistol.

As the metal thudded onto the wooden end table beside her bed, she stared at the weapon. "Why did you put that there?"

Grinning, Drago stepped toward the door. "I believe you'll need this after we leave. It's something you've wanted to do for some time, isn't it? This will help you fulfill your deepest desire." He waved at the couple, and they disappeared with her baby down the hall.

With one hand on the doorknob, Drago looked back. "Goodbye, Giachetta." The door shut with a click, and footsteps echoed away toward the stairs.

A bottomless well seemed to open before her, sucking into its depths all hope and joy and resolve. They'd taken her baby, and what did she have to live for now?

The same black terror she'd experienced when the Master had come before now crushed in upon her. From somewhere deep beneath the earth, a thick, swirling darkness boiled into every corner of the room. Icy fingers clutched her heart, squeezed, and she gasped. More than anything in the world, her shaking hands wanted . . .

To grab the gun.

To place the muzzle against her forehead.

And to pull the trigger.

FIFTEEN DAYS BEFORE

CHAPTER 2

MARGOT DURAND

Brussels, Belgium

Joel 2:28, 31 (HCSB): *I will pour out My Spirit on all humanity; then your sons and your daughters will prophesy, your old men will have dreams, and your young men will see visions . . . before the great and awe-inspiring Day of the Lord comes.*

Gripping the arms of the red velvet chair, Margot Durand sat rigid and expectant, her heart hammering before His Excellency, the Most Reverend Phillipe Bonheur, Archbishop of Brussels. For seven long minutes, the book-lined walls stared back at her, the wall clock ticked, and the archbishop flipped back and forth through her portfolio. Periodically, he set aside her traveling case with her collection of oil canvases. Then he'd peer again over his spectacles and page through her album stuffed thick with photographs of paintings she'd left at home.

But as a deepening scowl stretched the archbishop's heavy jowls, a cloud of doom seemed to gather about her.

Finally, he pushed back from the desk, smoothed his purple gown, and adjusted his glasses. He threw a wave at the desk. "How long have you been painting these so-called visions, mademoiselle?"

"Four years, Your Excellency."

"And in total, how many paintings have you?"

"Over two hundred."

His eyes widened, and his lips parted. "And where do you think they come from—these visions of yours?"

She swallowed. The archbishop wasn't reacting with the enthusiasm and awe her priest had. "Your Excellency, I believe they come fr–from God. But my father had the visions first. Only after he convinced me to start painting what he saw—only then did they also come upon me."

"First your father. And then you." The fingers of both hands, festooned with bejeweled rings, met in an arch, seemingly fighting each other. "And are you a faithful Catholic? Do you attend Mass each week? And go to confession?"

"Well, uh, since the visions, not as often as I should, Your Excellency. I now spend most of my time painting."

"I see. And your father—is he a faithful parishioner?"

She nodded.

The arch of his fingers collapsed. Briefly, he closed his eyes. "I do not know what to say, mademoiselle. When your priest brought this to my attention, I was skeptical. Such a case has never before crossed my desk. Now, having seen what you have painted, I am deeply troubled. And deeply worried for you, Margot Durand. And for your father and brother."

Her heart leaped hard against her ribs. "W–what are you saying? Do you not see what these paintings mean? The clear message they're telling us? The warnings, the—"

"I do see, mademoiselle, and that is what troubles me." He picked up one canvas and pointed. "This is a scene of destruction and carnage in our own city, is it not? Cars crashing. A plane diving into a building." He set that painting aside and chose another. "And this—fire and hail from a darkened sky, raining down on a populace fleeing in panic." Flipping through the pile, he chose a third. "Here we have a swarm of monstrous flying creatures with stinging tails attacking people hiding in a basement." He looked up. "These are horrific scenes out of Hell, meant to frighten, not inspire, people."

He chose yet another, peered closely, and stabbed a finger at it. "This poster behind the crashed vehicles, the one on the wall advertising this year's Expo." He raised both eyebrows. "By September first, those posters will be gone. Do you dare predict that these events will occur within the next two months?"

She swallowed. "I–I guess that's what it means. But I painted that one a year ago."

"Nonsense and falsehood." The archbishop dropped the canvases and sat back in his chair. "What is true, Mademoiselle Durand, is one of three things. First, either you are a deeply troubled young woman in great need of professional psychological help. Or, second, you expect me to put a stamp of approval on some nefarious scheme to make your family rich and famous. Yes, I have heard that all of this"—with eyes on fire, he picked up a newspaper and waved it—"made its way to your website and has gone viral. This article says thousands of people across the world are clamoring to buy your paintings."

He scanned the paper and read. "Luc Durand's weekly *Armageddon Blog*, with versions in three languages, now registers tens of thousands of hits each day from all over the world." His eyes narrowing, he frowned at her. "Do you deny this?"

She shifted in the chair. "No, Your Excellency. But my brother, Luc, put these out on the internet without my permission. I didn't even know what he was doing until people started calling us. And believe me, I have no plans to sell my paintings or even copies of them. But I am glad of one thing."

"What is that?" A sneer lifted one corner of his lips.

"That the world is finally seeing what I'm seeing. Because the visions came to me as a warning. And people need to hear and take heed."

"And who are you, an untrained parishioner, to judge what is a warning from God and what is not? Have you studied at seminary for three years? Are you an ordained priest, authorized by the Church to discern spiritual things?"

"N–no, I—"

"Of course not. And now you will hear my third explanation. Given the years this has obsessed you and the number of works you have created—and, I might add, extremely intense and frightening works, indeed—this option, I believe, is most likely the truth."

"W–what is that?"

"That you and your entire family have been possessed, not of God, but of Satan."

She gasped. "But how can you say such a thing? Neither I nor my father chose these visions. Father has always been a devout man. The visions came suddenly. They filled me with such a desire to paint them, I couldn't resist. I feel as if, through this art, God is calling me for some great mission." She clutched the arms of the chair until her knuckles hurt. "And people are moved by what I paint. One man even posted that, after seeing my collection, he converted to Christianity. Many are saying these are scenes from the book of Revelation, that they're warnings of a time to come, a time that's almost upon us. Your Excellency, do you not see that?"

"I do not, mademoiselle. The book of Revelation is obscure, and anyone can see anything they want in it." He collected the paintings and shoved them into her portfolio case. "I will tell you what I *am* going to do. The moment you leave, I will begin the process of excommunication for you, your father, *and* your brother. After today, none of you will ever set foot inside this cathedral again. This afternoon, I will put out a public statement declaring what the Church believes about this heresy, for that's what it is, mademoiselle—heresy. Perhaps that will take the air out of your internet notoriety. Your family's visions do *not* come from God, Margot Durand; they come from the Devil himself."

The archbishop's judgment was so sudden, unexpected, and harsh, it froze her to her seat. Her mouth opened, closed, opened again. "I—I don't understand." Tears streamed down her cheeks. "The visions are . . . from Satan?"

"I am certain of it." He crossed his arms.

"B—but, my sense of mission, my compulsion to bring these visions to the—"

"Even Satan can appear as an angel of light. There is nothing more to say." He shoved the case toward her. "Now please leave my office."

She stood and, with shaking hands, grabbed the case and turned toward the door. Through her tears, she could barely see the floor, but her feet carried her, echoing through the transept and down the vast corridor of the nave. After passing through the high wooden doors, she stumbled down the stone steps to the street. Out into a bright, sunny day.

How she got to the park, she didn't know. But when the bench appeared, she slumped onto it, laid her case beside her, and put her head in her hands. Then she sobbed.

People strolled past, staring, whispering to each other. Birds sang in the treetops. Out on the lawn, two children squealed as they kicked a ball between them. Indifferent to her pain, her failure, the world went on without her.

The archbishop must be right. For wasn't the Church the final arbiter of all things spiritual? Didn't the highest learned official of the Brussels church, not Margot Durand, possess the knowledge to decide what she was experiencing? Whenever she worked, when the brush brought new revelations to life, the desire to paint burned within her like some kind of possession, eating at her, driving her on, not letting her rest until she transferred her vision to canvas. And no sooner would she finish one piece than another obsession took its place. For four years, she'd been doing this. Now the highest ecclesiastical authority in the country had pronounced sentence, and, difficult though it was, she must accept it.

The verdict cut into her heart like a knife, but yes, she saw how it must be true. She had been possessed by Satan. And painting such vivid scenes of disaster, tragedy, and judgment—it wasn't helping, but misleading and frightening people.

Her body racked with sobs as another wave of grief ripped through her. Grief for being so stupid as to be misled. Grief for four, long wasted years. Grief for the loss of an obsession she'd come to enjoy, transposing vivid, albeit terrifying, dreams to canvas. And finally, grief for creating what the Church now considered works of the Devil.

Wiping her eyes, she raised her head to the sky. "Jesus, you let me work against you. Why oh why didn't you stop me? Are you even there?"

Head lifted, hands clasped tightly, she waited. But echoing back from the heavens came only . . . silence.

She lowered her gaze to the muddy, trampled dirt beneath her feet. Yes, her destiny was there, in the worlds beneath, not with the living above. If such worlds even existed. Gripping her head, shaking it side to side, she closed her eyes. Had God *ever* spoken to her? Or had it been Satan, masquerading as the Holy One to lead her astray?

Did any of them even exist?

Or had it all been a fantasy created by her foolish mind?

Even if she had another vision, she vowed—then and there—never again to take up brush, dip it in oil, and bring the future to life.

Then somehow, she sensed, as from a quiet whisper arising from the deepest recesses of her mind, that the visions had ceased and would not soon come again.

CHAPTER 3

THE TURNERS

St. Cloud, Minnesota

As the pastor gave Alice Fisher's eulogy, Dylan Turner squeezed his eyes shut, locking tears behind swollen lids. His aunt was the kindest, gentlest, most fun-loving, and intelligent woman he had ever known. Now she was gone.

Not only was her death tragic, it was also shrouded in mystery. She'd been racing north with a police car behind her, sirens wailing. Reportedly, she carried a child in the back seat. The first train had just left the tracks without crossing gates, and as Alice floored the accelerator, her car's front wheels touched the tracks beyond. Then came a second train roaring in from the opposite direction.

The child escaped with minor injuries.

Not so Alice. This was a closed-casket funeral.

But why was she running from the police? His aunt was ever law-abiding, honest, respectful of authorities. And who was this mysterious child? Alice was a widow, without sons or daughters, and living alone.

Nobody knew more than that. His family knew nothing about any child.

He raised bleary eyes to the casket. Its polished, knotty pinewood gleamed brightly, belying the grisly death—and the secrets?—contained within.

Seven years ago, Dylan had spent a summer with Alice Fisher at her cabin on East Gull Lake in northern Minnesota. That was after his uncle had died, shortly after Dylan had recovered from a long illness. In the two summers after that, his brother, Caleb, had joined them. During those halcyon days, the two brothers had grown closer to their aunt than they ever had to their parents. This coming September, the three even planned a two-week reunion—

With fishing. Biking. Canoeing. Rocking on the back porch, listening to the loon's haunting wail out on the lake. Hiking the nearby trails.

Reading together in the evenings before a crackling fire—she with her Bible, he and Caleb with novels from her vast collection. And of course, sitting at the dock's end, dangling their feet in the water, discussing life.

Only a month ago, he'd talked with her. There'd been no mention of a child.

"That was Alice Fisher's life"—the preacher's words snapped Dylan back to the present—"serving the church, helping the needy, bringing love to all in need, and worshiping her Lord."

On Dylan's right, Caleb sat grim-faced and rigid. Beyond Caleb, his mother, Kate, and his sister, Chelsea, sat red-eyed with Kleenexes in hand. On Dylan's left loomed his father, Adam Turner, CEO and founder of Turner Enterprises, a big supporter of atheist causes, and a lifetime opponent of everything Alice stood for. Father, of course, sat with crossed arms and a scowl.

The family hadn't been together since a Christmas almost eighteen months ago. Tonight, if Mother had her way and they gathered at his parents' mansion in Minneapolis for dinner, there'd be the usual emotional fireworks.

He wasn't looking forward to it.

"Alice knew the Lord Jesus, my friends." Dressed in a blue suit, the tall pastor had no trappings of religion dripping off him like some preachers. "We know where she's going, so let us grieve, yes, but with hope! For right now, she's in Heaven with the King of Kings, the Lord of light, the source of all love. And before we close, I'd like to read something Alice gave me two years ago to read at her funeral."

"Here we go," whispered Father, loud enough for the next row to hear. "Always the last to have your say, weren't you, Alice?"

Dylan shot him a look of impatience and again faced the front.

"I read from the book of Ephesians, chapter five." The pastor's head dipped to his text, brown hair slipping onto his forehead. " 'Imitate God, therefore, in everything you do because you are his dear children. Live a life filled with love, following the example of Christ. He loved us and offered himself as a sacrifice for us, a pleasing aroma to God.' "

Beside Dylan, Father shifted uncomfortably on his seat.

" 'Let there be no sexual immorality, impurity, or greed among you. Such sins have no place among God's people. Obscene stories, foolish talk, and coarse jokes—these are not for you. Instead, let there be thankfulness to God. You can be sure that no immoral, impure, or greedy person will inherit the Kingdom of Christ and of God. For a greedy person is an idolater, worshiping the things of this world.' "

As the preacher paused, his glance fell directly on Father. But the man who'd spent a lifetime creating the most successful security business in the country, possibly in the world, simply stared back.

Dylan suppressed a smile. Even in death—perhaps especially now—Alice tried to convince her atheist brother-in-law of the truth.

Father again leaned Dylan's way. "What did she ever do compared with my three-billion-dollar company?" he whispered. "Feeding a bunch of ne'er-do-well homeless panhandlers? Opening her home to every missionary pedaling false promises and foolish dreams to the gullible? And now we're stuck with her mortgage and her cat."

"Ssshhhh," came Mother's whisper from down the row.

The preacher's gaze returned to his text. " 'Don't be fooled by those who try to excuse these sins, for the anger of God will fall on all who disobey him. Don't participate in the things these people do. For once you were full of darkness, but now you have light from the Lord. So live as people of light! For this light within you produces only what is good and right and true.' " Pulling off his glasses, the preacher smiled.

"My friends, we live in trying times. We can choose to join either the sheep or the goats. Now the goats are taking charge, and for those who follow Christ, difficult days lie ahead. Alice chose to join the sheep, and because of that, she died."

Dylan sat up straighter. Did the man know something about Alice's death?

After setting the book aside, the pastor grabbed the podium, scanned the room, and settled his gaze again on Father. "If anyone here today does not know the Lord Jesus, I'll be available after the service to talk."

As Father again shifted in his seat, the worship band took the stage and led them in a song Dylan had heard once before—in his friend Blake's church in Oregon. The words lifted Dylan's spirit with a message that an all-powerful, all-loving God ruled over all. It reminded him that, though his aunt was gone from those she loved, she was now in Heaven.

At the luncheon afterward, the family sat together in a strained silence.

Chelsea munched on carrots and celery, carefully picked the ham out of her bun, and ate only the bread and cheese. Then she wandered to a far corner to talk to a distant cousin.

Mother picked at her food then abandoned the table, leaving Dylan with Father and Caleb. As she talked with her relatives across the room, she seemed to perk up.

Why didn't he know some of these people? Half of them were relatives on Mother's side, yet they never got together. Of course, none of Father's relations had flown in from "out East". Some past affront, real or imagined, kept that part of the family from ever interacting with their Minnesota kin. Or at least that's what Mother had once hinted.

Father waved toward where an animated Chelsea conversed with her cousin. "Why does she wear her hair like that? Her blonde hair used to be pretty. Now it's . . . pink and . . . frizzled."

"Curly, shaggy mullet, she calls it," said Caleb sitting beside Dylan. "It fits her."

"And why would she come dressed to a funeral in black jeans with holes in the knees, wearing a jeans jacket with zippers?"

"It's the style," said Dylan. "At least in New York. In some quarters."

"I don't understand her." Father shook his head. "She looks like a refugee from one of those apocalypse movies."

Dylan started drawing circles on his napkin. "Father, what happened to cause Alice to be fleeing from the police? That wasn't like her."

Brushing aside blond locks, Caleb raised gaunt eyes. "Good question."

Father scowled. "She was obviously in trouble with the police. Maybe she wasn't such a Goody Two-shoes after all?"

"I can't imagine her breaking the law unless she had a good reason." Dylan scanned the room, hoping to find the pastor and some answers. What he found instead was people laughing through their grief, happily getting reacquainted. He faced his father. "Why don't we grieve like these people? They seem to have a joy we do not."

"Don't you know?" Caleb gave a lopsided smile. "We're damaged goods. We're children of the great Adam Turner, and we aren't capable of feeling like other people."

No longer feeling that way about himself, Dylan ignored his brother's comment.

"I'll not deign to answer that." Father's jaw was set, and his lips tightened. "I'm your father, and you will show me some respect." He stood and crossed the room to his wife.

Dylan also rose, following his father, circling the room's perimeter, looking for the pastor. He found the man leaving a conversation in a far corner, just heading for the door. "Excuse me, sir?"

"Yes?"

"I'm Dylan Turner, Alice's nephew. She and I were close, and I'm wondering if you could tell me what you meant when you said she'd chosen the path of the sheep and that's why she died?"

His eyes narrowing, the tall preacher examined him from head to toe. He nodded then led Dylan to an empty table where they sat. "I remember your summer visits many years ago. You have a right to know."

"Thanks." He wiped strands of brown hair from his forehead. "But who is this child everyone's talking about? We knew of no child."

"Her name was Christina, she was six years old, and Alice was trying to adopt her."

Dylan gasped.

"Yes, it was all very recent. She'd heard about a family of missionaries murdered overseas, and the missions agency sent the orphaned daughter to Des Moines where the family once lived. But no close relatives would take her. The state then placed Christina in a foster home and put her up for adoption. Alice was touched by the story, and she drove down to meet the child. The two spent many long weekends together, getting to know one another. Alice told me that Christina was taken with her and desperately wanted to live with her."

"What child wouldn't?"

"Exactly. Anyone who knew Alice would agree. They made a home visit to check out her home, and everything seemed on track for adoption." The pastor's smile fell. "But then came the questionnaire and a problem with how she answered a question."

"What question?"

"When Christina reached the age of ten, if the child decided to change her sex, would Alice agree to the operation? Of course, she answered no. And because of that, they stopped the process."

Dylan sat back, his mouth open. "That's insane!"

"Criminally insane. It seems, in the State of Iowa today, one must agree to insanity before one can adopt."

"But why was she fleeing the police with the child in the back seat?"

"She was ready to give in and let the state have their way, but then she heard they were going to give Christina in adoption to a homosexual couple. Against my advice, she drove down, stole the child from the foster home, and was bringing her up here."

"So that's why she was fleeing the police."

"They caught up with her only a few miles south of here."

Closing his eyes, Dylan rubbed his temples. "The goats *have* taken over, haven't they?"

"I'm afraid they have, Dylan. And someday, they will reap a terrible judgment for what they are doing." The pastor stood and extended his hand. "I must be elsewhere this afternoon, but it was good speaking with someone who understands. Some who've heard the story—some here in my own congregation—think the state had a right to do what they did. But in this case, God's laws supersede the state's."

Dylan shook the pastor's hand then returned to the table and Caleb. When he repeated Alice's story to his brother, an incredulous Caleb closed his eyes. "What is happening to us, Dylan?"

"It couldn't get much worse, could it?"

Before they could comment further, Father returned to the table, muttering that they were stuck here until the women were done visiting. That stopped their discussion.

* * *

As ADAM TURNER DROVE HIS Mercedes Benz A-Class sedan down Interstate 94 toward Minneapolis, a cloud of silence enveloped the family. He alone seemed relieved that they'd left the church. But when Chelsea snapped at his every utterance and his sons refused to engage in conversation, he fell silent. To ease the tension, he switched on the satellite radio, catching the news.

"Today, delegations from the Palestinian, Israeli, and Arab worlds will join US and Russian representatives in Geneva for peace talks. The conference leader, a man known simply as Davato, the UN Assistant Secretary-General for Political and Peacebuilding Affairs for the Middle East, is not due to arrive for several days. Many have high hopes that Davato can break the stalemate and bring opposing parties to a resolution. Others aren't as optimistic. For decades, the Palestinians have been adamant that the Israeli state is illegitimate, that they will not negotiate with an Israel that has—"

"Turn it off," said Kate beside him. "I don't want to hear more bad news today."

Adam punched the button, killing the announcement. "Sorry. Did you tell the cook we're on our way?"

"I did." She threw a glance at their children in the back seat. "Tonight, I want all of us to eat together. It will be the first time in a year and a half we can all sit down at the same table as a family."

"How about let's not?" said Chelsea. "I want to look up some friends from school."

"Me too," added Dylan.

"Not tonight." Adam gripped the wheel tighter. "Your mother needs our support at this time, and for once, we're going to eat together. Also, I have something important to say to Dylan and maybe you, Caleb, something that could dramatically affect your futures."

"Dear." Kate laid a hand on his arm. "Do we have to do this tonight? Can't we just have one nice family meal together? A meal without issues?"

"No. They'll soon be off to New York or Italy or Chicago or wherever it is they go to escape their family, and I want to get this out of the way."

"Then by all means"—Caleb's mocking tone grated—"let's get the thing out of the way."

Adam twisted his fingers over the wheel. His own children had no respect for him. Well, tonight, when he presented his sons with the proposition of a lifetime, perhaps that attitude would change. Yes, surely it must.

He pushed the cruise control up another five miles an hour faster.

CHAPTER 4
A FAMILY DINNER

Minneapolis, Minnesota

In the formal dining room of the Turner mansion, Dylan's hands grasped the velvet-cushioned chair and pulled it closer to his plate. The only sounds came from a ticking antique clock down the hall and a jet passing overhead. An expanse of lawn outside ensured that any sound from a noisy neighbor would die in the distance. In the Turner clan, one must never get too close to the hoi polloi.

Dylan watched his mother lower her fork and smile in his brother's direction. "What are you working on right now, Caleb?" She was trying to make this family dinner pleasant and without argument. Wouldn't that be a first?

"I finished my novel and gave it to a friend to critique. But now, I'm working on my new blog. It's called *The Real Truth*. I've already got quite a following. Nearly two thousand hits a day."

"*The Real Truth?*" Dylan shot his brother a quizzical look. "The truth about what?"

"Wherever there are lies, my blog will ferret them out. When I get back, perhaps I'll write about how some of America's largest corporations have become enemies of democracy by censoring anyone who disagrees with their politics. None of them have the backbone to resist the demands of the radicals. They've utterly lost their souls."

"What are you talking about?" Father dropped his knife. "There's no such thing as a corporate 'soul'. Even if there was, you can't say we're enemies of democracy."

"No, I agree with Caleb." Chelsea smiled at him. "Corporate America has lost its soul. It's rotten to the core."

Caleb nodded in his sister's direction.

Father rolled his eyes to the ceiling. "Don't I hire gays and blacks and vegetarians and even Republicans? Don't I contribute to your causes, Chelsea? How does that make Turner Enterprises rotten to the core?"

"You don't get it." She grabbed her glass of wine. "It's all about the oppressors and those they oppress. Rich versus poor. Those in power versus those without. And the big corporations are the worst offenders of all."

"She's talking about *us!*" His voice rising, Father spoke to Mother with an upraised hand.

"So what is *your* solution?" asked Dylan of his sister.

Her face reddening, she saluted with her wine glass. "Throw them all out and start over."

"Then I suppose *you'll* be in power." Father's voice broke with a hint of laughter. "And then, of course, things will be much better."

"I can see it now." Caleb waved both hands over the table and laughed. "Chelsea the Great and her anarchist friends, trying to rule America without destroying it."

Dylan struggled to keep a straight face. Tonight, his sister was over the top.

"Make fun of it as you will." She slammed her glass down. "But we're going to tear everything down and start over from scratch!"

What was up with her this evening? Even earlier on the ride home, she seemed on edge. Now she was strident, spouting opinions too radical even for her. At least, he *hoped* they were too radical for her.

Father rubbed at his temples then smoothed his hair. "Enough of this." He pushed his plate away. "It's time for a family discussion and a serious proposal I'd like to make to my sons. First, to you, Dylan."

Oh no. Here it comes. He cocked his head, the perfectly charred steak churning in his stomach. "What kind of proposal?"

"Son, you've been adrift. At twenty-four, you haven't settled into a career or even finished a degree. You're wandering from city to city, country to country, without friends, except the ones who invite you to parties. You've got your trust fund, yes, but have you ever earned a dime on your own? You're chasing one foolish idea after another, with no purpose to your life, doing nothing productive. And I—"

"That was in the past. I've changed." His neck muscles tensing, he focused on his empty plate and its gold-embossed edges. Should he drop his bomb now? Or should he wait?

"Yes, but tonight I'd like to offer an alternative, one I hope you'll consider."

"What alternative?" He set his jaw. Every time Father proposed an "alternative", as he called it, another agenda was behind it. His fingers closed about the arms of the chair and tightened.

"An executive position with Turner Enterprises. You won't even have to start at the bottom. You'd be working directly under me, watching me as I run the company, as I—"

"No." He brushed aside his bangs. "You can forget that idea. I'll never work in some corporate office. Beside you or anybody else. The very thought makes me nauseous."

"You won't get such a chance anywhere else."

"I don't care." His face growing hot, Dylan forced himself to meet his father's gaze.

The man peered back, unspeaking, unblinking, then gave a sharp nod. "Is there nothing I can do to change your mind?"

"Nothing."

Father closed his eyes and rubbed his forehead. Opening his eyes again, he turned to Mother. "What did I do to deserve this? Legions of young men in my organization would die for an offer like this."

"I know, dear." She filled her wine glass again and drank. "But he's not interested."

"There's something else you need to know." Dylan took a deep breath. Now was as good a time as any. "My life has changed dramatically since last we met. I–I've become a Christian."

Caleb gasped, Father's jaw hung open, and Mother's brow twisted in puzzlement.

"Aren't they the ones causing all kinds of trouble right now?" Chelsea tilted her head.

"You've been listening to the lies spread by big media and big tech. Christians are against the woke agenda—or at least they should be—but only because it violates every command of Jesus."

"When did this happen?" Father turned a stunned expression on him.

"For the last three months, I've been with Blake at his cabin in Oregon, going to church with him and studying his Bible. Two weeks ago, I was baptized." He faced his brother. "Caleb, it's true. The Bible is really true. And the Jesus who came to earth over two thousand years ago was really the Son of God."

"So you fell for Blake's line, hey?" Blake was their college friend, now a ski instructor and mountain guide. But hard as Blake tried to convince Caleb of his faith, Caleb just wouldn't be moved.

"It's not some line." Dylan gripped the chair again. "If you're interested in truth—there it is."

"I thought we'd purged all such nonsense from our children." Father shook a fork at Mother then pointed it at Dylan. "This just proves what I said earlier—you're adrift with no anchor, with no serious goals in life."

"On the contrary, for the first time in my life, I've found an anchor that's real, that will hold fast no matter what. And I'll tell you something else—after studying and reading the entire Bible, I think we're long overdue for the end."

"The end of what?" Father raised an eyebrow.

"The end of the world as we know it." Dylan swallowed.

Caleb guffawed, Mother shook her head, and Chelsea tried on a silly grin.

Father's fork clattered onto his plate, and he peered at Dylan as if a homeless beggar had just entered the room.

By their reactions, it was a mistake. He should never have told them. But after looking hard at the world around him, he knew, deep in his heart—the human race was long overdue for a divine reckoning.

"This is even worse than I thought." Father drew a hand through his hair. "You've gone beyond aimless drifting. Now you've been taken in by lunatic fairy tales."

Shaking his head, he turned to Caleb, who started twirling the thin gold chain he always wore around his neck.

"What about you, son? Unlike your brother, you finished Carleton and graduated. I had high hopes you'd make something of yourself. So you finally finished that literary novel you were working on?"

"Yes, and a friend of mine, a famous novelist actually, is reading it right now."

"Who, dear?" Mother's gaze lifted from her glass to Caleb.

"Uri Baranov."

Her eyes widened. "Why, I've read some of his books. He *is* famous, and his books are *very* good."

"He's a dinosaur." Chelsea stabbed her last bit of broccoli with her fork. While everyone else ate steak, she was munching only on vegetables. "An old codger with outdated ideas."

"No, sister." Caleb narrowed his eyes at her. "He's a great man."

"We're getting off the subject." Leaning forward again, Father focused on Caleb. "I've looked into it, and novels like that simply don't sell. There's no future in it. And you've never published anything."

Dylan dropped his gaze to his empty plate. Why did Father always have to denigrate every goal, every independent idea coming from his children?

"So what?" Caleb sat up straight. "It's where my heart is. I must be true to that, not to the god of Mammon. And my blog is drawing in thousands of eyes each day. I can bring the truth to the world through that. It will be a springboard for my novels."

"Truth?" Again, Father rolled his eyes. "What do you know of truth? I'll tell you what's true—building a worldwide enterprise that employs tens of thousands, creating a company that might soon join the DOW, and putting out a product in demand by hundreds of corporations and dozens of countries."

"And it's a company with products used to control and spy on people." Chelsea crossed her arms, her gaze too intense, her lips pulling back as if she were about to bite someone. "Your product, as you call it, is—"

"Stop!" Father smacked the table with a palm. "We've been through this, and you'll not criticize my company. But I'm talking to Caleb now." He closed his eyes and drew a deep breath. "Caleb?"

"Yes?"

"What if I offered the same to you—an executive position at my side at Turner—"

"No!" In imitation of his father, Caleb smacked the table. "I've told you my goals, the writing I'm passionate about, and—no! Working for Turner Enterprises is not going to happen. Not in my lifetime."

For long moments, as Caleb returned their father's stare, Father's stern demeanor seemed to wilt. Again, he closed his eyes and rubbed his forehead. When he opened them, he fixed his gaze on Chelsea. "What about you, daughter?" But now his voice had lost much of its aura of command as though he knew the answer before he even asked. "Would you consider the same offer?"

"I'm happy . . . with my job at Cool Green Planet." But she spoke with effort, as though—finally!—she was trying to restrain herself. "How can you ask such a thing of me? You know how much I've worked against what corporate America stands for." Her face reddened. "The answer is . . . no."

Again, Dylan detected too much fire in her voice. But at least she was trying to moderate her passion.

"You have all the skills we need—research expertise, web design, marketing."

"No, no, and no, again. And I would never leave New York for a job in Minneapolis. Cool Green Planet is considering me for a post in their new Rome office. I've always wanted to work in Rome."

Father's shoulders fell, and he nodded. His gaze swept the table, landing on each of them. "So this is what it's come to? All of you going your separate ways, giving up the opportunity of a lifetime to work beside your own father in one of the most successful companies in the world? I don't understand this. I never will."

Dylan pushed back from the table. "If this is over, I'll be going."

"Me too." Without waiting for Father's reply, Caleb stood and headed for the door.

Chelsea followed.

Outside in the hall, Dylan stopped her before she left the house. "What's wrong, sis?"

She froze, locked gazes with him, then shrugged. "Nothing."

"No, I agree." Caleb exchanged glances with him. "Something's wrong. You can't hide it from us."

Her gaze swept from one brother to another. Then, as tears came to her eyes, Dylan stepped forward and hugged her.

"What is it? What's wrong?" he asked, his voice low.

"Nothing." She pushed away, wiped her eyes, and again started for the door. "I've got to go. I've got a girlfriend to look up."

After the door slammed behind her, he turned to Caleb. "What was that all about?"

"Yeah. Something's up with her. I've never seen her so worked up."

"I'm worried about her. But if she won't talk about it . . ."

Caleb shrugged.

"To change the subject—are you going on the Mt. Hood climb next week? It will be great getting up on the mountain. Blake will guide us."

"Blake?" Caleb smiled. "Sure, count me in."

"Good. I'm flying back to Oregon tomorrow. I've got a lot of studying to do before next week."

"The Christian thing again?"

"Of course." Dylan winked. "For the first time in my life, something has brought me peace. Real peace. You should look into it. But I'll see you there. Bring your gear."

"Is it safe to fly into Portland now? Have the riots stopped?"

"The National Guard has the airport well-secured. Driving to the mountain isn't a problem."

CHAPTER 5

THE AUTHOR

University Village, Chicago

Colossians 2:8 (HCSB): *Be careful that no one takes you captive through philosophy and empty deceit based on human tradition, based on the elemental forces of the world, and not based on Christ.*

The next day, Caleb drove back to his upscale apartment at University Village where the burly armed doorkeeper let him in. The following morning, he walked out his door, turned left down the hall, and crossed thirty feet of marble tiles. He knocked on the apartment belonging to Uri Baranov and his granddaughter.

The author brushed back a white mane and bid his young friend to enter. "Back from family duty, hey?" His weathered, chiseled face and tall, muscled build belied his seventy-five years. "How'd it go?"

"Exactly as expected." Caleb sighed. "Badly."

The author's black-and-white miniature Australian shepherd, Nika, lifted both paws to Caleb's knee and licked a hand.

But as he followed Uri into the living room, an unfamiliar man rose from a chair. "Caleb," said Uri, "this is Sergei, and last night after we talked about old times back in Russia, he spent the night."

Sergei nodded, but his face appeared haggard, his frame bent, and his thin white hair unkempt. Yet the man's piercing brown eyes—with a hint of bloodshot—held a sharp, wary look, as if everything crossing his vision were examined in great detail.

"Thank you for vodka," said Sergei, "for breakfast and company. But now I go." He exchanged kisses on the cheek with Uri then left.

As Uri resumed his seat on a wooden rocker, Caleb removed a stack of books from a leather easy chair and joined him. The smell of old cigar smoke mixed with the must from the books.

"Sergei's about ten years younger than me," said his host, "but we're old friends. Last night we spent time over a bottle of vodka. One thing to know about Sergei—if you want to be on his good side, you must join him over vodka. Anyway, it was late, and—how can I put this?—Sergei likes his drink. I, of course, didn't drink nearly as much."

"So he says." Tanya, wearing a blue jean jacket and ripped jeans, entered from another room. As she flicked strawberry blonde hair over one shoulder and leaned her lanky body against the doorframe, he waved a hello. She nodded in reply. "But last night, Uri couldn't have walked a straight line if his life depended on it."

Her grandfather waved her off. "Even Jesus ministered to prostitutes and tax collectors."

"Yes." She winked at Caleb. "What he did last night was *ministry*. Coffee, Caleb?"

"Yes, please." He shot her a smile. How many times had he intended to ask her out, but didn't have the guts to do it? Only a year or two younger than he, she was the second—or was it the first?—reason he so enjoyed his visits to Uri's place.

Uri leaned forward in the rocker with his hands on his knees. "Sergei once worked for the Russian FSB. But he ran afoul of higher-ups, and they imprisoned him in Chelyabinsk, a hellhole if ever there was. After I flew there and bribed his way out, he's been forever in my debt. We've become good friends."

"He was a Russian intelligence agent?"

"Yes, and now I'll take you, as a good and dear friend, into my confidence. Sergei is not his real name. Once we got him into the US, the CIA got their hooks in him, and for a time, he worked for this country. But again, he angered his superiors, they accused him of some crime he didn't commit, and ever since, he's been in hiding. You wouldn't know it to look at him, but Sergei is an expert in forgery, assassination, and he can penetrate nearly any security system or network in the world. He's got quite a setup somewhere in the city, away from his apartment, with all the equipment. He does occasional odd jobs that pay him quite well, indeed."

Caleb whistled.

"He has a lot of sins needing forgiveness. Someday, he'll turn to the Lord."

"That would take a miracle." Tanya brought Caleb his coffee with the milk already in it then sat across from the two men. "I'm glad you came, Caleb. Besides the reprobate who just left, you're the only other like-minded soul who can put up with him."

Caleb grinned, sipped his coffee, then waved at the manuscript on the nightstand beside his host. "Did you read it?"

"I did. All three hundred and fifty pages." Nika padded over to Uri and curled up beside him on the floor. "It needs a bit of editing, but on the whole, I like it. It's good. To spare no adverbs, it's actually very good. There is, however, one serious problem with what you've written."

Caleb leaned forward, his heart racing. That this most famous of all authors would declare his work "actually very good" was more than he could hope for. But there was always a "but", wasn't there? "What's the problem?"

"With the characters you've got and your conservative storyline, no one will ever publish it."

"Why not?" His stomach churned, and his hand went to the gold chain wrapping his neck.

As Uri grabbed a cigar from the counter and struck a match, Tanya scowled, but he ignored her. "You and I have the same problem, my friend."

"What's that?" Caleb leaned forward in his seat.

"Why do you think"—Uri puffed on the cigar—"no one will publish anything I've written in the last ten years?"

"I don't know."

"Outside the shrinking market called Christian fiction, a market mostly devoted to romance, the gatekeepers have abandoned the search for good literature." He blew smoke to the side. "The ranks of the book agents and publishers' acquisitions departments are now filled with young, progressive idealists. Having little or no understanding of history and bursting with radical idealism, they think all literature must support their personal political leanings. And in these times, if any of them expresses a view apart from the rest, they are ostracized and marginalized. Their careers are essentially 'canceled'.

"Yes, Caleb, their goal seems no longer to entertain, but to remake society. They want only manuscripts that check boxes on their political scorecards. Thus, my friend, do we both find ourselves on the wrong side of the culture."

"My book isn't that conservative." He grabbed the arms of the chair, his fingers tightening. How many weeks and months had he spent writing it? How many nights jumping out of bed to write down a sentence or two to make it better? Was Uri saying it would languish in oblivion?

"Neither does it promote a radical progressive agenda, and that's now what they're looking for. But the problem goes far deeper than publishing. Under the leadership of today's ruling elites, everything is political, and politics itself is spiritual." He waved his cigar toward Tanya. "She doesn't believe in God, Caleb? Did you know that?"

"No, I—"

A knock sounded on the door, and Uri rose to answer it.

It was Sergei. "Sorry, I forget package. Come with me to car."

"What package?" Uri's voice showed puzzlement.

"Come." Sergei waved. "Then you see."

Uri turned back to the room, rolled his eyes, and left Caleb alone with Tanya.

This was his chance, wasn't it? His big chance to ask her out. But instead of coming out with it, he dropped his gaze to the floor, and one hand grasped the other. "So what do you like to do with your free time?" *Lame, Caleb. Lame.*

As though expecting him to say something else, she cocked her head. "I help out at the food pantry on Saturdays. I read a lot. And of course I ride my bike."

"Oh yes, I've seen you out riding. I ride too, you know." He swallowed.

"Yes." A sly smile curled one side of her mouth. "I've seen you bringing your bike up the elevator."

"Yes." He sucked in air. Uri could return any minute, and the moment would be over. He needed to come out with it. For one moment, his eyes locked with hers. But again, panic gripped him, and his gaze shot toward the window. He swept a hand through his hair then forced his eyes to again lock with hers. "Tanya?"

"Yes?" She leaned forward in the chair. "Yes, Caleb, what is it?"

"Would you"—he swallowed—"would you consider going out to dinner with me?"

Smiling, she sat up straighter. "When?"

His heart beat faster. "Tonight?"

"Oh." One hand went to her mouth. "I'm sorry, but I've got a date tonight."

He closed his eyes and dropped his gaze. She was just saying that to put him off, wasn't she?

"But wait." She reached into her jeans pocket, pulled out her phone, and dialed. Looking up again, she smiled. "Maybe I can change it."

Hope rose as did the heat on his brow.

Someone answered her call, and she walked to the window, out of earshot. She was still talking when the door opened, and Uri reentered, followed by Sergei.

"I don't want your gun." Waving a hand and frowning, Uri seemed agitated. "I've got one already."

"You need unregistered gun." Sergei carried something wrapped in brown cloth. "One day, government come, take away registered gun. All governments the same. You need secret gun."

Tanya returned from the window with her phone in her pocket. But Caleb couldn't tell from her expression what her answer might be.

"You're paranoid." Uri whirled back to his friend. "I'm a Christian. What am I going to do with a gun? Shoot someone?"

"Sometimes, da. Is either you or them. Totalitarian peoples all the same. Want all peoples to think alike. Socialists all the same. Someday, they come for you. Especially for Christians. Is true." He unwrapped the cloth, revealing a black pistol. His eyes pleading, he extended the weapon toward Uri.

Uri's gaze focused on the gun then on the Russian. "Will it really come to this? Will I someday have to defend myself against such madness?"

"New political peoples like Communists in Russia. Always know better than everyone else. The camps, the knocks on door at midnight—they come. Then you see." Holding the gleaming black metal, he took a step toward his friend. "Take it."

Uri's eyes fixed on the hunk of black metal. Then his glance sought Sergei's. "But it's a weapon of death."

"Your death?" Sergei's bloodshot eyes pleaded. "Or theirs. Your choice."

CHAPTER 6
WARNINGS

University Village, Chicago

Caleb shifted in his seat as the Russian brought the gun across the room to Uri. "When crazies come to door, what happen to Tanya, da? Better they die, not you, not her." His free hand landed on Uri's shoulder. "I say this as good friend."

"All right." Uri sighed, received the weapon, then set it on the end table with a heavy clunk. "Now you might as well sit while Caleb and I continue our conversation. It applies to what we were just discussing."

"I stay only little bit." Sergei pulled up a wooden chair then turned to Caleb. "Beware, friend. Give him audience, and he is college professor." He winked.

"If that isn't the truth." Tanya sat next to Uri, and Caleb looked for any hint of what she'd decided. But her gaze was on her grandfather.

Uri reached for another cigar, lit it, and puffed. "Before you came, I was telling my young friend here why no one will publish his book. His novel is a love story, but it's also about a man struggling with the evils of the socialist revolution in Ukraine in World War I."

His eyes lighting up, Sergei nodded with approval toward Caleb. "Good. Socialism worst government ever."

Caleb's glance kept going to Tanya, hoping for a hint of whether she'd go out with him or not. But she seemed oblivious of the painful anticipation gripping his heart.

"As I was saying, our society is racing toward destruction, and the publishing world only mirrors what's going on everywhere else. Even though they run screaming in horror from the Bible, the elites in charge think they have exclusive knowledge of what sin is. But the Evil One has twisted their God-given sense of morality one hundred and eighty degrees, and they've got everything backward. In their eyes, good is now evil, and evil is good."

"Da, Uri. These peoples all the same. Socialists. Communists. Woke peoples. All the same. Turn good things into bad." Sergei's pleading glance wandered toward the kitchen, stopped on Tanya, and he lifted one hand in a question.

Tanya shook her head. "Forget it. I'm not giving you vodka this early in the morning."

Chastened, Sergei dropped his gaze to the floor. "Da. World is upside down. And Tanya is hard mistress of her kitchen."

Chuckling, Uri snapped his fingers, and Nika ran to his open hand. He rubbed behind her ears. "Upside down, indeed. The ruling dogma has become so absurd, it now insists people can choose, regardless of how they were born, whether to be a man or a woman. It's the absolute definition of lunacy. I ask you: In what other era or past society has human reasoning ever become so perverted, twisted, and opposed to God's will? If we continue this way, it will be the end of civilization itself. And perhaps that is their goal—to destroy the existing order." He tapped away the ash then fell silent as he focused on his cigar.

Sergei slapped a hand against his knee. "Same in Russia with Communists. Every good thing they destroy. No food at market. Nothing on shelves. Midnight knocks on doors."

"But, Sergei"—Uri sent a cloud of smoke toward the ceiling—"I know you don't believe, but the worst part about this is that they've abandoned God. Every country on earth is now working against God's will. The insanity, the iniquities, the rebellion of the human race are approaching a peak. What if God will no longer tolerate it? What if he has already passed judgment and abandoned us to our sins? Then the Apocalypse is just around the corner."

Startled by Uri's declaration, Caleb shot him a glance. Here he was, worrying about getting a date, wondering if his book would ever be published, and Uri was talking about the end of the world. A shiver raced down his spine.

"Nyet, I see no God anywhere." Sergei leaned back in the chair. "Where is he in Chelyabinsk when they bring cattle prod, dump ice water on naked body? Where is he with peoples in gulag? Nyet. There is no God."

"You're wrong, Sergei. There is a God, and when the world turns away from him, he abandons them."

"Nyet." Scrunching his face, Sergei rose from his chair. "You and your God again. I agree world is changing. Woke peoples like Communists. Bad times are coming, da. But enough talk. I must go. Is now good you have unregistered gun. In new world, when they come for old weapon, you have protection against the crazies. Is like old Soviet Union now. Someday, they come at midnight. Then you see. You use gun. Or they take you to camps."

Sergei's warning sent another shudder across Caleb's shoulders. He spoke with too much authority.

"Can't you stay a bit?" Uri stood from his chair.

"Nyet. I thank you for company last night." Sergei shook Uri's hands. "But you have guests, and I have much work today."

Everyone rose as Sergei left.

After he'd gone, Caleb's gaze settled on Uri. "He seems quite certain what's going to happen."

"Yes. His family saw the worst of the purges from the KGB, and his father died in the gulags. Then the FSB began acting just like the thugs they replaced."

"This is all very distressing." Caleb glanced toward his manuscript, stacked on the table near Uri. "But what about my book?"

"Yes." Uri settled back in his chair, crossed one ankle over a knee, and his chair creaked back. "Your book. There's not an institution left that they haven't corrupted, compromised, or co-opted. That includes publishing. And now everything has become about 'race'."

Oh no. He was off on a tangent again. When would they ever discuss his book?

"But aren't they right, Uri?" Tanya leaned forward in her chair. "Isn't this country racist at heart?"

"No, child!" His fist hit the arm of the rocker, his body jerked fully upright, and Nika lifted her head. "You need to study true history, not the biased, edited version they peddle nowadays. The ideologues have hijacked our past, reinventing it to suit their ideology. With their fiction in hand, they declare this nation was founded on slavery.

"Continuing with that absurd falsehood, they contend that everyone whose skin color is white is automatically racist at heart, that we've always been racist, and we always will be. And for that, we can never be forgiven." He sat back in the rocker, his head shaking behind a fog of cigar smoke, his gaze wandering to a far corner.

Yep, Uri had forgotten his book. His "actually very good" book. *Uri Baranov, the great author, had actually said that.*

"Think about that for a moment—a philosophy that forever withholds forgiveness, requiring us to forever wallow in past sins not of our making, forever regretting what our ancestors did long ago, forever hating ourselves for something we never had a part in, for something we can never change, with no way to move forward. It's the very antithesis of Christianity. It's part of a new creed, a new pseudo-religion, but one utterly lacking in forgiveness and mercy. It's a theology without love, founded on a deep hatred of all who disagree with their radical dogma. I can think of nothing to better divide us and pit us, one against another. Ah, my friends, we are in a spiritual, not a political, battle. If you believe in Satan, such a philosophy would be first among his tenets."

Uri stubbed out his cigar, went to the counter, and returned to his seat with two Fig Newtons. When Nika rushed to his side, sat obediently, and raised a paw, he dropped a piece into her open mouth.

In the pause, Caleb glanced again at Tanya, and—finally!—their eyes met. Maybe she'd give him a hint of her decision.

But no. She looked past him to the clock on the wall.

He took a deep breath.

Uri continued. "I must sound like an old man who's seen too much and lived too long, a mad observer in a world gone mad, watching the world tumbling headlong toward its destruction." He dipped a Fig Newton into his coffee and munched.

"No, Uri," said Caleb. "You're making a lot of sense. Too much sense." Again, he wrapped his chain around a finger.

"It's kind of you to say so."

"But you're scaring me."

"And scared we should be. For some time, I've watched this madness grow. And now the publishing industry is nothing but a shill for a progressive, atheist agenda. There might be some small publishers out there bucking the trend, but not many."

"Are you saying I must write according to some checklist?" He twirled the chain faster. "Or change my characters? Or my subject?"

"Yes, Caleb. The publishing and entertainment world today is like a man peering through a two-inch window covered with gauze, afraid to look right or left. They only want manuscripts that check their political boxes." He waved half a cookie in the air. "And with the anti-Christian ethos now sweeping the nation, they cannot tolerate in one's manuscript even a single mention of God, or horrors—Jesus! Unless, of course, disrespect or blasphemy is involved. Believe me, if I were starting out today, no one would ever publish *Hugo's Revenge*. In its day, it sold ten million copies."

Caleb rose, walked to the window, and looked down at the passing cars. "But I have to write stories going to the truth of who we are. In the Ukraine in World War I, there are no blacks or Hispanics or openly gay men. My main character is a white male because that's who I am and that's who they were. He's in love with a woman, and they're struggling against the horrors brought on by a totalitarian, socialist ideology. And like me, he's searching for truth." He turned back to the room.

"I have a confession." Tanya's glance caught his. "I read your manuscript, and I liked it. Somehow, it goes to the heart."

Touched by her response, he smiled. "Thanks."

Uri finished his now-soggy Fig Newton. "I applaud you for the universal themes in your work. But the gatekeepers will want a woman protagonist, preferably black. And—"

"Won't they then accuse me of cultural appropriation?"

"They might." He laughed again. "There's no winning with these folks. You also have two mentions of God—they've got to go. And you have no same-sex love affair. And you aren't promoting one of their favorite causes, such as the mistreatment of some minority or the dysfunction of the nuclear family or transgenderism or climate change. And they certainly don't want to hear about the evils of socialism. You'll also have to hire a 'sensitivity reader' who'll comb your work for the slightest hint of racism, sexism, and all the other leftist isms. She'll purge your document of all politically incorrect thought, anything remotely opposed to the new political agenda."

Caleb couldn't imagine hiring such a person, someone diametrically opposed to his philosophy. Would a publisher hire such a person even if he didn't want one? Would they mangle all his hard work? His breathing quickened, and his fingers clenched. He could never let that happen. He'd poured his very soul into that book. When he spoke next, it came out as a whisper. "Has the whole world lost its mind?"

"Yes." Uri shot him a sly smile. "It has."

What would be left of the message he'd wanted to touch readers' minds? Caleb's racing heart picked up speed, his every muscle tautening before his words burst forth. "But I'm opposed to their agenda with every fiber of my being." He crossed the room and plopped again into the chair.

Uri lit another cigar while a frowning Tanya walked to the window and opened it. "Assimilate, and you'll go far." He tipped ash into the tray and raised an eyebrow. "Resist, and they'll come after you." His smile widened. "They're the new Borg, Caleb, and they want your brain."

"They can't have it." Caleb tried to smile and failed. "They may not publish my book, but I've got my blog. There I can get at the truth, and no one can stop me."

Uri sat back, and the rocker creaked. "You're a fighter, standing up for what you believe. I applaud you. But there will be pain."

"Thank you. I think." The thought that all his hard work might be rejected because of the craziness sweeping the world twisted his stomach into knots. Casting a glance toward Tanya, he rose then started for the door. "Can you at least help me with editing?"

"Yes, my friend. What else have I got to do besides walk my dog? Work on that novel over there?" He waved toward a laptop sitting on a desk in the corner. "Yet another conservative opus that will never see print? You see, we're both alike."

"Excuse me, Uri." Tanya stood and crossed the room. "Caleb and I have something to discuss."

Grinning, Uri waved her out.

But when she said "discuss", Caleb's face flushed. She was going to turn him down, wasn't she? What else could she mean by that?

He entered the hall, followed by Tanya.

"What did your friend . . . say?" His heart was racing again.

Her face impassive, she searched his eyes.

He stood rigid, unmoving. Why was her answer so important all of a sudden? He hadn't decided to ask her out until the moment he entered Uri's apartment. He swallowed.

"My friend said . . ." Then her eyes, her lips, her entire face lit up with a smile. "He said we were through, that if I broke off our date for someone else, he didn't ever want to see me again. The answer, Caleb, is yes—I'll go out with you tonight."

His heart swelling, the blood pumping to his face, he said he'd pick her up at seven.

With the door half-open, she looked back. "But I warn you, I'm not a cheap date."

"For you, Tanya, I'll spend a fortune on tonight's dinner."

She smiled, entered the apartment, and closed the door.

He felt as if he were floating over the tiles toward his apartment. She'd actually said yes, and he was actually taking her out tonight. But he stopped, remembering the conversation with Uri, Sergei, and earlier, with Dylan. Then even the prospect of dinner with Tanya was unable to shake off their warnings.

It was all part of a growing pattern, wasn't it? The new political madness, the chaos in the cities, the anti-Christian mood sweeping the nation.

Something was coming, something that would change the world forever.

CHAPTER 7

DAVATO

Geneva, Switzerland

Nahum 1:5–6 (NLT): *In his presence the mountains quake, and the hills melt away; the earth trembles, and its people are destroyed. Who can stand before his fierce anger? Who can survive his burning fury? His rage blazes forth like fire, and the mountains crumble to dust in his presence.*

As the three black limousines rolled down the street with Lake Geneva on their left, UN flags fluttered on each side of the hoods. Before and behind the motorcade, police motorcycles wailed their sirens. The assistant secretary-general's was the last delegation to arrive, and, just as Davato had ordered, Carlo Scutari had made sure their entrance would turn heads. Davato opened his leather folio and found the day's schedule.

Back in Rome before this morning's flight, he had been in a pensive mood. He'd set down his coffee cup, turned to his aide, and said in Italian, one of the fifteen languages in which he was fluent, "How long have you been with me, Carlo?"

"Fifteen years, sir. Six with Worldnet. Six with the European Commission. The last three here at the UN."

Davato nodded. "And how long with the League before that?"

"Ever since I was eighteen. That would be another ten years."

"Do you often wonder if this will be *my* time?—*our* time?—if what the League of Abaddon has prepared for all these centuries will come to pass before we die?"

"Anything is possible, sir."

"I suppose it is." He'd lifted his gaze to the expanse of windows and the Rome skyline. "But there's always been someone like me, hasn't there? And if even the Master doesn't know when, one has to wonder—will this be our time? Will the time *ever* come?"

"I wouldn't express such doubts aloud, sir. The Master, you know?"

"Of course." He'd glanced at his aide with a knowing smile. If the Master were near, Davato would feel his presence. "But today, I am set an impossible task. How am I going to get these obstinate parties to come together? Their stubbornness, their inability to look past the clear benefits of compromise, and their obvious mental deficiencies are astonishing."

"Many people are counting on you, sir."

"They are, indeed."

That was this morning back in Rome, and now the three-car fleet with police escort approached the main entrance of Geneva's Intercontinental Conference Center and Hotel. The cars and motorcycles stopped before reporters and a crowd of the curious. He handed the schedule back to Carlo. Then his aide hurried around to open the door. He passed through a gauntlet of reporters firing questions about the upcoming meeting, but he merely waved and shot them his winning smile. "Later, my friends. We've only just arrived and have nothing yet to report."

His handpicked assistants and researchers left the other two vehicles. In the lobby, his underlings took a different elevator to less expensive quarters while he and Carlo exited at the top floor and the Executive Lake View Suite. He allowed only Carlo a bedroom inside his private, five-room chambers with Jacuzzi, living and dining rooms, full wet bar, and fantastic view of the city and Lake Geneva beyond. Besides secretarial duties, Carlo was also an expert marksman. And the Glock G17 he always carried confirmed his dual role as bodyguard.

While Carlo dropped their bags in the hall, Davato entered his room and threw his jacket on the bed. "When is our first meeting?" he called into the hallway.

"Fifteen hundred hours, sir."

He loosened his tie. "Time enough for a drink."

As Davato headed for the living room and the wet bar, someone knocked on the door. His aide opened to one of their researchers, a young woman with whom Carlo hadn't yet slept. She stood with pale face and downcast eyes.

"What is it, Genevieve?" asked Carlo.

"Sirs . . ." She threw a nervous glance over Carlo's shoulder toward Davato then breathed deeply. For some reason, though all the UN staff held him in awe, a few showed an inordinate fear of their boss. "Sirs, there's been an earthquake in the Middle East. Massive destruction. Terrible loss of life. I was told you should take a look."

As the woman left, a thrill raced up and down his spine. An earthquake in Israel or Palestine? He found the remote and switched on the television.

A woman announcer sat before a screen with a still shot of rubble and long rows of bodies. "Much of the West Bank and Gaza has been leveled," she said in breathless tones, "including parts of Jerusalem. Reports are coming in of incredible destruction in nearly every Palestinian town and village. Thousands, if not tens of thousands, are feared dead. Palestinian hospitals and emergency workers are overwhelmed. But wait"—she touched a hand to her ear—"we have more from Peter Davis, our correspondent in Jerusalem."

The scene shifted from the studio to a man standing before mounds of ruins. Dust hovered in the air. "I'm here at Temple Mount in Jerusalem," came the crisp, businesslike voice, "the holiest site in the world for both Jews and Muslims. Only hours ago, the shrine to Muhammad, the Dome of the Rock stood here. But as you can see, it's been completely demolished. When the earthquake hit, it was especially severe up here on Temple Mount. Oddly, much of the rest of the city was spared. And—"

The view shook, and somewhere off-camera, people screamed. "It's an aftershock. Hold on." For nearly a minute, the reporter fought for balance as the camera jiggled. "It's over," he said. "Let's pan over there." The screen panned to piles of stone debris surrounded by black-draped women mourners and hundreds of bearded men falling on their faces, over and over. "One can only wonder," came the reporter's hushed voice, "what turmoil and chaos this will cause in the Muslim world."

Davato switched off the set. "How fortunate! Our meeting this afternoon should be most interesting, indeed."

* * *

BY 15:05, THE ASSISTANT SECRETARY-GENERAL sat at the head of a massive circular conference table. They were meeting in the hotel ballroom, the only room large enough to accommodate such a gathering.

He scanned the delegates—the sunburned Israelis, the dour-faced Palestinians, the businesslike Americans, the black-garbed Iranians, the pasty-faced Russians, and the dark-skinned, sour-faced Turks. Also present were the Arabs in their turbans and white, ankle-length thwabs—the Egyptians, the Syrians, the Saudis, and on and on.

Forty dignitaries must be seated here today, with many more aides clustered behind them. Everyone wore an ear monitor. Microphones sat before all. On the room's perimeter, translators waited in plastic sound-proof booths. When he had a chance, he must praise Carlo. The logistics must have been a nightmare.

He called the meeting to order, stating the goal of a permanent peace while translators rendered his speech into each delegate's preferred language. He asked each envoy to introduce themselves. When everyone had announced their name and title, he smiled, leaned to the mike, and congratulated them on joining such an august body for this momentous, history-making event. "Having made our introductions, we will now break until tomorrow morning. I understand the hotel chef is excellent. Does anyone object to starting tomorrow at nine?"

The head Palestinian representative, a short man garbed in a kaftan and bearing a stubbled chin, raised a hand and leaned toward the microphone. "We request an adjournment of four or five days while we assess what has just happened in our country."

Davato looked to the others. All around the table, heads nodded. Turning back to the petitioner, he smiled. "Of course. Take as much time as you like. We understand the destruction was unprecedented and quite severe. Our condolences and prayers go with you." He scanned the others in the room. "I'll notify all parties after our Palestinian friends have appraised the situation, conferred with their counterparts back home, and are able to resume."

With that, he adjourned the group. But as Davato and Carlo stood alone in the elevator ascending to their room, he turned to his aide. "Something tells me there's more to this earthquake than meets the eye. Could the Enemy be involved?"

"The Enemy?" Carlo rubbed his chin. "If so, the quake could be a prelude to the events we've all been hoping for."

"Right now"—a slow smile curled Davato's lips—"anything is possible."

TEN DAYS BEFORE

CHAPTER 8
DYLAN'S DISCOVERY

Mt. Hood, Oregon

Daniel 12:4 (NLT): *"But you, Daniel, keep this prophecy a secret; seal up the book until the time of the end, when many will rush here and there, and knowledge will increase."*

Dylan jerked his gaze from the computer monitor. If what he was seeing on this website was true, it would change everything. He rubbed his eyes and stretched his arms. Light streamed through the cabin windows. The buzzing wall clock revealed it was six thirty in the morning. Had he been studying this woman's pictures for *nine* hours?

He stood, guzzled a glass of orange juice from the fridge, then stepped outside. A cool breeze trickled between the pines. Nearby, an owl hooted. Through a gap in the trees, the early morning sun glinted silver off the snows of Mt. Hood.

She was Belgian, but her site was available in English, French, and Dutch, and when he'd hooked his laptop to Blake's big monitor, he could see every frightening detail. The terrifying events they depicted, rendered with vivid colors and impossible artistry, stunned the mind, shook the soul, and brought sweat to one's brow.

In the three months since he'd become interested in Christianity, he'd already read through the entire Bible and many study books in the cabin's small library—twelve weeks of intensive scholarship, some with Blake's help. Last night, he'd even found a tome delving into the book of Revelation that explained at length what was coming. Using that reference, he'd cross-matched this already-recorded knowledge with Margot's paintings.

Then it was as if someone had grabbed his shoulders and shook him. Then he knew—the hand of God was upon this woman. This Margot Durand was a modern-day prophet. No one could have illustrated so many events with such frightening clarity over such a long period without divine guidance. And what her paintings told him was this—

The Apocalypse was imminent.

The world as everyone knew it was coming to an end.

And only those who knew Jesus as the Son of the living God would be spared what was coming.

Stepping off the porch, he breathed deeply of the chill mountain air and its sweet pine scent. Beside the mountain, a half-moon was setting. Overhead, wisps of clouds streamed east. This morning, the world was calm, peaceful, and up here, breathtakingly beautiful.

But all that would soon change. That this Margot Durand had been selected, in this day and age, to illustrate the coming events meant the time was short and he needed to save his family. His brother and sister were not believers. He had little hope for his father, but for his mother—maybe?

Taking his cell phone out of his pocket, he dialed Chelsea. It would be nine thirty in the morning in New York, and she'd be awake.

She answered almost immediately.

"Sis, there's something you need to see, and it's important." He dove straight into what he'd found, explaining what would happen when the end began and what he'd found on the Belgian woman's website.

He gave her time to find the site and peruse the pictures.

Moments later, she came back on the phone. "Dylan?"

"Yes?"

"I can't deal with this right now. I appreciate your eagerness with what you've found and all, but I just don't believe the world's going to end soon or that some Belgian woman can draw pictures about it. I've got to go. Bye."

He gripped the dead phone, squeezed his eyes shut, and swore under his breath. But the moment he did, he remembered he could no longer swear, that bad language was offensive to God, and he mumbled a prayer asking forgiveness.

Maybe he'd come on too strong? Maybe she'd go back and look at the pictures later? But something else was up with her. He'd noticed that back in Minneapolis. He'd call her again next week.

He raised the phone again and dialed Caleb. It would be eight thirty-five in Chicago.

When his brother answered, their conversation mirrored the one with Chelsea. Caleb was skeptical. He believed in God, and he believed in truth, but not in the truth of Christ. And after hearing the news about the end of the world from his brother—Caleb couldn't buy it.

After an awkward silence, Caleb told him about the woman he'd taken out on two dates and had asked out on a third.

"So is it serious?" Dylan asked.

"No. But in time it could get there."

"Good for you."

"Are you staying at Mt. Hood until I arrive?"

"Of course. Blake is returning tomorrow. This week, he led some people on a Mt. Rainier climb. Until he returns, I have the place all to myself."

"I'm looking forward to it." Caleb laughed. "As long as the mountain's still there and the world doesn't end before I arrive."

"Ha ha." They said goodbye, and Dylan leaned back against the cabin wall.

Two elk wandered out of the pines, munching grass beside the road. Bearing huge racks, the magnificent animals dipped their heads to eat, the sinews and muscles of their powerful flanks rippling. Did they know their time on earth was almost up? Did God give such wonderful creatures a sense of impending doom?

Looking at his phone again, he called up the Belgian woman's website. What if he actually spoke with her? When not traveling, he'd spent most of the last few years at his family's villa in Tuscany. He'd had language tutors since he was ten, and he knew both Italian and French. The site had no phone number, of course, but it did have an email contact.

He moved inside, brought up the site's contact page on his laptop, and typed his message.

Dear Margot,
   My name is Dylan Turner. I'm from Minnesota, and I am
a new Christian. I've studied your website in depth, and I am

blown away. Your pictures can only have come from God himself, and the message they bring is one that all the world needs to hear. I would like to call you and talk about this in person. . . .

He typed his phone number and sent the message. Then he sat back and yawned. Nothing would come of it. She'd think he was some kind of kook or he was trying to sell her something.

Moments later, his phone played Beethoven's Fifth.

The call came from overseas.

CHAPTER 9
ON THE RHÔNE RIVER

Avignon, France

2 Timothy 3:1–2 (NLT): . . . *in the last days there will be very difficult times. For people will love only themselves and their money. They will be boastful and proud, scoffing at God . . . They will consider nothing sacred.*

Barely had the porters dropped the bags in their cabin than Adam Turner faced his wife and complained again. "Two days stuck in Marseilles. Two whole days lost from our trip, and all the line will do is give us a voucher for a few hundred dollars off another cruise."

Opening one of his bags, he pulled out his laptop, powered it up, and sat at the desk.

"Who was to know, dear, that there'd be such widespread unrest?" Kate took a black velvet dress from her valise and laid it on the bed. "No cabs. No buses. No trains. Everything in France was shut down. For a time, the anarchists even prevented the crew from getting on board. What could anybody do?"

Adam shrugged, brought up his email, and perused the list. Nothing important since this noon when, finally, they'd left their Marseilles hotel. Next, he checked the news, finding an article about how the Geneva peace talks, resumed after the Palestinians returned from their quake-ravaged land, were again stalled.

He stood and entered the balcony of their expansive Grand Suite, one of only two on the ship. Out on the river, a seagull dove and reemerged, a fish in its beak. He breathed deeply. "At least we're finally here."

"There's a welcome meeting in the lounge in half an hour." She held up a diamond necklace. "With free champagne. You should change."

He reentered the room and kissed her neck. "What would I do without you?"

* * *

After the captain introduced some of the staff and made his speech and after several refills of champagne, Adam followed the group to the dining room where he grabbed one of the elegantly adorned tables and sat. Immediately, a tuxedoed waiter appeared, pouring one of the premium French wines for which he'd paid extra.

"It's so good to get away." Kate pressed a white napkin to her lap and examined the menu. "Tonight, I'm going to have the Belgian endive tarte Tatin with Rocamadour cheese."

"I will never get over why neither Caleb nor Dylan would take the position I offered them?" Adam picked up the menu, but his eyes wouldn't focus. "Do my children hate me?"

"No, dear. But look, we're moving."

His gaze followed everyone else's to the windows as the ship left the dock and headed out into the river. "At the office, I have two dozen résumés on my desk, all begging for the position they refused."

"You should leave work behind and enjoy the cruise." She set down her glass. It was already empty. She'd better not get drunk again like she did at the hotel restaurant last night.

Couples were filtering into the dining room and finding seats. This week, he just wanted to be left alone, but the captain had encouraged everyone to find someone new to sit by each day and to mingle. As he looked up from the menu card, a man and a woman were occupying the empty seats across from them. He stifled an urge to frown.

"We're the Turners," said his wife to the newcomers. "Kate and Adam."

"Cheryl and Bob Smith from St. Louis." The woman's smile, bright and cheerful, made Adam cringe. "This is our anniversary cruise. We're celebrating thirty years of marriage."

"Then congratulations to you!" Kate waved to a waiter to refill her glass then turned to the woman's husband. "And what do you do, Bob?"

"I'm a pastor at a small community church." His smile was disgustingly warm and welcoming. "How about you, Adam? What do you do to bring home the bacon?"

Adam's first inclination was to leap out of his chair, grab Kate's hand, and find a different table. But most of the seats were now filled, and he wasn't going to let some Bible-thumping preacher deny him a pleasant first meal on this cruise. He breathed in and held the man's gaze. "I'm the chief executive officer and founder of Turner Enterprises. Perhaps you've heard of it?"

Bob's eyes widened. "Yes. Of course. Who hasn't?" His gaze dropped to the menu.

After the waiter came to take their orders, Bob leaned toward Adam. "This is our first cruise. How about you folks?"

"This is our tenth." Adam raised an eyebrow. "All river cruises. Fewer people than on the big boats. I don't like crowds."

Bob nodded. As a waiter filled the newcomers' glasses with the standard wine, Bob sat back. "If I'm not mistaken, Turner Enterprises gave a large grant to the Freedom From Religion Foundation. Am I correct?"

"That's right. I'm an atheist and a big supporter of atheist causes." Adam let a smirk lift his lips. "I don't believe in fairy tales."

"Everyone is entitled to their opinion. For myself, I believe in an eternal, all-loving, all-knowing God who created the universe. And I guess we should leave it at that and enjoy our dinner."

"Yes, dear." Kate laid a hand on his. "Let's just enjoy our dinner."

But Christians and their preachers always raised his ire, and he couldn't help himself. He sipped his wine and set the glass down. "Can I ask you a question, Bob?"

"Sure, go ahead."

"Correct me if I'm wrong, but you people believe in an invisible being who, with a wave of his invisible hand, just magically made everything pop into existence? Aren't you a bit old to have an imaginary friend?"

Kate frowned in his direction, and under the table, a shoe kicked his leg. But planting his feet more firmly, he ignored her.

"Ah, but he's not imaginary. He's oh, so real." Bob smiled. "But maybe you are more of a logic person, so let's set belief and unbelief aside for a moment. Science tells us the universe isn't eternal. Both the Big Bang and the Theory of Relativity prove that. Science tells us some twelve or so billion years ago, the universe had a beginning. And anything that had a beginning must have had a cause. So something or someone must have *caused* everything to come into being. One could say someone was in the business of *creating* the universe. Ergo, the universe had a Creator. That's where logic and science lead us, and it happens to agree with the Bible. Genesis 1:1 tells us that, 'In the beginning, God created the heavens and the earth.' " He sipped his wine and set the glass down before continuing.

"That leaves us with the atheist viewpoint—your viewpoint, I presume—which says something arose out of nothing." Bob leaned forward in his chair. "So, Adam, can you explain to me how that works? How, exactly, can something arise from nothing?"

"Well"—Adam waved his hands—"maybe from an alternate reality. From another universe."

"But that just moves the problem out further. Who created those alternate realities or other universes? That doesn't solve the problem, does it?"

"Maybe some super powerful aliens." His face warming, Adam gripped his drink and squeezed.

"Still, then, who created the aliens? Same problem. No, my friend, some great and powerful force created the universe—a force we call God. And what's amazing is that this God is personal, and he loved us so much he sent his Son to die for us."

Adam lifted his glass and emptied it in one swallow. "That brings us to another thing that's always troubled me—a God who sent his own son to be murdered. What kind of father would that be? In Minnesota, we'd call that a crime, and the man who let it happen would be sent to prison."

"But God did it out of love, don't you see? His Son was a part of himself, one of the Trinity, and thus God was really sending himself to the cross. He allowed his own Son to be killed because, by Christ's death, we who believe in him are then saved. After we believe, when God looks upon us, it's Jesus on the cross he sees, not our sins. It is so counterintuitive to our human way of thinking, yet so brilliant, we have a hard time wrapping our heads around it."

"On that point, we can both agree." Clutching his glass so hard, his knuckles whitened, Adam beckoned waiter. "Garçon, more wine here."

"Perhaps we should now enjoy the meal," said Bob. "But thank you for the discussion."

"That's a nice dress you're wearing," said Cheryl to Kate.

"Thank you. The last time we were at our villa, I had it made in Florence."

As the first course arrived, Adam swore to himself that never again on this cruise would he allow himself to be seated beside Bob and Cheryl Smith, Bible-thumpers from St. Louis.

ONE WEEK BEFORE

CHAPTER 10
MARGOT'S FALL

Brussels, Belgium

As she'd done every day of the last week, Margot curled her legs beneath her on the seat before the bay window and stared at the traffic below. The people down there went about their lives as if they mattered, as if such things as hope, truth, and faith still existed. A tear trickled down her right cheek. Oh to have that back, to once again be like them, to have a reason for living and the hope of an eternal future!

But no. Ever since her visit to the archbishop, hope and even truth itself had been stolen. Now a shadow lived within her. And day by day, it grew, crawling further into her soul, sucking out the light, leaving in its place emptiness, a sense of great loss, and a nagging accusation. She tried fighting it, but that only left her weak, drained, tired. Now she was a boat adrift in a storm, with swirling clouds bearing down upon her, and her only guide was a captain whose name was darkness.

Someone knocked on the door, but she didn't turn her head. It was probably Luc. But just like yesterday and the day before and the day before that, she wasn't in the mood.

The knock came again. "Sis, it's me," came Luc's muffled voice through the wood. "Please open up."

"Go away." Now she turned into the room, toward the four posts of her unmade bed and the oak dresser cluttered with cups, saucers, and dirty plates. Beyond loomed the wood of the door, blackened by decades of varnish.

"I've got coffee for you. And I want to talk."

She closed her eyes. He wouldn't give up, would he?

Then she thought she heard—but couldn't be certain—a whisper from the other side. "Please, sis. Don't do this."

She extricated her legs from the bench, and, averting her eyes from the row upon row of paintings huddled against the far wall, she dragged her feet across the room. What point was there in keeping all those canvases now? Why not just burn them? She opened the door.

Smiling and standing in the hall, Luc held two cups of coffee. He lifted one toward her. "Just as you like it. With cream and sugar."

Nodding, she took it. She cradled the hot mug and started back to her bay window. Footsteps followed behind.

As she again folded her legs up onto the seat, he pulled a chair close and sat. "I'm worried for you, Margot. Since you saw the archbishop, you've barely left your room. You're hardly eating anything. You aren't painting. And you won't talk about it."

"There's nothing to say." Her voice sounded strange in her ears—remote, hoarse, stripped of life. Her eyes again sought the traffic below and its movement. For someone who was dying inside, the movement, speaking of life, was vaguely comforting. "I gave up my painting. I renounced my faith. I don't believe in . . . anything . . . anymore."

"I don't believe you."

"Well, it's true." Her throat strained as she spoke to the glass. "I thought I was doing the right thing, but I was deceived. I'm not even sure there is a God. Or a Jesus. Or a Devil. Or anything like right or wrong."

"You're talking nonsense. What about all those visions you had? All those wonderful paintings? Father still believes in them. So do I. So do a lot of people."

"Then you've all been deceived."

When she turned to face him, he brushed aside a mop of blond hair. Their glances met, and she stared into his eyes, so clear, so blue, so filled with concern.

Never had she seen such worry in his eyes, and it scared her. She dropped her legs to the floor and laid a hand on his knee. Suddenly, she felt like talking. "Luc, there's something wrong . . . with me." Her breath caught in her throat. "For four years I painted nothing but garbage. Works of the Devil, the archbishop called them." She gripped the mug tighter then turned back to the glass. "It all seems like a dream now—all that furious work. No . . . a nightmare. All for nothing."

"No, please." He gripped her hand, still on his knee. "You're not thinking right. Father and I are worried about you. We went to a

Protestant church this morning, and it was great worshiping God there. We don't need Archbishop Bonheur and his disbelief, his pronouncements of excommunication, or his fancy cathedral. Next week, won't you join us, and—?"

"No!" Scrunching her face, she pulled her legs back under her, up onto the pad so her whole body faced away from him. "There's nothing left for me in any church anywhere. Don't talk to me about church!"

For long moments, he sat in silence beside her, breathing hard. Finally, he stood and trudged to the door.

Alone again, she set the cup down, wrapped her arms about her chest, and rocked back and forth. As before, a lone tear trickled down her right cheek.

"If death means a welcome oblivion," she whispered to the window, "then let it come."

CHAPTER 11

CHELSEA

Greenwich Village, New York City

Matthew 24:12 (HCSB): *Because lawlessness will multiply, the love of many will grow cold.*

On Monday evening, Chelsea followed several steps behind Archer Harris down the street. The swarming mob was fifty yards ahead. The sixth precinct station was half a block beyond that. Archer had outfitted her with a helmet and face guard, and a gas mask hung from her belt.

He turned back to her and shouted, "Why so slow today?"

She ran to his side. "I'm just not into this right now."

"Well, babe, whether you're into it or not, it's happening." With his own helmet and plastic guard covering his chest-length beard, he looked like a wild man. "What's wrong with you?"

"Nothing."

"I don't believe you." He grabbed her shoulders. "Ever since you came back from Minneapolis, you've been checking your weight and puking after every meal. You becoming anorexic on me? You're thin enough."

"It's not that." She shook off his hands.

"Here." He shoved a glass jar into her hands.

A wick stuck out of the top, and she smelled gasoline—a Molotov cocktail. "What am I supposed to do with this?"

"Burn the station—what do you think?"

"Where'd you get it?"

He pointed to a pallet in an alley behind them where men dressed in black were doling out frozen water bottles, bricks, and more jars with gasoline and cloth wicks.

She ran back and exchanged her incendiary for a frozen water bottle.

"Why'd you do that?" He frowned at her bottle.

"I'm no arsonist. What if I caused someone's death?" She lifted the plastic helmet visor so he could hear her over the shouting. "I could never live with myself."

"They're only cops. They deserve to die. Come on." Then he led her toward the surging crowd.

Two hundred feet from the station, the police had hooked a barricade of linked bicycle racks, behind which stood a line of blue. Sparse though it was, with plastic shields, helmets, gas masks, and billy clubs, they presented a formidable defense.

She drew in breath. She believed in the cause with all her heart. But where would this end today?

Archer led her deep into the crowd. Around them, people screamed, shouted obscenities at the cops. Then they started hurling objects—bricks, frozen bottles, plastic bags of urine.

"Excuse me, sir?"

Chelsea turned her head.

Beside them, a man shoved a microphone into Archer's face. A cameraman stood behind him. "What are you protesting here today?" The noise from the crowd nearly drowned out his words.

"Protesting?" He turned a stunned look toward Chelsea. "Uh, why, the police. And the injustice."

"What injustice?"

"Their oppression." Again, Archer's glance pleaded for help. "Babe?"

She stepped in front of the mike. "We're fighting the oppression of the ruling classes." She lifted her visor and waved toward the station. "We're in a struggle between the oppressed and the racist oppressors. The cops are all white supremacists, and now it's either us or them."

Several from the crowd had heard and now formed a circle around her and Archer and the television crew.

The interviewer pointed at Archer's Molotov cocktail. "And your goal is to burn down the station house?"

Archer nodded, and Chelsea wondered if that was a good thing to admit on camera.

"And what will that accomplish?" The interviewer thrust his mike back to Chelsea.

"We're going after the centers of corruption and power. We want to bring it all down. We want to start over."

Some in the crowd now started a chant. "Bring it all down! Bring it all down!"

The reporter flashed a worried look at the crowd, at his cameraman, and the two backed away.

Archer grabbed Chelsea's arm. "Let's get up where the action is."

At the barricade nearest the building, he lit the wick and hurled the jar of gasoline toward the station. The bottle exploded in flames on the sidewalk just short of the building's façade, bringing a curse from Archer.

Chelsea now threw her water bottle. It hit an officer on the helmet, knocking him temporarily off his feet.

"Way to go, Chelsea!" Archer cried.

The crowd surged back and forth, struggling with the barricade. Tear gas canisters began landing near them, and she pulled her gas mask over her face.

But as she turned her head, Archer was on the ground, gasping for breath, clutching his ribs.

"Archer, were you hit?" She knelt beside him.

"Y–yes." He reached for a spot under his shirt on his right side. His body stiffened, and his face jolted. "I think something's broken."

"Let me see." She unbuttoned his shirt to expose the spot and winced. An ugly black bruise was spreading across his chest. "Must have been a rubber bullet. Your rib might be broken. We need to get you back to the apartment."

"I . . . guess. I can't throw anything more today anyway."

* * *

CHELSEA BROUGHT ANOTHER ICE PACK from the fridge and another beer for her patient, lying in an easy chair with his legs up.

"You're going to live. I don't think anything's broken." She gave him a half-smile. "But tomorrow you should go to the clinic and have that looked at."

Archer replaced the ice pack with a new one, took the beer, his fourth, and drank. "I hope this doesn't stop me from working."

She squinted at him. "Instead of painting, you could try selling what you've got."

He shrugged, grabbed the remote, and flipped on the television and the local news.

"The riots continued tonight in Greenwich Village's sixth precinct," said a woman anchor. "The devastated ranks of blue have barely been able to keep the protestors from burning one of the few remaining station houses. So far tonight, four officers have been hurt, one seriously. The force is down to a third its former size, leading to an explosion in murder, robbery, and carjackings across the city. Ever since the disruptions in 2020, such riots have broken out sporadically in cities across the country, pausing only during the winter months. Experts don't know when or if the chaos will ever end. . . ."

Archer switched from the news to a football game.

Chelsea picked up the beer she'd been working on and strolled to the wall where he'd hung his latest works. "Violent, chaotic, bold, and disturbing"—that's how one critic described his paintings after the big show she'd arranged and paid for. But after all the effort to show his art, he'd sold only two works, and those to a man she secretly hired to buy them. The paintings were now stacked in a basement, along with a pile of furnace filters, window screens, and bicycle tires.

"When was the last time you sold something, Archer?" She turned from the wall to face him.

"At the show." But his voice was distracted, and his eyes were fixed on the game where a fight had broken out between teams.

"Look at me." She planted hands on her hips.

He glanced up.

"I meant it when I said you should try harder to sell what you have. When you're not at the studio—a studio I paid for, by the way—you're just lounging around the apartment, drinking beer, doing nothing."

"Sure thing, babe." Again, the game captured his attention.

"I'm not a babe. In this day and age, Archer, no one is a babe."

"I know. You keep telling me that."

He was incorrigible. She slid a hand over her belly, imagining movement.

She didn't know if this was the moment, but time was running out. "Please turn off the TV. We have something important to discuss."

"Can't it wait?"

"No." She moved in front of the screen, and he glanced up again. "Please turn it off."

He frowned and turned down the volume. "What?"

There was no easy way to put this. She swallowed, looked at the floor. "I'm pregnant."

Archer flicked off the set. For long moments, he stared at her, and silence filled the room. Finally, he said, "We can't have a kid. You need to have an abortion."

"I . . . know." And then, as she stood before the father of this child growing within her—this unwanted, unplanned, uninvited child—tears filled her eyes.

She'd known for a month now but was paralyzed into doing anything about it. It had taken her weeks to come to the agonizing decision that she needed to abort the baby. But here was Archer, rushing to the same conclusion within seconds.

It left her feeling empty, soiled, used.

"Sorry, babe. I'd come to you right now, but I can't get up." He placed a hand on the ice pack on his chest.

She wiped her eyes. "I want you to come with me to the clinic. You need to be there, Archer. You really do."

An expression flitted across his face—a frown or a puzzled look, she didn't know. "All right . . . babe. Whatever you say. When?"

"I'm not sure. Maybe next week."

He nodded, and she ambled to a seat beside him. Archer flipped on the game again.

The way he reacted to her news—she could have been telling him her car needed a new muffler and she needed a ride back from the dealer. She whipped her head toward him, squinting, as if that would let her see him, understand him better. But his gaze was fixed on the game.

Sometimes, Archer was so cold and without feeling, he frightened her.

CHAPTER 12

FREYA LEWIS

Greenwich Village, New York City

1 Timothy 4:1 (HCSB): *Now the Spirit explicitly says that in later times some will depart from the faith, paying attention to deceitful spirits and the teachings of demons.*

Tuesday morning, Pastor Freya Lewis limped to her desk in the offices of the Church of Peace. Why she'd attended the riot yesterday, she didn't know. Possibly, it reminded her of the old days before she was ordained, when she regularly attended such events. In retrospect, the protest seemed badly organized with far too much violence, and she should have stayed home. Someone had thrown something—a bottle, a rock, who knew?—and it missed its target and hit her knee.

Slumping into her seat, she picked up the bulletin insert she'd been working on and read it once again.

> Are you physically attracted to people of the same sex?
> Perhaps so much that you both wish to marry?
> Were you born into the wrong sex, know it in your heart,
> and want to make a permanent change?
> What does the Bible say about it?
> Come to a discussion this Sunday afternoon on
> sex, marriage, gender, and identity.
> Moderated by Pastor Freya Lewis.
>
> –Everyone welcome.

Today, she needed to answer the question about what the Bible said. Surely, some verses somewhere would support her views.

Pulling up her browser, her main source for biblical answers, she typed in her query. The first answer she found was from Deuteronomy 22:5: "A woman is not to wear male clothing, and a man is not to put on a woman's garment, for everyone who does these things is detestable to the Lord your God."

She sat back and stared at the screen.

All right. That was written over two thousand—or was it three thousand?—years ago. And by a man. That was before our enlightened age, before we knew better. She knew in her heart people had the right to decide who they were, what gender they were. How could God go against a person's natural, innate desires? And didn't those same men also write rules about stoning people for trivial offenses? Yes, she could ignore that verse.

She tried her search again and found 1 Corinthians 6:9–10: "Don't fool yourselves. Those who indulge in sexual sin, or who worship idols, or commit adultery, or are male prostitutes, or practice homosexuality, or are thieves, or greedy people, or drunkards, or are abusive, or cheat people—none of these will inherit the Kingdom of God."

For some time, her eyes focused on what she found.

But here again, wasn't Paul, the author, another one of those men in power? And didn't he also have a thing about head coverings for women? How archaic was that? What did that guy know about today's enlightened culture? Why should anyone listen to such backward thinking?

She opened the flyer's source document on her laptop and highlighted the line pointing to answers from the Bible. If the Bible wouldn't support the position everyone knew was right, she'd not reference it. But as her finger hovered over the delete button, she hesitated.

It was troubling, wasn't it? The men who wrote those words were always against her. This wasn't the first time she'd looked to the Bible for an answer to a difficult contemporary issue. All too often, the ancient authors disappointed her. Who was right?

She had good company for her views. In today's sophisticated age, the Bible was becoming a "living document", changing with the times. Either that, or it would become irrelevant. Didn't most of the pastors she knew also believe the same as she did?

A knock came on the door, and Bill, the janitor, poked his head inside. "Someone to see you, Pastor."

"All right. Let them in." She shoved the laptop aside, put on a smile, and faced the door.

"Pastor Lewis?" An attractive woman with a curly, shaggy mop of hair, dyed pink, walked in.

Freya rose and extended a hand in greeting. "Come in. Haven't I seen you in church?" She waved toward a seat opposite.

"You have. But not very often. My name is Chelsea Turner."

The woman sat, and Freya noted her pert nose, cute and slightly upturned. She wore leather jeans with holes and a flowered blouse. "What can I do for you?"

"Something's been troubling me." She sat on her hands, glanced aside, then back to Freya. "And I'm hoping the Church has an answer for my dilemma."

"What is it, Chelsea?" They all came with problems, didn't they? And they expected their pastor to solve them.

"I–I have a boyfriend. We live together. But it's not working out." She breathed in deeply.

"And you're wondering if you should leave him?"

"There's more to it. I–I'm pregnant." The woman was looking at the floor.

"All . . . right." Yes, there was definitely more to it. "So what's your dilemma?"

"We both decided I should have an abortion, but the more I thought about it, I question whether it's the right thing to do. Pastor?" Imploring eyes looked up into hers. "Do I have the right to abort my baby? What do you think?"

Freya sat back and smiled. There was no issue in which she believed more strongly. "You have the absolute right to do with your own body what you will. It's your life, your choice, and if you've decided to abort the fetus, you should go ahead with it."

"B–but is it a baby?" Appearing uncomfortable, the woman shifted in her seat. "I've heard babies in the womb feel pain, have a heartbeat, have little fingers and toes, and—"

"It's just a fetus." Freya waved a hand. "If you're not ready for a child, you have a right to choose what to do with your life, your body. Don't let one mistake ruin your whole life."

"You think I should go ahead with it?"

"I do. But let's pray about it." She reached across the desk and grabbed the woman's hand. Then she prayed for Chelsea to make the right decision.

Shifting her feet and scrunching her face, the woman appeared uncomfortable with the prayer. Still, she thanked Freya, rose, then left.

Freya smiled, warmth filling her chest, feeling good about having given someone good, solid advice.

Alone again, she pulled the laptop closer. The troublesome line promising a biblical answer was still highlighted.

What good was the Bible when it disagreed with what everyone knew was right? Just as with her advice to Chelsea Turner, she must rely more and more on what her heart told her, on her own firm grounding in right and wrong, not on what some ancient, out-of-touch men said in some long-forgotten world that passed away ages ago.

Her finger hit the delete button.

CHAPTER 13

THE CABIN

Mt. Hood, Oregon

Matthew 24:6–7 (NLT): *"And you will hear of wars and threats of wars, but don't panic. Yes, these things must take place, but the end won't follow immediately. Nation will go to war against nation, and kingdom against kingdom. There will be famines and earthquakes in many parts of the world."*

Caleb followed the GPS on his phone and made the last turn through the woods. Having left the main highway a half mile back, his rental car now climbed through the pines. Blake's cabin, a log structure built nearly eighty years ago, came into view. On the right through the trees, Mt. Hood rose, regal and majestic, its snow-bright slopes glistening in the afternoon sun.

The Portland airport had been secure. Only the city center, now a mass of abandoned, burned-out buildings, still seethed with occasional rebellion.

During the hour-and-a-half drive from the airport, the traffic had been light on a Tuesday afternoon, and he'd turned on the radio. But the news was still about the Palestine earthquake, the devastating famine in the Sudan, and the renewed fighting in Afghanistan. He shut it off.

He focused his thoughts instead on his blog. The cabin had internet service, of course, and if he could find time alone, he'd write his next entry. He thought again about his aunt and her disastrous flight from the police. His months with Alice at her cabin had instilled a love of truth, universal values, and deep thinking. She was a welcome change from Father, a man so obsessed with growing his company and making money, little else mattered. Alice had influenced him almost as much as she'd influenced Dylan. Only not with the Christian thing.

He was still trying to process the tragedy and the outrageous law that caused it. In his heart, he knew she was right. Why he knew this, he couldn't say. Others believed the opposite. But his sense of what was good and what was evil seemed true. Blake would tell him he'd received that sense from God. Maybe he had. It was something to ponder.

Whenever he came to Blake's mountain retreat, he could lounge for hours with his laptop on the porch, smelling the pines, breathing the crisp mountain air. Somehow, up here in the brisk air, he could soak up the beauty, think about truth and lies, good and evil, and ideas came to him. Maybe he would even make sense of Alice's death.

He pulled the car to a stop beside two others, grabbed his backpack and the duffel with his gear, and mounted the wooden steps. Before he reached the door, Dylan opened it.

"Caleb, glad you made it." His brother let him in.

Blake, with his thick eyebrows, dark good looks, and black hair flowing to his shoulders, walked in from the kitchen. "Welcome to Mt. Hood. Ready for a great climb tomorrow?"

"I am so looking forward to this." Caleb plopped his bags on the pinewood floor. "You want to start tomorrow?"

"Tomorrow night." Blake returned to the stove and a boiling pot. A loaf of French bread, a box of spaghetti noodles, and a bottle of sauce waited on the counter. "We need to arrive at the parking lot at eleven p.m., check in, and start the climb by midnight in order to avoid the ice falls the next day. Do you have all your equipment?"

"I think so." Caleb followed Blake into the kitchen, took a beer from the fridge, then walked to the couch. "That means we'll need a good rest tonight?"

"Yes, we must sleep in tomorrow." Blake dropped pasta into the boiling water and opened the sauce.

"So how was the big date?" Dylan gave him a playful punch on the arm. "What was her name? Tanya?"

"Yes, Tanya." Caleb grinned. "And it was great. Actually, we went out twice."

"Serious?"

"Nah. Just friends." On the couch, Caleb shoved aside a book titled *Because The Time Is Near*. It was about the Book of Revelation. A Bible and another book on the same subject lay beside it.

"I assume these are yours?" Caleb rolled his eyes from Dylan to the ceiling.

"Good guess." His brother smiled.

"Have you heard about Dylan's discovery?" Blake waved a spoon from the kitchen. "About this Belgian woman who's painted these incredible pictures of the end of the world?"

"So he's been harassing you with that too?"

Blake dipped his spoon in the sauce and stirred. "I've been poring through her website and her paintings. I once took a class on Revelation, and she's drawn an incredibly startling, even alarming, portrayal of events as they might occur today. They are terrifyingly prophetic. I am impressed." He grinned at Caleb. "Dylan has become quite the Bible student these last months."

"What about you, brother?" Dylan sank onto the other end of the couch and draped an arm across its plush back. "You say you believe in truth."

Caleb shrugged. "I'm not ready to go there yet."

"All in good time." Blake stirred his pot. "This will be ready in about ten minutes. In the meantime, you can—"

The cabin shook. The floor moved. The couch bounced.

Leaping to his feet, Caleb fought for balance.

The wall timbers rattled and ground against each other. Chunks of joint mortar crumbled, showered to the floor.

Dylan was halfway to the door.

Blake shut off the stove and staggered after him.

The pinewood floor heaved and cracked. A picture dropped from its wall hook, crashed, and its glass case shattered.

Caleb tried to follow but lost his footing. His knee hit the floor, hard. Then he rose again, his heart thudding against his ribs.

Outside, trees crashed against each other. A car alarm sounded.

He staggered like a drunken man. Somehow, he made it through the door, onto the porch, to Dylan's and Blake's side. Following their lead, he gripped the log railing. But some invisible hand was shaking it back and forth.

From somewhere deep beneath the earth came a primeval wave of sound, a deep rippling and grinding from the depths. The subhuman cry of a continent in motion.

"Stay under the porch!" Blake shouted to be heard. "Keep away from the trees."

Another wave rolled beneath, lifting his feet off the porch. He grabbed the railing on the way back down. The earth itself seemed to groan, rattle, and moan. A tall pine fell, just missing the cars but crushing Blake's woodshed. Two more trees crashed into the yard.

Long, impossible seconds later, it ended.

Caleb was still standing, heart hammering, sweat pouring off his forehead.

"That was a bad one." Blake ran into the yard and whirled to face the cabin. "From the outside, it looks okay." He circled the cars. "The vehicles are okay too."

As Dylan shut off his car alarm, Caleb joined Blake in peering down the lane toward the highway. Every few yards, downed trees blocked the drive. "How are we ever going to get out of here?"

With hands on hips, Blake stared down the access road. "I've got two chainsaws. But one is hard to start. Clearing the way to the highway might take a couple of days." Shielding his eyes from the sun, he surveyed the mountain. "Obviously, our climb for tomorrow is off. And if there were climbers up there when the quake hit . . ."

"What then?" asked Dylan.

"There'd be slides. Not good." Blake pulled his phone from his pocket. "I can't help with search and rescue until we clear a way out. And we won't be able to schedule an ascent until we get a report about conditions on the mountain."

"I'm good with that," said Caleb. "I can stay as long as needed."

Frowning, Blake peered at his phone. "I'm not getting a signal. The cell towers must be out." He faced Dylan. "How about you? Can you stay?"

"Depending on the wait." Dylan looked down the lane. "I'm not sure."

"Why not?" asked Caleb.

"Because next week, I'm flying to Belgium. I've got plans to visit this woman who says the world is ending. I talked with her brother, and nothing's going to stop me from going."

Caleb scrunched his face, struggling not to gape. What on earth had gotten into his brother?

THE DAY BEFORE

CHAPTER 14

THE ARCHANGEL

In The Great Throne Room

Joel 3:14 (NLT): *Thousands upon thousands are waiting in the valley of decision. There the day of the LORD will soon arrive.*

In the great throne room of the Lord of Hosts—an expanse stretching for miles to the east, west, north, and south and reaching for a mile or more above—the archangel Michael bowed low. Something of great importance was about to happen.

Surrounding him in the room was a host numbering in countless millions, for Michael, his brother Gabriel, and a great army of lesser angels had been summoned. From the gathering multitude, he sensed an eager expectancy in the light shimmering above them. Since time began, no gathering like this had ever assembled before the Lord of Hosts, the Creator of all that was, is, and will ever be.

An electric excitement rippled from the top of his head, out across his wings, down to his feet clothed in light.

The floor shook as behind the throne thunder boomed and lightning flashed, turning Michael's focus onto the Lord of Hosts where it belonged.

Fire rippled over the four cherubim beside the throne. Each being possessed four faces, and each face pointed in a different direction—a man's in front, a lion's on the right, an ox's on the left, and an eagle's behind. The creatures had three pairs of wings. One pair covered their faces, and below these extended arms with human hands. With a second pair of wings, the creatures hovered. A third pair of wings pointed toward their feet, which were the hooves of calves, shining like burnished gold.

Beneath each cherub whirled a giant wheel containing an inner wheel. The outer rim, gleaming like polished aquamarine, touched the ground. Eyes circled the rims, eyes that saw everything.

Lightning flashed between the four creatures. They hovered above the revolving wheels and moved from one side to another, but without turning. "Holy, holy, holy is the Lord God of Hosts," they cried, again and again.

Thick smoke spread out from behind the throne, rising far, far above to a ceiling like a sea of brilliant crystals. Smoke curled and spread out above, even to the edges of the vast hall.

Michael bowed lower.

THE TIME OF WAITING IS OVER, reverberated the voice from the throne, and the sound, like the thunder of many waterfalls, rumbled through the vast hall from one end to the next, vibrating even in Michael's chest.

He raised his head toward the high seat towering far above them, toward the Lord God, Creator of the universe. There he sat, enveloped in light so brilliant, no words could describe it. He gleamed with the fire of many suns, a bursting radiance filled with all the colors of the rainbow.

THE WORLD'S INIQUITY IS RIPE FOR THE HARVEST. TOMORROW, WE WILL CALL OUR PEOPLE HOME.

An electric sense rippled through the vast throng. The light hovering over the angelic host shimmered, changing from blue to red, and increased.

TOMORROW IS THE BEGINNING OF THE END OF THE ADVERSARY'S REIGN, THE BEGINNING OF THE END OF EVIL, came the voice of rushing waters. *TOMORROW WILL BE THE FULFILLMENT OF PROPHECY. MICHAEL AND GABRIEL, ARCHANGELS OF THE HOST, STEP FORWARD.*

The cherubim, still facing forward and hovering over their giant wheels, moved to the side, opening a path. The lightning between them ceased.

Thus summoned, Michael joined his brother in approaching the throne of the Lord God. He bowed again.

RISE, ARCHANGELS OF THE HOST, FOR TOMORROW, THE TIME WE HAVE LONG AWAITED HAS COME. TOMORROW, YOU WILL FOLLOW THE SON AS HE BRINGS MY PEOPLE OUT OF THE WORLD. AS YOU RETURN, THE ADVERSARY WILL TRY TO TAKE THE CHOSEN ONES FROM US, BUT YOU WILL PROTECT THEM, COMFORT THEM, AND GUIDE THEM SAFELY HOME.

"Yes, my Lord God." Michael and Gabriel responded in unison, but their voices were like whispers in a hurricane beside the one who spoke the universe into existence.

MARK WELL THIS MOMENT, came the rushing thunder, FOR THE TIME OF WAITING IS OVER.

"Holy, holy, holy is the Lord God of Hosts," echoed the voices of the cherubim.

As Michael and his brother backed away, lightning and fire from the four creatures again jumped back and forth, and the cherubim resumed their positions at the throne's foot.

"*Holy, holy, holy is the Lord God of Hosts,*" echoed the voices of the countless angels beyond.

Michael and Gabriel joined in, and Michael again bowed low, his wings touching the floor of crystalline, translucent gold.

He felt the excitement building, not only within him but also within the vast throng filling the miles upon miles of the throne room. Indeed, the entire universe had been groaning, yearning, longing for the events of the days to come—

For the end of the Adversary's reign.

For the end of evil.

For the beginning of the end of a fallen earth.

And for the beginning of the blessed reign of the Son.

CHAPTER 15

DYLAN AND LUC

Brussels, Belgium

1 Corinthians 3:11–15 (HCSB): *For no one can lay any other foundation than what has been laid down. That foundation is Jesus Christ. If anyone builds on that foundation with gold, silver, costly stones, wood, hay, or straw, each one's work will become obvious, for the day will disclose it, because it will be revealed by fire; the fire will test the quality of each one's work. If anyone's work that he has built survives, he will receive a reward. If anyone's work is burned up, it will be lost, but he will be saved; yet it will be like an escape through fire.*

After the airport cab dropped Dylan at his Brussels hotel, he called Chelsea. He hadn't planned the call, but once he'd unpacked, taken a shower, and laid his phone on the dresser, he realized he hadn't talked with her since the quake cut off Oregon's cell service.

"So, you're in Brussels?" Her voice showed surprise.

"Yes. Tomorrow, I'm seeing Margot Durand."

"The prophecy woman? Does she know you're coming?"

"Maybe. I talked with her brother, and he's expecting me."

"You are so into this end-of-the-world thing. I'm surprised, Dylan. Why the sudden interest?"

"All of it is true, sis. Everything she's drawn is so real, so accurate according to the book of Revelation, and so frightening, I just know it's true. You have to believe me, Chelsea. I'm begging you—go to her site and study it."

"I tried going there, but . . . I just couldn't get into it. This is so not like you, Dylan. It's really taken you in, hasn't it?"

"I believe in it with all my heart." He took a deep breath. He hoped he wasn't sounding obsessed. "But what about you? At the funeral, you didn't seem quite yourself. I've been thinking about you lately."

"Thinking about me? That's nice." A pause at the end of the line. "As for Chelsea girl . . . she's a bit down right now."

"Why down?"

"It's Archer." Another long pause. "I–I'm not quite sure where he's at with me. It might not work out between us. If you know what I mean." But something about her hesitant tone suggested there was more to it.

"Never met him, but I can guess what you mean. Are you sure there isn't something else bothering you?"

Silence at the other end.

"Chelsea?"

"No, there's nothing else."

"Well, hang in there. Just thought I'd check in. But my phone is nearly out of charge, so I'd better hang up. I have one more call to make."

"Let me know how your visit with the prophecy lady turns out."

"Will do."

After he hung up and plugged his phone into the charger, he drew a hand through his hair. As kids, they'd often fought as brother and sister. But in adulthood, he and Chelsea had become good friends and confidantes. And lately, he was worried about her.

Always on fire for some cause or another, she'd now joined such a radical crowd, he feared she was out of her element. When she talked so forcefully about oppression, racism, and class struggle, he wondered if, down deep, she believed all that. She was, after all, a child of what she now called "the oppressors". Wasn't she, like Caleb and Dylan, simply rebelling against her father and all Turner Enterprises stood for? There was a lot to rebel against there, but all her talk of revolution and bringing down the system and starting over—he didn't buy it.

The ideology she espoused was also deeply troubling. It labeled most of the populace as "racist", "evil", and "white supremacist". To top it off, if you even mounted a defense against their outrageous charges, they called that proof you were what they said you were. He knew Chelsea, and it wasn't like her to believe in such drivel.

He didn't know this Archer, but if the man was as radical as he suspected, then he wouldn't be good for her. Had Archer sucked her into this?

Picking up the phone again, he called Luc Durand.

"Âllo," said the voice at the other end.

"Luc? This is Dylan Turner," he said in French. "We talked last week."

"Ah, Dylan. Are you here in Brussels?"

"Just arrived. How is your sister?"

"Not well, my friend. She is sad. Possibly depressed. As we talked last week, I am hoping that, if she meets one of the people she touched with her pictures, she will come out of her sadness and believe again. Can you come today?"

"How about tomorrow morning? I'm beat after the long flight."

"Tomorrow afternoon is better. I will take my father to church in the morning. You have our address?"

"You gave it to me, remember?"

"Yes. Thank you, Dylan Turner. I look forward to your visit. I believe it will help my sister."

"Until tomorrow afternoon then."

He hung up, undressed, and slipped into bed. He'd take a short nap, eat supper later, then walk around the city before turning in for the night. Tomorrow would be a big day. Tomorrow, he'd meet the woman predicting the end of the world.

* * *

FOR THE THIRD TIME, LUC knocked on the door. And for the third time, Margot ignored it.

"Margot? Please let me in." His muffled voice sounded through the dark wood. "I have something to say to you. Please?"

Sighing, she lowered her legs from the bench by the bay window, dragged her feet across the room, and opened the door. "What?"

Standing a full head taller than she, Luc drew a deep breath. "Tomorrow, someone's coming to meet you. This man so believes in your work, he flew all the way from America to see you. I want your promise you will speak with him. Will you?"

She dipped her eyebrows together in a frown. "From America, you say?"

"Yes, Margot. I spoke with him last week, and when he asked if he could come and visit with you, I said he could."

Crossing her arms, she took a step back. "You shouldn't have done that. I don't want to talk to anyone about those . . . those works of the Devil."

For a moment, Luc closed his eyes. "Please, Margot? He's come a very long way."

"I don't want to see him." She began shutting the door. "Now I want to be alone."

"At least think about it. Maybe you'll change your mind?"

She closed the door and began padding back toward her window seat, back to her view of the traffic where the world made no demands on her.

But before she was halfway there, Luc's forehead bumped the other side of the door. She stopped. She turned. Then he whispered. "What's happened to you, sis? Where is the Margot I used to know?"

She brought a hand to her mouth. His concern moved her deeply. Had she changed so much?

Feet clomped away down the hall.

She didn't want to see anyone tomorrow. But what if—for Luc's sake—she did?

* * *

It was three o'clock in the afternoon as Dylan lay in bed with the lights out. Usually, a short nap after an overseas flight helped prepare him for the evening. But tired as he was, he couldn't sleep.

Although confident of his own eternal future, he feared for Chelsea and Caleb, whom he loved dearly. He also feared for his parents. None were Christians. And if the end were near, if the Rapture took him and left them behind, who would guide them to the truth?

It gnawed at him like some kind of animal—that his siblings wouldn't believe, wouldn't save themselves from what was coming, that there'd be no one to show them the way.

And what about Margot Durand? He hadn't met her yet, but some sixth sense was drawing him toward her. Her art and her visions fascinated—yes, even obsessed—him. Even before they met, he felt a deep kinship with her. Someone needed to bring her back to faith, and Luc thought it might be him.

Why oh why wouldn't people believe? Why would they reject the bright eternal futures awaiting them?

Didn't they understand they were eternal beings, destined to live for time without end in one of two places? These last months, he'd thought a lot about eternity. And to be destined to live in Hell forever—he shuddered.

Was it that people didn't believe in their own immortality? Was that the problem? Did they not understand that the God who made the universe also made spiritual realms and spiritual beings to inhabit those realms? Was it also so hard to imagine that the moment a man or woman was birthed, God made them to be immortal creatures?

He gripped his hands together. He grieved for his brother's and sister's unbelief and for what it would bring them when the end came.

But his concern for their eternal futures was only part of what troubled him.

There was also this: He believed in Christ, and he was destined for Heaven, yes, but what had he done with his life? Lately, he had brooded on a passage from First Corinthians where it talked about the work we do here on earth and what we take with us into the next life. And as he examined his life before becoming a Christian—what had he done? Wandered from country to country, party to party? Explored mountain climbing, skiing, hiking, lying on beaches in the sun? Putting pleasure, the good life, and self above all else? But what good had that done anyone but himself?

If the Rapture came tomorrow, what would he take with him to the Kingdom of Heaven? A handful of good, yet unfulfilled, intentions?

He could not, must not, leave like that.

And people he knew and loved were in need of finding their way to eternal life, not to a timeless, never-ending death. If he didn't help them, who would?

Yes, before he left this earth, he was meant to do more. He was like an arrow in a quiver longing for a bow. The desire to fill this unmet need burned such a hole into the center of his being, tears now ran down his cheeks.

His heart was thumping wildly. He knew what he had to do, but it was scary, this decision he was about to make. More than scary, it was terrifying.

Still in his underwear, he slipped out of bed and fell to his knees. He closed his eyes and clasped his shaking hands.

"Oh Lord God, hear my prayer." His voice was loud in the empty room. "If the Rapture comes soon—and I think it will—those I love will be left here with no one to guide them to you. Lord Jesus"—he was breathing hard and fast now, his fingers digging into his palms so much they hurt, feeling like his whole body was thrust into this prayer—"please . . . leave me . . . behind. Yes, Jesus. When you take the others, please leave me here so I can bring your truth to the ones I love."

He was about to close when another request fought to the surface. "And then use me—yes, please use me—for whatever task you want me to fulfill. Let me do something that survives into the life beyond, something that shows my love for you. This I ask, from the bottom of my heart. Lord Jesus, hear my prayer."

Sweat was dripping off his forehead as he finished. He'd never prayed so hard.

But it felt right, and now he breathed easier.

When he slipped back into bed, he fell instantly asleep.

CHAPTER 16

THE CLINIC

Greenwich Village, New York City

Chelsea sat in the waiting room, her heart beating fast, her glance going every minute or so to the door. Where was Archer? He'd gone to his studio this morning, but he'd promised to meet her here before the procedure. She looked again at her watch. Only two minutes and they'd call her. He wasn't coming, was he?

How had it come to this? How could she, of all people, be sitting here, pregnant, with a boyfriend who cared more about almost anything other than being with her on the most difficult day of her life? What was wrong with him?

What was wrong with her?

When she was younger, she'd once dreamed of being a mother, of marrying a handsome, reliable man, and having a family. But that was long before she realized how archaic and old-fashioned was that dream. At least, everyone kept telling her that—everyone in every movement she'd ever been a part of.

Forget about marriage, they said. A woman has a right to exist apart from a man. You have a career and rights, they said. Don't buy the lie that you have to give all that up for an outdated tradition. What do you need with kids anyway?

What she got instead was Archer, a difficult live-in roommate, a bad artist with anarchist tendencies who couldn't pay his share of the rent, and a seat in an abortion clinic.

Her breath caught in her throat, and she wiped a tear from her cheek. *If anyone deserved a pity party for herself right now, it's you, girl.*

The door to the next room opened, and she had a glimpse of the procedure room chair, its metal footrests, and a whiff of antiseptic. "Chelsea Turner?" said the nurse.

"Y–yes?"

"We're ready for you."

Feeling as if she might throw up, she rose, walked woodenly toward the nurse, and entered the room.

* * *

Archer stood before his latest painting, *Pig On Fire*, and frowned. He'd worked on this every day for the last week, and it was as complete as he could make it. But now, after standing back and seeing it—really seeing it—in the harsh light of day, he'd come to a terrible conclusion.

It was crap.

Perhaps the worst thing he'd ever done.

He turned his back on it and walked to the window. The sun was bright, not a cloud in the sky, and in the stark light of day, the sun revealed that his latest work was indeed—

Total.

Utter.

Crap.

Whirling, he grabbed the three-by-five-foot canvas and shoved his foot through it. Then he struggled with the wooden frame, bending it until the joints separated. Then he rolled the entire mess up and threw it across the room toward the door.

He pulled out a new, smaller canvas, set it on the pedestal, and stared at the blank space. Perhaps he should do something more abstract? Something that didn't require him to draw an animal. Something with bold, dark colors to release his anger and frustration. But what?

A glance at the wall clock told him he'd missed Chelsea's appointment. She'd wanted him to be there, but what difference would that have made? He was better off here at his studio. She'd be angry, but so what? He could sleep here tonight on the cot in the corner. Tomorrow, she'd be over it, and they would make up.

It rankled that he had to rely on her to keep this studio, pay for his supplies, and even arrange for that disastrous show. He couldn't even help out with the rent. But wasn't that the story of his life? Always grubbing for scraps and relying on the charity of others.

His father had been an alcoholic, and his mother died when he was ten. Nothing in the world ever came easy for Archer Harris, whereas

Chelsea's father handed her everything she ever wanted. And though she railed against the upper classes, wasn't she part of them? She scorned her father's money, but she took it anyway. And now Archer took Chelsea's money, which in turn, she took from her trust fund. Looked at that way, their arrangement was only fair. He was only getting what was owed him.

And why should he have to babysit her at a doctor's appointment? He'd be of no use there at all.

Picking up a new pallet, he squeezed out some black, red, and yellow paint. He dipped a new brush with thick bristles into the black.

Then he dabbed and splattered enough onto the canvas, so it dripped all the way to the bottom. Good. Now for some bold slashes of red.

* * *

CHELSEA OPENED THE DOOR TO her apartment and walked in a daze into the kitchen. The whole time she'd laid on the procedure table, she'd closed her eyes, trying to think of something else. Still, what crept on demon feet through her mind were the sounds of suction, the smell of blood, the doctor asking the nurse if he'd got it all, and the nurse replying that, yes, he had.

Now she was sore, and she slumped into a chair and stared out the window. The bright noonday sun belied her mood of unending, unrelenting sadness.

She feared this mood would only deepen, darken, and never depart.

The only bright spot in this otherwise awful day had been Dylan's call this morning. What if she called him back and told him what she was going through? Right now, his was the only shoulder she wanted to lean on.

But no. She couldn't tell anyone about this. It must forever be her secret. Besides, it was now late evening in Brussels. After the long flight from Portland, he'd probably be in bed.

Struggling to stand, she drank a glass of orange juice from the fridge, then trudged toward the bedroom. Maybe sleep would take away this looming sense of utter despair?

CHAPTER 17

THE MOUNTAIN

Mt. Hood, Oregon

Caleb parked his rental car at the Timberline Lodge, and Blake went inside to register their climb. He opened the hatchback and removed the packs. When Blake returned, they took an inventory of their equipment.

Shell pants and jacket. Insulated jackets with hoods. Three pairs of gloves of all weights. Lunch, energy snacks, and water bottles. Carabiners, climbing harnesses and helmets, crampons and ice axes, rope and belay devices, first aid kits, glacier glasses, and trekking poles. They were already wearing wool long underwear.

"Looks good." With Blake's approval, they repacked everything into their backpacks and locked the car.

"It's nearly midnight." Blake turned to Caleb with a smile. "Ready?"

"I am. Let's go."

Leaving the parking lot, they began their ascent. They were taking the south-side approach, and their first stop would be the Silcox warming hut at seven thousand feet. The first leg of the climb followed the ski run, and the lift towers rose on their left, black scarecrows without lights, with dark patches on the slopes where the summer sun had burned through to the dirt. The air was crisp, the snow crunchy, and few climbers were on the mountain tonight.

Blake had assured him that slides from the quake should have taken down the worst of the mountain's loose ice and rock. "It's probably safer now than it's been all summer," said his friend and guide.

Last week, the men had spent three days removing downed trees from the access road. By the time they'd freed a path to the main highway, mountain rescue operations had recovered five bodies. That's also when Dylan left for the Portland airport to wait for his Brussels flight. "If there's another quake," he'd said, "I don't want to miss it."

Dylan's deep-seated desire to see the prophecy woman impressed Caleb. "But don't be surprised, brother," he'd said, "if you're disappointed."

To that, Dylan only smiled and said he wouldn't be.

After Dylan's departure, Caleb had spent time on Blake's porch, letting the mountain's crisp air, its perfect serenity, rejuvenate and restore him. He mused on what to write next. Yet he had difficulty coming up with a subject.

* * *

As the two men reached the warming hut, a chill wind whipped across the slopes.

"We just knocked eleven hundred feet off the climb." Blake pointed to the shed. "Want to rest a bit?"

"Sure." Caleb's feet crunched over frozen snow to the log shelter, open on one side and facing east away from the prevailing winds. He joined Blake and sat in one corner. On the far bench, another party of three climbers was also taking a break.

"Hey, David," Blake shouted to a man in a yellow parka. "Have you been up here since the quake?"

"No, but I hear it's okay."

He turned to Caleb beside him. "David goes to my church. He's also a guide."

Caleb removed his pack and leaned back against the log wall.

"Tell me again, what's your blog about?" Blake pulled out a candy bar and munched.

"It's about truth wherever I can find it." He, too, found a bar and began chewing. "We hear mostly lies nowadays and from all directions. We're bombarded with all kinds of nonsense from social media, entertainment channels, news media, and political leaders. And after all the recent censorship, people are hearing only one side of things. So far, the cancel people and the trolls have left me alone. Or else they haven't found me yet. My goal, as I see it, is to seek what people don't know and write about that. But deep truths. Not trivial stuff."

Blake nodded. "I've always known you to look deeper than most. But at college, I thought you were going into journalism. You got your degree in that, didn't you?"

"Yeah. But the news media have become so radical, so biased, I could never work for them. I want to do something important, something meaningful, with my life."

Blake caught Caleb's glance. "That's admirable. But your brother said something about an offer to work for Turner Enterprises."

"Never." Caleb gripped a pole tighter then rammed one into the frozen dirt. "If I did, I'd end up becoming my father. He's obsessed with money and power. He wants Turner Enterprises to be the biggest, most powerful company in the industry, perhaps in the world. But there's no end to his striving. He'll never be satisfied."

"I sense a bit of resentment there." Blake cocked his head.

"You could say that. He's run all our lives, and yes, he recently offered both of us an executive position with Turner Enterprises." Caleb waved his hands, dropping crumbs from his candy bar. "But if I did that, I'd end up just another Turner lackey. And in ten, twenty, thirty years— what would I have done with my life? Nothing worthwhile. No, someday I want to publish novels, important works that get at the truth of who we are, where we're going, and what matters in life. I've already written one, but I'm told it's too conservative."

"Wow!" Blake slapped a hand on Caleb's knee. "I wish I had that kind of ambition."

The three climbers opposite them left the hut and headed out. "See you up top," said David.

Blake waved as they departed. Then he faced Caleb. "I applaud your search for truth, but there's one truth that's more important than any other. What about the Son of God? There's a truth that's important for all eternity."

Frowning, Caleb eyed his friend. "What about him?"

"Why don't you look into him. Maybe write about what you find?"

He shrugged. "I don't believe in him."

Blake brushed crumbs off his shell pants. "But what if he is who he says he is? What if the Bible is true? What if your brother is right, and this woman, Margot, is receiving visions that line up with the book of Revelation, telling us the end is near? Because that's what I see. And if all that is true, then I'd think the news that the Apocalypse is about to happen and that Jesus is the only way out would be the most important, earthshaking truth anyone could write about."

Caleb had heard it all before. Except for the part about the Apocalypse. "How can God have a Son? I can't get my head around that. But I'll promise you this—if what Dylan's woman says is true, then maybe I'll believe."

"By then it will be too late." Blake stood. "But it's time we started out again. We need to get off the mountain before nine o'clock tomorrow to beat the ice falls."

Soon, they were trudging over frozen tracks made by hundreds of climbers before them that summer. The slope steepened, the wind picked up, and Caleb was glad for the shell pants and long underwear.

* * *

By four in the morning, they'd reached the Upper Palmer Lift House, the last area accessible to skiers. Caleb scowled at the climbers being dropped there by snowcat, skipping the full climbing experience.

"We've added another fifteen hundred feet of vertical." Blake leaned on his poles and watched a group leaving a snowcat and heading up. "How you doing?"

"Great." Caleb sucked in breath. He knew from maps that the Triangle Moraine lay ahead. But all he could see now was a hulking dark mountain silhouetted by the stars.

"First light will be in about an hour, but the climbing gets harder from here. Let's go."

Caleb followed his friend and guide up the mountain, toward the dawn.

WHEN IT HAPPENED

CHAPTER 18

THE TRUMPET CALL

In The Great Throne Room

1 Thessalonians 4:16–17 (NLT): *For the Lord himself will come down from heaven with a commanding shout, with the voice of the archangel, and with the trumpet call of God. First, the believers who have died will rise from their graves. Then, together with them, we who are still alive and remain on the earth will be caught up in the clouds to meet the Lord in the air. Then we will be with the Lord forever.*

The archangel Michael stood with Gabriel and the vast multitude of the heavenly host at the exit from the great throne room. Before him, ready to lead, stood the Son of the living God, shining now like a thousand suns. His hair was as white as the purest snow. His eyes, piercing and deep, were aflame with fire. And his feet gleamed like polished bronze.

Jesus beckoned to Michael and Gabriel then spoke. And his voice was the sound of thundering waterfalls. THE TIME HAS COME TO BRING HOME THOSE WHO ARE OURS. AS THEY RETURN, YOU WILL PROTECT THEM FROM THE ADVERSARY. LET US GO.

The Son of Light, the King of Kings, the Savior of Mankind, led them out of the vast hall, floating fast over the heavenly city's main street.

Michael and Gabriel, both holding trumpets, followed first. Michael glanced behind at the glow of excitement pulsing above the millions of angels pouring out of the throne room. Had there ever been such a vast angelic throng heading toward earth? As they passed through the miles upon miles of heavenly city, hundreds of thousands of souls emerged onto the streets of translucent, crystalline gold to watch in awe.

They left the city for the vast countryside beyond then entered a tunnel exiting the heavenly dimension, the one leading to earth. Faster and faster now, they traveled. They broke through the barrier of light protecting the holy realm. Surrounded by swirling darkness on all sides, Jesus led them at an increasing pace.

Their goal was to protect and comfort the redeemed and to thwart the plans of the Adversary. For, once Lucifer discovered what was happening, he'd surely mount an attack on God's people.

Michael had known the Adversary since the beginning, back when his name was Lucifer. Back when Lucifer prized wisdom and obedience.

Of all the angels, Lucifer had been, by far, the most beautiful. Truly, his beauty shone as bright as his robe of precious stones—its red carnelian, pale-green peridot, white moonstone, blue-green beryl, and green jasper. Back then, everyone thought him blameless, and Michael had revered him and called him friend.

But after the Lord of Hosts gave Lucifer power to lead the others, something in him changed.

So much did Lucifer fall in love with the splendor of his own existence, so much did he bask in the glory of admiration from his brothers, he forgot by whom he was made.

Pride entered into him. And he sinned.

One day, he approached Michael and the others. "Has not the Lord of Hosts given me the power to lead you?" he asked. "So now I, the brightest most beautiful star in the Heavens, will lead the angels instead of the Lord of Hosts. I am as great as He—surely you see that?—and if you swear your allegiance only to me, together we can do great things."

After a third of the brothers agreed to follow Lucifer, Michael was sickened to his core. In secret, he met with Gabriel, also shocked by what was happening, and together they approached the Lord God Creator.

But the Lord of Hosts already knew, and when the number of the rebels was complete, the Creator cast Lucifer and his followers into the outer darkness.

In that moment, Lucifer became the Adversary, God revoked the former status of the rebels, and the angels became demons. Lucifer then declared all-out war on his former brothers. Now the only sanctuary from his evil was Heaven itself. Everything else was in need of defense.

A light appeared at the tunnel's end and quickly expanded. The earth appeared below with its cities, farms, and villages. Jesus nodded to Michael and Gabriel beside him.

He put the great trumpet to his lips. Gabriel did likewise.

After countless millennia of waiting, the ethereal blast that issued forth from those instruments echoed and rang and reverberated around the earth, a tremendous ethereal vibration falling only on the ears of the redeemed, a sound calling the people of God out of the world.

The last trumpet of the church age, calling God's people home.

CHAPTER 19
DYLAN AND MARGOT

Brussels, Belgium

1 Corinthians 15:51–52 (HCSB): *Listen! I am telling you a mystery: We will not all fall asleep, but we will all be changed, in a moment, in the blink of an eye, at the last trumpet. For the trumpet will sound, and the dead will be raised incorruptible, and we will be changed.*

It was early afternoon under a sunny sky, and Dylan left the taxicab below the three-story building and took a deep breath. How long had he waited for this moment? What would happen when he finally met the woman whose visions had drawn him across two continents?

The Durands lived on the third floor, and in the tiny downstairs foyer, he entered the one-person elevator and pushed the button. At the top in a stuffy hallway, he knocked, and the door opened.

"Dylan Turner?" The young man speaking his name bore a mop of blond hair, a thin mustache, and eager blue eyes.

"Yes, and you must be Luc?"

Luc bid him enter, and they shook hands. "I am so glad you have come, Dylan. We are so worried about Margot, and your interest might be what is needed to snap her out of this sadness, this unbelief that has taken hold of her life."

Dylan's heartbeat quickened. Wasn't this expecting a bit much from him?

Luc took him into the living room before a television set where an old man with thinning gray hair sat watching a soccer match—but of course here they called it football. The old man rose, and Luc introduced his father, Claude.

After exchanging greetings, Claude turned down the volume. "Luc tells me that for some time you've believed deeply in Margot's paintings and want to meet her?"

"Yes, sir. I flew in from Portland, Oregon. I've felt a powerful urge to come here and meet your daughter."

"And you are a devout Christian?"

"Yes, sir. I am." Saying that to a stranger felt good.

Claude drew a hand across the liver spots on his forehead. "My daughter has withdrawn from the world, Dylan. What is worse, she has renounced her faith. We fear for her. If you can convince her that her visions, and mine, are important and come from God—well, I will pray for your visit with her."

Dylan nodded, thanked him, and Luc led him down the hall to a closed door.

"After we talked yesterday," whispered Luc, "I told her you were coming, but she did not want to see anyone. Maybe today, she will change her mind." He knocked.

"You have a visitor, Margot," Luc said to the wood. "Please open the door."

Silence.

"Please, Margot. He has flown halfway across the world to see you."

More silence.

Luc tipped his head back, eyes closed, lips pressed taut. "Please, sister," he whispered.

Footsteps padded across the floor, and a short, black-haired woman with bangs and dark eyebrows opened the door a crack. Underscored with dark circles, her eyes peered out at him. And those eyes, so wide open and honest, seemed to penetrate deep into his.

Taken aback, he sucked in breath. She was beautiful, not in a classic sense, but in a real, earthy way. This unassuming yet vulnerable woman was not whom he pictured as the author of the visions that so obsessed him. "Hi," he finally said, "I'm Dylan." He smiled. "Can we talk?"

As she examined him, he shifted from one foot to another, feeling like a fool. Was that all he could think of to say? What if she said no? He'd flown thousands of miles, and after one glance deep into his soul, she was going to say no.

"Come in, then, Dylan." A brief smile flitted across her face, a winning smile that broke her somber visage. "And yes, I'll speak with you a bit."

Luc laid a hand on Dylan's shoulder and grinned. "I will be watching the game. Good luck." He whirled and headed back down the hall.

Margot shut the door then led him to a bay window overlooking the city. She started to sit facing away, toward the street, then seemed to change her mind and sat facing him. "You flew all the way from America?"

Dylan pulled up a nearby chair. "From Portland, yes, and thank you for seeing me."

"It's no use, you know?" She brushed aside a black bang, and that simple action sent his heart aflutter. "No one can convince me that I haven't made a terrible mistake."

"You mean about the paintings?" He motioned to the rows of canvases stacked against the far wall, so many they occupied one entire corner of the room. "There's something about them, Margot—may I call you Margot?"

"Yes . . . Dylan."

"There's something about them that drew me in from the moment I saw them. They've become something of an obsession with me. You were given an incredible gift."

Her lips pinching together, she shook her head. "I wasn't. It was all a delusion, a trick of the Devil."

Dylan's face scrunched in pain. "But how can you say that? I've shown them to a friend of mine from college, a Christian who's studied Revelation. He says they're an accurate depiction of what the Bible says."

"He did?" She tipped her head.

"Let me ask you something. Before you started painting, did you ever read the book of Revelation?"

"N–no. The priests say that's their job."

"Then how were you able to paint so many images that seem to come straight from Scripture, adding so many specific, frightening details that you brought the future, the Bible's apocalyptic predictions, alive?"

"My archbishop says they just frighten and don't inspire people. He says they're works of the Devil."

He waved a hand. "Let me tell you something: When I started reading Revelation for the first time, I, too, was frightened." He brushed aside stray hair and flashed her a smile. "It's meant to be frightening. It's about the end of the world."

"Where did you say your home is?" She cocked her head.

"I flew from Portland, but I grew up in Minneapolis. My parents also have a villa near Florence, Italy, and that's where I spend a lot of time. It's become my second home."

"It must be nice in Italy. Warm. Sunny. Without so much rain."

"It is."

She smiled, and again, it sent his heart aflutter. "What do you do with your time, Dylan?"

He looked down. "Not much, I'm afraid. I read. I travel a lot. And go to parties."

"Surely you do more than that? You said you went to college?"

"Only for two years. After I left Carleton, I mostly wandered—much to my father's dismay, I might add."

"I would love to travel." Carrying a faraway look, her eyes sought something in the distance. "Where have you been?"

"Tuscany, of course, and most every country in Europe. The Cinque Terra in Italy. The Swiss Alps. The south of France. Sometimes, I visit my sister in New York, my brother in Chicago. Lately, I've spent a lot of time in the woods near Mt. Hood, Oregon. Hiking, biking, skiing. Whatever's fun." He frowned at his feet. "I'm afraid I've mostly wasted my life."

"Oh, I don't know. That all sounds wonderful. Your family must be rich."

"You could say that. My father's the CEO of a big security company. But he and I don't have much in common." Feeling his jaw muscles tightening, he looked toward the window. "Correction—we have *nothing* in common."

"I–I'm sorry." She laid a hand on his then jerked it back. "That must be difficult. My family has a close relationship. Or at least, we did." Now she looked away as well. "Until I stopped believing."

He nodded toward the rows of paintings. "Can I see them?"

Under her brows, her eyes darkened, and her jaw tightened. "I wasted four years of my life on them. Are you sure you want to see them?"

"Please?"

"All right. But only because you came such a long way." She stood and led him toward the stacks of canvases.

On the phone, Luc had said she'd painted two hundred visions. But flipping through the outpouring of so many years of divine inspiration nearly stopped his breath. Dylan paused at one painting showing opposing armies on a vast battlefield. Another pictured people in the street fighting over bread. Another illustration was of a man preaching before a crowd in a cellar with a watcher at the door. Each scene was finely detailed, with color, perspective, and a remarkable—one might say unearthly—sense of realism.

"You are a great artist." He walked to the next row and flipped through canvas after canvas. Through visions of earthquakes. Comets falling onto a devastated earth. Fire and hail raining from the sky. All scenes of terrible destruction. He faced her with widened eyes. "I've seen the internet photos, but in person, these are . . . breathtaking."

"I haven't painted a stroke since I saw the archbishop."

"He was wrong, Margot." His face hardened. "I'm here to tell you that, whatever he said, he was dead wrong."

"But he's the Church. And only ordained, educated priests can interpret signs and visions. That's what the Church says. I should have known that before I started. He said they were"—as if in pain, her thick eyebrows tried to meet—"works of the Devil."

Dylan shook his head. "Listen to me, Margot Durand." He took her hands in his. "I'm only a new Christian, but I've studied, and what I see here is not, cannot, be the work of the Devil. These were inspired by . . . God. Yes, they are—"

He staggered, feeling dizzy.

A terrible feeling of loss shook him, starting in his head and rippling down his chest to his legs.

Somehow, he sensed it—something good and right and necessary had just been ripped out of the world. It was as if, in a split second, the world turning on its axis had lost something important. A chill shuddered, convulsed through his body, piercing deep into his soul.

Margot's hands flew to her cheeks. And the fright and surprise in her eyes told him she, too, sensed something terrible had just occurred.

"What . . . happened?"

"You felt it too?" Agony twisted her face. "I—I don't know."

From outside came the sounds of cars crashing.

They both ran to the bay window.

The street was a scene of chaos. A number of vehicles must have lost control simultaneously. A nearby Volkswagen crashed into a light pole. At the intersection to their right, a Peugeot rammed into two other cars. On their left, a bus crossed into oncoming traffic and smashed head-on into a delivery truck.

In the distance, a passenger jet was plummeting from the sky, heading for one of the city's tallest buildings. As they watched, breathless, gripping each other's hands, the plane ripped into the top floors, followed by a ball of fire rising through the upper stories.

"Your . . . painting." Breathing fast, Dylan looked to Margot and waved at the scene. "This is it. Right here."

"Yes." Wild eyes glanced back into the room.

They both ran to the stack of canvases, and Margot directed him straight to the one they'd flipped past a moment ago. She pulled it out and brought it to the bay window.

Dylan held it up. It was an exact depiction of what was happening outside—the same Volkswagen and light pole, the same bus and truck colliding, and in the distance—the same plane crash and burning building.

"My visions." She caught his glance, and her mouth opened. "They were true."

"Yes. It's happened. The Rapture." Dylan's heart was beating hard. "The believers have been taken."

"And I wasn't." She slapped her hands over her eyes. "Oh, what a fool I am. I believed the archbishop, not my visions."

She started sobbing, and not knowing what else to do, he drew her toward him. She gave herself into his arms, and he held her.

"But you?" She looked up into his eyes. "If you are a Christian, why weren't you taken?"

"Because I prayed yesterday to be left behind. Someone has to bring the truth to my brother and sister." He peered into her eyes. "And to you."

"You did that?" Her eyes widened, a slight gasp slipping past her lips. "For me, too?"

"Yes."

But now that his prayer had been answered, his gaze fell again on the destruction outside, and the reality of what he'd done was only just sinking in. For weeks now, he'd studied and read about what was coming—a time of terrible tribulation, judgment, and destruction.

A time of terror that he and Margot Durand and all those left on earth would now have to face. A shudder began in his shoulders and rippled down his spine.

What had he done?

CHAPTER 20

THE RIVER CRUISE

On the Rhône River

Matthew 24:37–41 (HCSB): *"As the days of Noah were, so the coming of the Son of Man will be. For in those days before the flood they were eating and drinking, marrying and giving in marriage, until the day Noah boarded the ark. They didn't know until the flood came and swept them all away. So this is the way the coming of the Son of Man will be: Then two men will be in the field: one will be taken and one left. Two women will be grinding at the mill: one will be taken and one left."*

The cruise up the Rhône was nearing its end, and tomorrow they'd be docking at Lyon. The afternoon sun burned hot on the third deck terrace where Adam Turner sat in a lounge chair with Kate beside him, sipping his glass of Chateauneuf du Pape, one of the region's best wines. On the table before him, his tablet was open to his investment account.

"While we've been touring the river, enjoying the scenery, the excellent food, the fine wines, I've made forty million dollars in our personal stock account. The business account has done even better." Adam gazed at the device with admiration, perhaps a hint of love.

"Can't you put that thing away for at least one day?" Kate squinted against the sun, now peeking under the umbrella. "We're here to relax."

"Relaxation, my dear, is seeing a twenty-percent increase in the company's investments this year alone." He sat back and glanced at the forested hills as the ship turned a corner of the river. "That's what gives me pleasure."

But as he set his glass on the table, Cheryl and Bob Smith passed nearby. Seeing the two empty chairs at their table, the St. Louis pastor stopped. "Can we sit? We haven't seen you two since the trip started, and tomorrow is our last day."

Adam had tried his best all week to avoid them, but now they'd caught him and Kate sitting at a table with two free chairs. He gave a dismissive wave to the seats opposite, and the Smiths sat.

"How have you enjoyed the cruise, Adam?" asked a smiling Bob.

"It's been fine." Adam avoided eye contact and shifted in his seat. Pretending to avoid the sun, he swiveled his chair to face away from the Smiths toward the river. Maybe they'd take the hint and leave. With high hills on both sides, the river here wound through the French countryside, and the sun glinted off the rippling water. A hundred yards ahead, a steel railroad bridge with concrete pillars loomed over the river.

"These little villages are so quaint." Kate was waving her wine glass again. "They're filled with so much history. It's like being in school all over again."

Cheryl laughed. "How true, my dear. How did you like the wine tasting at Tournon?"

"It was wonderful," said Kate. "Although I think the California wines are just as—"

A sudden sinking feeling, as if Adam were coming down with a nasty bug, hit him hard, swirling in his head.

Kate screamed, and he whipped his head toward her. She pointed a finger at the empty chairs where the Turners had sat. They must have left rather abruptly. He frowned at his wife. "What's the matter with you?"

"Th–they disappeared."

"Good. I didn't want them sitting here, anyway."

"N–no, Adam. You don't understand. They . . . just . . . disappeared." Her right hand was shaking, spilling wine all over her dress. "One moment they were here. And the next . . ." She closed her eyes.

"Get a grip on yourself. You—"

From down the terrace came a shout for help. Another woman was crying, a man was shouting something, and now a crewman in a white coat was running down the deck, his eyes wide. Adam stood up, grasped his arm, and stopped the purser before he passed. "What's going on?"

"Th–the captain." The man waved toward amidships. "One moment he was there. And the next"—wild eyes searched Adam's—"he wasn't. He was in the wheelhouse. The door's locked. No one's running the ship!"

"Then get someone to open it." Why didn't these people show more gumption?

"I can't find the copilot." This time, the crewman waved toward the bow. "And look!"

Adam's gaze swept forward where the man pointed. The ship was headed straight for a concrete bridge abutment.

As the purser ran to the bow, Adam raced to the wheelhouse. Inside, it was indeed abandoned. But as he peered through the glass walls, his gaze settled on a white suit jacket, pants, shirt, and a captain's hat. All in a heap on the floor. Had everyone suddenly lost their minds?

He glanced forward again. The ship was still aimed at the concrete piling. Looking around, Adam found the only thing he could use—a deck chair. He lifted it, slammed it hard against the glass. Nothing. Again, he tried to break through, but it didn't even cause a crack.

He glanced again toward the bow. Even if he could get to the wheel, there wasn't enough river left to turn the ship. Others on the terrace also realized the danger. They were standing and pointing. Some were running toward the stern.

The ship entered the bridge's shadow. The pillar grew larger.

He ran back to Kate, still sitting at the table, still stunned by what she imagined she'd seen. "Come on!" he shouted. "We have to get out of here."

"W–what?" She raised startled eyes. Was she drunk again?

"Get up!" He grabbed her hands and yanked her to her feet.

The deck jerked out from under him.

His head hit the floor.

An earsplitting crunch of metal and glass followed. The ship lurched sideways. Tables and chairs tipped onto the deck, skidded, and screeched toward the port railing. Adam and Kate slid along with the furniture. They came to rest against the piled-up chairs.

"Are you all right?" He drew a hand across his forehead. It was bleeding.

"I th–think so."

Moans and crying now came from the other passengers, lying or standing in various positions against the port rail or caught in the mess of downed chairs. One woman began screaming.

He tried to stand, fought a wave of dizziness, then helped Kate to her feet.

The ship had plowed straight into the concrete piling. A twelve-foot section of port bow was missing. Now, the current was bringing the stern around into the main channel, sweeping the ship away from the abutment, farther from shore. Then they were drifting sideways down the river. But the deck angled oddly toward the port bow.

"We're sinking." His heart was beating fast. "We need life preservers."

"Sinking?" Her startled gaze swept the deck.

His glance, too, swept the deck, but he found not a single crewman. "Come on."

He led her across the deck, tilting more all the time. Everyone had life preservers in their cabins, but theirs was one deck below, and he wasn't going down there now.

Hadn't there been some hanging in the stairwell? He opened the door, but passengers from the lower decks swarmed out, blocking the way. He rejoined Kate just ahead of the mob.

The deck now angled so much it was difficult to walk, but somehow, he led Kate to the port rail and a point free of the tangled furniture. "It's going to sink." His heart thumping hard against his ribs, he gripped her hand, stared into her wild, frightened eyes.

"This can't be happening." Her head wouldn't stop shaking. "They just disappeared. And now the ship is sinking."

"Stop it!" The deck's angle increased further. "The ship's going down. Get ready."

He'd barely said the words when the deck lurched to port, and like a catapult, it launched him and those around him into the air and over the railing.

Still holding Kate's hand, Adam hit the water and went under.

CHAPTER 21

THE CHURCH OF PEACE

Greenwich Village, New York City

2 Timothy 4:3 (NLT): *For a time is coming when people will no longer listen to sound and wholesome teaching. They will follow their own desires and will look for teachers who will tell them whatever their itching ears want to hear.*

Chelsea woke Sunday morning needing to hear words of comfort and reassurance. Last night, Archer never came home, not surprising after his failure to appear yesterday. She was still sore, but after a cup of coffee and a piece of toast with jam, she walked the mile and a half to the Church of Peace in Lower Manhattan. There she found a seat, hoping the words of Pastor Freya Lewis would ease her troubled soul.

The woman stood at the front wearing a green, floor-length frock and a sash across her chest decorated with the symbols of the Jewish star, the Christian cross, the Islamic crescent moon, the Buddhist white parasol, the taijitu with the black-and-white yin and yang of Taoism, and a globe symbolizing earth wisdom. The topic today was love, and Freya Lewis, who often identified herself as Christian, had a unique approach to the subject.

"God is love," said Freya Lewis in conclusion. "And when we love another person, no matter who they may be, God approves. Jesus boiled all of the law into two commands: Love God. And love others. That means it's okay to love your same-sex partner. And if your love is so deep you wish to marry, then who can say no? Yes, I believe the God of love blesses such a union. And this afternoon at two o'clock, I will host a discussion on matters of sexual preference, changing your birth sex, and choosing your sexual identity."

That, for Chelsea, fairly summarized the message. It wasn't what she needed, but it calmed her troubled mind. She didn't really believe in God or Jesus or the Church. But once in a while, attending these little rituals brought her comfort, peace, and a feeling of belonging. The singing was always uplifting.

When the service concluded, she joined a line of people filing out the door to shake hands with the pastor on the steps outside. In front of the church was a narrow plaza in the process of renovation, with a new maple surrounded by rocks but missing a metal grate. She passed the tree and was almost to Freya Lewis when the young man in front of her started a conversation she couldn't help but overhear.

"Thank you for your message," said the man, dressed smartly in new jeans, a black shirt, and a white tie. His long black hair fell nearly to his shoulders. "But I suggest you know neither your Bible nor the God you are preaching about."

Freya Lewis cocked her head and frowned. "What makes you say that?"

"You've focused entirely on only one of God's attributes—his love. And in doing so, you've ignored a vital truth. God is also good and holy. To love God is to obey him, and he says we shouldn't sin. And because God is perfectly holy, good, and just, he must judge sin. Indeed, the very nature of a perfectly holy God requires him to judge sin. And what you've preached today about homosexuality is, in God's eyes, an especially abhorrent version of sin."

The pastor's eyes widened, her mouth opened like a fish's, and she seemed unable to respond.

"Yes, Pastor Lewis, God has a particularly dim view of same-sex 'love' as you call it. Just listen to Romans, chapter one." He had the Bible open on his phone, and he began to read.

" 'So God abandoned them to do whatever shameful things their hearts desired. As a result, they did vile and degrading things with each other's bodies. They traded the truth about God for a lie. That is why God abandoned them to their shameful desires. Even the women turned against the natural way to have sex and instead indulged in sex with each other. And the men, instead of having normal sexual relations with women, burned with lust for each other. Men did shameful things with other men, and as a result of this sin, they suffered within themselves the penalty they deserved.' "

Around him, a crowd was now gathering. The young man cast them a wary eye but continued reading.

" 'Since they thought it foolish to acknowledge God, he abandoned them to their foolish thinking and let them do things that should never be done. Their lives became full of every kind of wickedness . . .' I'm skipping ahead here, but it goes on. 'They know God's justice requires that those who do these things deserve to die, yet they do them anyway. *Worse yet, they encourage others to do them, too.*' "

The man slipped the phone into his pocket. "Well?" he asked.

The church congregants were now frowning, shifting their feet, leaning closer to hear every word.

"That was only a . . . man . . . speaking." Freya Lewis was breathing hard, her eyes narrowing.

"It was Paul, an apostle appointed by Jesus himself." He eyed his growing audience uneasily.

"You are a . . . hater."

"Not me, Pastor. Those are God's words, not mine." The young man took a step back from the encroaching throng. "And what you're preaching is apostasy straight from the mouth of Satan."

"Hater! Hater! *Hater!*" came an explosion of cries around him.

He whirled and started to run.

Seething with anger and hate, the crowd picked up rocks at the base of the tree and began throwing them. "Hater!" they screamed. Rocks fell beside and beyond the man. One nearly missed a young woman in a pink dress leading a small child by the hand.

For a moment, a red-faced Freya Lewis watched two of her congregants chase him down the street, occasionally stopping to hurl more rocks.

It was Chelsea's turn, and she stepped forward. "Thank you, Pastor. I mostly agreed with what you said."

Freya Lewis's focus was still on her receding opponent. She breathed deeply, smoothed her green frock, and faced Chelsea. "You're welcome." Slowly, recognition came to her eyes, and she tried a smile. "And did you come to a decision on what we talked about?"

"I took care of it yesterday, and . . ." But as the words formed on her lips, Chelsea's eyes moistened, her throat began to close, and she could barely finish. "The baby's gone."

"I'm glad you decided." But the pastor's eyes were still distracted, glancing occasionally toward the fleeing young man, and her manner indicated she wanted to be elsewhere.

Chelsea took her leave and started down the sidewalk.

But she hadn't gone fifty feet when an odd feeling twisted something inside her head. It was as if between steps, she'd dropped fifty feet from a cliff top, and her heart was still back on the ledge above. She sucked in breath.

Frozen where she stood, her breath coming fast, she whirled toward the street.

Everywhere, chaos was erupting. Vehicles were losing control, crashing into cars, storefronts, pedestrians. People were screaming or standing openmouthed, staring at empty spaces on the concrete. The young woman in the pink dress was crying, staring at a pile of clothes on the sidewalk. "Where is my baby?" she cried.

A passenger-less motorcycle veered crazily toward her, and she jumped back as it skidded on its side, sparks flying, engine whirring, wheels spinning. It knocked over a newsstand, broke through a pharmacy's glass front, and screeched to a halt, its front wheels breaking into the store.

To add to the sense of unreality, a pile of clothes and shoes littered the sidewalk beside her.

Had the entire world gone crazy?

Behind her, someone screamed, and Chelsea spun.

A van was racing out of control. It bounced over the curb, heading for the line of congregants, heading for Pastor Freya Lewis. Everyone but the pastor scattered.

Freya Lewis turned—slowly, too slowly—toward the vehicle.

Run, Pastor. Run!

Chelsea's heart flipped upside down in her chest. Her hands flew to her mouth.

Freya Lewis tried to run. But there was no time. The van hit her body with a loud crunch, launching it into the air before lurching to the side.

The body smashed against the bricks fronting the Church of Peace.

Then it dropped, limp and unmoving, onto the sidewalk.

CHAPTER 22

FREYA'S JOURNEY

Greenwich Village, New York City

Isaiah 5:18, 20 (NLT): *What sorrow for those who drag their sins behind them with ropes made of lies, who drag wickedness behind them like a cart! . . . What sorrow for those who say that evil is good and good is evil, that dark is light and light is dark, that bitter is sweet and sweet is bitter.*

When the bus slammed into her, Freya Lewis felt a moment of shock and disorientation before the world went black.

When she returned to consciousness, she was confused. It was odd, but all her senses had heightened a hundredfold, and she was more aware, more alert, than she'd ever been.

She stood now above a woman's crushed, bloodied, and mangled body. Gazing closely, she discovered the woman's hair was like her own. How odd! The woman also wore the same dress Freya had put on this morning. What a coincidence! And how terrible for the poor soul!

A few of Freya's congregants approached, but they ignored her and rushed to the woman's body. One man knelt over it, feeling for a pulse. Then he backed away, shaking his head.

"I'm over here," she called. "I'm all right."

The man looked straight at her, and though she waved, he didn't acknowledge.

Something wasn't right.

A thought crawled from the back of her mind to the front, and she shivered. But it was too surreal to believe.

Was she dead?

When she touched her arms and chest, she squeezed solid flesh. It felt different, more solid, even more sensual.

From somewhere, voices were calling her name. "Freya, Freya. Come with us."

Relieved that somebody finally recognized her and could talk to her, she glanced around. In the alley beside the church, a fog had gathered, within which moved the silhouettes of a number of people, but the mist concealed their faces. This, too, was strange. But she sensed warmth and love from them.

A sense of unreality rose up within her. Fighting a wave of dizziness, she stepped closer.

"That's it, Freya," they called. "Come with us. Come closer."

Three more steps, and the fog deepened. When she glanced back, the street, the crashed bus, and the church were cloaked in dim shadows.

A tremor rippled down her back.

"Yes, Freya," they called. "This way. Only a bit farther."

She walked further, and swirling shadows replaced the fog. Turning back, she took a step toward where the street had been. But it was gone.

"No, stupid, not that way." The voices were harsher now, more insistent. "Come with us."

"Who are you?" The sense that they were friendly was fast disappearing.

"Your friends, Freya." But the tone was mocking. "And we love you."

"Is this Heaven?" She mouthed the words, but she feared the answer.

"Yes, Freya, this is Heaven, and you must come with us." But the mocking laughter that followed sent chills across her shoulders. Something was terribly wrong here.

Unable to return to the street, she took more steps toward them.

The dark figure of a woman stepped from the shadows. "Yes, Freya," said the voice, followed by cacophonous laughter. "Welcome to your new home. This is Heaven, and you'll be with us forever and ever."

A sudden, unreasoning fear tightened her throat. The woman was lying.

A whiff of sulfur and rotten flesh washed past her, and she gagged. The darkness around her gathered and grew. But it was unlike any darkness she'd ever experienced. It was thick and deep and without end.

She also sensed that some necessary, comforting ingredient that had always been present in the world was missing. She was utterly, totally, alone.

From the side and behind came raucous laughter, and she whirled. Two more shapes stepped out of the dark, but their noses, mouths, and eyes were distorted caricatures of humanity.

"We want to love you, Freya." A woman darted forward and touched her arm.

But the stroke of those fingers was like icicles dragged across her naked flesh, and Freya jumped back. And yes, now she realized she was naked.

"Yes, Freya, we love you." Out of the shadows, another woman lurched toward her, grabbed her breast, and its hand slid away. But where its claws had raked was now a mass of pain, a gaping wound.

Freya screamed and stared at the ragged, bleeding flesh. "No!" she shouted. "This cannot be."

"But it is, Freya." A third shadowy figure, another woman, jumped in front of her, and as it embraced her, she gagged at the whiff of rotting flesh from its mouth. When it pulled away, a ripple of pain spread down her back where claw marks had scraped.

A fourth shadow leaped out of the dark and ripped away a hunk of her shoulder. A jolt of searing, shivering pain shot through her torso.

Screaming, she turned and tried to run, but behind her followed dozens—hundreds?—of the twisted, satanic caricatures of men and women.

Were they demons?

As she stumbled on, the flesh they'd torn from her body grew back. And the fear that had gripped her a moment ago now increased a hundredfold, becoming a suffocating blanket of terror, a soul-trembling, gut-searing kind of raw horror burrowing deep into her soul. And she now realized what was missing from this world—the love, compassion, and mercy of God.

"You are ours, Freya," they shouted, their words mocking, insistent. "We are yours forever and ever."

"Jesus!" she shouted into the darkness. "Why have you left me here?"

A figure of brilliant light appeared in front of her, and the demon-people vanished into the darkness.

"Why are you here, Freya Lewis?" came his words, and she sensed such a powerful love mixed with such deep sadness that tears streamed down her cheeks. "You led your flock not to me, but to the Adversary. You knew my words, but you twisted them and refused to listen or obey them. You led your people not into righteousness, but into terrible iniquities of the flesh. And you promoted the murder of little ones yet unborn. I didn't leave you, Freya Lewis. Long ago, you left me." And before she could respond, the brilliant light vanished.

Around her now, the crowd of shadowy figures increased and closed in. Darting in and out, they grabbed at her arms, her legs, her breasts, her private parts. And wherever their claws raked, they ripped away pieces of flesh and left searing, unbearable pain. They screamed horrible obscenities. They mocked her. They laughed. They belittled her and told her what a fool she was.

When she was nothing but a bloody mass of pain, a pile of shredded flesh clinging to bone, crying and writhing and gnashing her teeth on the ground, they backed away into the depths. As the flesh grew slowly, painfully back, she knelt and vomited, but her stomach was empty.

When she was whole again, she stood and searched frantically for a place to hide. But around her was only the endless abyss of darkness, the horrible memory of what they'd just done to her, and the thought that there was no end to this.

Picking a spot, tears streaming down her cheeks, she fled toward it.

From the dark, they rushed at her again. "Forever," they cried. "Forever and ever and ever."

CHAPTER 23

THE DINER

Greenwich Village, New York City

Archer Harris woke with a headache. Perhaps it was the ten shots of whiskey he'd downed before going to bed last night. Or maybe it was because he hadn't eaten anything since yesterday noon. In any event, he walked the four blocks to Mac's Diner, the small restaurant he often frequented. On a Sunday morning, he'd have the place all to himself.

He bought a paper from the vending machine outside, then entered, and slumped into a booth. Without the usual commuter crowd grabbing a quick bite, only he and two other men occupied the place.

"CHAOS IN ST. LOUIS!" screamed the headlines as yet another weekend of riots, murder, and anarchy erupted in the nation's heartland. Good for them.

His favorite waitress, Sandy, appeared beside him with a coffee pot and mug. Today, she wore calf-length leather boots, a short red skirt, and a blue jean jacket over a white blouse.

He tilted his head and flashed a smile. "I thought you didn't work Sundays?"

"Liza's sick, and Mac called me in." She poured his coffee. "It means I'm missing church. But a gal's got to make a living."

"I've been wondering: What's a pretty thing like you do with her Saturday nights?" He poured cream into his mug.

"Saturday nights? I do laundry." She frowned. "What'll you have?"

"With that outfit, I bet you're into country and western. Or maybe line dancing. With a beer in one hand and a guy in the other."

"No beer. Don't like the taste. And I just like the western look." She put a hand on one hip while sashaying sideways with the other. "What's your name again?"

"Archer. And I'll have two eggs over medium with bacon and toast."

"Got it." She left him and took the order to Mac, the ponytailed owner and cook behind the counter.

The other two customers stood and paid Sandy at the cash register. The bell over the door tinkled as they exited to the street.

Over sips of coffee, Archer nursed his aching head. Beyond the window, cars waited at the intersection. For a Sunday morning, traffic was light. The sun was out and already hitting the streets. In Archer's New York, there were few early morning shadows.

Turning to the next page, he skimmed the headlines. PALESTINIAN QUAKE LOSS SEVERE. And: OVER TWO HUNDRED THOUSAND DEAD. And: NO VILLAGE LEFT UNTOUCHED. And: OREGON TEMBLOR CLEANUP UNDERWAY.

As the waitress set two plates before him, Mac brought a broom from around the counter and began sweeping the floor.

"I know a little country-western bar not far from here." Archer caught her gaze and grinned. "I'm usually not doing anything on a Saturday night."

She began refilling his coffee. "And now, I suppose you're going to ask me out?"

"It's possible." He grabbed his cup and dumped in sugar. "Do you have a guy?"

"No, but even if I was looking for one, I doubt you're my type."

"And what's your type?" He poured cream after the sugar.

"For one, he wouldn't be sitting here on a Sunday morning nursing a hangover." One hand went back to her rising hip. "He'd be in church."

"Okay." He sat back in the booth. "You caught me. And I suppose that's never happened to you?"

"Sometimes"—she started to smile—"I admit it has, but—"

But she never finished her smile. Or her sentence.

With Archer watching, with his focus only on her, she simply vanished.

One moment his eyes were feasting on the silky auburn hair, the engaging smile, the roundness of her hips. The next, he was staring at the counter beyond.

The coffee pot shattered to the floor, followed by her clothes drifting down.

At the same moment, something lurched inside his head. But he was too rattled to take inventory of the feeling.

He stared down at the red skirt, the blue jean jacket, and the white blouse, all scattered around her leather boots and soaking up spilt coffee.

Then he laid a hand on his forehead, wondering if he had a fever. But no, he wasn't sick. Only hungover.

"Hey, Mac!" He shot a glance toward where Mac had been sweeping.

But Mac's clothes also lay piled at the end of an abandoned broom. Mac, too, was gone.

From the street came the noise of rending, screeching metal. Out the window at the nearest intersection, a black sedan had rammed headlong into a van, and the cars behind were piling up. Then a white SUV jumped the curb and smashed into the jewelry store across the street. It crashed through the bars on the display window, rending metal and showering broken glass over the sidewalk. A burglar alarm began clanging.

He stood and raced out the door. On the sidewalk, a man knelt before a pile of women's clothes. His mouth agape, he raised frightened eyes to Archer.

What was going on?

At the far intersection, cars were also clogged. Another accident?

He crossed the street, empty here, and ran to the jewelry store, closed on a Sunday. He approached the SUV. Had the driver left the vehicle? Then he saw jeans and a flowered blouse on the seat. So whatever had happened to the waitress had also happened to this driver.

Reeling, he stepped back. People were disappearing, evaporating into thin air.

Then he put his finger on the odd sensation he'd experienced when the waitress had vanished. It was as if some invisible restraint he'd struggled against all his life had just been removed. And he was free.

The store's alarm was still clanging, but he didn't expect any cops to come. The entire world had just gone crazy, and now, surely, they had bigger fish to fry. Sweeping broken glass off the hood, he crawled over it, past the twisted metal bars, until he was inside. Behind the counter, he found a plastic bag. He picked up a piece of the car's fender from the floor and approached the line of glass cases. The light was dim, but the first locked display held diamond rings. With the fender, he smashed the glass and began filling the bag.

The next case held rings, diamond and emerald bracelets, ruby earrings, expensive watches. He stuffed them, too, into the bag. Case after case, he emptied until the plastic bulged. Then he opened the front door from the inside and strolled back across the street.

Inside the diner, he had the place all to himself. If people everywhere were vanishing, leaving their homes and stores unguarded like Mac's, how many other opportunities had just opened up? Who was there now to stop him from doing anything he wanted?

A smile widened his lips. Whatever had just happened—even if it was the Apocalypse—perhaps he was meant for this?

His phone buzzed inside his pocket, and he answered. It was Chelsea. She was rattled, scared nearly out of her mind, and wanted to meet.

"I'm at Mac's Diner," he said. "Only a short walk from your church. I'll be here."

After he hung up, he sat down before his plate and picked up the fork. He hoped the eggs were still warm.

CHAPTER 24

THE LAST ASCENT

Mt. Hood, Oregon

By five thirty, the sun had been up for half an hour, shedding a crystal-blue light from a cloudless sky. The two climbers passed Devil's Kitchen and arrived at Crater Rock. Following Blake's lead, Caleb sat on the slope and pulled crampons over his boots.

Steam rose from a nearby fumarole, and the smell of sulfur itched in his nostrils. Off to the side, snow had melted around a circle of hot rocks, reminding him that Mt. Hood was indeed an active volcano.

Catching his breath in the thin air, Caleb glanced to his friend and guide. "If you don't mind . . . I'd like to stay another week at your place. Your cabin is good for my muse."

Blake brushed snow from his pants and grinned. "On one condition."

"What?"

"That next Sunday you come with me to church."

Caleb finished snapping the crampons in place. "All right. For another week up here, I can do that."

"When your brother stayed here the last few months, he finally seemed to find peace."

"And you're going to tell me it's because he found Jesus?"

Blake cocked his head. "Don't say I didn't try. But we'd better start out again. We need to be off the mountain before the ice falls begin."

For the next four hundred feet, they traversed the Hogsback, an ice- and snow-covered slope. One group of four climbers was ahead of them while another trudged behind. With each step, Caleb breathed out white fog.

At the bergschrund crevasse, Blake drew them to a halt and pointed to a five-foot gap. "It's gotten wider since the quake."

Caleb gazed into endless white depths and shuddered.

"We'll have to go around." Blake led them to the left, and they followed the gap until it narrowed to only two feet. "We can do this."

He crossed first, and Caleb easily followed.

They trekked back to the main route and headed up toward the most difficult part of the ascent—the Pearly Gates. The way steepened, and Caleb found himself inside a chute, leaning against a forty-five-degree wall of ice. He slammed his ice ax onto the slope above and, with each step up, kicked his crampons into the frozen surface below. Around his waist, a rope led to Blake above. Caleb's blood was pumping fast.

His friend glanced back. "I'm sorry for this, Caleb. If I'd known this was all ice, I'd have taken you up the Old Chute instead."

"That's okay." Caleb was breathing heavily from climbing in the thin air above eleven thousand feet. "It's good to get a different climbing experience. But I must say, for my first real alpine climb, I'm enjoying this."

"You'll be ready for Mt. Rainier before you know it."

A sudden gust of bitter cold washed down the chute, but he welcomed it on his face.

Blake's ice ax drove into the frozen snow above, sending a few chunks bouncing back down. "We've only an hour to reach the summit. We're right on schedule."

"Great." Caleb kicked a boot into the ice, thrust his ax ahead of him, and—

A sudden feeling of vertigo churned in his head. He sucked in cold air.

But his disorientation was more than physical. It was as if some necessary component in the fabric of the world had just vanished. As if all the world's hope had been gathered up, ripped from its roots, and replaced by despair.

He looked up.

Blake was gone.

And Blake's backpack was tumbling down the slope toward him.

CHAPTER 25

BLAKE'S JOURNEY

Mt. Hood, Oregon

1 Corinthians 15:52b (NLT): *For when the trumpet sounds, those who have died will be raised to live forever. And we who are living will also be transformed.*

One moment, Blake's hand was grasping his ax, and he was kicking a crampon into the ice, ready to climb higher up the chute. The next, a trumpet blast reverberated down the mountain, vibrating his body, his mind, and his soul, reaching deep and touching every molecule and atom of his being. It was a "sound" unlike anything he thought possible, a single musical note, yet so complicated, it contained thousands upon thousands of undertones, harmonies, and melodies. And somehow, when the blast hit his ears, he was able to hear and distinguish and absorb every multifaceted, multidimensional wavelength.

He experienced a moment of disorientation.

When he recovered, he realized his body had fundamentally changed, and he was in the air, flying. Suddenly, he had never felt so good, so happy, so free. The muscle aches from climbing, the biting cold on his face, and the difficulty breathing the thin air had all vanished. A sense of peace unlike anything he'd ever imagined settled in and around him. Time itself also changed, and he knew, intuitively, that what was happening to him now was occurring in a quadrillionth of a second everywhere on earth.

Still rising fast, he looked down. There was Caleb, his gaze fixed on the slope. Blake's pack was frozen in midair, about to tumble toward his friend.

If Caleb weren't thrown off-balance, he'd be all right. He had the skills to climb back to the bottom by himself.

Blake was above the peak now, and wherever he looked, he could focus, whether it be ten feet or ten miles away. He cast a glance to the far horizon, toward Portland, and he could see the burned-out hulks of buildings, the people wandering the streets. Others of the redeemed, including children below the age of assent, were rising into the sky. But the numbers were too few. He gazed below and saw the mustache on the leader of another group making its way up the chute about two hundred yards behind Caleb. Plumes of frozen breath from the climbers formed solid clouds around them.

From high above came singing—clear, melodious tones so sweet and ethereal, they would bring tears of happiness to mortal eyes. The music filled him with incredible joy. Beside him, two beings of light appeared, smiling, welcoming, guiding him. He sensed their love for him, even as the three of them rose faster into the sky. Far to the right and left, a hand-ful of others, also accompanied by angelic creatures, rose from the earth. Among them, he recognized his friend David.

Where before his mind was clouded, now it was crystal-sharp, and he understood things his earthly mind could never have comprehended. This was the Rapture, and those who possessed the Spirit of God within them, those who had declared their love for and belief in Christ, were being taken out of the earth. With only a fleeting thought to those left behind, he looked up.

Across a sky that moments ago had been clear, bright, and azure came a massive surge of roiling, churning clouds. From one end of the earth to the other, the clouds covered the horizon, and within this heavenly mist shone all the colors of the rainbow. It centered on a being brighter than the sun, brighter than the millions of others around him, brighter even than the glowing heavenly army flying beside him.

It centered on Jesus, Lord of Lords, King of Kings.

And as Jesus traveled across the sky, he gathered up all who were his, all whose names had been written in the Book of Life, and all the chil-dren below the age of assent.

Blake sensed his journey was happening moment by moment. But from an earthly perspective, he knew it was happening—had already happened?—instantaneously. In whatever realm he was now a part of, the nature of time itself had fundamentally changed.

By now, he had risen several thousand feet above Mt. Hood. The surrounding land spread out below, with its rippling foothills, sprawling towns, and green forests. But out of everything he was experiencing—even more than his new, perfect body, the comforting angelic creatures, the incredible feeling of peace, and his ability to fly—the one thing that stood out above all was the love he felt from the great being of light.

When Jesus looked down upon him, Blake had not imagined such love could exist anywhere, from anyone. No earthly words could ever have expressed it. Nothing he could ever have imagined could possibly describe it. An indescribable peace, joy, and elation filled and lifted every corner of his being.

And he sensed that finally, after struggling his entire life, he was going home.

Because time was so different, he was not at all surprised when Jesus began a review of his life. In the tiniest fraction of a second, Jesus walked with him through all the major events he'd ever lived through. . . .

All the good and the bad.

All the people he'd hurt, the people he'd helped.

Every sinful, lustful thought or deed, every harm he'd ever done to anyone.

Every relationship, good and bad, and how he'd loved or not loved.

Every person he'd ever helped.

All that he'd done to further the church.

All the people he'd told about Jesus.

He'd not been perfect, not by any means. And as he reviewed his life before this being of perfect love and righteousness, he regretted all the opportunities he'd wasted—the people he could have helped, those he could have told about Christ and didn't, and the lost opportunities for serving, giving, and furthering the kingdom of God. But when the review concluded, Jesus forgave everything, every bad thought and deed, every moment of doubt or falling away, and he welcomed Blake with a love that reached deeper into the recesses of his soul than anything he'd thought possible. In the end, Jesus's love overwhelmed everything, and Blake knew he was welcome into the eternal family of God.

He joined the millions assembling before the roiling clouds, and the procession continued around the earth. Beside him flew a vast and diverse multitude. He knew intuitively that they were African tribesmen, Andes hill people, suburban American housewives, London factory workers,

Russian peasants, Persian innkeepers, and Roman soldiers. They came from every age and every land—those who had put their trust in Jesus or, before his coming, in the promises of God.

All were flying beside Jesus and the two great angels bearing the trumpets that called the redeemed out of the earth—first from the dead in their graves, then from the living.

The angels, whom Blake knew as Gabriel and Michael, blew on their great trumpets, and the sound reverberated around the world, calling more and more believers to their side.

Now he joined in the music arising from millions of voices, all singing in a thousand languages that, somehow, meshed together in a perfectly harmonized melody praising the King of Kings and Lord of Lords.

It was the Rapture, and Blake reveled that he was going home.

THE MOMENTS AFTER

CHAPTER 26
THE PAINTING

Brussels, Belgium

Margot lifted her head from Dylan's shoulder and eased away. "I've been such a fool." She looked into the eyes of this newcomer from whom she sensed such warmth and understanding. That he'd prayed to be left behind to save others touched her deeply. "I should have trusted God, not the archbishop."

His gaze moved from the scene of destruction unfolding out the window back to her. "You believe again, don't you?"

"Yes." She wiped a tear from her cheek. "But it's too late."

From down the hall came the sounds of the football match, but the sportscaster's tone had changed to one of alarm.

"Father!" She whirled away from Dylan. "And Luc!" She rushed across the room and through the door. Down the corridor and into the living room. As she ran, she knew what she'd find, and her breath came faster. Before the television, she stopped.

Her hands gripped the sides of her head.

Father's clothes lay on his chair, his slippers on the floor.

Luc's clothes were strewn over the couch beside Father's.

She rocked her head from side to side. Of course, they'd been taken. Throughout, they'd been faithful, whereas she, wallowing in grief and anger at herself and at God, had embraced disbelief. Dropping her hands, she struggled to breathe. "They're gone. My family's gone."

The pain in the eyes of this American whom she barely knew mirrored her own, and he nodded. "What do we do now?" he asked.

"Listen." She pointed at the television.

"Something odd has happened," said the sportscaster, "and they're calling a halt to the game. The German goalkeeper is no longer at his post. Neither is the French fullback. There seems to be some confusion on the field, and—wait. Something's happened in the stands as well."

The camera showed someone leaning down to whisper in the announcer's ear, and the man's face scrunched in a frown. He faced his audience. "They're calling the game. Apparently, a number of sudden, unexplained disappearances have just occurred here at Lotto Park in Brussels and elsewhere—"

Margot picked up the remote and shut off the television. "I'm a fool. I turned from my own visions and renounced my faith. And now I've been left behind."

"And I prayed to stay here, thinking I could save my siblings. And you." He shook his head. "I hope it was worth it." Then a laugh escaped him, and she lifted a puzzled glance.

"What?" she asked.

"Aren't we both a fine pair of fools?" The smile he gave her then was so genuine, she wanted to smile back.

But the regret, the loss of her family, the knowledge that again she'd been wrong, oh, so wrong—it tore at her heart. New tears ran down both cheeks.

Again, he took one of her hands in his. "It will be all right," he whispered.

Somehow, his words comforted, and she wiped her cheeks.

"Let's go back to the window," he said.

She followed him back to her room, and they stood before the bay window looking down at a city struggling to recover from the initial chaos.

"Look!" Dylan's startled gaze focused on the painting they'd left leaning against the wall.

When she saw it, she gasped.

She'd painted the scene two years ago. It depicted the Rapture happening on the streets beyond where they were standing now. But when she'd painted it, the perspective showed only what was outside the building.

Now the viewpoint had changed. Now the painting encompassed the interior of the bay window itself. And somehow—during the time she and Dylan had gone to the living room—two figures had been added—

Two figures standing side by side, staring down through the window onto the street.

Two figures who were unmistakably Margot and Dylan.

"W–what?" She stepped back, cast a glance at him, then again at the picture.

"It's us, isn't it?" Dylan was breathing fast, his eyes fixed on the picture. "Showing us as we stood here only moments ago."

"It's not possible." She clutched a hand to her chest. "How can such a thing . . . ?"

"Margot, this is telling us something." His voice rising in pitch, Dylan whirled toward her. "We were meant to be here. Both of us. Here in this place. Together."

Her gaze went again to the painting. Was it possible?

"Something or . . . someone . . . led me here to you, to your apartment." He waved a hand. "I didn't understand what it was, but for weeks, a powerful obsession told me I needed to see you. Then yesterday, something led me to pray to be left behind. But this painting—the only explanation for what brought us together is . . . God."

"Yes." She knelt to the canvas and examined the new brush strokes. The paint was dry, and the technique was hers, as if she'd painted it herself. It was as if the figures of her and Dylan had been there all along. She rose. "You're right. But why?"

"Why?" He smiled. "It must be for a reason. God has brought us together to fulfill some purpose."

"But what?" A thrill now beat in her chest.

"I don't know."

"Dylan Turner, it must be true." She wiped the lingering moisture from her cheeks, grabbed both his hands, and returned his smile. "We were meant to be together."

CHAPTER 27
TROUBLE ON THE WATER

On The Rhône River

Still holding Kate's hands, Adam Turner hit the water and went under. But he lost his grip on her. Kicking furiously, he rose to the surface and gasped for air.

He paddled in a circle. His gaze swept the river. But he couldn't find her. His wet clothes made treading water difficult. Still, he searched. All around him, men and women were trying to keep their heads above water. But she wasn't among them.

For long minutes, he paddled in circles, fighting the current. Once, he even dove beneath the murk but saw nothing. Weary, he treaded water, tried to catch his breath.

He had to face it. Kate was gone.

The current was fast carrying him and the other survivors downriver, away from the ship. It had sunk at the bow upstream where ten feet of stern stuck at an angle above the water, but it wasn't moving.

He was nearing exhaustion. Now, he regretted not going to the health club more often.

A few yards nearby, an elderly, white-haired man wearing a life preserver floated face up, his eyes closed. Adam detected no movement. Was the man dead?

He swam toward the man and struggled to release the clips to free the arms and chest from the vest. He'd just unsnapped the last buckle when the eyes opened, stared at him, and something incoherent issued from the man's mouth.

Adam yanked the vest free from grasping hands then paddled a few yards out of reach. Well away with his prize, he pulled the preserver over his chest and, breathing heavily, snapped it on.

When he glanced back, the man had gone under. All the better. Explaining what he'd just done would have been . . . difficult.

He thought about making one last effort to find Kate. But she'd never returned to the surface, and he'd now drifted far downriver. If only she'd learned how to swim.

But he was used to setbacks—in business and in life. Painful though it was, he must move on.

The current was swift, and the bank was passing quickly beside him. He began swimming toward shore. But he made little headway until he broke free of the main channel. Beside him swam a few other survivors.

Once in calmer waters, he was able to reach the bank. He climbed the muddy wall and fell, exhausted, onto the grass. All up and down the river, other passengers were also leaving the water. Townsfolk appeared and began helping the survivors.

He stood and struggled out of the vest. Pulling out the phone still in his pocket, he looked for a signal, but the display was blank. He shook it, but water had ruined the device.

An old man with a walking stick appeared beside him. "Parlez vous français?"

"No, I speak English."

"Dans la rivière, I see what you do." An expression of disgust twisted the man's face, and he raised his stick at Adam. "You let the man to die."

Momentarily taken aback, Adam stepped away. But he recovered his composure, shoved his accuser's stick aside, and strode toward the village. The old man tried to follow, but Adam soon left his pursuer behind.

It was only a half mile to the main square. There, he pulled out his wallet. Fortunately, he still had that. And his credit cards. At the largest café, he sat in the sun and breathed his relief.

But when the waiter saw him, mud-streaked, wet, and disheveled, he asked Adam to leave. Trying to keep calm, Adam explained to the startled servant what had happened in the river. Then he waved a soggy, hundred euro note, ordered a coffee with brandy, and asked to borrow the man's phone. After a moment's hesitation, the waiter agreed, and Adam called his Paris office.

"Our ship sank in the Rhône," he said to a man identifying himself as Louis. "The captain and crew were negligent, gone from their posts, and we hit a bridge. My wife . . . she drowned." Adam took a deep breath. "I'm going to sue them for everything they've got."

"I am terribly sorry, monsieur." Louis's voice at the other end was rattled. "But have you not heard? All over the world, people are disappearing. Everywhere there is pandemonium. No one knows what is going on."

"Disappearing? All over the world? Are you sure?"

"Oui, monsieur. Everyone is afraid. Everywhere is total chaos."

His gaze drifted past the table and across the square. So what Kate was trying to tell him was true. The Smiths had truly disappeared. So had the captain and copilot. What was important now was to return home.

"I need to rent a car. I'm in . . ." He looked across the way to a sign on a shop. "Vienne, I think. Can you arrange for me to get a vehicle here? Lyon isn't far. And get me reservations at a good hotel in Lyon for tonight. And a flight to Minneapolis tomorrow."

"Oui, monsieur. One moment."

Long minutes later, Louis returned. "You'll be staying at the Cour des Loges Lyon. But all the rental companies are closed on Sunday. I would suggest a taxi."

"All right. Thank you."

When the waiter appeared with his coffee and brandy, Adam reluctantly returned the waiter's phone and sat back.

Strange and sudden disappearances?

Chaos everywhere?

Once he was back at company headquarters in Minneapolis, he must learn all he could about what had just happened. One thing he'd learned in life: Wherever there was disaster, there was also great opportunity.

CHAPTER 28

CHELSEA AND ARCHER

Greenwich Village, New York City

When Chelsea pushed through the door into Mac's Diner, Archer was sitting in a booth before an empty plate. On the floor, a man's clothes had crumpled near an abandoned broom, and a woman's outfit lay beside Archer. Still unnerved by the bus crash and what she'd seen on the walk here, she slumped into a seat opposite and shivered.

"Archer, I don't know what's happening, and I'm scared."

"I don't know either, babe, but look." He pulled a bag up from the seat beside him and emptied its contents on the table. Diamond rings. Emeralds. Gold watches. A veritable cache of jewelry. "I'm rich."

Horrified, she stared at the pile then at him. "Where did you get that?"

He pointed to a jewelry store across the street where a van had smashed through the window.

"But that's theft."

"No one's going to care anymore, babe." He picked up a diamond ring and let the light twinkle through its prisms. "The cops are plenty busy. Want this?"

"No. It's . . . stolen."

"So what?" He dropped the ring and gestured to the clothes strewn on the floor. "Mac's gone. So's the waitress. In fact, everyone's gone. Have you had breakfast yet?"

"Just some toast. But I'm not hungry."

"Sure you are. I'll make you some eggs. Mac's not with us anymore. He won't mind."

Chelsea gazed at the piles of clothes and shut her eyes. "A bus just killed a woman pastor in the place where I was standing only moments ago. And on the way here, I saw accidents on every street. Archer, people are disappearing!"

"Yeah, they are." He stood and went to the griddle. He fished in the refrigerator, after which came the sound of frying eggs and bacon. Then he popped some bread into the toaster. "It's a new world, babe, and I fit right in."

"What are you talking about?" She wrapped her arms about her chest, trying to control her shivering.

"Look." He walked to the cash register, opened it, then waved a handful of bills at her. He stuffed the bills into his pockets. "Now they're paying me to eat here." He laughed.

"Archer, that is wrong. You can't just—"

"Just what?" He looked up from his frying. "Take what I never had because I wasn't born to it? Babe, I'm thinking this thing was made for me."

"No matter what's happened, theft is theft—even if you have no money and someone else does."

"You're always talking about how we need to tear down the system and take power from the oppressors and give it to the oppressed. Well, here we are. It's a new world, and I'm doing just that."

"But not this way."

Moments later, he brought her a plate with eggs, bacon, and toast. "Here. Breakfast's on me."

She looked at what he'd made, then at Mac's clothes and the empty restaurant, then realized that she *was* hungry. "But I'm vegan."

"Can't you eat the eggs? Nothing died to make them."

"All right. Just this once. But you take the bacon." He grabbed the bacon, and she pulled the plate toward her. As she ate, she opened her phone's browser to a news site and read the headlines.

Unexplained Disappearances Rock Nation.
Babies Ripped From Mothers' Wombs.
Air Traffic Grounded Nationwide.
President Urges Calm, Refuses To Declare Emergency.

She only finished half her plate before pushing it away. "The nation is in turmoil, people have disappeared for no reason, and I'm having serious trouble dealing with this." She crossed her arms. "Aren't you the least bit curious about what's happened? I mean—the world has just gone nuts, and you're running around stealing stuff."

"Sure, I'm curious. And yeah, I'd like to know what's going on." He shoved his jewelry collection back into the bag. "But so what? It happened. And there must be more stores around—even apartments—where the owners have disappeared. Do you know what that means?"

"The world might be ending?"

"Don't you see?" He cocked his head. "I've never had a break my entire life. Now I see a great future for someone like me. Babe, I'm going to be rich—filthy, stinking rich. I can take whatever I want, whenever I want, and no one's around to stop me. Just look!" He pulled out the wad of bills from the cash register and laid them beside the bag.

Chelsea sat back in the booth and narrowed her eyes at him. What was happening here? She'd never seen this side of Archer before. Sure, he'd always been covetous of other people's advantages, wealth, and privilege, but she thought he was grounded in at least *some* morality. His art often depicted a search for justice and a realization that something was wrong with the world. Sure, his paintings were crude, bold, and angry— What revolutionary ideals weren't? But this blatant theft of other people's property . . . Something inside her rebelled.

"So you're going to do more of this?" She waved her arms at the bag and the cash.

"Why not?"

"Maybe because it's wrong?" Her forehead scrunched.

"If no one owns it anymore, is it wrong to steal it?"

"How do you know Mac didn't have a son or a daughter or a brother? How do you know the owner of that jewelry store won't come here tomorrow and find you've stolen a lot of his inventory?"

Archer shrugged. "Not my problem."

"And I suppose not coming to the clinic yesterday wasn't your problem either?" Even as she stood from the table, the soreness reminded her of the procedure.

"Oh, about that—sorry, babe. Got wrapped up in a project and lost track of the—"

"Sure thing, Archer." She walked to the door and stopped. "You're always losing track of something, aren't you?"

"I'll be home for you this afternoon, babe. I promise."

"Maybe not." She put a hand on the door. "Since you're so rich all of a sudden, maybe you should just get your own apartment?"

Archer's jaw dropped, and for a moment, he seemed taken aback. Maybe more rattled than he'd been after the world around him went nuts. And what did *that* say about him?

She pushed through into the street, turned right, and walked past the window behind which he sat, still gaping at her, still searching for a reply.

CHAPTER 29
CALEB'S DESCENT

Mt. Hood, Oregon

When Blake's pack smashed into Caleb's legs, his feet slipped from their holds, his ice ax lost its grip, and he fell backward down the slope. He flipped onto his belly, but, oh no—now he was sliding down the chute headfirst.

The slope was icy and steep. If he didn't stop, he'd keep going for five hundred vertical feet or more, right into the bergschrund crevasse. Or he'd pass over it into Devil's Kitchen, toward its superheated, bubbling fumaroles.

He tried to grab the ice walls on either side of him with his gloves, but they only sprayed ice crystals and snow onto his goggles. Spreading his legs, he tried to kick his boots into the curve of the wall, but his feet, with the spikes facing uphill, couldn't find a grip.

Still sliding, he threw both arms to one side and somehow flipped himself around onto his back. Now he was headed downhill feet first, his back resting on his shuddering knapsack. He kicked hard into the snow on both sides, but the studs only threw up another hail of ice and snow into his face. When his spikes tried to grip the ice wall, they sent a violent pulsing up his calves, gripping, then releasing, gripping, then releasing.

His speed was increasing. He hit a bump. For a few seconds, he was airborne.

He was a human bobsled, racing out of control down the mountain.

Below, he was fast approaching the second group who'd barely started up the Pearly Gates. Seeing his approach, they spread out and stretched a rope between them. As he neared their makeshift lifeline, the slope lessened, and he raised his hands.

He reached for it—and yes!—grasped, and held on. That slowed his descent, and he finally rammed both boots into the snow and came to a stop.

Clumps and balls of snow and ice rolled down the chute beside him.

For one moment, he lay on his back, the blood pumping hard through his veins, his heart racing. Then he stood and looked back up the mountain.

What had happened to Blake?

His friend had been above him, leading the way, talking one moment, gone the next.

What . . . had . . . happened? He peered up the chute into the shadows. Was that Caleb's ax up there, stuck in the snow? He could barely make out Blake's boots. And Blake's clothes—hung up on shards of ice.

It was as if his friend had been ripped bodily out of his clothes and . . . simply . . . vanished.

His hands found the top of his head. Then he remembered Dylan's phone calls trying to convert him to Christianity, Dylan's incessant talk about the Rapture, and how Jesus would someday come for his people and whisk them away.

Blake was a Christian. What other explanation could there be?

He was breathing fast, his thoughts spinning. It wasn't possible, but how else could he explain this? It went against everything he believed, yet—he'd just seen it with his own eyes.

One moment, his friend was above him.

The next, he was gone.

Blake had been raptured, and Caleb was left to face the terrible events that so obsessed Dylan, events depicted in the Belgian woman's paintings that Caleb had so easily dismissed. And now he wondered if Dylan, too, had been taken.

The other group began walking back to him, and he met them halfway.

"What happened?" asked a woman about his own age. Her freckled face, with its pert nose, nestled so tightly inside her parka, could have belonged to a snow pixie. The thought was so incongruous with his situation, if he hadn't been so disoriented, he would have laughed.

"My guide, my friend Blake, was ahead of me." He sucked in air. "Then he . . . just . . . disappeared." Caleb pointed to Blake's pack that had stopped some distance up the slope. "That was his."

"What do you mean?" Another man, older, with a weathered face, possibly a guide, stepped close. "What happened to Blake?"

"He just disappeared. One moment he was there. The next . . ."

"I don't understand."

"He vanished into thin air."

Guffaws erupted from three of the six-member group.

But then the pixie woman's cell phone rang, and she answered. Another phone belonging to a black-haired young man, possibly a college student, also rang.

For long moments, as the two conversed, their voices intense, their eyes serious, the others listened.

Finally, the pixie woman hung up and faced the others. But her face was long, her eyes wide.

"He's right." She could barely get the words out. "It's happening everywhere."

"Yeah." The college student's tone was breathless. "All over the world, people are disappearing."

"It's the Rapture," said Caleb. "And those of us who weren't Christians have been left behind. Folks"—his glance sought each of the six—"this is the end of the world as we know it."

All that answered him were six startled faces, the whistling of the wind through the chute, the cry of a hawk overhead, and the scream of a woman from another group barely visible down on the Hogsback.

CHAPTER 30
ENTRANCE TO HEAVEN

In The Kingdom Of God

1 Corinthians 2:9 (NLT): *No eye has seen, no ear has heard, and no mind has imagined what God has prepared for those who love him.*

In the tiniest fraction of a second, Blake had followed the great procession of angels, the newly raptured, and the redeemed of the church age. They had circled the planet, gathering all who belonged to the family of God. Then this being of infinite love, this Jesus who shone with the light of a million suns, brought them to a tunnel leading away from the earth—a tunnel invisible and inaccessible to mortal eyes—and they entered.

Faster and faster, they flew through the passage. Around them swirled a deep blackness, and just outside the tunnel walls, the angels accompanying them brandished flaming swords.

From out of the shadows appeared millions of other angelic creatures, but these carried no light about them, only darkness. Their faces were twisted into masks of hate, rebellion, and anger.

Blake knew instinctively they were demons, former angels banished from the heavenly realm for some past insurrection and disobedience. Each carried jagged black swords, sickles, and hammers.

Outside the tunnel walls, the heavenly host engaged the demon army in battle. Seemingly everywhere at once, Gabriel and Michael swung their mighty swords, longer than many of the demons they fought. The massive, fiery blades clashed with thunderous force against the demons' black weapons, shedding sparks and fire.

For one moment, Blake felt fear. The forces against them numbered in the millions. The enemy swarmed the vast space around the tunnel, even as the procession traveled faster and faster toward their destination.

One demon broke through, his sword cutting into the tunnel wall itself. But Michael appeared instantly. His blade sliced down and broke the demonic weapon in half, driving the dark twisted creature away.

HAVE NO FEAR, came the voice of Jesus, and his words were like the rushing of many waterfalls. They filled Blake with peace, calm, and compassion. THEY WILL NOT WIN.

Onward they flew as the demons harried and pursued them. A disc of light appeared ahead and grew larger. With Jesus leading, they passed through it.

Blake glanced back. The demon horde was stopped at the disc. The barrier of light trapped them forever in the outer darkness.

Led by Jesus, the great multitude of the redeemed and the angels entered a new and wondrous realm, and Blake gasped in awe. Its peaceful light and beauty were so intense, it filled him with indescribable joy.

He'd entered Heaven itself.

* * *

HE CAME TO REST AND stood on a kind of ridgetop. Drifting down around him came music so beautiful, so intricate, it could never have been made on earth. More than sound, it was a multithreaded symphony cast over multiple frequencies—as if through light waves, radio waves, and infrared and ultraviolet waves, all at once. And somehow, in his new body, he could hear every impossible note. Here in this place, had God created a new kind of physics? Whatever the medium, the music was so complex, expertly woven, and pleasing, he could listen to it forever.

It was the same with his vision. He was looking down into a lush, green valley surrounded by distant, shimmering mountains, a scene so peaceful and eye pleasing, he wished his whole body could smile. The grass on the slopes beneath him was of uniform length, about a foot high, every blade perfect and waving in unison. The blades parted as he walked—no, floated—over it. And each blade glimmered with a thousand—no, a million—shades of green, gold, russet, blue, violet, red, and more colors he'd never before seen and had yet no words for. Every changing color, hue, and shade was a feast for the eyes.

Off to his left, a forest of tall pines covered the slopes, their perfect trunks each rising a thousand feet or more into the sky, thousands of giant stately columns. When he focused on their tops, he could see the smallest detail on the tiniest cone on the highest branch.

He sent his gaze to the horizon and the farthest blue-black peak. Up there, mountain laurels bloomed with brilliant whites and purples and blues and glistened brightly on the crags. The mountaintops shimmered as from snow or from a million multicolored crystals. But it couldn't be snow, for here was no heat, no cold, only perfect weather.

Farther to his right, a golden city of light hovered above the plains, its walls extending so wide, rising so high, he couldn't see the sides or top. Embedded in its translucent walls of shimmering, effervescent gold stood a giant gate of milk-white pearl, now yawning open. Visitors clothed in glowing light were entering and leaving.

He marveled again how all anxiety and fear had fallen away. The love of Jesus, his Savior, filled every corner of this place, washing over all, lifting him, buoying him, reminding him that it was Christ who had created it, Christ who had brought him here.

A crowd of familiar faces appeared before him. Greeting him first was his mother, dead five years now, smiling and opening her arms. They hugged, and for a moment, it was as if their souls merged and she exchanged her love with his. Then he told her how much he missed her.

When she'd died of cancer at fifty-five, she'd been thin, emaciated, made hairless by the chemotherapy. But now she appeared as a young thirty-year-old, her long blonde hair curling in waves to her shoulders, her eyes and face clear and bright and smiling, her body youthful and emitting a warm glow. Beneath the glow, she wore her favorite flowered dress. Everyone seemed dressed in their favorite clothes, the ones they felt most comfortable in. Just seeing her filled him with such happiness, he could almost shout. And somehow, though he would never have recognized her back on earth, he knew this thirty-year-old better than he'd ever known her when she was alive at fifty-five.

Greeting him next were his father, dead for seven years now, his grandparents, and distant cousins, uncles, and aunts. Also, friends from long ago, taken from life too soon. And members of his church, good friends who'd passed on.

Then a young man, also about thirty, approached. "Hi, Blake, I'm Brian, your younger brother."

"But . . . you died when I was four." He gaped. "I never knew you."

"And now you do." They embraced, and again Blake could barely keep his happiness in check. For all those who'd died in youth had grown here to the same age as Christ.

Again, he noted how time was so different. He could speed it up or stop and savor this moment of greeting forever. He did, and his reunion went on and on and on.

When it was over, they parted, and he marveled again at how he wasn't really walking, but floating, flying, wherever he thought to go. Then Blackie, the collie that had been his constant companion until about four years ago when a car ended his life, bounded out of the forest. Blake knelt, the dog licked his face, and they both felt each other's happiness, in the process discovering another new sense.

At the bottom of the valley grew a vast swath of flowers. Just by thinking, he floated there among them. He entered a field of giant daisies, petals as long as his arms, stalks taller than he. Each flower emitted a scent so pleasant and multilayered, he breathed deeply, floating along a winding lane through their midst, savoring their tranquility and incredible beauty.

Then a realization hit him. This was just the beginning. The heavenly realm was far deeper, vaster, and more complex than what he'd just seen. He'd barely touched the tip of his little toenail over the threshold, and it would take an eternity to explore and relish all that lay beyond. Even then, he'd not have seen it all.

As he passed to the far side of the flower paddock, he came face to face with Jesus, the one who'd led him here, the one in whom he'd believed, trusted, and followed. Though the light of a million suns shone from him, Blake could see him just fine. Jesus's smile, focused now on Blake alone, seemed to hold all the love that, if it had been gathered from every person on earth in one place—Jesus's love would still far exceed it.

"Is it to your liking, Blake?" Jesus's eyes were smiling.

"I like it just fine."

"I thought you might." Jesus laughed. "Welcome home!"

ONE DAY AFTER

CHAPTER 31
THE BIKER

Spearfish, South Dakota

Caleb pulled his rental car into a motel lot in Spearfish, South Dakota and parked near a motorcycle and a van. After returning from Mt. Hood to Blake's cabin, he'd tried to get a flight home. But because so many pilots, air traffic controllers, and security personnel had been taken, and because so many planes had fallen from the sky, the President had imposed a nationwide air traffic shutdown until they sorted things out. At five in the morning, awake and unable to sleep more, he threw everything into his rented Toyota and started for Chicago.

After a few stops, he'd been on the road nearly fourteen hours and couldn't drive another mile. The trip had been harrowing, driving through one ghost town after another, creeping through unmanned gas stations without a living soul. He'd narrowly avoided abandoned cars, appearing at random in the middle of the highway, had seen others wrapped around signs, crashed into bridges, or flipped upside down in the median.

It was now eight in the evening, and after checking in at the motel's front desk and dropping bags in his room, he crossed the highway to a small diner. Not only was he dead tired, he was famished.

Inside, an older couple sat at a booth. Two teenagers occupied a far table. Caleb plopped onto a stool at the counter and grabbed a grease-stained menu stuck between condiments.

When the waitress arrived, he ordered a cheeseburger, fries, and a Pepsi then browsed the news on his phone. At least here, he had a signal.

UFO SIGHTINGS EVERYWHERE! screamed the headlines.

He shook his head. Had the whole world lost its mind?

Barely had he started reading when a man with a ponytail took a stool two seats to his right and laid what looked like a Bible on the counter. He wore black biker leathers, and he set his helmet on the far counter's side. Doffing his jacket revealed a muscled arm with a beautifully rendered Celtic cross, and above that, a woman unfurling what looked like wings.

The biker glanced toward Caleb. "It's all in here, friend." He patted the leather-bound, dog-eared book. "Everything that's happened. Everything that's about to happen."

Taken aback, Caleb raised an eyebrow. It was rare to find a Bible-believer so open about his belief, especially one dressed like this man. But why wasn't he taken? "You're not the first person to tell me that. You going to Sturgis?"

"I was, but two days ago, considering what happened, they canceled the rally. I usually get there early, but now I've just been hanging around."

"I'm not surprised it was canceled. The whole world's on hold."

"On the contrary, it's on the move. Things are really happening."

"You're right, but I'm not sure they're all good."

" 'We know that all things work together for the good of those who love God: those who are called according to His purpose' Romans 8:28."

"I suppose you're right again. But you sound like a Christian—why weren't you taken?"

He drummed his hands on the counter. "Did you ever wonder if some were chosen to stay behind?"

"I . . . uh . . . no."

"You weren't a believer when it happened, were you? But now you are."

"I . . . uh . . . I wasn't. But I'm fast coming around. I guess I am now. My brother was heavy into the book of Revelation, and he warned me before the vanishing. But I was too stupid to listen."

"You and most of the world. But we're in a dangerous time right now. The barriers between this world and the one below are breaking down. Dark spirits are roaming unchecked upon the earth."

Caleb shifted in his seat and faced away. You couldn't be too careful with strangers you met on the road, especially if they started talking like this guy. He tried to change the subject. "Where are you from?"

A slow smile lifted the corners of the guy's mouth. He nodded to the waitress as she set a mug of coffee before him. "Here, there." He lifted the cup to his lips and stared at the furred, stuffed jackalope mounted on the wall. "Everywhere."

The waitress brought Caleb his Pepsi, and he sipped. "What do you do when you're not going to bike rallies?"

"I help people. Folks like you."

"That's a really nice thing to do—helping strangers you've never met before."

"It's what our Lord did for us and what we should do for others."

"Right."

"And, Caleb?"

Stunned, Caleb whipped his head toward the man. Like a fish gasping on the bank, his mouth opened, and he sucked in air. How could this stranger know his name? He hadn't given it to anyone since entering the diner.

"As it leads you after the Savior, follow your heart, for I sense it is true. And remember this."

He stared into the man's eyes, so blue and deep. He imagined he'd never seen eyes so kind, so gentle, and so . . . ethereal. "W–what?"

"Beware of dark places under the trees at night."

"Here ya go." The waitress dropped his plate on the counter, and he turned to her, moving his hands to make room. But the second his gaze returned to the mysterious stranger—he was gone.

The Bible, the helmet, the leather jacket, and the biker himself—gone. Caleb shot a glance toward the exit, but neither was he walking toward the door.

All that remained was a half-empty coffee cup, a ten-dollar bill, and the words still reverberating through Caleb's mind: "Beware of dark places under the trees at night."

TWO DAYS AFTER

CHAPTER 32

CHAOS

New York City

Adam Turner stepped off the plane at New York's JFK Airport and hurried through the terminal. His phone finally had a signal, and he booked a room at the Surrey, one of the city's most expensive hotels. With him, he had only the carry-on bag he'd bought in Lyon, stuffed with what he'd scavenged the day before his flight. His ticket had been for Minneapolis, but midflight, a rattled pilot announced that the FAA had ordered yet another airspace shutdown for the entire country. After the event everyone in the US was now calling Vanishing Day—V-Day for short—there hadn't been enough air traffic controllers, flight maintenance, or security personnel to ensure safe travel anywhere in the country. Now he was stuck in New York, at least until tomorrow. By then, everyone hoped the situation would stabilize.

He followed signs for the off-site transportation and taxi platforms, finally stepping into a cab.

"I hope you're not going to Jersey," said the cabbie, who appeared to be of Indian descent. "There's a Boeing 747 blocking the Lincoln Tunnel in Midtown, and they haven't yet cleared the other bridges of the wrecks."

"No. Take me to the Surrey."

As they drove through Queens, the scene out the cab window was surreal. Many storefronts had been broken into with glass strewn over the sidewalks. Everywhere, police cars, buses, and other vehicles were either crashed, abandoned, or vandalized. Some were nothing but charred hunks of metal. Few people were out, and they passed several youth gangs strutting down sidewalks as if they owned them. The cabbie sped past these, even running a few red lights to avoid them.

"Is no one working today?" Adam asked. Only then did he notice the cabbie's pistol in a holster inside the open glove compartment.

"For most people, not since V-Day. They say next week things will get back to normal. But I doubt it."

Pulling out his phone, Adam called up the market news. When the website came up, he gasped. The DOW had dropped another twenty-five hundred points since he'd changed planes at Paris's Charles de Gaulle airport. For the last two days, while Adam had been stuck in France, he'd watched television monitors relay the grim news—the DOW had crashed over fourteen thousand points with no end in sight, and this even after circuit breakers had kicked in. With the French cell service overwhelmed and out of commission, it wasn't until now that he could do anything about his accounts.

His shaking fingers were barely able to punch the number of his broker. When the man answered, Adam tried not to shout into the phone. "Sell everything in my personal and business accounts!"

"I already had stop-loss orders on most issues." He could barely hear the man's shaken voice above the background yelling. "But liquidity is so bad, orders aren't filling. It's taking days to get an order through. Then we're only getting a fraction of what the stocks were once worth."

"Well, keep at it until you dump it all." He hung up, wiped his brow, and shook his head. Was the whole world going nuts?

By the time the cab dropped him at the Manhattan Mall, he was sweating, and his heart was pounding. This was far worse than he'd feared.

At the nearly empty mall, he completed his emergency wardrobe from the few upscale shops still open. But after spying a gang of young toughs heading his way, he hurried to the exit. Where were the cops?

His shopping complete, he took a cab to his hotel. Safely in his room, he poured a tall brandy from the bar, switched on the news, and sat.

Brent Edwards, the familiar anchor, wiped his brow and adjusted his glasses. "Demographers have now estimated that on V-Day the US lost thirty percent of its population, including twenty-one percent of adults. What's worse, all young children and babies, one entire generation, have disappeared." The newscaster paused as if staring with unbelieving eyes at the teleprompter. "Also of great concern are losses in the military, with an estimated forty percent of America's fighting men and women simply vanished, including many of the top brass. Analysts fear this has put the country's defense in serious jeopardy. Some aircraft in flight crashed, and naval vessels everywhere are returning to homeports to consolidate and refit crews.

"Though no one knows for certain, losses in Africa and South America may be similar to America's. In Europe, it's estimated that up to five percent of the adult population is gone, though Japan came through unscathed. We have no official word from China, of course, but unofficial sources are giving figures of six percent, with virtually no losses in the ranks of the ruling Chinese Communist Party. But in China, as elsewhere, all the children were taken. These are all sobering numbers." The anchor wiped his brow.

"Everyone is now focused on the cause of the vanishing and whether it could happen again. One now-discredited theory focused on the Christian Rapture. Interviews with survivors initially suggested that the majority of those taken were Christians. But experts, pointing to the loss of all the young children, even in Muslim countries, vehemently dispute that theory."

Appearing uncomfortable, Brent cleared his throat and went on. "A second proposal blames the disappearances on climate change. Somehow, goes the proposal, an altered climate created a tear in the fabric of the universe leading to random disappearances. But only the most die-hard climate scientists are promoting this theory.

"Instead, many experts are now getting behind a theory emerging from Princeton and Harvard. It's based on the recent rise in UFO sightings across the world. The military has also just released fifty years of previously secret video showing almost monthly occurrences of what they term Unidentified Aerial Phenomenon. Given this, experts now theorize that the vanishing was due to a massive alien abduction."

Adam sat back in his chair, his mouth open. "Aliens!" he said to the screen. "It makes as much sense as anything else."

"Whatever its cause," continued the announcer, "economist Melvin Silverman of the Brookings Institution is here to assess V-Day's effects on the economy." Brent turned to a man sitting beside him on the anchor desk, a man with stringy hair, a thin face, and a paisley bow tie. "Melvin?"

The economist blinked then stared at a point somewhere to the right of the camera lens. "In the short run, the country—and the world—has too few consumers chasing too many goods, so except in instances of hoarding, we'll see some serious deflation. That means the value of all currencies will go up, which is bad news for anyone in debt. Based on the number of missing adults, about thirty percent of all US households are simply no more. Understand that these are households who'll never again be able to pay their mortgages, car loans, and credit card debt. There's not a bank in the country able to survive the number of defaults we'll soon see. Many, if not most, of them will go under."

Brent swallowed as his gaze settled on his guest. "But surely, Melvin, that's too pessimistic. There must be a bright spot in all this?"

"In the short run, yes. There will be plenty of food and manufactured goods. In fact, the food pipeline's got thirty percent more than we can eat. But we did an informal poll of twenty farming communities across what some call fly-over country, and many of them are now ghost towns. We now estimate the rate of disappearances in farm country at close to sixty percent, much higher than in the rest of the country. Once we consume the food now in the pipeline, there will be severe shortages, hoarding, and food inflation. In the long run, how to replace all those farmers, till their land, plant their crops, and harvest them is going to be a serious problem."

"So, you're saying the farm economy has . . . collapsed."

"Completely."

"Right." Brent seemed flustered and at a loss for words. When he composed himself, the camera focused only on him. "In other news, the United Nations General Assembly, a deliberative body that, unlike the US Congress, lost not a single member, met in emergency session today to discuss the deteriorating world situation and . . ."

Adam shut off the television, went to the bar, and poured himself a second brandy. He walked to the window and, for the hundredth time since the event, tried to call his Minneapolis headquarters. This time, he got through.

"Adam!" Marvin Polk, his vice president, answered. "I'm glad you finally called. It's been absolute chaos here." Despite the rushed sentence, a strain underplayed Marv's weary voice. "With the market crashing and the loss of key executives and employees everywhere, there's been a cascading series of business failures all across the country."

"Calm down, Marv. What about us? What about Turner Enterprises?"

"I've talked with many of our customers and suppliers, and, Adam"—his voice rose again—"everyone is way beyond panic. In the last three days, our stock has dropped eighty-nine percent with no end in sight. And Standard and Poors just downgraded our bond rating to the lowest available junk bond status."

"They can't do that! We're solid!" Though the phone was now shaking in his hands, Adam tried to calm his voice. "When I left, we were in great shape. It can't be all that bad."

"B–bad?" The word trembled through the speaker. "It's worse than bad. We're facing bankruptcy. We have a big bond issue due Thursday, with another due next week, and First National is asking if we can pay. But we no longer have the reserves we once did. Even our money market funds are folding. Adam, we're facing default."

The words shot through him like a nail gun through a palm. "Default? How . . . is that . . . possible."

"It's a financial panic like nothing we've ever seen. The Fed has dropped rates to zero, pumped all kinds of liquidity into the system, but it's not working. The German and French markets are near five-decade lows. It's not just us. It's everyone. Many of our suppliers and customers have told me in confidence that, by week's end, they, too, will go under. Adam, we're facing a total financial collapse far worse than the Great Depression, and nobody knows how to stop it."

The news so stunned him, Adam ended the conversation, saying he needed to think. How could everybody have lost their minds all at once? Worldwide panic and fear? Unrestrained selling? Surely there was some way to keep Turner Enterprises—his baby, his life's work, the focus of his existence—from going up in flames?

Slumping into an easy chair, he set his brandy aside and held his head in his hands.

For maybe five minutes, he tried to calm his racing heart. Somehow, he'd find a way out of this. He always had. But tomorrow, not today. Right now, he was too exhausted.

Though he barely had the energy for it, he must call Chelsea. In France, he'd been cut off, unable to reach any of his children since V-Day. Now he was in the city, and he had no excuses. Taking a deep breath, he made the call. "Chelsea, this is Father. I'm in New York."

"Here? In the city?" A short pause. "With Mother?"

"Just me. I was unable to reach you until now. I was headed home, but our plane had to land because of the nationwide shutdown."

"Yeah, it's crazy everywhere. Where's Mother? Still in France?"

"Chelsea." He closed his eyes. This was why he'd put off the call. "Your mother . . . didn't make it."

"W–what do you mean? Where is she then?" A hint of panic had constricted her voice.

"We lost our captain. The boat crashed into a bridge. Chelsea, the boat sank. Your mother—she drowned."

The line went silent. "Chelsea?"

What returned was the sound of her breath, inhaling quickly. "Y–yes." She breathed hard into the phone. "Where . . . are you staying, Dad?"

"At the Surrey. Can you meet me here at the restaurant for dinner? Then we can talk. In about ninety minutes?"

"I'll be there." Rare for his firebrand daughter, her voice dropped to a whisper. "Have you told Caleb?" She drew in a sharp breath. "Or Dylan?"

"No. The French cell service was out, and I just landed. It's been an exhausting day, a long flight, and . . . can you tell them?"

Another long pause. "Yes, I'll tell them."

"Thanks. See you in a bit."

Drained from events and the flight, he downed the last of his brandy and laid down to rest before going downstairs to meet his daughter.

CHAPTER 33
CHELSEA'S DINNER

Greenwich Village, New York City

After Father hung up, Chelsea went to the couch, plopped into it, and wiped tears from her cheeks. Then she stared at the one painting Archer had left behind. It hung there, a blob of dark, dripping colors on the living room wall. She was glad now that two days ago he'd packed all his things and departed. Along with everything else, she couldn't deal right now with insensitive, self-absorbed, larcenous, hotheaded Archer.

But her mother had drowned in France, and Archer's chaotic, depressing colors on the wall matched her mood. Dropping her head into her hands, she sobbed. If someone had nailed her to the wall right now, she'd be like Archer's painting—a picture of grief, depression, and mourning.

Where could she turn for solace and comfort?

Dylan. She needed to call Dylan. Speaking with him was always comforting, and besides, she needed to tell him the grim news. But a glance at her watch told her it was nearly midnight in Belgium. The time zones again. She'd have to call tomorrow.

With the phone still in her hand, she punched Caleb's number. It kept ringing until his answering service kicked in. She punched the number again. On the third ring, he picked it up.

"Chelsea?" In the background, she heard tires humming over asphalt.

Upon hearing his voice, she breathed her relief. "Yes, it's me. Where are you?"

"Somewhere in Wisconsin. With everything shut down, I couldn't get a flight out, so I'm driving back from Oregon. How are you?"

"I . . . I'm . . . okay." But her voice cracked.

"You don't sound okay."

"You're right. I'm not." She sniffled. "Caleb, I have terrible news. Really terrible news."

"What?"

"I just got a call from Father. He's here in New York. But Mother"—she sucked in air—"she's gone. On V-Day, their boat crashed and sank. And she drowned."

A long silence. "Drowned?"

"Yes. I'm meeting Father tonight. His flight was grounded when they entered US airspace."

"I can't believe it. She's really . . . gone. Hold on. I'm pulling off the road." The engine and tire noise abated. "This is awful, just truly awful. Just a minute." She thought he heard his breath catch. After another long silence, he came back on. "So now, really . . . how are you?"

"Not good. I'm down. Really down." How could she tell him she'd just had an abortion, she'd just kicked out her live-in creep of a boyfriend, and her city and her world were falling apart around her?

"I'm sorry, Chelsea. I wish I were there with you now."

"Th–thanks."

"Did you try to call Dylan?"

"It's midnight there. I'll call tomorrow."

"Chelsea . . . I'm not sure Dylan will be with us anymore. He was right about what happened, right all along."

"Right about what?"

"About the Rapture. Because that's what happened on V-Day. All the Christians were taken out of this world."

"But the news says it was aliens."

"They're wrong. I know because Blake was climbing with me, and he . . . just . . . disappeared. He was a solid Christian, and he vanished into thin air, just like Dylan said was going to happen. And if Dylan was a Christian, he may have been taken too."

The news that Dylan may also be gone so stunned her, her mouth opened, and she gasped for breath. But didn't the alien abductions make more sense? Maybe Dylan hadn't been taken?

"Chelsea? You there?"

"Yes. I saw piles of clothes on the sidewalk. Cars without drivers crashing. Chaos everywhere. But the news is saying not all the missing were Christians, so I'm not sure about this Rapture theory. I'll try reaching Dylan tomorrow. This is all so sudden and troubling."

"I know. Call me the minute you reach him—if you reach him."

She agreed, but when she checked her watch, it was time to grab a cab for the Surrey. They said goodbye, and she hung up.

In the bedroom, she changed into her most expensive dress. Tonight, she needed to be with someone she knew, especially family. In the restaurant, she'd be on her best behavior, not goading Father about their disagreements, trying her best to get along.

But when she descended the stairs, unlocked the front, and stepped out onto the street, she froze. Hanging around the porch next door were the same gang members who'd moved in yesterday. She glanced right then left. No one else was on the street, and no cabs anywhere in sight. This was just like yesterday.

"Yo, mama," said one of them, "get over here and keep me warm." He snickered, and the others beside him laughed. "I'm cold."

She ducked back inside the foyer and locked the door.

Then Frank, a young, always impeccably dressed teller who worked at a nearby bank, plodded down the stairs. He poked his head out the door then stepped back inside and locked it. "They're still here."

"Yes."

"I wouldn't go out there now, if I were you, miss. I'm sorry, but I forgot your name." He shoved his glasses back on his nose.

"It's Chelsea." How many times hadn't she given him her name?

He peered through the barred glass. "Yesterday, they robbed and beat to death the man in the apartment across from me. His body is lying down the street. I barely made it back here before they got me too."

"Really?" She shuddered. "Guess I'm not going tonight."

"Did you see the UFOs over the river yesterday?"

"No." She cocked her head. Frank had always impressed her as being a bit of a nerd, the type who would be into that sort of thing. "Are you sure they were UFOs?"

"Definitely. There were five of them. They hovered for a while. Then they shot across the sky really fast. It was impossible what they did."

"Weird. Extremely weird." Unsaid was that this was also her opinion of Frank.

"You got that right."

She left her neighbor, ascended the stairs, and called her father. When she explained she couldn't leave the building, he asked where the police were.

"Good question. For some time even before this happened, they haven't responded to anyone's calls. Now it's probably even worse. It's not safe to leave tonight. I'll have to skip dinner with you."

"I'm sorry, Chelsea. I would have liked to be with you."

"Me too." As she said the words, she missed being with her father more than she ever remembered. Now she regretted being so angry with him the last time they met.

She said goodbye. After changing back into jeans, she went to the kitchen and pulled out a cardboard box of Chinese food she'd brought home before V-Day. As she sat down with a bottle of wine and stared at her limp and soggy veggie chow mein, she realized the restaurant where she'd bought this food was now a burned-out shell.

How had the world changed so much, in only a few days' time? And all for the worse.

CHAPTER 34

CALEB'S RETURN

University Village, Chicago

After Caleb returned the rental car, he had difficulty finding a taxi. Then, as the cabbie drove him the ten blocks to his apartment, he gaped at the numerous crashed vehicles, the burned-out buildings, the empty streets.

"Where you coming from?" asked the young Jamaican as he dodged a wreck blocking his lane.

"Oregon." Caleb leaned back on the seat. His roller bag and backpack lay beside him. He'd left his climbing gear at the cabin.

"Hope it's safer out there, mon." The driver glanced in the rearview mirror. "This city is out of control."

"It was a hairy trip. Abandoned vehicles everywhere. Some places nothing but ghost towns."

"Yeah, mon. You live in the city?"

"Yes."

"Well, it's changed. Not safe anywhere. And last night, five UFOs hovered over the river. Then they shoot across the sky faster than any plane I ever seen. And you know what? Five minutes before, those same UFOs were over New York. Everyone's saying the aliens did it."

"You sure they were UFOs?" He'd heard the same thing on the radio.

"Yeah, mon. I'm sure."

They drove the rest of the way in silence. At his apartment, the armed doorman was gone. Also, someone's dried-up milkshake and desiccated french fries had spilled across the entryway, and no one had bothered to clean it up. Usually, the maintenance on his upscale apartment building was flawless.

The elevator opened on the third floor with its usual loud clatter. Someday, he must speak to the concierge about the noise—if they still had a concierge. As he fumbled for the keys to his apartment, a door opened down the hall.

Tanya peeked out, saw him, and hurried to his side. Nika padded down the hall after her.

"Caleb, I'm so glad you're back." Her voice was thick, her eyes swollen.

"Come inside." His key turned in the lock, and he waved her in first. "You look terrible."

He set his bags down and led her and Nika into the living room where she plopped onto the couch. He sat beside her, leaving a few feet between them. Nika shoved her muzzle against his hand, begging for a pet, and he obliged.

"Grandfather—he's gone. Like so many others." With her arms around her knees, she dropped her head between her legs and spoke to the floor. "I'm so scared. I don't know what to do. The city's gone nuts."

"It's the same everywhere. I just drove from Oregon, and in some places in the middle of the country, there's hardly anybody left."

Sticking out of her pocket was the handle of a pistol. She pulled it out and set it on the couch between them. "This was his. I've been carrying it around. But I've never fired a pistol in my life."

"I have."

"Then you take it. He's got Sergei's in the safe." She looked up. "Will you go with me to the store? It's not safe out there, and I'm almost out of groceries."

"Sure, I'll go." He moved the gun to the coffee table.

"Thanks." Sitting back, she appeared to breathe easier. "The news says aliens were behind it, that aliens took all the missing people. They're also claiming that the ones taken weren't all Christians. But they're wrong. Grandpa often warned me that someday the Rapture would come. But I didn't believe him."

"I know. My brother said the same thing. I didn't believe him either."

"Grandfather left me a note. It was in the safe." She reached into the pocket of her jeans and unfolded a paper. "He said that, if he and a lot of other people ever disappeared suddenly, I was to open it and read it. At the time, I thought he was nuts." She handed it over, rubbed her hands together. Then she shoved her long blonde ponytail over one shoulder. "I've been carrying it around, reading it. Again and again. Here—"

Caleb smoothed the folds and read.

Dearest Tanya,

If you're reading this, then I and many others have been taken out of the world. Jesus, the one and only Savior, he who took part in creating the universe, predicted that one day this would happen. I don't know what the news media, always so corrupt and biased, is telling you. But what's happened is called the Rapture of the Church, and it is the beginning of God's final judgment on the world.

I've often wondered why, in recent years, we've seen so many disaster movies about the end of life on earth. Could it be that God has put some kind of antenna in mankind's collective psyche to warn us what's coming? Maybe I'm wrong, and you will never have to open this letter. Men have been predicting the end since the time of the apostles.

But if you're reading this, then what Jesus warned us would happen has happened. He gave us warnings to look for, portents I have followed over the years, signs that in my estimation have been fulfilled. Thus, this letter.

The supersign was the regathering of the Jewish people into the modern nation-state of Israel. That, of course, happened before our time, in 1948.

Following this was the creation of the European Union from the remnants of the old Roman Empire. Although nations come and go, the EU is still a fait accompli.

But it was always the third major sign I was unsure of. For some time, I've watched events unfolding, and as I write this, I fear—not for me, but for you—that this, too, is complete. What is the last major sign?

Apostasy in the church of Christ.

I was deeply concerned when last year, even as more priests were accused of pedophilia, the Pope gave his approval to bless same-sex unions. I also suspect he believes in a universal religion.

Not to be outdone, one Protestant public figure after another was caught in out-of-wedlock affairs, not just with women. We also heard about more of these highly public pastors having private jets and enormous mansions, the same ones telling folks to save their souls by sending them dollars to fund their lavish lifestyles. Their sermons are nothing but self-help pep talks with little or no biblical content.

Then there are the preachers declaring that God is just a cash machine, and that, regardless of God's will, if only we had enough *faith*, we would all live prosperous, healthy lives. Tell that to the apostles. Not one of them was rich. All but one died a martyr's death.

Do they not know what Jesus said? That where your treasure is, there your heart will be also. To blame every sickness or malformity on a lack of faith is to deny the existence of evil and the effects of the Fall. It also declares that what they call *faith* is a power higher even than God himself. It is true heresy.

Even worse, most of the mainline denominations have finally embraced homosexuality and same-sex marriage—a sin especially abhorrent to a perfectly holy God. Some of these same churches also care more about "saving the planet", an idolatrous goal if ever there was, than they do about the murder of the unborn in the womb. This country is killing enough babies each year to populate a city the size of Fort Worth, Texas.

Instead of biblical teaching, the modern church now brings us prayer labyrinths, universal salvation, and the denial of Hell—this while their congregations question God's existence, whether Jesus is the only way to salvation, and whether, if they just live a good life, that's all they need to get into Heaven.

Yes, granddaughter, the big, mainstream denominations today have strayed far from the words of Jesus and the apostles. And apostasy in the Church completes the signs preceding the end.

Now, you ask, what about Tanya? If you are reading this, then I have failed to convince you of the truth of the Son of God, and for that, I beg your forgiveness. Ahead of you lies the Tribulation—seven years of terrible trial, destruction, and God's judgment. There is only one way out for you now, and that is to grab one of my Bibles, start in Matthew, and read the New Testament. Then pray for your unbelief.

Even for what lies ahead, if you turn to Jesus, believe in him, and trust in him, your lot will be far better than otherwise.

That is my only advice, dearest granddaughter. I hope you take it.

With all my love,

Uri

P.S. We cannot deny that UFOs exist. But they're not what they seem. Why do I mention this? Because if the world is now seeing increased UFO activity, do not be misled. They are not aliens. They are demons sent by Satan to lead people away from the truth of the Rapture.

My first proof—of a kind—is what I've found about the conditions necessary for any one planet to support life. My conclusions? The chances for extraterrestrial life existing anywhere else in the universe are so infinitesimally small, it is impossible for complex life to exist anywhere. It only exists here because of divine intervention.

My second proof exists in reports from those who have experienced lifelong periods of repeated abductions by "aliens". Over the decades, these supposed aliens have told their victims they came, variously, from the moon, Mars, Venus, and Alpha Centauri. They can't keep their story straight. So they are liars, a sure hallmark of Satan.

Before they were abducted, some of these unfortunates also dabbled in the occult. Finally, though none of them were Christians before it happened, some converted later. Then when the UFO "aliens" visited them again, and when these new Christians invoked the name of Jesus, guess what happened? The "aliens" fled. What better proof do we have that these supposed "aliens" are demons sent by Satan? These are all documented incidents and proof enough for me.

Caleb set the letter aside and raised his glance to Tanya. "Except for the part about aliens, this is what my brother was trying to tell me. And now we're both here, left behind to live through"—he waved a hand across the room—"this."

It was the wrong thing to say. Didn't he always say the wrong things to women at the worst possible times? Tanya's face scrunched as if in pain, and her eyes welled with tears. Again, she dropped her head in her hands. "I should have listened. I've been such a fool."

"You and me both." He scooted closer and laid a hand on her knee. "It will be all right, Tanya."

Wet eyes found his. Then she wrapped her arms around him, and he hugged her.

For a time, he held her. When they parted, he remained close beside her. Nika, too, was now licking her hands. "I'm ready to say my brother was right, and I was horribly, horribly wrong. I've seen enough evidence, and though it's too late"—he took a deep breath—"I do believe, with all my heart, that Jesus is the Son of God."

Tanya wiped her eyes and faced him. "Me too, Caleb. Uri was right. Jesus is real, and I, too, believe."

They exchanged smiles.

Then he sat back, grasped his hands together, and gazed toward the window and the sunlight streaming onto the beige carpet. As he'd spoken his belief out loud, a surge of joy, of inner warmth, welled up within him. He crossed to the window and watched a mass of brilliant white cotton passing overhead, fluffy clouds sunlit with reds and oranges and yellows. "It feels good to have said that—to say I believe."

Padding footsteps approached, and she stood beside him. "I feel the same way." She caught his gaze. "It lifted me up. To have said that made me feel happy and warm inside. And complete."

"It means something, doesn't it? This feeling?"

"I think it does."

"I think God is welcoming us." His gaze followed the clouds. "It also means this business about UFOs and aliens is wrong. People are being misled."

"I know. They're seeing UFOs everywhere. Here and across the world. And people are falsely blaming the UFOs for V-Day."

"My cabbie even saw them here in Chicago. But once again, 'the experts' have got it wrong. They usually do." He whirled back to her. "People need to know the truth about what happened. This was the Rapture of the Church, not an alien abduction."

"I agree."

"Tanya, this is why I'm here." His heart beat faster. "To bring folks the truth. From now on, that's what my blog will be about." Then he frowned. "But I know so little about the Bible."

She smiled. "Uri has a number of them. Also books that help you understand them. I'll bring you some."

"Thanks." He pointed at the street below. "There are others out there, folks just like us, confused and looking for answers. Someone needs to counter the lies they're hearing. Someone needs to bring them the truth."

"I can help." She went to the door. Nika padded after her, but she made the dog sit and ordered her to stay. "Ever since it happened, Nika's stuck to me like glue. I'll go get Uri's books."

CHAPTER 35

THE FIRST SEAL

In The Great Throne Room

Revelation 6:1–2 (HCSB): *Then I saw the Lamb open one of the seven seals, and I heard one of the four living creatures say with a voice like thunder, "Come!" I looked, and there was a white horse. The horseman on it had a bow; a crown was given to him, and he went out as a victor to conquer.*

For the first time since arriving in the heavenly realm, Blake entered the throne room of the Lord of Hosts. With each passing moment in Heaven, he found something new and startling to amaze him. But the throne room exceeded all that went before. Far more than a room, the space extended for miles in all directions. A mile above, the ceiling gleamed with brilliant, sparkling colors, as if composed of a billion prisms. Everywhere across the translucent, crystalline floor millions upon millions of believers also gathered, all waiting with breathless expectation for the event to come. Also present were angels beyond counting. In the farthest corner he stood, gazing with wonder, awe, and reverence up toward where the Lord himself was seated.

Cloaked in light more blinding than the brightest sun, the Father sat upon a throne high above the vast throng. Blake glanced once but looked away—his unworthiness rose up within him like a dagger of accusation. But Jesus's sudden reassurance of salvation allowed him to look again without shame.

The throne itself gleamed golden with a light so bright, he could barely see the embedded emeralds, jasper, amethyst, and diamonds. They sparkled and pulsed from every surface. From behind the two-story seat, lightning shot out, and thunder rumbled. Fire and thick smoke boiled above the Father, licking, roiling, climbing even to the ceiling, and spreading out from there.

Awesome and terrifying to behold, the four cherubim with four faces—of a man, a lion, an ox, and an eagle—waited below. Each of their six folded wings was twice as long as a man's body. Between the creatures issued waves of fire, flashes of lightning as they hovered over giant multicolored wheels as they spun, sparked, and whirred.

On both sides of the throne sat twenty-four elders, great leaders of the redeemed from the church age. Among them, Blake recognized apostles.

Sitting high above them all, the Father raised in his right hand a scroll, written on both sides, but secured with seven seals. Blake knew intuitively, as he knew so many things after his arrival, that the scroll contained the title deed to earth. It had been written at the dawn of creation, foretelling the events of the end now unfolding.

Standing half again as tall as a man, the archangel Gabriel approached the cherubim. And when he faced the room and spoke, his voice thundered. "Who is worthy to open the scroll and break its seals?"

Blake stilled, sensing how important this act was. Breaking the seal would begin the time of the Antichrist, the events of the Tribulation, and the final defeat of evil, sin, and the Adversary.

A hush swept the assembly as the twenty-four elders, the vast numbers of the redeemed, and the crowd of angels looked around expectantly. After arriving in Heaven, Blake had felt no sorrow or anxiety, only an uplifting, ever-present joy emanating from the presence of Jesus and the deep, indescribable love Jesus held for him—yes, even for Blake personally. But now, he nearly despaired. Was there no one in all creation worthy enough? Would no one step forward to open the scroll? As he looked at the faces beside him, he realized he wasn't the only one experiencing such negative emotions for the first time.

There was movement at the front by the throne. He struggled to see what appeared to be a lamb stepping forward, but a wounded lamb. The Lord of Hosts reached down, handed this lamb the scroll, and then Blake saw the creature for who he really was—the Lord Jesus.

But today, Jesus wasn't surrounded by brilliant, glorious light. He didn't gleam with fire and all the colors of the rainbow. No, today, he appeared as a mere man in a simple robe. Visible now were the holes in his wrists and ankles where the foot-long spikes had punched through.

There, too, was the wound in Jesus's side where the Roman centurion had plunged his spear. And on his forehead were the marks left by the crown of thorns the soldiers had smashed upon his head.

Today, Jesus appeared as the man who had given up his earthly life for the sins of the world. And for the first time since Blake had arrived in Heaven, a tear ran down his cheek. But someone had been found worthy, someone had stepped forward, and his despair morphed into joy.

When the elders and cherubim saw who had taken the scroll, they raised their hands in the air, uttered cries of rejoicing, and then bowed low before the Son of God. From the long tables on either side of the throne, they took a harp in one hand, symbolizing all the prophecies leading up to this moment. In their other hand, they took a bowl of incense, containing all the prayers of the redeemed.

Then the elders and the cherubim sang a song never before heard in Heaven. They praised this Jesus who alone was worthy to take the scroll. He was a complete innocent, slaughtered by evil men so his death could purchase a people for God—a people born of every tribe and language and people and nation.

A new earth was coming, a perfect world ruled by Christ and the people he had redeemed, a world without sin, pain, suffering, or death. And for all eternity, they would love God, be loved by God, and live with God. And what made all that possible was the sacrifice of a perfect life—the death of God's Son.

Jesus grasped the scroll and broke the first of the seven seals.

The wax cracked and fell away. The snapping echoed across the hushed multitude.

This act, this breaking of the first seal, would bring the time of the Antichrist and the first judgment. The Rapture had removed the redeemed from the world, but in so doing, it had also removed the Holy Spirit, the third person of the Trinity, part of God Himself, and all the good that he brought through them. Of course, the Holy Spirit was still present in the world, ready to redeem countless millions in the coming Tribulation. But with the absence of God's Spirit working through his people, the world now roiled with chaos, anarchy, hate, and violence.

Even before the Rapture, the world was experiencing a preview of universal lawlessness. The people had rejected God, and God had abandoned them to their sins. So even before the Rapture, God's judgment was already rising against them.

The multitudes remaining now longed for peace and stability. And Scripture decreed this would come from the Antichrist.

But it would be a false and temporary peace, for the man of lawlessness was a spawn of the Adversary, a creation of the great Deceiver. Even so, he was part of God's plan.

Here then, was the beginning of God's final judgment on a sinful, rebellious world.

It was the beginning of the end of Satan's reign on earth.

CHAPTER 36

THE COMING OF
THE MASTER

Geneva, Switzerland

2 Thessalonians 2:6–8 (HCSB): *And you know what currently restrains him, so that he will be revealed in his time. For the mystery of lawlessness is already at work, but the one now restraining will do so until he is out of the way, and then the lawless one will be revealed.*

Davato sat in a high-top chair at the bar in his suite, swirling and contemplating the ice in a nearly empty glass of whiskey. Beside him on the counter stood an empty bottle. Somewhere in the next room, Carlo was typing on his laptop.

The last four days had been torture. The Christians had been taken out of the world, so his time had come. The moment it happened, an odd feeling had swelled inside him, as if some ever-present shackle, some odious and unseen restraint, had been ripped from its source and whisked away. Reveling in a moment of joy, he'd glanced at the delegates seated around the conference room table—at the frowning, puzzled faces, the shaking heads, the sudden, faraway stares.

Of course, not a single member of the UN party had vanished that day, and he'd tried to keep the meeting going. But with all the cell phones buzzing and aides interrupting with urgent dispatches from home, he called a second temporary halt.

Now here it was, the afternoon of the fourth day, and tomorrow, they'd meet again. Yet in private conversations, he still couldn't get the troublesome Palestinians to agree to anything.

He emptied his glass and walked to the next room where Carlo was working. "Will you go down to the lobby bar and bring me another fifth?"

"What about room service?"

"I'll need a refill long before they come."

Ever faithful and obedient, Carlo stood and left.

Alone again, Davato walked to the window in the main room of the Executive Lake View Suite. Far out on the water, a stiff breeze raised whitecaps. Below, hotel guests scurried about like mites swarming over carrion. Some were surely from the League. They would be watching him closely now.

The League now expected much from him. When he negotiated the withdrawal of Iranian forces from Syria two years ago in Tehran, he'd been lucky. After a combination of Israeli air strikes and cyberwarfare had taken out much of Iran's nuclear program, Iran and Israel seemed on the brink of all-out war. Somehow, he'd convinced the two parties to negotiate. Secretly, he suspected the Iranians agreed only because they needed time to rebuild what the Israelis had destroyed.

Here in Geneva, he hoped the massive destruction of nearly every Palestinian village and the leveling of the Dome of the Rock and Al Aqsa Mosque on Temple Mount would soften the Palestinian position. It hadn't. Even after seeing their devastated homeland, when the towel heads returned to Geneva, they remained intransigent. Their hatred for Israel was always greater than their desire for peace.

What was wrong? After the Christians were taken, why wasn't he able to sway these sheep? This should be the beginning of his time. Yet, at every turn, he'd been stymied.

He started to turn away from the window, when—

Darkness—and a smoke so thick he could touch it—swirled into the room, filling every corner. It was—

The Master himself.

Only a few times before had he experienced the Master's presence. The first was in his teens when he questioned why the League had chosen him. Next, it was right before he joined the UN. But then, the Master's presence had been light, fleeting, only enough to motivate and give him a glimpse of what lay ahead.

Today, the Master held nothing back. And Davato reveled and rejoiced in what settled upon him.

Incredible dark energy poured into him all that he lacked, all that he needed to fulfill his mission. Power and ego and strength of will, like an intoxicating, exhilarating drug, swelled every fiber of his being. Ruthlessness and cunning and strategic thinking sharpened his brain.

Where before he saw the world through a smoky lens, now he peered through a translucent pane of clear crystal.

Where before his mind trudged through a muddy bog, now it raced across an open track with the wind behind him.

Where before he was a garden snake, nipping at the Enemy's heels, now he was a twelve-foot cobra, rising with hood flared, fangs full of venom.

Your time has come. The Master's words formed like dark crystals inside his mind. *You are the one we have been waiting for.*

"Yes, Master." Whispering with eagerness, shivering with restrained power, and bursting with pride, Davato bowed low. "Thank you, Master."

You have what you need. The words buoyed him. *Now go forth and rule.*

Then the dark presence departed.

Davato returned to the window and looked down on the insects below, all so insignificant and weak. "I know what to say to them now," he whispered to himself, "what will convince these obstinate Palestinian sheep to sign the treaty."

Carlo opened the door and entered the room carrying a package. But after two steps, he froze, his eyes wide. "W–what happened to you?"

Davato grinned. "He came upon me."

Carlo's mouth opened, closed, opened. "The Master?"

"Yes. Call the Israeli ambassador and have him meet me here, alone, in one hour." Davato faced the window again, eyes narrowing, arms crossing. "My time has come. And now, the world will be mine."

EIGHT DAYS AFTER

CHAPTER 37

THE TREATY

Geneva, Switzerland

Daniel 9:27 (NLT): *The ruler will make a treaty with the people for a period of one set of seven, but after half this time, he will put an end to the sacrifices and offerings.*

Bearing a winning smile, the assistant secretary-general for the Middle East, Asia, and the Pacific led Carlo Scutari into the hotel conference room and strolled to the microphone. Standing nearby was Azaan, the dark-skinned UN press secretary from India. Davato scanned the crowd. Would there ever be a press so eager to ask questions as the group assembled here today? He gripped the podium and nodded to a few individuals in front, adding a personal touch.

"Good afternoon, ladies and gentlemen, *mesdames et messieurs*. You've heard the press briefing. Now I understand you have a few questions for me?"

Hands shot up across the crowded room, and he pointed to a prominent American newsman a few rows back.

"For years," said the towheaded man gripping his mike, "we've been hearing that the Palestinians would never give up control of Temple Mount. Yet, today, they seem to have done so. Do you expect this agreement to last?"

"Thank you for your question, Ron. I do, because, in return for relinquishing all claims to the site, they will receive funds for a complete rebuilding of every Palestinian town and village. The earthquakes have so destroyed their country, without that kind of help, it would otherwise take decades to rebuild. Yes, the agreement will last."

He pointed to a German man furiously waving his hand on the right.

"What finally convinced the Arab world," asked the reporter, "to abandon its long-standing demand that Israel gives up its settlements on the West Bank and Golan Heights?"

"A promise of reconstruction." Davato smiled. "And lots of money."

As laughter rippled through the crowd, more hands shot up, and he pointed to an Arab woman in the second row wearing a hijab.

"The press release said that the UN and the Israelis are paying for the rebuilding. How much is Israel putting up?"

"We are each funding fifty percent of the reconstruction. Half of the UN funds are being released tomorrow. We've also arranged for construction crews from Germany, the UK, France, and Italy to arrive next week." Unsaid was how much those construction contracts swayed a few votes.

His finger then singled out a woman from the Netherlands.

"With Temple Mount now in Israeli possession," she said, "are they planning to rebuild the Temple soon?"

Silence swept the crowd. This had been the great flash point in the past.

Davato gripped the podium with both hands and manufactured his most serious face. "I understand that within days plans are in motion to clear away the debris and begin construction on the Temple. This, too, was allowed under the agreement that all parties signed."

He looked over the sea of waving hands and chose a man from the BBC.

"Everyone is saying that, after decades with no progress, this treaty is truly remarkable. What was the catalyst that finally broke the logjam?"

Davato smiled, stepped away from the podium, and waved to the dark-skinned press secretary.

His face beaming, Azaan approached and lifted his chin to the microphone. "It was accomplished, my friends, only through the superb negotiating skills of our assistant secretary-general." He waved a hand toward Davato who nodded in turn.

"It was this man alone who created a contract all parties could agree on. As you know, Davato is no stranger to leadership. He was, of course, the founder and CEO of Worldnet. He was once Italy's EU representative before he became president of the European Commission. But he sacrificed that high position to become a UN assistant secretary-general, all because of a deep, personal desire to achieve peace in the Mideast. In these negotiations, I, personally, have never seen such wisdom and nego-tiating skill, giving something to all parties involved. The world owes Davato a great debt for his sacrifice to this cause and for what he has done here today." Clapping in Davato's direction, Azaan stepped away from the podium.

The entire room joined Azaan in lengthy, explosive applause.

Self-satisfied and beaming, Davato resumed his position and finished the briefing. He answered every question with aplomb and gained their complete admiration. But he'd only given the world a glimpse of his new-found intelligence, his considerable powers of persuasion, and his newly enhanced charisma—those and his brilliant suggestions were the missing elements that concluded this troubling affair. Everyone got something, with the Palestinians giving up their cherished Temple Mount site for cash and the promise of a massive reconstruction.

As he and Carlo Scutari rode their private elevator to the top floor, Carlo smiled at him. "Everyone's astounded by what you've done, sir. And if I may say, you are a different person than you were a few days ago. You are truly the one the League of Abaddon has long awaited."

"Thank you, Carlo, for saying as much." Then he frowned and laid a hand on his aide's shoulder. "But this is only the beginning. We have much to do in a short amount of time. I'm expecting a call this afternoon from the secretary-general himself, inviting me to give a speech next week in New York before the entire General Assembly."

Carlo uttered a gasp. "Why, that is wonderful. But, sir, how did you organize that?"

"I have my ways." He smiled. Sometimes it was good to remind Carlo he wasn't indispensable, that Davato could arrange events without his aide. "But before I give that speech, we must conclude the matter we talked about yesterday. Were you able to contact the individuals in Marseilles and employ the man I told you about?"

Carlo's smile evaporated, and his gaze found the floor. "I was. And they assured me he is the best man for the job. He's never been caught, and his record of success is excellent."

"And do they understand how exceedingly important it is that there be no trace leading back to us or to them?"

"They understand completely."

"And how will he proceed? Did they say?"

"With an untraceable poison. It will appear as a heart attack. They will also have a doctor available to prevent any autopsy from learning the truth. And with the president's history of heart disease, everyone will assume it was a natural death."

"Good." The elevator stopped, and they crossed the hall to the top-floor suite.

With the old Swede out of the way and the accolades pouring in from all over the world, and with the seeds planted over the years in strategic places within the EU, Davato was certain to become the next president of the European Council.

From there, he would begin the process of reuniting the old Roman Empire into a new nation, but one ruled by a single individual—a man prophesied, bred, and uniquely fitted for the job. And it would all happen before the end of the year.

CHAPTER 38
MARGOT'S REVIVAL

Brussels, Belgium

With Dylan carrying the shopping bag beside her, Margot sauntered through one of Brussel's outdoor food markets, purchasing peppers and onions here, a head of cabbage there, carrots, lettuce, and fresh-baked bread at other stalls.

After her family had been taken, she couldn't stand to be alone. So the day after the event and after staring again at the painting showing them both together, she'd asked Dylan to move his things from the hotel to her father's room at the apartment.

She was glad he'd agreed, glad he'd crossed the Atlantic. His presence had been comforting.

"If I stretch my imagination, I can almost see the world as normal again," she said. "Except now there are fewer stalls. And no children. And there's a wariness in people's eyes, as though they don't trust anyone anymore."

"Who can blame them?" said Dylan. "Especially with all the looting, the robberies, and the break-ins."

"We never had that here before. They say it's far worse in America." She smiled. "Aren't you glad you're here?"

He reached out and squeezed her hand. "Yes."

She breathed deeply of the fresh air. While she'd been holed up in her room in the weeks before the vanishing, she hadn't ventured outside even once. Now, neighbors were emerging from their apartments, and some cafés were reopening, filled with people desperate to resume their normal lives. It was like the end of the lockdowns after the Chinese virus hit in 2020. When they neared an empty table on the sidewalk, she pulled him toward it.

"Let's sit and order some wine."

They did, and when the waiter brought them two glasses and a plate of cheese, she sipped the wine, ate the tangy cheese, and could almost be happy. For some time they lingered, saying nothing, only sipping, munching on the cheese, watching people stroll by as they left the market.

She sank back in her chair, breathing deeply of the hundreds of scarlet and gold begonias trailing meter-long strings from a nearby basket. Because of the catastrophe, they'd canceled the Flower Carpet event in the Grand Place, but some florist had hung her display on a pole in the market. A few meters away in the street, a bearded man pushed a creaking cart, its bed ripe with tomatoes. "I'm glad you came, Dylan. I don't know what I would have done without you."

If men could blush, she thought he might have just then. "Something led me here and brought me to you. And something led me to ask God to remain behind." He cradled his glass. "You and I were meant to be together for some purpose. And it isn't just to be together." He smiled. "If you know what I mean."

Now she felt like blushing. "Y–yes. I know what you mean." While staying at her place, he'd been the perfect gentleman. But she'd grown so fond of him in the last week, she'd almost come to think of him as her—what? Boyfriend? She suspected it might come to that. But not yet.

Somewhat embarrassed, she changed the subject. "I've always believed we were put here to help others, to be God's hands and feet and voice." She clasped her hands, stared at them, then looked up again. "As Christians, we should be like the lighthouses on the coast that used to guide the ships away from the rocks to a safe harbor."

"Well said, Margot. I agree completely."

A man in a leather jacket at the next table lit a cigarette, sending smoke their way. From somewhere beneath the table came the cooing of a pigeon searching for scraps.

"But, Dylan," she went on, "why, specifically, *were* we thrown together—you and I?"

"I don't know. Perhaps we are to wait for the answer. There's a lot of that in the Bible—waiting on the Lord. Eventually, we'll find out. Your painting changed for some reason."

"Can I ask you a personal question?"

He sipped the wine, set the glass down, and nodded.

"You've said that, before you became a Christian, you wandered a lot. But your parents were rich. What was going on with that?" She brushed aside a lock of hair. "But no. Maybe that's too personal. You don't have to answer if you don't want to."

"I guess you have a right to know." He stared at his half-empty glass then caught her gaze. "When I was eleven, I became sick with an undiagnosed illness. For five years, I was confined to a bed, and I withdrew from everyone. My folks sent me to one doctor after another. But they couldn't pinpoint a cause. Then, mysteriously, for no reason, I got better. Ever since, I've been obsessed with finding something I can't even put a name to. Maybe because of that, because of all the time I missed being a normal kid, wherever I've gone, I've felt like an outsider. And so I wandered."

A motorcycle rumbled past on the street, and their gazes followed until the noise subsided.

"Even at home, I never really belonged. My mother—rest her soul—was always lost in an alcoholic haze. And my father is . . . how can I say this? He's got a different morality, a different set of values, and we don't get along. None of my siblings get along with him either."

"I'm sorry." She touched his hand. "It sounds like you had a difficult childhood."

"Yes. Only my brother and sister seem to understand me. And Blake, of course. But after speaking with Caleb last week—Blake is gone." He finished the last of his wine. "And that's why, for the last few years, I've roamed from place to place, country to country. I've spent time skiing, mountain climbing, beach combing, doing almost anything to make up for being bedridden for so long. But what I was really doing was seeking some kind of meaning to my life. And now"—a wide smile lifted his lips—"I've found it."

"What are you saying? What kind of meaning?" Folding her arms on the table, she leaned forward.

"When I became a Christian, I found my place in eternity, my place in the family of God. And I realized that everything I'd done before that moment was a waste. None of it pleased God. So I'm glad I wasn't taken.

I know that service can't save you. Still, I can now make up to God what I failed to do before—make my life mean something to somebody. Maybe now I can take something with me into eternity, something of lasting value. There are a lot of lost people in this world like my brother and sister. Maybe I can help them."

"Dylan"—her eyes searched his, and their gazes locked—"that was an incredibly selfless act."

"Maybe. Maybe not. But there's more. After I met you, I found another reason to be glad I stayed behind. For whatever plans God has for me, I know this: You, Margot Durand, are part of them. And lately, I've been taking great comfort in that."

As she gazed into his eyes, so blue and kind, tears filled hers. That almost sounded like a proposal, though she knew he hadn't meant it that way. He was so honest, open, and vulnerable. Had he also just confessed that she was the salve for a wounded soul? Wiping her eyes, she reached across the table and grabbed his hands. "Thank you, Dylan. That's the nicest thing anyone has ever said to me."

He lifted her hands to his lips.

When he kissed her fingers, a little shiver ran up her arms, and she caught her breath.

The waiter brought the check, interrupting the moment. Dylan released her then threw some euros on the table.

"Let's walk back," she said. "It isn't far."

They left the market and started the trek home, each with a bag in their arms.

* * *

Only a few blocks from the market, the spires of the cathedral where Margot's family had attended rose beside the street. She stopped. One of the huge doors was open a crack.

"What's wrong?" Dylan asked.

"Nothing. Follow me."

She mounted the steps and, with him beside her, pushed through into the vast interior. Inside, no lights were lit, but the afternoon sun glinted through the stained-glass windows high in the clerestory. It was not enough to break the shadows filling the empty pews below or the stalls bearing unlit candles before the gloomy statues of saints or the chancel up front, now shrouded in darkness. "Everyone's gone," she whispered. "All the priests. All the parishioners."

"Not everyone." Dylan pointed to a dark form lying prone across the chancel steps. From that direction came a faint moan.

Their footsteps echoed down the nave toward the sound. Then the dark figure, wrapped in red robes, moved an arm. When they were only a few meters away, it rose, and the emaciated visage of His Excellency, the Most Reverend Phillipe Bonheur, Archbishop of Brussels, turned to face them. But stains smeared his rumpled robe, and he hadn't shaved in days.

At first, he seemed not to know her. But recognition hit, and his face twisted into a grimace. Tears streamed down his cheeks, and his mouth opened.

"Margot Durand!" He fell to his knees and brought his hands together before her as though in prayer. "Margot Durand, against whom I have greatly sinned. Forgive me, child! Forgive a prideful old man for not believing you, for putting my faith in ritual, tradition, and saints, and not in the Son of the Holy God whose wrath has fallen upon me." He waved a hand over his robe. "You see, don't you, how he has left me?" Then a question seemed to cross his brows, and his gaze caught hers. "B–but why are you here? Why weren't you taken?"

"You told me my visions came from the Devil." When she spoke, she surprised herself at how cold and distant her voice sounded. "Archbishop, I believed you. Because of that, I lost my faith."

His visage twisted with pain. "Oh no, No, NO!" He gripped the sides of his head and shook it from side to side. "Oh no, my child. Now, I am doubly damned! What have I done? Can you ever forgive me?"

As she stared at this pathetic figure, she felt only disgust. How many others had he led from the true Jesus by his blind devotion to empty ritual, his obsession with keeping the mechanism of the church going while ignoring the hearts of its people? But then she saw how broken and repentant he was, and she felt only pity for him.

"I do forgive you, Archbishop. And be assured, I have regained my faith." But then she whirled away from him. "Come, Dylan. Let's get out of here."

As Philippe Bonheur mumbled his thanks, she strode from the cathedral.

CHAPTER 39
TROUBLE IN THE STREETS

Brussels, Belgium

After Dylan and Margot left the cathedral, it was nearly dark. As had happened every night since the vanishing, the streets emptied. Never before had Dylan felt unsafe in Brussels, but with all the recent robberies, he now looked askance at every passerby, few though they were. If their arms weren't wrapped around the bags they carried, he'd reach for her hand.

"I don't like this." Her gaze swept from side to side. "The neighbors said gangs have been roaming the streets in our neighborhood after dark, and we still have two blocks to go. We've never had gangs before, and the police aren't prepared to deal with them. Where did they come from?"

"Apparently, it's the same everywhere. Except for his presence in the few believers like us, the Holy Spirit has mostly abandoned the world to its sin. That's left us with violence, anarchy, and chaos."

"Oh no. Look there!" She pointed, and Dylan squinted. Three shadows huddled in an entryway. Three youths peeked out and gazed in their direction.

"This is not good." The nearest intersection was half a block away, and this street had no alleys. "We can't go around. We'll have to pass them."

He led her to the other side of the street. When they were opposite the group, he increased the pace.

"Hey, you!" One of the youths stepped from the shadows. "I need ten euros." He spoke French with an Algerian accent. But his voice squeaked. "How about it?"

"Walk faster and don't look at them," Dylan whispered.

"Hey!" a different voice called out, and steps clomped across the street. "He's talking to you. Answer the question."

Still walking, Dylan glanced back. All three were now striding diagonally across the cobbles on an intersecting path. "I don't have anything on me right now," he responded in French. "Try me tomorrow."

"Are you playing with us?" said a third voice, deeper, older. "How about thirty euros? That sounds better. Or maybe a hundred. Do you have a hundred euros, monsieur?"

Dylan shot another glance to the side. Their pursuers were closing in. He whispered to Margot. "How far to the apartment?"

Skin ashen, voice tight, she pointed ahead. "At the intersection, only a few meters."

"Then let's—run!" He broke into a sprint, and she followed.

But the moment they did, feet began slapping the pavement behind. Having spent the last years skiing, climbing, hiking, and jogging, he was in good physical shape. But Margot had cooped herself up for weeks and now had trouble keeping his pace. And they each held a bag from the market, slowing them further.

At the intersection, he checked his speed so she could catch up. They turned the corner. Down the new street he ran, the groceries bouncing, Margot falling behind again. They were losing ground.

With only twenty meters to go, one of their pursuers was closing in. They weren't going to reach the apartment in time. He'd have to make a stand.

Margot turned at the entrance, dropped her bag, and fumbled for the key. He came to a halt in the entryway and set down his bag. Slapping hands on his knees, he tried to catch his breath.

The three youths closed in and formed a semicircle.

"Where's our money?" said Squeaky Voice. "Let's have it."

Dylan reached into his pocket. His hand crumpled around a bill. He looked right, then left, sizing up his adversaries. They ranged from sixteen to twenty five—all of them punks. "All I've got is ten euros."

"You're lying," said the oldest, his voice deep, his hair a tangled mop of wiry brown. "Give us your wallet."

"Take the ten and leave." Behind him, the lock clicked and the door creaked open.

Dylan began to turn, but the big one, more solidly built, older and taller than the others, lunged. "Enough of this," he said.

Dylan spun back toward him.

He'd never fought anyone before, and as the man's right fist swung, he tried to duck. Not fast enough. The blow caught him on the chin. The impact jerked his head back, slamming his skull against the doorframe, sending a shock through his spine. Before he could react, a second youth's fist punched his ribs, knocking the breath from his lungs.

As he gasped for air, a boot found a target on a shin, and he jerked his leg back in pain.

Smirking, the big one waved the others aside. "Leave him to me."

The stocky youth shot out with a fist.

Remembering his time with the high school wrestling team, Dylan ducked, and as the arm passed his head, he grabbed the arm and spun the man around. He threw his hand over his opponent's neck and put him in a headlock.

With one, lightning-fast movement, he thrust one hand into his pocket, removed the ten-euro note, and slapped it into the man's open mouth. "Don't forget what you came for."

Planting his foot on the man's buttocks, he pushed with all his might. The youth flew forward, lost his footing, and sprawled over the cobbles. He broke his fall, his hands scraping over the bricks. Cursing, he eyed his bloody hands and rose to his feet.

"Get in!" shouted Margot from behind, and Dylan whirled.

He took a step into the foyer.

But something hard and heavy rocked his head from behind.

Inside the building now, he threw his weight against the door to close it. Dizzy and seeing spots before his eyes, he fought for balance.

Beside him, Margot flipped the deadlock into place then shot him a worried glance.

All he remembered next was his legs buckling beneath him.

Then the world went black.

* * *

HE WOKE, LYING IN THE foyer. Above him, Margot knelt, and tears ran down her cheeks. Her hands held a bloody rag.

"You're awake!" She dabbed the back of his head with the rag, and where it touched, he winced. "One of them hit you with a brick from behind—the coward! I was so worried. You've been out for the last hour, and I couldn't lift you. Can you stand?"

"Yes." But when he pushed himself to a sitting position, the room spun in crazy circles. Closing his eyes, he waited for the dizziness to pass. He grasped Margot's hand and struggled to his feet. Then he focused on her. "Are *you* all right? Did they hurt you? Did they get anything?"

"No. They didn't get what they wanted. You were so brave." She pointed toward the elevator. "Let's get you inside."

When he tried to smile, his face cracked, and it hurt. The thugs had hit him there, too, hadn't they?

They crammed themselves into the tiny elevator and rode to the third floor. Inside the apartment, she tended his wounds at the kitchen table. The alcohol stung. She applied two butterfly bandages to the cut on the back of his head. Fortunately, nothing was broken.

"Do you have any brandy?"

"Father has—had—some, and you probably need it right now." She went to a cupboard and brought back a bottle.

He poured half a glass and sipped. "It's no longer safe here. We need to leave the city."

"But where to?"

"My family's villa in Tuscany. I've spent a lot of time there."

"That sounds wonderful. When should we go?"

"Maybe in a few days. Right now, I'm too dizzy to drive."

She leaned down and kissed his forehead. "We can wait."

CHAPTER 40
CONSEQUENCES

University Village, Chicago

Mark 16:17 (NLT): *These miraculous signs will accompany those who believe: They will cast out demons in my name . . .*

Focused on the fifth entry in the new thread, yet another attempt at broadcasting the truth, Caleb typed the last sentence. Then he sat back and eyed today's title—"Aliens or Jesus? Who Took Them?" Since returning from Oregon, he'd increased his readership by over 400 percent. He even had to contact his web host provider to get a more expensive server. With so many replies to his posts, he spent each morning trying to answer some of them.

"You need to get away from that thing," Tanya called from the kitchen. She and Nika were now spending half the time in his apartment, and he was glad of the company. "The lasagna is ready."

"I'm done." Smiling, he clicked on the button to post, and it went out to the world.

He stood and stretched his back. Before leaving the desk, he reached down and brought up his email to see how many needed a response tomorrow.

But as he scrolled down the list, he froze.

There it was again—another note from Morgoth.

The name itself was chilling and vaguely familiar. After looking it up, he'd discovered that Morgoth was the first Dark Lord in J.R.R. Tolkien's *Lord of the Rings* trilogy. Even more troubling were the contents of Morgoth's messages. He sat and read.

This is your third warning, Caleb Turner. You have one day to stop promoting your theory that some mythical god pulled citizens out of the world. This is not a joke. I know where you live. Persist and there will be consequences.

— Morgoth

"Caleb?" Tanya called again. "Food is ready."

"Come here and look at this." His glance remained riveted on the screen, and his heart was beating fast.

She sidled over, rested a hand on his shoulder, and leaned closer to the laptop. "Oh no. Not another one."

"Yes. And it's beginning to scare me."

"Me too."

He shut the laptop cover. But this didn't make sense. He rubbed the pulse at his temple. "Why should anyone care if I promote the Rapture over the alien-abduction theory?"

"Good question." Grabbing her ponytail with one hand, she held it. "This guy must be some nutjob. I suppose the police can't help?"

"After all the defunding, the retirements, and *that*"—he waved toward the window—"there aren't many of them left. No, we're on our own."

She threw her ponytail over one shoulder. "What are you going to do?"

"Nothing." He turned toward the kitchen. "Let's eat."

But as he sat at the table, he couldn't stop the unease creeping across his shoulders.

* * *

THE NEXT DAY, CALEB WELCOMED Tanya's presence as she spent the afternoon in his apartment with Nika. Lately, while he typed or studied, she would read, watch television, or nap on the couch. Three times a day, they'd take Nika for a short walk. He enjoyed her company, and they'd become good friends.

Following their usual routine, they ate supper together. Then she and Nika left. He'd been sitting at his laptop all day, and now he needed some fresh air.

He grabbed a sweatshirt and Uri's pistol, took the elevator down, and stepped outside. The stars were out, and a chill was in the air, unusual for early August. His glance swept the street, but the news reported that the gangs had moved to the south. Tonight, the streets were empty.

At the park, he crossed the field and passed under the line of trees. The nearest streetlights were a hundred yards distant, and with no moon, the night was dark. A symphony of crickets overlaid the echoes of a distant trumpet echoing out of some open window.

Once again, he thought of his mother and the news that she'd drowned. Robbed of the funeral, he'd also been robbed of a proper mourning. Perhaps this was why his thoughts kept returning to her. After learning the news from Chelsea, he'd called Father, but as always, their conversation was awkward, brief, and Father had shed little light on the event. The ship had crashed into a bridge abutment and sunk. Father had barely escaped alive. Mother had drowned. And his father was deeply worried about his business.

Still walking, he stopped beneath a tall elm. It was good that they'd planted trees in the middle of the city, good to find a bit of nature among the cars, lights, and crowds—or what used to be crowds. Tonight, even the sounds of distant traffic were missing.

For some reason, the crickets stopped chirping. A shiver crawled along his shoulders and down his back. Was it the early August chill? Slowly, he turned to look behind him.

There. Before that tree. In the shadows. The silhouette of a man?

Only a dozen feet away stood a figure, silent and motionless, nearly hidden by a dark trunk.

"W–who are you?" Caleb's hand slipped into his pocket. His fingers gripped the pistol, found the trigger.

But the solitary figure said nothing, and as Caleb squinted to get a better view, the edges of the dark form seemed to waver, to merge with the night.

"My name," came a hoarse guttural voice, "is Morgoth."

An uncontrollable quivering ran up and down Caleb's arms and legs. He wanted to turn and run. Too late, he remembered the cryptic warning from the mysterious biker in the South Dakota diner. It was night. And he was under dark trees.

"You were warned, and you didn't listen." The voice grated, unnerved.

He backed up. But the shadow darkened and grew larger.

What, exactly, was standing before him? If not a man, then what?

His heart beating faster, he whirled away from the dark presence. He took a step, but his right foot became an iron ingot, a hunk of metal, and he couldn't raise his left foot. He struggled with all his might, but he was fixed to the spot.

A cloud, a thick mass of swirling darkness, surrounded him. He tried to scream, but no sound issued from his mouth.

His hands reached into the pocket for the pistol, but his fingers refused to close on the weapon.

He couldn't flee, couldn't scream, couldn't even raise the pistol. Some powerful force of bone-chilling evil was dragging him, pulling him, pressing him down. Flat on the ground, the smell of dead leaves filled his nostrils. His heart beat wildly, a frightened animal trapped in the grip of a predator.

A hundred invisible fists began pounding on him—

Beating his arms. His legs. His head. His chest.

Pain pummeled every part of his body, striking him without mercy.

All he could think to do was to pray. "Jesus, help me!" Those words alone escaped his lips, but as a hoarse whisper. "Save me, Jesus! Protect me from this evil."

The beating stopped. The dark presence left.

For long moments, he lay sweating on the grass beneath the trees, his nose in the leaves, in agony with every intake of breath. But he was alone.

Then the crickets resumed their chirping.

When he stood, he could barely walk for the pain. Every limping step toward the apartment was sheer agony. He exited the elevator on his floor with its accompanying loud clank. But before he slipped his keys into the lock, they fell through his fingers. He looked down, but he couldn't even bend over to pick them up.

Tanya peeked out from her apartment then raced to his side. Nika was close beside her.

"Caleb!" Her eyes wide with fright, she picked his keys up from the floor. "What happened to you?"

"I was attacked."

She unlocked his door, and they pushed through into the foyer where he leaned against the wall for support.

"T–there are welts . . . all over you." The shock in her eyes frightened him. "H–how did they do that?"

"There was only one." He breathed in deeply. "It was Morgoth. But he isn't a man. He's a–a demon."

Frowning, she grabbed an arm. "You need to lie down. Come with me." But where she touched, he winced. She led him to the bedroom where he sat on the bed. As she helped him remove his shirt and jeans, every movement caused shooting pain.

Dressed now only in his underwear, he glanced at his chest, his arms, his legs. Welts covered his entire body. "Ice. Get some ice."

"What do you mean—a demon did this?" Her eyes, moving up and down his body, seemed to hold as much pain as he felt.

"It was a shadow, an otherworldly creature. It was Morgoth. It was filled with evil—I *felt* its evil—and it said I hadn't listened. But when I prayed to Jesus, it left me."

"So . . . it really was a demon?"

"It was. We're in a spiritual battle, Tanya, and someone or some *thing* doesn't want me spreading the truth."

"I'll get some ice."

Moments later, she returned with a bottle of beer, two Tylenol, and two washcloths wrapping cubes of ice.

"I'm not going to stop." He downed the pills with a swallow of beer. "This attack tells me I'm on the right path, that what I'm doing is more important even than my life. I'm not going to stop."

Pain in her eyes, she bit her lip, looked again at the bruises covering his torso, and shook her head. "Caleb Turner, you are the bravest person I've ever met." She knelt and kissed his forehead. "You're also the craziest."

When she finally left him that night, he prayed to the Lord of light, the Son of the most holy God. He asked God to heal him and to show him what he was to do with his life. And he asked for divine protection for himself, his brother and sister, and for Tanya. He prayed, and he didn't stop praying until an hour later when peace settled over him and sleep called.

SEVENTEEN DAYS AFTER

CHAPTER 41

THE VILLA

In the Tuscan Countryside

John 4:24 (NLT): *For God is Spirit, so those who worship him must worship in spirit and in truth.*

Under an azure sky, between tall cypresses waving in the breeze, where verdant vines bursting with grapes wrapped the hillsides, Dylan turned the rental van onto the long drive leading to the family's villa. Before leaving Brussels, Margot had insisted they bring with them her entire portfolio. The back of their rented diesel Citroen van carried all her paintings.

The trip had been fraught with threats. Fortunately, the German Autobahn was cleared of pileups. But on the drive through Switzerland, they passed one ghost village after another, some with barricades and armed men demanding a toll for passage. Dylan paid them, hoping no one would ask about the paintings in back. Then on the plains of Lombardy, the chaos worsened. He bypassed Milan, but on the Italian Autostrade, he was forced to make sudden stops and detour around random, uncleared pileups. And in several villages, bands of youth threatened motorists with tire irons, knives, and axes until they paid for passage. Everywhere, order seemed to have broken down.

He'd wound through the roads of the Apennines and entered Tuscany. When they turned onto the villa's gravel drive, he let out a relieved sigh.

"It's beautiful, Dylan." Margot beamed as they passed olive trees, more grapevines, an expanse of lawn, and approached the three-story country house. "I'm so glad we're here."

"We'll be safe now." He pulled the van onto the cobbled space beside two other cars. He recognized the first, a green Fiat belonging to the caretakers, Bettino and Allegra Pisano. They were Catholics, but how devout, he couldn't say. The second car, a black Alfa Romeo, he didn't know.

Commanding the hill, the villa was a completely restored mansion with an all-stone exterior, red-tiled roof, and covered patio. After parking, he grabbed their bags and led Margot up wide steps to a second-floor living room where he knocked.

White-haired, round-bellied Bettino opened the door, gasped his surprise, and beamed. He waved Dylan into a sun-drenched room with cushioned wooden chairs where sat a familiar man. "Buongiorno, Signore Dylan, I am so glad you have returned," Bettino said in Italian. "His Most Reverend Excellency Emilio Gallo of Prato is visiting today. You remember the bishop? His villa is only two kilometers over the hill."

"Of course." Dylan dropped his bag, and as the bishop stood, they kissed each other's cheeks in greeting.

Today, the bishop wore tan slacks and a black, long-sleeved shirt. "But, Bettino, you must no longer call me bishop. I no longer deserve that title."

In English, Dylan introduced Margot, and for her sake, everyone switched to English. Bettino asked about the family, and Dylan filled him in. Bettino also informed them that Allegra, his wife, had been taken.

"I am so sorry," Dylan said.

"She is where we all should be now. But I am sorry about the signora. She was a kind woman. So many taken—it breaks the heart." Bettino drew a hand through his hair. "But they are with the Lord, no? These news reports about aliens—bah! What do these news people know?"

Unsaid was that Dylan's mother had drowned and wasn't taken, and she was probably *not* with the Lord. "Yes, their theory about alien abductions is rubbish. On the day people vanished, we believe Jesus came to take his own."

"On that point, we are in total agreement." Bishop Emilio raised an empty glass.

"Margot and I now both believe—too late—that Jesus is the Son of God." He need not relate how Margot had lost her faith or how he had prayed to remain behind.

"Ah, my friends, I am glad to hear it." Emilio's voice cracked. "If only we had all held right beliefs before . . ."

"But please, everyone sit." Waving to chairs, Bettino crossed to a table and a five-liter red bottle Dylan recognized as holding the villa's own vintage. "The bishop was about to leave, but I will get everyone wine, he will stay, and we will talk more." Before Dylan could object, Bettino was pouring two more glasses and refilling Emilio's and his own.

When all were seated, the bishop waved his glass. "Ever since the event, Bettino and I have been meeting. Two lost souls in a ravaged, sinful world, no?" But no joviality accompanied the strained words. "We share the fact that we are here, and so many of our countrymen are not. In the north of Europe, I understand, this is not as true." His gaze wandered to the window and the bright Italian sun. "But here in my diocese, I, the bishop in charge, was not taken." His gaze somber, he drank deep then faced the newcomers.

"I am glad for your newfound faith, Dylan Turner, but I confess to you that I gave my heart to the Virgin and not to Christ. I believed in her with all my soul. Each night I said many Hail Marys to her. I put my trust in her. And each day I would light candles for her in the cathedral." A grimace twisted his lips. "Now we know how much false belief it takes for a man to remove himself from the Book of Life. My worship was not in the spirit. It was not in truth, but in falsehood." He closed his eyes and hung his head. "What fools we all were! Even the Pope remains behind—he who blessed the sexual union of men with men and women with women, and who hinted of many ways into the Kingdom of Heaven."

In the silence that followed, Bettino's pained glance moved from the bishop to Dylan to Margot.

"But Bettino and I have talked long enough, and you must be tired after your long flight." Emilio emptied his glass, rose, and bowed. "I am glad to have made your acquaintance, but now, I must take my leave."

They followed him down the outside stairs. Then his Alfa Romeo sped away across the drive.

Bettino gripped Dylan's hands. "I am so glad you returned—you and the beautiful signorina. It is good to have life in the villa again. I will go now and prepare supper. Call if you need me." He climbed the steps to the kitchen.

With the smells of frying sausage drifting down from upstairs, Dylan and Margot brought her paintings from the van and began stacking them in the first-floor salon. But as she set one picture against its companions, she sank slowly to the floor, sat cross-legged, and stared.

"What is it?" he asked.

"Look at this." She pointed. "Do you see anything different about it?"

It was a scene in a basement. A man stood at a podium, looking out over about thirty others, each with a skullcap on their heads. They appeared to be orthodox Jews with twisted ringlets of hair—payots, they were called—hanging beside their ears. Candles lit the room, and one man stood watch by the door.

The speaker's face was clear, with smiling brown eyes, waves of curly black hair atop his head, and the shadowed beginnings of a beard and mustache. The man held a book with unique lettering on its cover.

Dylan drew a quick breath and stepped closer to the painting. "The face wasn't there before, was it? And now he's holding a book."

"Yes, and that book"—she caught his hand and gazed deep into his eyes—"it's one of Luc's. See the fancy gold lettering with the initials *LD*. That's Luc's Bible, and it's over there." She jerked her head toward one of the boxes they'd brought in from the van. "I never painted his face. Or that Bible." She let out a long low breath and whispered as if afraid to speak the fact aloud, "Those details appeared while we were traveling."

Dylan threaded their fingers together. "What does it mean?"

"This man is important to us. Somehow, we're connected with him."

"But how?"

She shrugged.

"Margot." A shiver raced down his back. "God is speaking to us again."

* * *

After stacking all the paintings in the salon, they climbed the stairs to the kitchen where Bettino was still cooking. Dylan then explained to him about Margot's incredible gift and what they'd discovered in the painting downstairs.

Bettino stopped chopping garlic, crossed himself, and looked with widened eyes at her. "May you someday join the saints, signorina. If we had a real Pope in these troubled times, you'd be canonized."

"I'm not so sure, monsieur. But maybe we should keep this a secret between us?" She smiled, and he nodded.

After supper, as the sun was setting over the Tuscan hills, Dylan wandered outside and sat alone on the patio. The cicadas buzzed, and in the distance, an owl hooted. Out on the lawn, a hoopoe with its fantail-feathered head, black-and-white striped body, and long beak pecked at something in the grass.

Still in his pocket, his phone played "Rock Around the Clock", his latest tune, and he answered. "Caleb?"

"Hello, brother. We haven't talked in a while, and there's a lot to tell."

"What about?"

"Over a week ago, I was attacked. I had welts everywhere, and I hurt all over. I was only able to get out of bed yesterday. Today, for the first time, I went for a walk."

"Oh no." Dylan stiffened and gripped the phone tighter. "What happened?"

When Caleb explained, Dylan was so stunned, he couldn't speak.

"Dylan?" came the voice at the other end.

"Yes. What are you going to do now?"

"The moment I'm better, I'm going to resume my blog."

"Be careful, Caleb." Dylan sucked in breath. His brother was attacked by a demon? A shudder rippled down his back. "This is spiritual warfare. We're both, finally, on the right side of this. I applaud what you're doing, but just . . . be careful. But if you were injured, were you alone?"

"No. I'm with my neighbor, Tanya Baranov." A pause. "She's been taking care of me."

Dylan smiled. "The woman you asked out?"

"She's a peach. A real beauty."

"Are you two . . . a number?"

"Just friends. Really good friends. And we need each other."

"I understand. Margot and I are . . . well, we're like that too."

"Have you heard from Chelsea lately?"

"Two days ago, I called her before we left Brussels. She's not doing well, and I'm worried about her. She's holed up in her apartment, afraid even to step foot outside. Apparently, it's worse in New York than any-where else, with gangs roaming the streets unchecked, people being beaten and robbed, and apartments being broken into every day. She needs to get out of there."

"Yeah. People are asking for martial law, but the President is so weak and antimilitary, she's afraid to do anything. In almost every city, order has completely broken down."

Dylan rose from his seat and paced into the yard. Now he wished he were in New York, able to whisk her to a safe place. "I hadn't realized it was that bad. What can we do for her?"

"Nothing, I fear. I'm still laid up, and until order is restored, it's dangerous to travel anywhere in the US right now."

They agreed to keep in touch, and he hung up.

But as he slipped the phone into his pocket, he feared for his brother. That a demon had risen to attack Caleb for telling the truth was more than troubling.

Was the Tribulation beginning already? Had the gates of the under-world been thrown open? Were the forces of darkness already loosed upon the world?

CHAPTER 42
THE NUMBER OF A NAME

In the Tuscan Countryside

Revelation 13:18 (NLT): *Wisdom is needed here. Let the one with understanding solve the meaning of the number of the beast, for it is the number of a man. His number is 666.*

The next day, Dylan, Margot, and Bettino gathered before a television in a downstairs room as Dylan tuned the satellite box for a British channel in English.

"In the market yesterday, they told me I should hear this speech." Bettino poured three glasses of the villa's wine from a large glass jug. "I'm sorry to have kept you so long in the vineyards. I hope we didn't miss much. This wine is from the vines you just saw."

"That's all right." Margot took a glass. "We enjoyed the walk. And the tour."

"Who is this Davato?" asked Bettino. "I haven't kept up with the news. Lately, it's been too depressing."

"He's the new president of the European Council," said Dylan, "appointed just this week after his predecessor died of a sudden heart attack. About two weeks ago, when he was at the UN, he arranged the historic peace deal in the Middle East."

As the channel sharpened, the president was just wrapping up his presentation.

"Peace between Israel and the Arab world was too long in coming." Davato's voice rang through the huge chamber. "But that accomplishment was only the beginning. What we need now, more than ever, is to lead the world out of the chaos, anarchy, and economic disaster that has, since the Great Calamity, traumatized the world community."

Glancing around the vast hall of the UN General Assembly, he gripped the podium with authority. His face reminded Dylan of some classic painting of a great general, but softer, more pleasant, more genteel. With a firm jaw and engaging deep-dark eyes, he looked like everyone's ideal of a trustworthy favorite uncle. His long silver hair swept back across his forehead, presenting a dignified appearance. His voice, though musical and pleasing to the ear, carried the timbre of unquestioned command.

But no, the voice was far more than that. The voice mesmerized, and the words from this man's mouth seemed to cast a spell on the listener— even through the television. Against his better judgment, Dylan wanted to believe, follow, and obey it.

"Thus, today," continued the voice, "I call upon this great body— and upon the citizens of every peace-loving nation of the world—to come together as one, to set aside petty national differences and together put the world on a path back to prosperity, peace, and even to unprecedented progress."

Thunderous applause broke across the room, but the speaker merely glanced at the floor in a stance of humility.

"Fellow citizens of the world," he went on, "the old has passed away, tragically ripped from its roots. In its wake, we need a new regime, one that rises from the ashes of a terrible atrocity that, through no fault of our own, has fallen upon us. Now we must start anew, but not as separate peoples, fighting and seeking ill for our neighbors. Now we must unite as one people, with strength, courage, and a loving heart for all men.

"But some might say such a thing has never before been done. Some will object that man is at heart evil and that ideological and age-old national and tribal rivalries will never allow such a thing. Yes, some will always be naysayers, throwing stale dogma and old-fashioned ideas at any plan that might lead us to a new and glorious future. But let us reject such negativity. For that kind of thinking is what holds us back." Then he smiled, and his glance searched those seated closest to the podium.

"Let me tell you a secret about something hidden within each of us, something we all know, deep in our hearts, is true, one to which the purveyors of outdated doctrines will object. But I contend that, when we shine a light on this secret, make it our goal, and bend government to that end, we will break down all the artificial and unnatural barriers we have built up over the millennia and unleash a new era of humankind.

212

"So now, my friends, I reveal the great secret that, until now, has been hidden: Within you, me, and every person on the planet lies the essence of a divine nature, a great goodness, and a deep inner wisdom. For too long, ideology, dogma, and a warped view of humankind have stifled it, buried it, called it evil, and tried to suppress it. To reach a new age of humanity—one with unlimited, unbounded progress—we must tap that potential within each of us, give it the freedom to go where it will, and let it grow. Before we can plant the seeds of a permanent peace, the precursor to progress, we must release what was chained. Yes, we must free our inner spirits, nourish them, and let them roam where they will. And with that, fellow citizens, we will begin a new age."

As applause again filled the hall, Dylan shifted in his chair. Bettino seemed mesmerized by Davato's words, but something about what the president said made Dylan uncomfortable. Release the inner man? Wasn't it when Hitler freed the "inner man" that Germany decided to wipe out the Jews? Wasn't it after every thief, murderer, and rapist freed their inner selves that they performed their crimes?

The president continued, and a shiver raced down Dylan's spine.

"But how can we free this secret strength so long buried within us? And how can we accomplish such a monumental task on a worldwide scale?" He gripped the podium, and his glance swept the hall. "The answer lies in a first small step—joining together the peoples of Europe into a new united nation, one far stronger than before, one that breaks down the false barriers of nationality. But that is only a start, for how can we ignore or slight the citizens of Africa, Asia, Australia, or North and South America? They, too, must be allowed, when the time is ripe, to join in, creating one government that unites every country on earth. Yes, a strong, united Europe is a good beginning, but it is only the start of turning around this horrible catastrophe."

The camera panned over the UN delegates filling the hall, their faces eager and rapt with attention, fixed on the figure commanding the podium, the room, the broadcast.

"From there, we will build on our progress, united in purpose, united in government, to foster an environment fertile to the task of freeing humanity's inner light. But before beginning our task, we must leave behind any dogma, ideology, or false thinking that holds us back. Thus, I call upon every Buddhist, Hindu, and Jew, every Christian, Muslim, and Mormon to set aside petty theological differences and join us in creating a new age of humanity, one with a greater promise, a higher goal than anything ever before seen on this earth. Let us look deep within ourselves, each and every one of us, and find our hidden purpose, our buried strength, and with this as our sword and shield, go forward. Together, let us create a new world order that elevates the inner man and woman, that puts humankind high on the divine pedestal it deserves. This, my fellow citizens, is my humble call to the world."

He bowed his head, and after long seconds of stunned silence, the assembly broke into spontaneous, wild applause. Dylan himself had the urge to clap, and when he looked aside to Margot and Bettino, their glances told him they, too, were caught up in the man's spell.

When the clapping subsided and a panel discussion began praising the speech, Dylan switched off the set.

"He is very convincing." Bettino looked up. "Do you think he can do what he promises? The world needs a leader like this right now."

Dylan shook his head. "Something about him troubles me. He speaks fine words. But his appeal to our inner nature is . . . wrong. Where is God in all this? Where is Christ, the only one who can bring us salvation? He talks about the need to do away with dogma, but by this, does he mean Christian teaching and the Bible? Instead, he offers us another dogma—his own. Only he doesn't call it that."

Margot's brows furrowed. "You're right. He almost had me convinced."

"I need some paper and a pen."

Bettino cast him a puzzled glance, but Margot brought him what he asked.

On the top of a sheet of paper, Dylan wrote the letters of Davato's name. Then he put the letters of the alphabet in a column on the left. For the letters *A* through *I* he assigned the numbers *1* through *9*. For the letters *J* through *R*, he assigned *10* through *90*. The last group of letters through *Z* he assigned in increments of one hundred each, giving *100* to *S*, *200* to *T*, and so forth.

Sitting across the room, Margot looked askance at him. "Are you sure they didn't knock something loose inside your head back in Brussels?"

"I think she just told a joke." He returned her smile. "No, there's a number theory called gematria. I read about it back in Blake's cabin in Oregon. By assigning a number to each letter of the alphabet, we can determine the number of a person's name."

"Oh no." She covered her mouth with her hands. "What is . . . his number?"

He looked up the letters of Davato's name then summed them. When he finished, he stared at the result.

"Well?" she asked. "What is it?"

"Six-six-six. It all makes sense. He alone made the peace treaty with Israel. When he speaks, he mesmerizes all who listen. His list of accomplishments is amazing. He's in charge of the EU, and now he's calling for the nations of the world to unite and free the inner man." He sat back in the chair. "Without a doubt, Davato is the Antichrist."

Bettino frowned at the ceiling and crossed himself.

"Then the Tribulation has begun," said Margot.

"We knew it had. This only confirms it."

CHAPTER 43
CHELSEA'S PLIGHT

Greenwich Village, New York City

On their third attempt this week to go to the store, once again, Chelsea and her neighbor made it only a block before running into yet another gang. Today, she and Frank, the nerdy young man living in the second-floor apartment, had gone out together, hoping for strength in numbers. But now they were both sprinting back to their building with ten young toughs close behind.

"Hey, you! What you runnin' from?" came a voice from behind.

"Oh, crap," whispered Frank, running beside her.

"Sweet mama, you don't know what you missin'," said another.

"I think I have an idea!" she shouted back.

Frank made it to the door first, his key already slipping into the lock.

She bounded past the newly spray-painted bricks and obscene graffiti and up the steps. The moment she rushed inside, Frank slammed the door behind her and turned the deadbolt. Fortunately, the windows, now broken, had always been heavily barred, and the outside door was steel.

As the group shook the bars, pounded on the door, laughed, and shouted curses at them, both she and her neighbor caught their breaths in the foyer.

"I'm out of food." Breathing heavily, Frank leaned over and grabbed his knees.

"Me too." Chelsea also gasped for breath. "And everything else."

The lights in the hall were out again. Frank pushed his glasses back up his nose and headed for the stairs. She joined him. With blackouts happening several times a week, sometimes twice a day, they no longer trusted the elevator.

At the second floor, he headed down the hall. Before she started higher, she pointed toward the empty apartment across from his. "What do you think? Is it time?"

"I think it is. We're desperate. I have a crowbar."

"Let's start with that one. I'll wait for you."

After the first week when neither could leave the building, they'd discovered that, of the six apartments in the building, only four were occupied. Before the event, two had been for rent, and on V-Day, one occupant had been taken. And then, only days after the vanishing, the man living across the hall from Frank had been robbed and beaten to death. That left only Frank and Chelsea.

As she waited, she wondered what Dylan was doing now. After her conversation with him two weeks ago, she was glad he wasn't taken. He told her he'd prayed to be left behind, and that's why he was still here. But she was skeptical. After all, what was one supposed to believe about what had happened on V-Day?

Since the event, she hadn't worked. Multiple times, she called the Cool Green Planet office, but no one answered. When she brought up their website, she learned that, like many other companies, it was bankrupt. She'd always prided herself on being able to make her own way, but now she was dependent on her trust fund. At least she had that.

Frank emerged, and she followed him down the hall to their target. With a crowbar, mallet, and screwdriver, they went to work. It took half an hour to break in. In the kitchen, she took inventory of the fridge and cupboards. "There's enough here to last both of us for weeks."

He grabbed a bag of chips and a Pepsi from the refrigerator and sat.

"The hamburger is bad," she said. "But the sausage is good, and there's a lot of it. I used to be vegan, but given the circumstances and my shrunken stomach, I'm giving that up right now. There's also a lot of rigatoni, tomato sauce, and in the freezer, some bread. How about if I make supper?"

"Sounds good."

As she began cooking, Frank searched the rest of the apartment and returned with a pistol and ammunition. "This might come in handy next time we try to leave."

"Better to be armed than beaten to death." How quickly one abandoned one's pacifism when your neighbor's corpse was moldering somewhere down the street.

Frank switched on the counter television, and they listened to the latest disaster bulletin. "After two and a half weeks of anarchy in nearly every city in the country, the President held a press conference on the White House lawn. She finally dropped her support of the climate change hypothesis in favor of the alien abduction theory. Then she gave the following surprising announcement."

The screen switched to a clip showing the liberal President, wearing her trademark grin, standing before a handful of reporters. Machine-gun-bearing marines surrounded them. Indeed, since V-Day, troops had ringed the entire capital.

"Our country is in a state of unprecedented crisis." She dropped the grin for a facsimile of seriousness. "Civil order has broken down, with anarchy and violence in many cities and towns. Some have been calling for me to declare martial law. Until now, I have been loath to do that. Instead, I have pleaded with the public for restraint and forbearance. But it's clear that our cities have become battlegrounds, and I have no choice but to declare martial law. Today, I am authorizing the National Guard to protect citizens of any state whose governor requests such assistance. I am also suspending the Constitution. I take this action with great reluctance, but given the dire nature of this crisis, I feel—"

Frank began switching channels. "She should have done that weeks ago." He stopped on a local station with two talking heads: ". . . it's long overdue and too late. But the problem is she has decimated the military. Even before V-Day, this President called her generals warmongers and the Pentagon an obscenity. She's dramatically cut the military budget. She's called for defunding the police. We simply haven't enough soldiers or cops to quell the violence. Here in New York, they'd need two divisions to control the gangs that, overnight, seem to be running the place. It's just as bad in Portland, Seattle, LA, St. Louis, and Minneapolis, but—"

Frank shut it off. "At the first chance I get, I'm leaving the city for good. I've got a brother in the North Carolina mountains. My car's in a garage about a mile away. If I could just get to it, I'd go live with him."

"Yeah, I don't know where I'd go, but I'm ready to leave. Who knows when it will ever again be safe in this city?"

"If you want"—he looked at her with pleading eyes—"you can come live with me in North Carolina."

She took a deep breath and stifled an urge to squirm. "Thanks for the offer, but I'd probably fly to Chicago and my brother's." She couldn't imagine living with Frank anywhere.

When the meal was ready, they sat and ate. Then they divided the former occupant's food, toilet paper, and soap between them. Tomorrow, they agreed to break into the third-floor vacant apartment.

It was either that or starve.

THE MONTHS AFTER

CHAPTER 44
A PRIVATE MEETING

Rome, Italy

Daniel 11:36, 39b (HCSB): *Then the king will do whatever he wants. He will exalt and magnify himself above every god, and he will say outrageous things against the God of gods. He will be successful until the time of wrath is completed, because what has been decreed will be accomplished. . . . He will greatly honor those who acknowledge him, making them rulers over many and distributing land as a reward.*

As Carlo Scutari ushered the president of the European Commission into Davato's penthouse suite at Worldnet headquarters, Davato crossed the room with his hand out. "Welcome, François, have you been here before?"

"I have not." They shook hands and exchanged kisses on the cheek.

Davato guided the newcomer to one of the plush chairs set before a low table and a window overlooking the city. Below, lights glimmered all the way to the horizon. "A Grand Marnier for François." He shot a glance to Carlo. "One for me also."

As the aide padded across the room to the bar, the two exchanged pleasantries.

Years before, when Davato himself had been president of the Commission, he had worked with François Desroches at EU headquarters. He knew the man as dependable and not averse to twisting a few arms when needed. With François's tall, slim frame, sculpted Gallic face, and wavy black hair, he was also popular with the ladies. Carlo's investigations had uncovered a number of secret and embarrassing affairs that could someday be useful if ever the man decided to go his own way.

"I am impressed by Worldnet's offices, monsieur." François waved a hand toward the window. "Twenty stories of steel, glass, and concrete atop one of the seven hills looking over the ancient city—how did you do it?"

"I have connections. We also own the building across the pond. Being on the edge of the historic district, we are somewhat discreet."

"But why have you asked me here? You said it was urgent."

"It is, my friend. The world, and Europe especially, are teetering on the edge of a precipice. We're in the grip of a financial, societal, and governmental panic unlike any the world has ever seen. Banks and companies everywhere are collapsing. Everyone is predicting a deep and lasting depression—the worst we've ever seen. Hysteria and chaos are spreading like a cancer across the world. In every country, order is breaking down. In every city, anarchy and chaos are the rule, and the police are overwhelmed."

Carlo brought their drinks, and Davato waved him off. The more private their conversation today, the more at ease François would be. Nodding, Carlo left the room.

"I agree, Davato. But what can one do? We've never experienced such a disaster."

"Yes, but the military situation is even worse. Europe can no longer rely on the protection of the US. The Great Calamity has gutted the American military and its Congress, leaving them with the weakest President in generations. Her country is faced with a disaster far greater than ours, and this woman—she formerly called the police terrorists and her generals warmongers—for weeks left her cities and towns to the rule of gangsters until, after a huge outcry, she declared martial law." He stifled a grin. She was more than he could ever have hoped for.

"With the US weakened, I expect China will soon make a play for Taiwan and Southeast Asia. If the American President acts—and it's not certain she ever will—that will fully occupy their armed forces. No, Europe can no longer rely on American might to save herself."

"Your insight is prescient, monsieur." François set his glass on the table and rubbed his brows. "What you suggest is troubling, indeed."

"There's more. I have recently intercepted transmissions that, within weeks, will order all US troops out of Germany and Poland. Russian President Petrov knows of this order, and my sources tell me his nation has designs on the Ukraine, Belarus, Lithuania, Estonia, and Latvia. And after that—who knows? Poland and Romania?"

"A Russian invasion?" François's face paled. "Surely he's not planning to invade the West?"

"That's exactly what he's planning. We don't know when, but I suspect he'll start by cutting off Europe's natural gas supply. We were fools ever to rely on Russia for our energy. Our wind turbines and solar panels can only provide so much, and on some days, they are completely unreliable." Unsaid was that the climate change madness that had swept the continent and the world—a paranoia the Abaddon League had worked hard everywhere to foment—had brought a welcome increase in government control of nearly every aspect of life in nearly every nation on earth.

"Since the vanishing, our intelligence has not kept up." François ran a hand through his hair. "I'm surprised and disturbed by your information."

"Much of the world's internet traffic now passes through Worldnet servers. And this is between you and me—I have programmers in certain places whose allegiance is to me, and they have successfully altered encryption algorithms to provide me special access."

As Desroches's forehead twisted in shock, Davato laid a hand on his shoulder. "All the better to serve the peoples of Europe and the world, François. But now, come to the window and see the city at night."

As they took their drinks to the glass stretching the entire length of the room, twinkling city lights spread out over the seven hills below.

"It's beautiful at night, no?" Davato waved his tumbler at the panorama.

"It is, monsieur."

"What a shame if this and so many other centers of culture, art, and history fell to the Slavs. We here in the West appreciate a free and open society, do we not? But events have brought us unexpected calamity. And the world is looking for someone to lead them to a solution."

"Do you have something in mind?" Desroches cocked his head.

"I do." Davato now employed the voice of command few could resist. "And I am putting my trust in you, François. You are hearing this before anybody else."

The president's creased brows told Davato his ploy was working, and he led the man to a square glass table surrounded by low leather couches.

When they were seated, he punched an icon, a display lit up, and a brightly colored map of Europe appeared beneath the glass. "This is Europe today." He spread a hand over the nations of the EU, lit in blue, with the Islamic nations in brown, and those of the Russian orbit in red. He punched another button, and some of the EU countries turned yellow. "What can you tell me about the ones in yellow?"

François looked up. "Weak economies. Weak militaries. Some have balked at our joint efforts."

"Exactly. Now let me ask you a question. What is the one thing people seek now more than anything else?"

"Peace. Stability. Security."

"Right again. And only a strong nation and a strong leader can provide it. The nations in yellow will never be strong partners in such a venture—at least not at first." He punched another icon and some of the blue countries joined the yellow ones. The blue had now been pared to Italy, Spain and Portugal, France, Germany, Belgium, the Netherlands, Luxembourg, Greece, Austria, Hungary, Slovenia, Switzerland, and Serbia. "These, I contend, must be the core, the strong backbone, the base of a new and powerful Europe able to provide the peace, stability, and security the world so desires."

"But Switzerland has never been part of the EU. And Greece—it's a mess."

"Granted, but geographically, culturally, and historically, they belong."

"I don't understand." François looked up from the map.

"I am suggesting something entirely new. A new nation, to be precise. A nation powerful enough to counter the Russian threat, but built on the foundation of history, culture, and geography. Instead of the weak entity we call the EU, our new creation will exude strength and power. I propose to unite the countries in blue into a new empire. We shall call it the Unitum Imperium. After the old Roman model."

"The United Empire?" François's mouth hung open. "A bit ambitious, is it not?"

"An ambitious and grand name for a grand idea. This, my friend, is how we will end the chaos, disorder, and anarchy now gripping the world. We will create a new and powerful empire, one strong enough to lead the world and march forward into history. But this is only a first step."

For some time, François examined the new map. Slowly, a smile stretched his lips. "Yes, monsieur. I see your vision. You have possibly captured the hidden desire behind those who formed the EU so many years ago, one which we never really achieved—a powerful, united Europe. Not multiple countries arguing among themselves, but one grand and mighty nation." He faced his host. "But who will lead such a venture?" The moment the words left his mouth, he smiled wider. "But of course. You are the logical choice. The only one the people will follow."

"I am humbled by your faith in me. But, yes, I will allow my name to be put forth as a candidate. For such a nation must be led by a man like no other, and—dare I say it?—a man unlike any the world has ever seen. Perhaps a man with ambition, abilities, influence, and power to rival, perhaps even exceed, God himself. But if such a being even exists, after the vanishing, he must surely be an impotent and feckless creature, unworthy of anyone's worship." He laid a hand on François's and squeezed. "Don't you agree?"

François looked up from the map into Davato's eyes, seemed to shiver, then swallowed. "Y–yes, of course."

"Good." Davato removed his hand. "But before we mention this to anyone, you and I have much convincing to do behind the scenes. We must approach these countries' rulers in secret. They must be persuaded that this is the only way."

"It will be difficult."

"But not impossible. And I have ways to sway the recalcitrant."

"What kind of ways?"

"Sometimes, François, certain details are better left unsaid."

"Of course." Again, a chill seemed to pass over him, and he looked away. "Never mind."

"We must also get the populace, the common folk, behind us. They will help sway their leaders. You heard my UN speech and how well it was received. Everywhere across Europe, I will soon give public speeches like that one, but with even greater force, all aimed at achieving our desired end. Once the masses hear my vision—the promise of peace, stability, security, and prosperity—they will clamor for it. And for me. Then their leaders will be forced to follow. And you, François, will have been part of it from its inception. And I promise you this—those who are with me from the beginning, I will greatly reward."

His guest beamed and raised his glass. "I am with you, my friend. Tonight, let us toast the saving of Europe."

Davato raised his glass, and the two tumblers clicked. "Yes, François, but this is only the beginning. Once Europe is united to our cause, we will take our vision and unite the world."

CHAPTER 45

THE VAN

University Village, Chicago

"Come here and look at this." For the second time, Tanya tugged on Caleb's sleeve as he sat at his desk.

"One minute." He finished typing the sentence then stood. It had taken weeks to recover, but today he was completing his third blog entry since leaving his bed. He only had a few more paragraphs before hitting the button to post, and he hated interruptions. "Okay. What's so important?"

She led him to the window, parted the blinds, and pointed across the street. "That van. It was there yesterday. It's back again today."

"So? People park there all the time. It's a free country. Or at least it used to be."

"But there are men inside. I've seen them. And they don't get out. And when that youth gang passed the van a moment ago, after they looked inside, something scared them, and they ran away."

"Hmm. But those are real men, aren't they?" Twisting his chain around his neck, Caleb stared at the vehicle for a while then grinned at her. "You don't suppose demons know how to drive, do you?"

"Laugh it off if you want, but it's troubling."

"What can we do about it?"

"Nothing, I suppose."

"I've got to finish today's entry."

He returned to his laptop. But he'd lost his train of thought, and he just stared at the screen. Were they really out there because of him? Could it be some kind of warning?

When he remembered how he wanted to finish, he typed the rest, reread everything, then hit the send button.

Nothing happened. Backing out of where he was, he went to the main dashboard where he found a flashing red message from his web host provider. "Due to an unexpected heavy volume of incoming traffic, we have temporarily suspended your site," said the message. "We apologize for the inconvenience and are working on the problem."

For some time he stared at the message then picked up his phone and called the help desk. After a series of transfers, he was routed to someone who seemed to understand what was going on.

"Your site, my friend, is under attack. It's been that way for the last three hours. Someone is sending thousands of incoming junk messages to your site each second. So we've temporarily disabled it. Because you've signed up for our high-end professional package, we're tracing it to its source. That's a new feature we recently implemented."

"When will that trace complete?"

"I don't know. No—wait." Caleb heard typing, a pause, then more typing. "They just finished. It's coming from somewhere in Italy. The area around Rome, I believe. And yes, right now, we're blocking all traffic from that IP address. Give us a few minutes, and your site should be online again."

"Okay, thanks."

He sat back, saved his work, and returned to the window where Tanya was sitting, still watching the van. When he told her about his website, she raised a worried glance.

"They're watching you, Caleb. And if you don't stop, they're going to come after you."

He didn't respond, only watched the van.

A man opened the vehicle's door, got out, and glanced toward their third-floor window. He held something in his hands.

Caleb stepped away from the window, but he could still see through a crack in the blinds.

As the man lit a cigarette, Caleb saw what it was the man held.

Something metallic. With a short barrel. Some kind of automatic rifle.

* * *

The next morning, low on supplies, they needed to visit the market, but he wouldn't take his car parked out front, as it was opposite the van.

With Uri's gun in his pocket, they exited by the building's back door into the alley. It was ten o'clock, cloudy and raining, and no one was about.

At the end of the alley, they turned left, entered the main street, then headed right.

He shot a glance back to the van as a man with long black hair got out. With his back to Caleb, he lit a cigarette beside the vehicle.

"Wait a sec." Caleb slid out his phone, zeroed in, and when the man turned, he snapped a photo. "I don't know what good this will do, but I've got a picture of him." Since he didn't think the man or the others had seen him, they hurried on.

The market was only two blocks away, and they arrived without incident. Outside, two men with rifles guarded the entrance. Inside, they completed their shopping from decimated shelves.

With both backpacks bursting and each carrying a full bag, they began the trip home. But as they turned the corner into their alley, a man in a raincoat was lounging at the apartment building's back door. Caleb recognized the short blond beard. He was one of the watchers.

"What should we do?" whispered Tanya.

"It's our place. We're going in. Here." He passed her the bag he carried. He stuck his hand in his pocket, and his fingers closed about the gun's cold metal.

As they approached, the man's eyes narrowed, and he leaned back against the door.

Inside his pocket, Caleb slipped a finger against the trigger.

"Going somewhere?" The man pushed back his hood, revealing a scar across his cheek and an unkempt mop of blond hair. Stocky and smirking, their antagonist was about forty.

"Please move." Caleb waved with his free hand. "We don't want any trouble here."

"Ah, but you already have big trouble." Now the man was grinning. "Stop what you're doing, Caleb Turner, and we'll leave you alone."

That they knew his name was troubling, but he stifled a shiver. "Get out of the way." He pulled the gun from his pocket and aimed it at his opponent's stomach.

His mouth opening in surprise, the man stared at the weapon and raised both hands. "Okay, okay, I'm moving. Don't shoot." He stepped aside. "But next time, you won't get away with using that. You know what you must do. Until then . . ." He grinned wider.

Caleb unlocked the door, he and Tanya entered, and he slammed the bolts shut. In the aftermath of the Chinese flu pandemic and the city-wide riots that followed, the apartment's entrances, like so many other upscale residences, had been hardened. Double-thick steel doors. Small outside windows with iron bars. Brick fronts.

Once inside, he leaned against the wall, his heart pounding, sweat running off his forehead.

"That was scary." Tanya set the bags down and peered out the window. "He's still there."

"I don't care who they are or what they want. I'm not going to stop."

He took his sack from her, she picked up her bag, and they climbed the stairs to his apartment.

He'd sent the demon away with a prayer to Jesus. But how do you get rid of a van full of men with guns?

CHAPTER 46
TROUBLING MESSAGES

In the Tuscan Countryside

It had been weeks since arriving at the villa, and for days a powerful urge had been building within her. Searching through the boxes beside the canvases in the downstairs salon, Margot found her easel and tubes of paint. She set up her pedestal and laid a blank canvas upon it.

Beyond the window, sunlight washed a view of the Tuscan countryside—tall cypresses, vineyards, verdant hills, and a winding stream.

She opened the pane all the way to let in the sounds of two larks engaged in melodic combat. Breathing deeply of the warm air, she felt a sense of profound relief in this place of peace and safety.

Once again, she was a believer, and today she marveled that she could ever have let that archbishop turn her away from the Christ, the Son of the living God, the one who had given her an incredible gift of prophecy. Her rejection of God had brought such a terrible melancholy in the week before the vanishing, she'd briefly contemplated suicide.

Since Dylan's arrival and his admission that he'd prayed to be left behind for the sole purpose of helping others, she wondered: Was it possible that she, too, had never actually lost her faith? After she'd turned away from God, had Christ forgiven her, then left her on earth for some divine purpose, knowing she would eventually return to him?

More and more, she entertained that thought—especially now that the urge to paint was as strong as ever.

Out on the lawn, a hoopoe pecked at worms, and the sight of this small creature, created by God so beautiful and free, oblivious of the plight of man, buoyed her. Today, she felt the presence of the Holy Spirit strong within her.

After pulling on her blue painting smock, she searched for the right brush and returned to the blank canvas. It had been almost two and a half months since she'd touched paint to canvas, and the brush in her hand felt good and right.

"Are you going to paint, Margot?" Dylan walked in.

She glanced aside. "I have this sudden strong desire—here in this place of safety and beauty—to create something."

"Wonderful. I'll leave you to it." He kissed her on the forehead and left by the outside door.

Shivering a bit after he pulled his lips away—why were his little affections doing this to her lately?—she took a pallet and squeezed tubes of yellow, brown, and black onto their own circles on the pallet. With the yellow and brown and a dash of blue, she mixed a new color. Dipping her brush into that, she brought it up to the canvas then stopped.

She had no idea what she was going to paint. All she knew was that a powerful urge, just like she'd felt hundreds of times before, was speaking to her. "Dear Jesus, I give myself to you," she whispered. "Speak through my work and lead me where you want me to go."

Her brush touched the fabric. Then she saw. The scene appeared before her in fine detail. And her brush moved of its own accord.

She began to paint.

* * *

ALL MORNING AS THE TEMPERATURE rose, Dylan walked the hills near the villa, wondering what Margot's latest vision would bring. That her gift of prophecy had returned was encouraging. He hoped he had something to do with it. The two of them now shared a deep bond.

They'd been waiting for God to reveal why they'd been brought together. The picture in her apartment that had changed, showing both of them looking out at the Rapture of Brussels, was surely a sign they were meant to be together.

But lately, their relationship was becoming something more than partners bent on a mission. Was he falling in love with her? Each time she smiled, said his name, or flipped the bangs from her face, a warm glow seemed to fill him, and he didn't want to leave her side.

Wiping the sweat from his forehead, he opened a gate, left the vineyards, and entered an olive orchard. He walked until noon then returned to the house and stuck his head in the salon.

"How's it going?" he asked.

But Margot was so deep into her work, at first, she didn't even realize he was there. Finally, she looked up, briefly, and mumbled something incoherent. Then her brush returned to her canvas.

Standing behind her and looking at what she was painting, he saw the façade of a run-down stone house. It was European, possibly Italian. The street cobbles in front needed repair, as did the half-pipe roof tiles. In the foreground, she'd begun the outline of a man.

Puzzled, he asked if she wanted lunch, but she shook her head, no.

Upstairs, Bettino had prepared fresh bread and a salad with eggs, bacon, tomatoes, and cucumbers, and, of course, wine. At the table, Dylan ate alone and searched for new tunes for his phone.

* * *

WHEN MARGOT FINALLY STOPPED PAINTING, it was after eight o'clock, the sun had set, and the smells of frying meat drifted down from the kitchen upstairs. She stretched, doffed her smock, and cleaned her brushes. Then she stepped back and examined her finished work.

"You're done?" Dylan's voice came from behind, and she whirled.

"Yes." Her bangs had grown longer these last weeks. Now she wiped them from her forehead with a palm, and this brought a smile to his face.

"Ah, the mad artist wakens from her trance. You haven't been very communicative today."

"Sorry. That happens sometimes." She smiled. "The urge to paint came on so powerfully, I had to give in to it. Then the world just seems to . . . fade. And all that matters is . . . the vision."

"But you're finished." Dylan peered at it. "This one's dark. Scary."

"I think the house is in Italy. It's old and unkempt. And there's a man with a scar on his right cheek holding a pistol in his left hand. He must be standing watch."

"Yes." Dylan frowned as he pointed. "But what's that on his right hand? That hand is closer than anything else."

"I painted the man in the foreground as the only figure, and his hand is the painting's main focus. I felt I had to paint that tattoo in fine detail."

On the back of his hand was a six-sided figure—a hexagram. From each outside corner, a line extended halfway to the middle then stopped. In the center was a globe with the outline of Europe and Africa. And in each blank space between the lines were six smaller symbols.

"Weird." Dylan's face showed puzzlement. "What does it mean?"

"I don't know. I only know it's important. And troubling."

"Yes. The man and the gun and the tattoo—creepy. What are those letters? Cuneiform? Some ancient language?"

"No clue."

"You've painted a mystery." He shivered. "But come. Bettino is making supper upstairs. I told him to wait until you were almost done."

"Thanks. I'm famished."

* * *

TANYA HAD JUST LEFT THE apartment, and Caleb sat at his computer, trying again to bring up his website. This morning when he'd attempted to log on, a message appeared saying his account was unavailable, locked for maintenance, and he should try again later. But this was his fourth try today, and now it even said his login was unrecognized. On a hunch, he tried his Facebook, Twitter, and Instagram accounts. But for each of them, he also received a message that his login was invalid.

Had he been deplatformed?

He grabbed his phone, intending to dial his web provider's help line, when the elevator's typical clunk sounded through the walls. Seconds later, someone began pounding on the door.

It wasn't the knock he and Tanya had agreed upon.

His heart beating faster, he rose and went to the door.

But when he looked through the peephole, someone on the other side was blocking his view. No one should have been able to enter the building without either him or Tanya letting them in, and they never admitted strangers. After the vanishing, they were the building's only occupants. "Who's there?" he called.

"You know who, Caleb Turner," came a man's voice. "You didn't stop, and now it's time to pay the consequences."

His heart racing, he stepped back then ran to the living room window. Down at the street, two men on the front sidewalk returned his gaze. Both held stubby automatic rifles.

He was trapped. Without an exit.

Something heavy and metallic crashed into the door, and his heart flipped upside down inside his chest.

They were coming for him, and he couldn't do anything about it.

He found the pistol, dropped it in his pocket, and ran to the laundry room. Maybe hiding there would give him enough time to let someone know what was happening. He closed the doors and pulled the phone from his pocket. Should he call Tanya? But no. By the sound, she'd know what was happening. He hoped she and Nika stayed hidden.

He found the number in his contact list and punched it. Once, twice, three times it rang.

Please, Dylan. Please answer.

"Hello," came his brother's greeting, and Caleb let out the breath he was holding.

"There's no time." His words came out tense, strangled. "They're coming for me."

"Who's coming for you?"

In the background, some kind of heavy sledge slammed against the outside door, rocking the walls, sending shudders through the apartment.

"Men who've been watching the apartment from a van across the street. They just shut down my website. Now they're battering down the door. I'm hiding in the laundry room. Dylan"—his breath was coming fast—"I fear they're going . . . to kill me."

"Kill you? Because of your website?"

"Yes. No. I don't know." He closed his eyes. "They warned me, but I wouldn't stop."

The smashing of metal against metal came louder. Then the door crashed into the foyer. A voice in the hall gave directions to start a search. Footsteps pounded down the hallway.

"They're inside!" He was whispering now. "They're coming for me. Got to go."

He dropped the phone and kicked it toward the washing machine. Shaking, his hand pulled out the pistol.

The louvered laundry room doors opened.

Three men stood in the hall. Two held pistols. A third man with long stringy hair pointed an automatic rifle. "Don't be stupid, Caleb," he said. "Drop it!"

What choice did he have? His fingers let go. The gun clattered to the floor.

The stringy-haired man waved his stubby weapon, and rough hands yanked him into the corridor. They held him while a fourth gripped his forearm and held it steady. A fifth man, short and bald, appeared. He began filling a hypodermic needle with clear liquid from a vial.

Caleb's wild gaze focused on the man, then the hypodermic. He struggled. But strong hands held him motionless.

"You're going to . . . drug me?" His eyes narrowed on the approaching needle. He tried to jerk his arm away, but they held him in a vise grip.

A jab of pain. The needle punctured the skin, then slipped into his vein. The plunger depressed. A hot, burning sensation crept up his arm.

Then his world went black.

* * *

MARGOT HAD BEEN EATING DINNER upstairs with Dylan and Bettino when Dylan's brother called. After a few exchanges, Dylan had put the conversation on speaker so everyone could hear. The last thing that had come from Caleb's phone had been a loud crack, then a scuffling sound, and then Caleb's last horrifying words: "You're going to drug me?"

She strained to hear more, but all that came across the ether was the tromping away of feet, followed by silence.

"They took him." His face twisted in anguish, Dylan slammed a fist against his thigh. "He wouldn't stop blogging, and now they've taken him."

"What are you going to do?" She brushed away stray locks.

He stood, paced to the window, and returned. "I'm going to Chicago. I don't know how, but I'm going to find out who did this and why. Then, somehow, I'm going to find him."

She gazed at this man who'd crossed the ocean to meet her and to save her, this man who now meant so much to her, this man in obvious distress. She stood, wrapped her arms around his chest, and hugged him. Then she whispered in his ear. "Without me, Dylan Turner, you're not going anywhere."

CHAPTER 47
THE FLIGHT

New York City

When the phone rang, Chelsea leaped from the shower just as it fell silent. Naked and dripping, she wrapped a towel around herself. Seeing the call came from Dylan, she rang him back. "What's up?"

"I probably should have called earlier. Five days ago, Caleb was kidnapped. Tomorrow, we're flying to Chicago to find out what happened."

Stunned, she leaned against the counter. "Kidnapped? Are you sure?"

"Yes. I was on the phone with him when it happened. We heard the whole thing."

"We?"

"Margot is with me. She's coming too. All week, we've been trying to get a flight, but it's been nearly impossible. I waited to call until I knew when we were arriving."

"What do you want me to do?"

"Join us. Your sleuthing skills might help."

She knew what she would say. Frank and she had talked about leaving the city, and since they'd eaten most of the food from the two apartments they'd broken into, they would soon be starving. Again. "Count me in. Where are you staying?"

"We're booked at the Marriott. It's the closest to Caleb's, and they're still in business. If you get there before us, leave a message."

"Okay. If I can get to JFK safely, I'll be there."

After hanging up, she dressed, descended to Frank's apartment, and knocked.

Once he answered, she said, "I need to get to Chicago as soon as possible. And since we're nearly out of food, this is as good a time to leave as any. If I can arrange an escort to your garage, can you drive me to the airport?"

"Sure."

"You still going to your brother in North Carolina?"

"Yes. It will be safer there." He pushed his glasses back on his nose. "But what kind of escort?"

"Leave that to me. Be ready to go in an hour."

Back in her place, she packed two bags then picked up the phone but stopped, frowning. The last thing she wanted was to involve Archer in anything, but he was now her only hope of getting past the gangs. Taking a deep breath, she dialed.

"That you, babe?" His presumption of familiarity made her cringe.

"Yes, and I need a big favor."

"Ah, she kicks me out, and now she wants a favor?" In the background, at least two other men snickered.

"I need to get to a parking garage about a mile from my apartment. My neighbor has a car there, but the gangs have taken over our block. We need an escort."

"Well, now, an escort for two. Let me see. What do I get in return? You kicked me out, remember?"

She breathed in deeply. "What do you want?"

"Cash would be nice. And some gold. And let me see—what about diamonds? And how about a night or two in my bed?"

"Not going to happen, and you know it. I have a gold necklace, a set of diamond earrings, and I can give you two hundred dollars. That's all I've got. But I'm not sleeping with you again, Archer. Not in this life. Not ever. After we get the car, Frank is driving me to the airport."

"Frank, is it? Is he your new live-in?"

"Just a neighbor." She gripped the phone tighter. She mustn't lose her cool now. "How about it? The gangs are really bad over here."

"Just a minute." She heard him talking in the background. After a while, he returned. "All right, babe. We'll be there in half an hour. Be ready to pay."

They hung up, and she went to find Frank.

* * *

CHELSEA AND HER NEIGHBOR LEFT the building and met Archer and four of his new buddies, looking like grunge band wannabes. Two carried pistols. Archer and the last man—a burly, tattooed ape with a ponytail—wielded automatic rifles. "No one's gonna mess with us, babe," said Archer. "Where's our payment?"

She passed him what she'd promised, including the two hundred, half of which came from Frank. But Archer didn't need to know that. Or the fact that she still had three hundred hidden in her bra.

"So, this is Frank?" Archer grinned, and as he circled her neighbor, Frank seemed to wilt.

"Yeah, that's Frank." Frowning, she waved him on. "Cut the crap, and let's go."

As Archer's crew sauntered with her down the center of the street, they passed one of the gangs that had harassed them for the last month, gangs who'd claimed Chelsea's block as their own. But after seeing the armaments of the opposition, the youths simply stared, hugged a stairwell in silence, and let them pass.

"They won't mess with real firepower." Archer waved his rifle and sidled closer to her.

But as he slid his hip against hers and a free arm reached toward her shoulders, she sidestepped away.

He shot her a glance and walked on. "Did I tell you I've got new digs, babe? More rooms, with a Jacuzzi, with every modern convenience known to man. The former occupant decided it was in his best interest that we switch apartments, and—what do you know?—the geezer bought all my old paintings to boot. He's now living in my studio."

"Well, bully for you, Archer." She refused to glance in his direction. "I suppose that's the only way you'd ever sell your work, huh? At the point of a gun."

"Hey, now." His voice rose. "Let's be nice. I'm doin' you a big favor."

"Right. A real favor. How about we just walk?"

At the parking garage, they climbed the stairs to the fourth floor. But as they passed one parked car after another, half had been broken into, and shattered glass littered the pavement. She held her breath until they found Frank's beat-up Ford. It was untouched.

"Okay, Archer, here's where we part." She slipped into the passenger seat and threw her bags in back. "It's been real."

Archer and his group stood aside as her neighbor started the car and pulled out.

Frank drove them down the circular ramp to the street. There was little traffic, and as they approached a stoplight, another gang waited at the corner.

Frank dutifully stopped at the light, and the youths began sprinting toward the car.

"Floor it!" she shouted. "Don't stop!"

He hit the accelerator, and in this manner, with him sweating, they sped through every intersection. They headed east until they reached the airport, securely held by the National Guard.

As they parted, she laid a kiss on his cheek. "Thanks for everything. You take care on your way south. Text me when you get there safely, okay?"

With that, they parted.

* * *

Twenty-four hours later, after sleeping on JFK's departure lounge floor, Chelsea landed at Chicago's O'Hare airport. She rented a car for triple the usual rate—at least her credit cards still worked—then drove to the Marriott. By the time she checked in, found her room, and called her brother, it was early evening.

"We arrived a few hours ago," said Dylan. "Let's meet in the hotel restaurant for supper."

As she took the elevator to the ground floor, she wondered what Dylan's new companion was like and if those two were now a couple.

But when she saw her brother's tall, lithe frame at the restaurant entrance, his brown hair long and falling around his ears, tears blurred her vision. "Dylan!" Running to him, she wrapped her arms about him, holding him tight before releasing him. "So much has happened. Mother gone. Caleb kidnapped. The world falling apart." She wiped her eyes and stepped back. "But you're looking good. And tanned. Must be that Italian sun. I am so glad to see you."

He smiled then turned to the short, black-haired woman beside him. Margot had thick dark eyebrows and bangs curling around her cheeks. Hers was a kind of plain, down-to-earth beauty, not the kind you'd see in magazines. And when she smiled, her whole face lit up. "I'm so glad to meet you, Chelsea." She extended a hand, and Chelsea took it.

"Dylan has been talking about you ever since we met." Margot squeezed her hands and returned the smile.

Crossing the marble floors, they found a table away from the TVs, and she sat across from them.

After they ordered, Dylan leaned forward. "Chelsea, how have you been? I've been worried about you. I wish we could have been together through all this."

A painting on the wall depicting the aftermath of the Great Chicago Fire drew her glance. "I went through some difficult times with Archer." She focused again on Dylan. "But that's over. I've moved on. I'm okay now."

"So you never met Father when he was in New York?"

"No. I haven't been able to leave the apartment for weeks. When I last talked with him, he was quite upset about the business. I gather it's in real trouble."

"I suspected as much." Dylan frowned. "But there's a question I need to ask you, and it's important."

"What?"

"What do you believe about the vanishing?"

She shifted in her seat. Why'd he have to bring that up? For the first time since *it* happened, she was feeling safe after being trapped in her apartment. "I–I'm not sure. Everyone says aliens took the missing people. Didn't they?"

"As usual, the media is lying. They've always been anti-Christian, anti-God, and aliens didn't do it. What happened was called the Rapture. It was Jesus who took his people out of the world, not aliens."

"But all the UFOs everyone's seeing—what about them?"

"That is Satan trying to deceive people, sending demons to lead them away from the truth. If you followed Caleb's blog, you'd know that."

"I have to admit, I didn't follow him. Did you really pray to be left behind?"

"I did. I wanted to save you and Caleb. And Margot. That's why I wasn't taken."

She stared into his eyes. He believed this stuff. Ducking her head, she frowned at her reflection from the glass-topped table. If all the people who vanished *were* Christians, then—that would prove Jesus was real, wouldn't it? She jerked her head up. "Why wasn't Margot taken?"

Margot leaned toward her. "Because an archbishop told me my paintings were works of the Devil, and I renounced my faith. But now I'm a believer again."

Dylan nodded. "And now we're wondering if she ever lost it, if maybe she was left here to join me in some divine purpose."

"If all the Christians vanished, why wasn't my pastor taken?" Her frown, her wrinkled forehead reflecting back from the tabletop. "I was just getting out of church when it happened, and a bus ran her down. She didn't vanish."

"I don't know. We've seen an archbishop and a bishop of the Catholic Church who were left behind, and that was because of false belief. The Pope too. Just because someone is part of a church doesn't make them a true Christian. It's a heart thing."

Hadn't Freya Lewis hinted there was more than one way to get into Heaven? And after she had advised Chelsea to get the abortion, Chelsea was still troubled by what she'd done, whether it was the right thing.

Dylan reached across the table and laid a hand on hers. "Caleb also told me that, while he and Blake were climbing Mt. Hood, Blake disappeared ahead of him. Blake was a solid Christian if ever there was."

"Yeah, Caleb told me the same." Was it possible? Had only the Christians disappeared? If that was true . . .

"So what about it?" asked Dylan. "Do you believe now?"

"It seems possible. Let me think on it."

"Fair enough."

Their food came, and Chelsea tore into the steak she ordered, medium-rare, heaped with mushrooms, and slathered with garlic and butter. With a loaded baked potato on the side. After weeks of deprivation, she was not going back to the vegan thing.

After dinner, since it was already dark and Dylan and Margot were exhausted after the overseas flight, they decided to wait until the morning to begin their investigation.

Besides, the gangs often didn't emerge until afternoon.

CHAPTER 48

BARUCH ABRAMOVICH

Jerusalem, Israel

Jeremiah 33:14–18 (NLT): *"The day will come, says the LORD, when I will do for Israel and Judah all the good things I have promised them. 'In those days and at that time I will raise up a righteous descendant from King David's line. He will do what is just and right throughout the land. In that day Judah will be saved, and Jerusalem will live in safety. And this will be its name: 'The LORD Is Our Righteousness.' For this is what the LORD says: David will have a descendant sitting on the throne of Israel forever. And there will always be Levitical priests to offer burnt offerings and grain offerings and sacrifices to me."*

Baruch Abramovich topped the steps to Temple Mount. He crossed the plateau and approached a flatbed trailer where, until a few days ago, the bulldozers had parked. Up on the bed, his friend David Benjamin was kneeling, examining a huge block of white stone.

David jumped down from the specially designed trailer. "Shalom, Rabbi," said the tall, blond-haired immigrant from Denmark.

"Shalom, David."

They shook hands then hugged. Baruch's astonished gaze swept the plateau. "All of it—it's gone."

David nodded. "The Al Aqsa Mosque. The Dome of the Rock." He spread his arms. "Every last stone and brick—gone!"

"They've desecrated this place for over thirteen hundred years. Do you know how many times I've walked up here and shuddered at the sight of those abominations? I can't believe they're finally gone."

"God did most of the work for us. All that was left was rubble. But I'm glad you came. The Torat Kohanim cannot thank you enough for your group's contribution. Three million shekels? My friend, that was far more than expected. Because of you, we've been able to put immediately into motion all the plans we've had for the last hundred or so years."

Baruch waved a hand in dismissal. "We merely shared with the people what you Levites have been preparing in secret. For the Third Temple, I'm sorry we couldn't raise more."

"Too modest, Rabbi." David smiled. "I know how earnestly you canvassed from house to house."

"I only told them about your preparations." Baruch grinned, thinking back on everything David's Torat Kohanim had accomplished over the years. . . .

An academy only a twenty-minute drive from here, an institution training priests in sacrificial worship and ritual. They'd even constructed a life-sized replica of the Temple.

A one-hectare lot bursting with pristine stones cut from a Dead Sea quarry, none touched by metal, all ready for installation.

Hundreds of gold and silver instruments and vessels, handcrafted by artisans, enough to fill a warehouse, all ready for Temple service,

And their North American breeding program has finally produced a pure, red heifer with which to purify the altar.

"No, David, it wasn't my poor entreaties." He laid a hand on his friend's shoulder. "It was your diligent preparations. But there's a rumor you can complete the work by July? Is that true?"

"It's possible. And just think—that our efforts should herald the coming of the Messiah . . . the very thought gives me goose bumps."

"Is that the foundation stone?" Baruch waved toward the truck bed.

"It is. We cut it from the quarry using wooden mallets and wedges and diamond-edged wooden saws. No metal has ever touched its surface. Water from the Pool of Siloam has blessed it. We designed specially hardened wooden tongs to lift it. We're planning a big ceremony to lay it next Wednesday. I hope you can come."

"Count on it. And when the Temple is complete, the Assembly hopes to be among the first to worship here."

"I will ensure you the best seats. But how goes it with you, Baruch?" His brows rising, David tilted his head. "I heard you've run into a bit of trouble?"

"Nothing I can't handle."

"No, you must tell me. I heard you're receiving threats. Is this true?"

Baruch shrugged. "I'm afraid it is." A hand searched in his pocket and brought out the creased paper. Unfolding it, he glanced at it again before passing it on. "Two days ago, this came in the post. It's the third warning they sent me."

A Nazi swastika was scrawled above a handwritten message. "Stop your teaching, Jew, and disband your group," it said, "or pay the consequences."

David's face scrunched with concern. With a shudder, he handed it back. "This is bad, very bad. Reminiscent of the holocaust. To see this here, in Jerusalem, our homeland!" He shook his head. "Who are they?"

"I don't know. But it doesn't matter."

"What will you do?"

"Continue leading my flock, of course. Nothing will stop what God has ordained."

"I will pray for the Lord's protection."

"Thank you." Baruch checked his watch. "But I must go, or I'll be late for my class at the synagogue. And I have to stop at home first."

After saying goodbye, he crossed to the steps. Minutes later, he passed under the Dung Gate into the old city. The quake had damaged only a few of the buildings nearest Temple Mount, and geologists were still puzzling over why the destruction was mostly confined to the mosque and the Dome. Why did they not look to God for the reason, he whose wrath finally cleansed Temple Mount of Islam's obscenity? Was their faith that shallow?

He entered streets that had experienced only minor shaking.

Open-front stalls lined the way where men sold trinkets, T-shirts, and leather goods. The smells of falafel and pizza mixed with incense and sweat. He walked down a narrow, stone-walled lane, passing a handful of tourists, far fewer than before the day of the catastrophe.

But he was late. He increased the pace.

Like so many others in the quarter, his two-story building was fronted by stone. He slipped his keys into the lock, but the door opened of its own accord. Odd. Hadn't he locked it?

Warily, he pushed through into his modest first-floor apartment. Nothing seemed amiss. Still puzzled, he went to his desk where he retrieved his copy of the Torah and his notes for the class he was teaching today. But the moment he whirled, ready to depart again, footsteps slapped the tiles and swept around the corner from the kitchen.

Three men blocked his way to the door. Two were muscular, with swarthy complexions, wearing tan slacks. The third was a short bald man, holding a handgun.

"W–who are you?" His heart beating faster, he froze. "What do you want?"

"We want you, Baruch." The bald man waved his gun, and the other two circled to both sides of him.

He stepped back until his spine hit the desk. "I am only a poor teacher."

"Three times you were warned, and still you continued." The bald man nodded, and faster than Baruch could react, the two men closed in from both sides and grabbed his arms. His books dropped to the floor.

The leader pocketed his pistol then removed a hypodermic from his jacket pocket. Baruch's eyes widened with fear as the man filled the syringe with clear liquid from a vial. The man flicked the full cylinder then approached.

Breathing fast, Baruch wriggled, tried to break free, but the men held him motionless. "Why are you doing this? I'm no threat to anyone."

Silent, with grim concentration, the bald man grasped his forearm, jabbed the needle into a vein, and depressed the plunger.

"May the Lord forgive what you are doing." He said the right words. But his eyes were fixed on the needle, and inwardly, he prayed for himself.

As the hot liquid burned up his arm, Baruch's gaze settled on a tattoo etched on the back of the man's hand—a hexagram with lines running from each corner to a central globe with the outline of Europe and Africa.

The last thing he remembered was his legs giving way, rough arms holding him up, and then—darkness.

CHAPTER 49

CLUES

University Village, Chicago

On Wednesday morning, Dylan, Chelsea, and Margot waited until the National Guard passed the hotel during one of their daily patrols. Dylan drove his rental car behind the armored procession, turning off at Caleb's street. After parking out front, he led them to the downstairs entrance, but the door was locked and barred. He pressed all six buzzers and waited.

Finally, a woman's voice spoke through the speaker. "I don't know you. Go away."

Dylan looked around. On the ceiling, a camera lens hid behind a glass panel. "My name is Dylan Turner. This is my sister"—he pointed—"and this is a friend. Caleb Turner was my brother, and can we—?"

"I'll come down and let you in. The opener buzzer thing is broken."

Moments later, a tall slim blonde opened the door, looked both ways up and down the street, then waved them inside. "We've had a lot of trouble with roving bands lately, so I'm careful about letting in strangers." She locked the door behind them. "My name is Tanya Baranov, and welcome! Caleb was a dear friend of mine."

"Yes, he mentioned you." Dylan introduced everyone, and she led them up the stairs.

She stopped on the third-floor landing. "Since they took him, I'm the only one left in the building. After V-Day, the other woman who used to live on our floor never returned. The rest of the building was either for rent, their occupants never came back, or they left."

They followed her down the corridor to Caleb's apartment where the doorframe had been ripped from the walls. The door itself lay in the hall inside, banged in, beaten-up.

Tanya shivered and wrapped her arms around herself. "I'm so glad you are here. I had just left him that evening, but when I heard them battering down his door, I was afraid to go out. Before that, Caleb was getting weird emails warning him to stop what he was doing. And then he had that encounter with a demon."

"Yes, he told me about that." Dylan glanced aside to Chelsea, now rolling her eyes to the ceiling. He turned to Tanya. "Did you see who took him? Can you tell us anything about them?"

"Not really." She rubbed her chin. "But wait! He did take a picture of one of them getting out of their van. But they probably took his phone."

"No, they didn't. When they came for him, the connection was still up, and we heard the sounds of a struggle. He called from the laundry room. The phone must still be there."

"Then follow me." She led them down the hall and through the laundry's louvered doors.

He flicked on the lights. Sticking out from under the washing machine lay a phone. It was out of juice, but he found its charger on the kitchen counter and plugged it in.

A few minutes later, he opened the picture gallery and flipped ahead to pictures from a few weeks ago. He scrolled past several photos of Tanya and Caleb and past a man who was probably Tanya's grandfather. He stopped on a snapshot of a man with long black hair smoking beside the van. He expanded the picture.

"He got the license plate!" Dylan wrote it down. "That's good. But even with this, how do we find out who owned the van? I'm no cop."

Dropping her gaze to the floor, Tanya seemed deep in thought. Then her face brightened. "Wait here. Uri may have left us a way."

Puzzled, Dylan nodded. As Tanya ran back to her place, the others followed Chelsea who meandered through Caleb's flat.

"How long did you say he's been gone?" asked Chelsea.

"At least a week," answered Dylan.

"Finding him is going to be tough." She grabbed a framed picture of the three siblings in a boat on the Mississippi when they were younger. "By now, he could be anywhere."

Margot stood behind her, gazing at the picture. "You three were close, weren't you?"

"Yes."

"We'll find him." She laid a hand on Chelsea's shoulder, but Chelsea only bit her lip and kept staring at the photograph.

Moments later, Tanya returned with a white envelope. "Uri had this in his safe." She handed it to Dylan.

On the outside was written a single word: *Sergei*. Dylan pulled out a sheet of paper containing only a phone number. "Who is Sergei?"

"A spy. First for the Russians, then for the US government, but he ran afoul of his superiors. Now he's in hiding, but he has skills that might help us. And he owed Uri big time. My grandfather bribed his release from a Russian prison."

"He's worth a try. But since you're Uri's granddaughter, maybe should you call him?"

He passed his phone to her, she dialed, and someone answered. Tanya explained who she was and that she needed a favor. After listening to Sergei's response, she faced the group. "He says he won't deal with people he's never met. But he *will* rendezvous with us in a nearby park at two this afternoon and check us out. If we pass inspection, he'll think about it."

Dylan and Chelsea nodded, and she relayed their agreement. After she hung up, she frowned. "But there's one condition he insists upon."

"What's that?"

"We must bring a bottle of vodka. And we must share it with him. Or else, no deal."

"What's the problem?"

"I hate vodka."

* * *

BEFORE LEAVING THE APARTMENT, DYLAN received a pistol from Tanya. "Grandfather had a second pistol in his safe, a gift from Sergei," she said. "Caleb had the other one, but I don't see it anywhere. They must have taken it."

"In case we encounter gangs?" he asked, and she nodded.

She led them down a cement path under a line of trees to Vernon Park. At the bench Sergei had indicated, all four squeezed together onto the seat.

"I know this place." She shivered and pointed toward the oaks. "Caleb said this is where the demon attacked him."

"The demon thing again? Really?" Chelsea looked askance at her. "Are you serious?"

"Yes, Chelsea." Dylan laid a hand on her knee. "We're in a spiritual battle, and it's real. Caleb told me that, the instant he prayed to Jesus, the demon left."

"Before he prayed," added Tanya, "the thing covered him with welts that took weeks to recover from." She shook her head. "If you had seen what happened to him, you'd be a believer in demons."

Chelsea pressed her lips tight, perhaps keeping silent with great effort. But the look on her face told Dylan she thought they were all crazy. What would it take to convince her that God, Jesus, and the spiritual world were real?

They waited in silence.

When he checked his watch, twenty minutes had already passed. Where was this Russian?

"Look," said Margot.

Across the field, a man and a boy of about twelve lifted a kite to the wind and ran with it. The sail rose, and as they led it over the grass, they came closer. When the two were within thirty feet of the bench under the trees, the man shot them a sideways glance. Moments later, he handed the kid a bill and the kite string then walked toward them.

Shoulders hunched, he strolled the cement path, stopped, and deep-brown eyes pierced each of them in turn.

Dylan shifted on his seat.

"Who are these people, Tanya?" His voice was thick with accent.

Tanya introduced everyone, and he nodded. "And do you honor my request?"

"Yes." She lifted a quart bottle from inside its paper bag. Opening the cap, she took a swallow, grimaced, then passed it to him.

Sergei raised the bottle, drank a shot, wiped his lips, then passed it to Dylan. In this way, they each drank two or three swallows.

"Da. Very good." Sergei wiped his mouth and set the bottle beside him. "Now, we are comrades, and we talk. What have you for me?"

Tanya turned to Dylan, and he passed the Russian a piece of paper with the van's license number. "Can you tell us who owns this vehicle and the address where it's registered? It's important."

Sergei unfolded the paper and rubbed it flat between his fingertips. In contrast to the white stubble covering his chin, a touch of red pinked cheeks that, long ago, seemed to have been scoured by coarse sandpaper. White hair, unkempt and thin, fell to his shoulders. "Why do you want to know this? What do you get me into?"

Dylan explained that his brother was kidnapped because he was blogging about the truth behind the vanishing. But he left out the part about the demon.

"Ah, so it is *that*." He narrowed his eyes. "Da, I help you. If this has anything to do with lying, backstabbing government—and it has the smell of them or something like them—I help you. But something I learn—you cannot trust anyone, and nothing is what it seems. Danger hides whenever your feet leave your door. I let you know what I find. But tomorrow, after I access my equipment."

They shook hands, drank another round at Sergei's request, gave him the bottle, and parted.

A bit light-headed, Dylan walked with the others back to Caleb's apartment. Before they arrived, he turned to Tanya. "Your grandfather had some interesting acquaintances."

She grinned. "I could say the same about Caleb."

CHAPTER 50
COMPANY AFFAIRS

Minneapolis, Minnesota

Just after eleven in the morning on Thursday, Adam Turner slumped into a chair on his patio. He lifted his gaze over the expanse of lawn—unmowed, untrimmed, and full of weeds. A cloud passed overhead, and a shadow darkened the terrace and his two-acre lot. How appropriate, he thought, and symbolic—a shadow to snuff the light from his last day on earth.

A few drops of rain splattered the deck, hitting the mail on the table beside him, then stopped. He stared at the wet circles on the papers and shrugged.

Earlier this week, he'd let go all his help—his cook, his butler, his gardener. The mower was in the utility shed, and if he'd had the gumption, he could have pulled it out and mowed the grass himself. It had been years since he'd mowed a lawn. But in a few minutes, an uncut lawn wouldn't matter.

Once again, he stared at the Glock G19 pistol lying on the table beside the court documents.

The official seal from the trustee at the bankruptcy court stamped the notice. "Your presence is required at 9:00 a.m., Friday, in Civil Court for a creditor's meeting," it said. "At the Hennepin County Government Center, Room C-332." There, he would be sworn in and grilled about his financial situation. Then the lawyers would proceed to pick apart, in excruciating detail, the wreckage of his life.

Shoving the notice aside, he reached for the tumbler of whiskey beside the mail and the gun. He took a long swallow, set the glass down, picked it up, and savored another long drink.

How could it be that, in a few short weeks, his life had fallen apart?

His spouse, his substantial personal investment account, all the accounts of Turner Enterprises, and virtually everything else associated with his baby, his life's work, the worldwide company he'd spent his life creating—gone!

He closed his eyes and with one hand wiped away a tear. Holding his wrist out, he examined this new thing, this moisture issuing from his eyes. When was the last time he'd cried? When he was twelve, and the class bully had shoved him to the ground after ripping up his homework? He hadn't even cried when Kate went down in the river. But that day, of course, he'd been stunned by events and fighting for his life.

For the hundredth time, Adam Turner stared at the Glock.

Could he do it? Could he pull the trigger?

But why not? Corporate bankruptcy affairs were months of interminable hearings, embarrassing meetings, endless grilling as one court official and lawyer after another went over and over his books. And when they did, they'd find that, not only was he broke, he was also guilty of insider trading.

Picking up the gun, he turned it over, hefted it, then set it back down. No, not yet.

He had one more duty to perform, something he'd put off for too long, something he had to do before he could leave in peace. Peace—now there was a cruel word.

Picking up the phone, he dialed Dylan's number.

"Father?" came the startled reply at the other end. "Where have you been? Whenever I called you, all I got was your answering service."

"Sorry about that. I've been . . . busy. But how are you, Dylan? And have you heard from your brother and sister?"

From the other end—silence.

"Dylan?"

"Chelsea is all right. She's with me here in Chicago. I'm staying at Caleb's apartment right now, but Caleb—he's disappeared. Father, he's been kidnapped."

The news didn't sink in. "What did you say?"

"Caleb's been kidnapped. We're here trying to learn who took him."

Adam gripped the phone tighter. "Have you called the police?"

"No. There are so few left, and so busy with the gangs, they can't help. It's up to us. But now that I've got you on the phone, Chelsea and

I noticed our checking accounts are almost out of funds. You could help by transferring something to us today."

Adam sucked in breath and gritted his teeth. This was one of the reasons he was calling. "Dylan, on that front . . . I have bad news. Your trust funds are—how can I put this?—they're broke."

"What! I thought we each had over a million in our investment accounts?"

"You did. But the company—actually, all our investments—are bankrupt. I'll transfer whatever I can to you, but it will only keep you going for another week or so. You'd better reduce expenses. And I'm afraid you'll have to find another source of income. I'm sorry, but in a few days, Turner Enterprises will be no more."

"Dad, are you serious?"

Never before had Dylan used that term to refer to him, and Adam sucked in air.

"I . . . I'm sorry," said his son. "I know how much that company meant to you."

"Thank you." Another tear made its way down his cheek, and he brushed it away with force. "Is your sister there? I'd like to speak with her too."

"She's taking a shower in Tanya's apartment down the hall. Tanya was a good friend of Caleb's. I can have her call you when she gets out."

"All right. I'll wait for her call."

They ended the call, and Adam hung his head. Now Caleb, his favorite, had been taken, and the one thing he could do to help—providing funds—had also been stolen from him. Grabbing his phone, he brought up the website with his personal account, but so little was left. What he transferred was barely enough for a few nights in a five-star hotel and a few good meals.

He glanced again at the Glock. Chelsea's call gave him another reason to wait.

"Hello?" A man in a US Postal Service uniform appeared around the side of the house, and Adam jerked his head toward the intrusion. The carrier bore a thick envelope.

"What do you want?"

"I have a DHL Express package you must sign for. It's special delivery from Italy, and it looks like it's important. Can you please sign here?" The carrier approached, but when he saw the gun, he froze.

Adam pushed the pistol aside and held out his hand for the pen. The deliveryman relaxed, stepped closer, and took his signature. He handed over the package then hurried across the lawn toward the side of the house.

Adam stared at the thick, white catalog envelope, postmarked Roma, Italia. No one sent junk mail by DHL Express, and if it were a demand from some lawyer or collection agency, it would bear a US postmark.

Breaking the seal, he pulled out a packet of legal documents and a smaller envelope. Inside, he found a letter dated yesterday on thick manila paper with an embossed logo of a globe showing Europe and Africa and the motto, "Security and Information for the World." He read.

To Adam Turner, Esquire,

Veritas Systems is a European company with worldwide offices and a bright future providing security systems, telecommunications, computer hardware, information services, and software to a variety of corporate and governmental operations. Our goal is to thrive and grow after the disaster inflicted upon the world by the Great Calamity.

We have many divisions, and after scouring the world for the right candidate, we are pleased to offer you the position as head of our Technology and Security Department. An essential part of our offer is our right to purchase from you, for the sum of seven hundred million dollars, all the equipment and interests of Turner Enterprises.

The contract for purchase is enclosed.

If this position interests you, we request that you call the number below and, no later than two days after receipt of this offer, be ready to appear in person at our Rome headquarters. If you accept, please bring with you the signed contract. We also extend an offer of employment to those of your former staff whom you wish to retain.

We do have one condition. Anyone joining our venture is required to move to one of our facilities in Belgium or Italy.

Also enclosed is an envelope containing a cashier's check for one million dollars, made out to your person. Whether you accept or refuse our offer, you may cash this check to settle any outstanding affairs. Consider it a token of our good faith.

Sincerely,

Aldo Conti, Vice President,

Veritas Systems

His heart pounding, Adam stared at the letter and read it again. He opened the envelope, found the check, and could barely hold it without shaking. He removed the contract and skimmed it—the usual stuff.

Considering that, in a few days, Turner Enterprises would be worth the price of a vanilla latte, the offer was incredible. How could he have such good fortune!

He kissed the letter, rose from his chair, and raised his hands to the sky.

After gathering all the papers, his whiskey, his pistol, he headed for the house. He must cash the check this afternoon, hire back the household help, stop the bankruptcy proceedings, inform certain staff at the office they were still employed, put money in the children's funds, pack his things, and get an evening flight for Rome.

First, he texted Dylan. "Fortune has just smiled on the Turner family," he typed. "The bankruptcy is off. By tomorrow, your trust funds will be good. I'll talk to Chelsea later."

Then he dialed the number in the letter. Aldo Conti himself answered.

CHAPTER 51

A TRAIL OF EVIL

University Village, Chicago, Illinois

Deuteronomy 32:17 (NLT): *They offered sacrifices to demons, which are not God, to gods they had not known before, to new gods only recently arrived, to gods their ancestors had never feared.*

After Dylan received his father's text, he told his sister about their conversation, and they both agreed—the whole exchange was odd.

"One minute he's talking bankruptcy." Chelsea shook her head. "The next, he's declaring good fortune and filling our accounts. Who can figure?"

"Regardless," said Dylan, "when he said we had to cut expenses, it gave me the idea to check out of the Marriott. Traveling back and forth all the time will be risky, and if Margot and I are living here at Caleb's, maybe we'll find more clues?"

"Chelsea, if you want, you can stay with me," added Tanya. "I've got room."

Following that plan, Margot and Chelsea left for the hotel to retrieve their things. Meanwhile, Dylan removed the door and its frame from a vacant apartment and installed them in place of Caleb's beat-up portal. He replaced the lock with the one from Caleb's door, for which he found an extra key.

He'd barely finished when Tanya rushed down the hall with Chelsea and Margot close behind. "Sergei responded."

"Did he find the address?"

"Yes, and it's close." She passed him a scrap of paper. "But there was no owner or company name. For some reason, the building's owner was removed from the property records. He said a record without a name should not happen. Without a name, he says he can't search further."

"Very odd." Dylan glanced at the paper, then at his watch. "It's eight o'clock. We've still got time to check this out before the ten o'clock curfew."

Everyone but Tanya said they'd go. Before leaving, he slipped the pistol into his pocket. Outside, Margot slid into the front seat, Chelsea into the back, and Dylan drove them west on Roosevelt Road.

Only a few blocks away, Margot pointed to a cardboard sign outside a church building: "Sunday services at ten. Everyone welcome."

"So there are others," she said, "who haven't fallen for the alien-abduction theory."

"That's the first open church I've seen since V-Day," said Dylan. "Maybe we should check it out?"

Three miles farther down the road, a barricade of vehicles blocked the way. The sound of gunshots echoed down the street.

Frowning, Margot craned her neck. "Sounds like trouble."

"It's the National Guard." Dylan leaned out the window. Soldiers had taken positions behind armored vehicles and were firing semiautomatic carbines at opponents in the intersection. "They're fighting a gang. I'll get around this." He turned the wheel, drove north for a mile, headed west, then returned to a main thoroughfare free of fighting.

Five more minutes, and his GPS led him to the address, a one-story brown brick structure. A sign above the entrance read, "Grandi Capelli. Fine Italian Hats." He parked.

But when he tried the door, it was locked. Beyond the partly soaped windows, dust and debris littered a barren floor.

"It's empty," said Margot. "Now what?"

"There's a light on in that bookstore." Chelsea pointed. "Let's ask there." She led them across the parking lot and knocked on the glass door.

Holding a pistol, a mousy-haired woman put her face to the barred glass. "What do you want?" came her muffled voice.

"Do you know what happened?"—nearly shouting, Dylan gestured next door—"to the Italian hat company?"

Dropping the gun into her dress pocket, she opened the door as far as the chain allowed and peered out the crack. "Odd folks, they were. Supposedly a company headquarters. But all I saw were the same three men in suits. None looked Italian. Never saw a single hat. Only shipments of office supplies delivered to the back door." She undid the chain and opened the door all the way.

"About two years ago, the place closed down. A month after that, the owner of the print shop behind me stopped by. He said that an odd group was using the building late at night. Now, I'm not one to abide a mystery, so I began staying late, doing inventory, even reading my own books. Books and a glass of white wine—now that's relaxation. Don't you agree?"

Dylan nodded.

"Anyhoo, nothing happened until the following Monday. It was late, about eleven thirty, I think." She stepped outside and waved toward the hat company building. "Then the whole lot around the place filled up with cars and folks going inside. It was odd, extremely odd. At first, I thought the owners had rented it to some kind of church. But, believe me, these folks weren't church people. Black clothing. Grim faces. Long black robes. Extremely weird." She grimaced.

"I recognized two men from the hat company. I had to solve this puzzle, so I marched right over. I stopped one of them and asked, point-blank: Did he have a church or something going on in there? And you know what he said to me?"

"What?"

"In language so foul and abusive, I can't repeat it, he told me it was none of my business and I should leave at once. So I skedaddled. Now, I often drive by the place before bed. And every once in a blue moon, they're here, late at night, dozens of cars. Sometimes they're chanting. It's creepy. Weird. I bet the building's owner doesn't even know what goes on over there."

"Is the space for rent now?" asked Chelsea.

"There's no sign out front." The woman put her hands on her hips, bunching up the denim of her dress. "If it's empty, the owner should rent it out, put an end to what goes on at night." She shook her head. "Something's not right over there."

Dylan thanked her, and they returned to the parking lot.

As Chelsea headed for the car door, Dylan headed instead for the trunk. "I'm not going back yet. I'm going inside."

"You're—what?" Chelsea stood with an open mouth as he grabbed a toolkit and a flashlight then slammed the trunk lid.

Out on the street, lights from passing vehicles and signs from across the road lit the Grandi Capelli entrance. He circled instead to the back of the building, entering a narrow alley lined with trash bins. Shadows fell on the back door. It was locked, of course, but with a padlock. Pulling out a hammer, he glanced in both directions. No one was about.

He tightened the shackle then swung the hammer repeatedly against the side of the lock until the padlock released—a trick he'd learned from the internet after losing a key to one of his padlocks. "Okay, we're in."

Chelsea looked at him as if he'd lost his mind.

Margot merely shrugged.

Dylan switched on the flashlight and stepped into a dark hallway.

"What do you expect to find in here?" asked Chelsea.

"Who knows? But we can't give up because of one locked door." He flashed his light inside a restroom on his left. Empty. Then into a storage room on his right—bare of everything but broken-down cardboard boxes. As they headed deeper into the building, shadows bounced along the walls.

He shed his light into two more vacant rooms that must have been offices. Squares on the walls testified to where pictures had once hung. The carpet was beaten down where desks had once sat. In a third room lay a stack of firewood and timbers, odd for an office building.

But as he continued down the hall toward a set of double-wide doors, a sense of foreboding rose within him, and his hand hovered over the push bar.

"I don't like this," said Margot from behind. "This place gives me the shivers."

He touched the cold metal, hesitated again, then pushed through into a wide expanse of floor that could have been a gym. Black paper covered a row of windows just below a twelve-foot ceiling. The floor was concrete, clean and bare except for a painted shape, forty feet in diameter, filling the space's center.

He shone his light on it then took a deep breath.

It was the same hexagram Margot had painted on the hand of the man guarding the Italian house. Thick lines ran from each corner, stopping halfway before the center and a globe with the outline of Europe and

Africa. In the spaces between the lines were six letters in some unknown, possibly ancient, language.

"I painted that symbol." Margot whirled toward him and laid a hand on his shoulder.

As the group stood transfixed, his light played over the hexagram.

"You painted *that*?" Tanya waved a hand at it. "I've seen it before."

"You did?" Dylan faced her. "Where?"

"When Caleb and I went to the market, a man blocked our way to the back door. Caleb forced him aside with the gun. The man had a tattoo just like that on the back of his hand. At the time, I didn't think anything of it."

"But l–look. Up there." Margot pointed to the far wall.

Dylan raised his light higher and gasped.

Hovering above the room was a picture of a naked man with a beard. He sat cross-legged on a globe. He bore the head of a goat, and it sprouted wide, curling horns. Black wings unfurled from either side of his body. Goat's hooves were folded beneath him. Woman's breasts bulged from his chest. And on his forehead—a Jewish star.

Scrawled in red under the painting was a name—Baphomet.

Below on the floor was a charred area, now swept clean.

As Dylan stared, his heart beat faster. Darkness seemed to gather in the space around him. A shivering chill started in his shoulders, spread down to his arms, drilled deep into his chest, then slid down to his legs.

"Baphomet?" Her eyes wild, Margot grabbed Dylan's arm, pulling him close. "It's some kind of demon. And I feel its presence . . . inside me."

Its eyes seemed to come alive and peer back at him. Then he saw what it saw, and he shuddered. Margot gripped his arm tighter.

Back through the years, the thing took him, showing him what went on in this room below the figure on the wall.

Here did men and women in black robes gather and perform unspeakable rites with their victims. They gutted living things—men, women, animals. They dismembered them and offered them, piece by piece, to the fire raging beneath the wall demon.

Then it took him further back, back before the days of Christ, back to the time of Stone Age druids and forest shamans, and even further back. He tried to fight it, but the thing pressed its vision upon him—

Men and women, wearing clay or fur masks topped with the horns of killed beasts, danced naked around bonfires under starry skies, inside circles of standing stone. They called to the demon in strange tongues. They praised and bowed before Baphomet, a minion of Satan, a sculpted idol of wood and sometimes bronze. They invited its evil into their hearts, giving themselves up to a wild dance around raging fires.

And in their ceremonies, their victims—men, women, or children—lay bound and gagged on stone altars, ready for sacrifice by the knife, the ax, the rope, or the fire. And after the deed was done, they would flee into the night and lie together, men with women not their wives, women with men not their husbands, coupling in wild abandon on the ground in the dark, an unholy group obscenity, for this was their worship before Satan.

"Did you see it?" Margot's grip tightened around his arm, wakening him from its spell.

"Yes. Let's get out of here." He grabbed Chelsea's and Margot's hands and tried to pull them toward the door.

But a dark cloud swirled about the room, and the light from his flashlight dimmed.

The other two clung to him, and they huddled together.

Bow and worship. Its words formed inside his mind. *Join us and be free.*

"Never!" he shouted.

Some unseen force pressed in upon his chest from all directions, and breathing became difficult. He gasped for air, fearing his lungs would collapse.

"Dear . . . Jesus," whispered Margot, her speech labored, "protect . . . us."

As she prayed, Dylan's flashlight grew brighter. The pressure on his chest lessened. "Jesus, Lord of light," he joined in, "protect us and lead us from this place of evil."

He and Margot prayed together. Then, as if they'd flipped a switch, the darkness receded, and the pressure on his chest ceased. The figure on the wall returned to what it had been when they entered—just an obscene painting.

The evil had been pushed back.

Through the double doors they sprinted, his flashlight bouncing down the hall, past the empty rooms, into the alley.

Outside, the others ran to the car. He stooped to retrieve his tools. But when he rose again, he noticed a tiny blue light above the door. Peering closer, he discovered a camera. Was it recording what it saw?

He rejoined the others at the car. Squealing out of the lot, he merged with the traffic on Roosevelt Road heading east. He didn't breathe normally until they passed the second stoplight and the familiar arches of a McDonald's. With only a half an hour before curfew, already traffic was thinning.

On the drive home, no one said a thing, but when he glanced at Margot beside him, she was mumbling a prayer. And in the rearview mirror, Chelsea's face was pale.

At the stoplight where the guard had battled the gang, uniformed soldiers now held the intersection, and an ambulance was hauling away the wounded.

They arrived at the apartment just before curfew then gathered in Tanya's living room.

He went straight to Uri's brandy bottle and poured a tumbler.

"You all look spooked," said Tanya. "What happened?"

When they told her, she plopped into a chair, her eyes searching each of theirs in disbelief. "Are you sure that's what you saw?"

"No doubt about it," said Chelsea, her face still pale, her hands trembling. "I don't believe in ghosts or demons or gods or anything like that. But after tonight—well, you had to experience it. I'm still shaking. Do you have some wine or something to calm my nerves?"

Tanya nodded and brought full glasses for the two women.

Nika went to Chelsea's side and began licking her hands.

Dylan found a seat. "What we learned is that Capelli Romani is a front for a group of demon worshipers. And the group goes back to the Stone Age."

"How does that help us?" asked Tanya.

"I don't know." He faced her. "But Caleb is in a lot more trouble than we'd thought. These people are more than kidnappers." He set his glass down and rubbed his forehead. Then he straightened. "Let's call Sergei back. If he's as good as you say he is, maybe he can discover something now that we have the owner's name?"

Dylan called Sergei with the information but kept their encounter with the demon out of the conversation.

"With name, I search more," said the Russian. "But tomorrow, not tonight. Is possible I now find something, da?"

They went to bed that night exhausted and drained. But before sleep called, Dylan prayed to the God of the universe, asking for protection from the forces of evil.

CHAPTER 52
THE NO-FLY LIST

University Village, Chicago, Illinois

The next day was Friday. After the demon encounter and with the world turned upside down, they sought the familiar, the comforting, whatever reminded them of better days. While Chelsea and Tanya watched an old movie on disk, a romantic comedy, Dylan walked with Margot to the nearest park. And since the guard patrols had—today, at least—pushed the gangs to the south, he even left the pistol behind. It was late October, the air was chill, the trees red and golden, and their feet swished through leaves on the sidewalk.

Margot grasped his hand and threw him a coy smile. They strolled together, breathing the crisp air, listening to the robins, watching a group of teenaged boys—all above the age of decision—playing soccer on the field. Whenever he glanced aside, she smiled back.

"I'm glad I came to America with you," she said. "But I fear what happened yesterday."

"Me too. But we can take comfort that God is with us."

"I know." She smiled again and squeezed his hand. "And so are you."

The wind—or had it been the teenagers?—had piled leaves under the trees. With a mischievous sideways glance, Margot ran to the pile, raised both arms to the side, and fell backward into it. Leaves whooshed out, then whooshed back, nearly burying her, and she giggled.

Not to be outdone, Dylan raced to a spot beside her, stretched out his arms, and fell backward into the mound at her side. The leaves flew up, then down, and when he opened his eyes, Margot had rolled over and was kneeling above him. He looked up into her smiling eyes, so wide and honest and brown with a touch of blue. Before he knew what was happening, her lips lowered and touched his.

Electricity shot through him. His hands grasped her head and pulled her close. When he released her, his breath quickened.

"I'm coming to like you, Dylan Turner." She plucked a leaf from her hair. "Yes, quite a lot." Then she backed away, scooped up a pile, and dumped it on his face.

Grinning, he shot to his knees. "So that's how you want to play?" Gathering an armload of leaves, he stood and unloaded it over her head.

For a time, they both tried to see who could deposit the greatest heap of crinkling, desiccated foliage on the other, but it was hopeless. The leaves were a poor choice with which to engage in mock battle. Finally, they stood facing each other, breathing fast, smiling.

Then he drew her close and kissed her again.

On their stroll back to the apartment, they held hands, and he couldn't remember a time—either before or after V-Day—when he'd been as happy as at that moment.

But it wouldn't last. The memory of yesterday's encounter was all too fresh.

The rest of that day, they waited for Sergei's call.

* * *

LONG AFTER SUPPER, AS THEY sat around Tanya's kitchen table, sipping wine, making small talk, Dylan's phone played his latest tune, a fugue by Mozart. It was Sergei's long-awaited call, and Dylan put the Russian on speaker so everyone could hear.

"I search property records," said Sergei. "I have certain secret methods, and I browse IRS and Illinois databases. Grandi Capelli exists, but barely. They report no income last two years. Why their name is not with state vehicle registration is big mystery. Such things should not be. I look further, and Veritas Systems owns Grandi Capelli. Is big Italian computer and software corporation, but nothing to do with hats. Very odd.

"I search more, go deeper. Veritas also has owner, and name is Conventus Romanus. Is holding company, and I think big. Very big. Owner of many, many companies. But this, also, is big mystery. Conventus Romanus website says nothing."

"Where is the Veritas headquarters located?" asked Dylan.

"Rome. I have address."

"And Conventus Romanus?"

"Hard to say. Is mother to many babushkas—in Rome, Marseilles, New York, London, Tokyo, Brussels, Miami, Paris, Madrid. All point back to mother company."

"All right, Sergei. Thank you."

"You are at Tanya's place, da?"

"Yes."

"Be careful what you say in other apartment. Anything could be bug. Badge, credit card, any small thing. Do not speak serious plans there. Only small talk."

"Okay, thanks." Then he hung up.

Dylan glanced around the table. "Let's look at those websites."

Tanya carried over her laptop, and they gathered around.

When Chelsea brought up the Veritas Systems site, it dealt in hardware, software, telecommunications, database, and information technology. Nothing out of the ordinary. There was a picture of a tall office building in Rome next to a pond.

Next, she searched for Conventus Romanus. Just as Sergei had said, more than a dozen companies referenced, in oblique terms, an association with the name. After trying several combinations, she found the company's home page.

A slogan in bold letters appeared at the top: "Truth, Peace, Charity, and Virtue. This is Conventus Romanus." But nothing else appeared on the screen except space for a login and password. She tried everything she could think of but couldn't get past it.

"Very odd, indeed," said Tanya.

"But we know Veritas Systems is in Rome, and that's a solid lead." Dylan turned from the computer.

"There's also this." Tanya's eyes lit up. "Caleb told me his website had come under attack, and his web host provider had traced it to the area around Rome."

Then Margot spoke. "And I think—though I'm not certain—that the house I painted is Italian."

Dylan nodded. "Then we should be in Italy, not here."

"What would we do when we got there?" asked Chelsea.

"I don't know. But we won't learn anything more here."

"I don't have a passport, so I can't help you in Europe," said Tanya. "Besides, I can't leave Nika."

The others agreed to continue the search in Italy.

"Then it's settled. I'll get a flight for tomorrow for the three of us." Dylan brought up his preferred airline's website and entered his name and departure information.

But when he hit enter to book the flight, an odd message popped up: "International travel is restricted for passengers on the no-fly list. Contact your nearest TSA office for further details."

"Let me try." Chelsea entered her information but received the same message.

Dylan then tried Margot's information with the same result. He switched to a different airline and tried again, but no matter what they did, the same message appeared.

"We're being blocked." Margot faced the others. "We can't leave the country."

"It's late." Dylan sat back. "This must be a mistake. Let's try again tomorrow."

But as he and Margot closed the door inside Caleb's apartment and they headed each to their own beds, a shiver ran down his back, and he knew—

The message was no mistake.

CHAPTER 53
CHELSEA'S OFFER

University Village, Chicago, Illinois

It was early Sunday morning, and after Sergei's warning, the four amateur investigators decided to take all meals in Tanya's kitchen. Chelsea was nearly finished with a breakfast of pancakes and bacon cooked by Tanya.

Having found the most generous human at the table, Nika sat obediently beside her, one paw in the air, begging for another dropped morsel. Chelsea obliged with another bit of bacon.

Dylan finished first then opened his laptop and tried again to buy tickets. But the same message reappeared. "I don't know what else to try." He slammed down the lid. "We dare not call TSA. I—"

Chelsea's phone rang, so she pulled it from her pocket and answered. "Father? It's good to hear from you."

"Chelsea, I have great news for you." An excitement the man rarely exhibited rang through the phone. "When I talked with Dylan a few days ago, Turner Enterprises was facing bankruptcy. The situation was . . . bleak. But now everything's changed."

"What happened? You sound so happy."

"I've been offered a job with an important company here in Rome. That's where I am now. Not only that, they're buying Turner Enterprises for seven hundred mil. I'm their new chief of security and technology—can you believe it? It's a dream come true."

Her eyes widened. "I'm happy for you, Dad. But we've been trying to get tickets to—"

"But, Chelsea, you haven't heard the best part. This company is growing fast, I have a lot of positions to fill, and one's perfect for you. So I'm offering you a job as assistant personnel researcher on my floor. It comes with a salary of one hundred thousand euros. That's a lot more than you're making now. You'd have to move to Rome, of course, and they would want you here as soon as you could come."

"Wow!" She took a deep breath. To work in Rome had always been her dream. And the salary was attractive, especially since she was now without a job. She hated being dependent on her trust fund. But working for her father was, well, problematic. "But listen, Dad, our search for Caleb has run into a dead end, and—"

"Oh, right—Caleb. I've been so busy, I've barely had time to think. What about a ransom demand? Is that what they're after?"

"We . . . don't know." Somewhat taken aback by her father's previous lack of interest in Caleb's disappearance, she frowned. "There's been no communication from them since he was taken."

"Hmm. Maybe I should hire a private investigator. No one steals my kid and gets away with it."

She took a deep breath. Did they really want Father poking his nose into this? "Can I get back to you on that?"

"Certainly. But let me tell you the rest. The company I'm working for was fast becoming one of my main competitors. Its name is Veritas Systems, and it's worldwide with many divisions and offices in many countries and . . ."

But as soon as he said the name, her thoughts spun out of control, and her heartbeat hammered her ears. Was her own father now working for a company involved in some way with Caleb's kidnapping?

"Chelsea? Did you hear what I said about getting a ticket?"

"Oh, sorry. I am so blown away by what you said—I can't think straight."

"I understand. It's a great offer. But what do you say? Will you accept? I can email you a ticket. Just say the word."

"I'd like to think about it and call you back."

A long silence at the other end.

She tightened her grip on the phone, its edges cutting into her fingers. "Dad?"

"I guess. Though I don't understand what there is to think about. This is the opportunity of a lifetime. These are difficult times. You'll not find a better offer."

"I'll call you back in a bit." She hung up, then slumped forward onto the table, her head in her hands. "You won't believe this," she said to the tabletop.

"What?" asked Dylan.

She lifted her head. "Father offered me a job as a researcher with an Italian company that just bought Turner Enterprises for seven hundred million dollars. He's in Rome right now. He's their new chief of security and technology. But the name of the company is—get this—Veritas Systems."

The news so stunned the other three, for a time no one spoke. Then Dylan broke the silence. "He can't know anything about Caleb's kidnapping. He got the job only a few days ago. But . . ."

"But what?" asked Margot.

"Veritas's link to the kidnappers is tenuous. They own the building, but it's been vacant for two years. Someone could be renting it on their behalf without them even knowing what goes on there. The bookstore lady even said as much."

"Sergei did say it was a big company," said Chelsea. "And hats have nothing to do with computers. If the company is that big, you could be right."

"Whoever is behind this—Caleb's kidnapping, putting us on a no-fly list—they've got a long reach, and they're powerful."

"But there's something else. Father also offered to hire a private investigator to find Caleb." She pressed both hands against the sides of her head. To decide what to do now was almost as difficult as going to the clinic to end her baby. She whispered, "What should we do?"

Dylan's gaze narrowed. "I wouldn't trust anyone he'd hire. They could be associated with Veritas. Tell him we're giving up the search and leaving the city but to go ahead and hire his detective. Tanya"—he turned to her—"is it all right, when that detective comes, to give them your name?"

She grimaced. "I suppose. But what should I tell him?"

"Just what you saw. Of course, leave out the demon encounters. And the phone. And the warnings to stop blogging. Without that info, I doubt a detective will find anything. We don't want him involved in our search. Just tell him about the van, how the men broke into Caleb's apartment, and how they took him."

"All right." Tanya sat up straighter. "So it seems I do have a part to play in this after all."

Chelsea stood, walked to the window, and returned. "But what about the job offer? What should I do?"

"We were already going to Italy to check out the company," said Dylan, "and with you working for Veritas—that would be even better. Even if the company is not connected to the demon tattoo people, you'd get yourself a job in Rome like you always wanted."

"What did you say your position would be?" asked Margot.

"Assistant personnel researcher."

"So," added Tanya, "you'd be checking backgrounds for applicants and employees."

"Which means you'd have a high level of security clearance," added Dylan.

"Possibly."

He nodded. "Call him back and tell him you'll accept the job. And if he can break through this 'no-fly problem' and get you a ticket, maybe he can do the same for us? But don't tell Father about the connection between Veritas and the hat company. He's our father, yes, but . . . I still don't trust him. Or any detective he hires. And his line may be bugged."

"So you want me to be a spy?"

Her brother grinned at her, looking much like Caleb when they were about to play a prank on Dylan. "Yes."

She turned away from them and again walked to the window. She'd be living in Rome, something she always wanted. Yes, she'd be working for Father, and that would be difficult. But her sense of adventure was fast overcoming all other reservations. And if it would help find Caleb— she whirled back. "Okay. I'll do it."

Dylan grabbed her shoulders and planted a kiss on her cheek.

As her hand grazed where he'd kissed, she returned his affection with a smile.

She called Father back and told him that, with all leads to Caleb's disappearance exhausted, Dylan and Margot were leaving the city, going back to the villa in Tuscany.

Overjoyed that she would take the job, Father would try to get her, Dylan, and Margot off the no-fly list and get her a ticket. He also agreed to hire a private investigator to check into Caleb's kidnapping.

Minutes later, he called back saying she was off the no-fly list and her ticket was on its way. He was also sorry, but for some reason, he couldn't clear Dylan's and Margot's names.

Before she could object, he hung up.

She scowled at the phone. "He's sending me a ticket, and I'm able to fly now. But, Dylan, he couldn't clear your name or Margot's. He couldn't have tried very hard. Or else some very powerful people are blocking you two."

"I have an idea how to get around this." Dylan's gaze focused on something across the room. "You just go. Somehow, we'll get to Italy. Then Margot and I will wait at the villa for whatever you find."

"Okay. But, if I'm to catch my flight, I have to leave for the airport this minute."

After Chelsea went to her room and packed, they said goodbye in Tanya's living room.

She laid a hand on her brother's shoulder and kissed him on the cheek. "We're getting into this way over our heads. You both take care now."

"You, too." Dylan hugged her, followed by Margot.

But as Chelsea lugged her bag out to the street, she wondered who was now taking the greatest risk.

CHAPTER 54
SPIRITUAL WARFARE

University Village, Chicago, Illinois

After Chelsea left for the airport, Dylan called the Russian. When he explained that someone was blocking them from buying airline tickets, silence filled the other end.

"Sergei?"

"Da. I'm thinking. Persons with government connections put your names in database, block travel."

"What can we do about it?"

"Do not try again from computer with same IP address. I come your place at noon, take new photos, make new passports. Then we buy tickets from anonymous website with bitcoin, da?"

"Bitcoin?"

"Is currency for gangsters, criminals, and peoples hiding money from government. I come after noon, da?"

"Yes, Sergei. This is much appreciated."

"Where is car you drive? Where parked?"

"Out front. Why?"

"Leave it there. Be certain no one follow and walk to rental agency. Then rent new car to drop at airport. Park on different street and walk back to apartment."

"O–kay."

He then asked Dylan to text him the make, model, and license number of the rental. "But now is new requirement. With extra work comes extra payment. Another bottle of vodka, da?"

Smiling, he asked Tanya, and she said that yes, Uri kept a supply in the cupboard for just that purpose. After he relayed the news, Sergei hung up.

But when Dylan announced he was going to rent the car, Margot stopped him. "Today, I want to go to church. Remember the sign we saw Friday?"

"Yes."

Tanya gave him a questioning look, and he explained. Then she said that she, too, would go with them. It would be her first church service, ever.

"Then we'll drive my car to this church, and I'll get the rental when we return. I'm still reeling after what happened at the hat company. I could use something like that right now."

Before they left, he dropped the gun in his pocket. Just in case.

The church was less than a mile away. He parked, and as they walked through the open front door, Dylan didn't know what to expect. All the believing pastors and Christians should have been taken in the Rapture. Who was left to lead a church service?

A smiling young woman in her twenties with straight black hair greeted and waved them past the foyer through more double doors toward the pews. The sanctuary held maybe a hundred and fifty, max, but today only about twenty-five people of different ages and races had wandered in. Just like Dylan, Margot, and Tanya, the others were warily checking out their neighbors.

"Welcome to the First Church of the Apocalypse." A middle-aged man with curly black hair stepped to the front. "At least that's what we're calling our motley collection of refugees from V-Day, those of us who were too dumb, too prideful, or too stubborn to realize the truth when it mattered. If anyone can think of a better name, let me know. But before we begin, how many of you believe aliens took the Christians out of the world? Raise your hands."

Dylan looked around, and not one hand rose.

"Just as I thought. My friends, we here today are now the smart ones. My name is Brody Cooper, and I will lead you in worship. I studied in seminary but quit after a year. I never really believed, you see. I never really"—for one moment, the words seemed to stick in his throat—"never really . . . had Jesus in my heart. Now, of course, it's a different story.

"To begin, Mary will lead us in song. The words will be up on the screen. Mary?" He stepped aside, and the young woman who greeted them took a guitar to a stool up front while Brody brought out a mandolin.

They sang three songs, and for Dylan, they were uplifting. He'd only been attending church for about three months, and once again, he realized what he'd been missing all his life. He also realized that worshiping God not only gave him pleasure, but he also sensed that it pleased God.

After the singing ended, Brody set his mandolin aside and took the front.

"One more thing I will mention—we've received warnings not to proceed with this event, our first service since V-Day. I've gotten nasty anonymous emails. And after our sign went up outside, I received a letter filled with the vilest epithets and language, warning that harm will come to me, personally, if we continue. So, if anyone here today is worried about repercussions from your visit, you may leave now. We won't hold it against you."

Only one older man stood and waved his hands as if to say, "I want nothing to do with this." Then he hurried from the building.

Brody thanked the rest for staying. "So, dear people, the warnings we've received have given me the topic for today's message: Waging Spiritual Warfare."

The sermon was exactly what Dylan needed to hear. Brody Cooper talked from Ephesians six, verses ten through seventeen, and the subject was protection from the strategies of the Devil. " 'For we are not fighting against flesh-and-blood enemies,' " he said, quoting Scripture from Ephesians six, " 'but against evil rulers and authorities of the unseen world, against mighty powers in this dark world, and against evil spirits in the heavenly places.' "

He then talked about the weapons to use against Satan's wiles— truth, righteousness, prayer, faith, the peace of Jesus's salvation, and the knowledge that the Spirit of God resides within every believer.

By the end, Dylan felt cleansed of the evil they'd experienced at the hat company, and when he glanced aside, both Margot and Tanya were beaming.

After the service, Dylan held the other two back until they were last in a line of people shaking Brody's hands at the door. When their turn came, Dylan introduced himself, then congratulated Brody on the message and called him pastor.

"No, my friend. I don't deserve that title. If I'd had any sense, I would have believed long ago."

"Begging your pardon, but I think you can claim the title now. But you said you received warnings not to proceed with this service. We've had the same experience but for a different reason. My brother was running a popular blog trying to convince folks that the Christian Rapture, not aliens, caused V-Day, and—"

"I *know* that blog." Brody's eyes lit up. "I followed *The Real Truth* until someone shut it down."

"Not only did they shut it down, but they also kidnapped my brother. We're trying to find out where they took him, and two nights ago"— Dylan glanced at the floor—"well, let's just say we had a first-person, close encounter of the worst kind with the forces of darkness."

For a moment, Brody said nothing. Then he laid a hand on Dylan's and Margot's shoulders and prayed for their protection. Afterward, he said, "I wish you well, Dylan Turner. Our troubles are not as serious as yours, but if you ever need to place to hide, contact me here at the church. If necessary and if we're no longer meeting here, drop a note in the little box beside the back door. Just your name and phone number. The previous church used that to collect prayer requests, but we can use it for discreet communications."

"Thank you. We're following a lead that should take us out of the country, but if we're ever back in Chicago, we'll stop again." They shook hands and parted.

Outside, as they walked to the car, Margot spoke. "It seems others are also battling with the forces of evil?"

"Yes," said Dylan, "and whoever the enemy is, they seem to be everywhere."

He drove straight back to the apartment. Since the National Guard had stepped up patrols the last few days, the route was clear, at least for now, of gangs.

They climbed the stairs. But as Dylan approached the apartment, the door hung open. Someone had drilled a hole in the lock.

"Oh no." Tanya's hand covered her mouth, and she stepped back.

He drew the gun from his pocket. Slowly, he pushed until the door swung in.

Taking hesitant steps, he entered, glanced around, then gasped.

Every piece of furniture had been flipped on its side. Every cushion had been ripped with a knife. On two walls, obscenities in black paint defamed the name of Christ. In the living room, broken glass from a picture frame lay scattered atop books pulled from the bookcase, their spines broken or ripped apart. A bottle of red wine had been emptied onto the carpet, leaving a spreading stain. Shards of the bottle's broken glass lay smashed on the fireplace hearthstone.

"I'm checking my place." Tanya ran out the door and down the hall. Moments later, she returned as Dylan and Margot entered a bedroom. "My apartment is okay," she said, her voice relieved.

In the bedroom, the mattress was cut, and pillow feathers covered the floor.

"Who would do such a thing?" Margot spread her hands toward another obscenity scrawled across a broken mirror with soap. "And why?"

"To warn us."

Dylan left the guest bedroom and crossed into the kitchen. "What's this?" He pointed to the table where lay a thin box, about ten inches square and wrapped with a red ribbon and bow. He picked it up and shook it. Pieces of something bounced around inside. He shot a questioning glance to Tanya and Margot.

"Open it," said Tanya.

"What if it's a bomb?" asked Margot.

"It's not heavy enough." He pulled off the bow, slipped off the ribbon, and eased open the lid.

Excrement filled the interior. Gagging at the stench, he dropped it and jumped back.

"How awful." Margot winced.

He approached again. In one corner, a bit of gold chain was hidden beneath the feces. Lifting the package, he carried it to the bathroom and dumped the excrement into the toilet. Beneath was a plastic baggy containing a note.

After extricating the bag and chain, he washed them—and his hands—thoroughly in the sink. He recognized the chain as Caleb's.

Then he read the note. "If you do not stop what you are doing, you will pay the consequences."

Closing his eyes, he backed to the wall, leaned against it, and wrapped his hands around his head.

Margot read the note, saw the chain, and gave him a puzzled glance.

"That was Caleb's necklace," whispered Tanya. "He never took it off."

"What should we do?" asked Margot.

"Nothing." He raised a finger to his lips and drew them into the hallway. "They were in there. They might have bugged the place. Now, it's even more important that we leave the country. And with new passports, I doubt they'll find us in Italy."

"How did they know about us?" asked Margot.

"They must have been watching the place. And there was a camera above the hat company's back door that I never told you about. That must be how they learned we were digging into their business. And now they're warning us to stop."

An hour later, Sergei buzzed from downstairs, and they let him in. When he saw the mess in Caleb's apartment, he shook his head, whistled, and drew them far down the hall. "Now is important you hide, not go out again. Stay out of apartment but turn lights on and off and pretend you are here. I get passports and tickets and come tomorrow. I also get you new phones for Europe. Drop old phones in trash at airport. Tonight, you stay with Tanya. I think they do not know she is involved."

In Tanya's apartment, Sergei took passport photos of Dylan and Margot.

"Did you get rental car?" he asked.

"Not yet. I drove mine to a church this morning."

Sergei frowned. "You do not listen. What I get for dealing with amateurs. Get rental and text me make, license, and where you park." Then he left.

Dylan followed him out the door then walked to a rental agency two miles away. After he parked several blocks away, he and Margot moved to Tanya's and waited for Sergei's return. Everyone was spooked by what happened, and every so often, Dylan went to the window and peered out. But no one seemed to be watching the building.

CHAPTER 55

ESCAPE FROM CHICAGO

University Village, Chicago, Illinois

All the next morning, a Monday, they waited, and all afternoon, but still no Sergei. Before noon, a steady drizzle painted the sky a dirty gray and wet the concrete below. That afternoon, as Dylan repeatedly checked the street for watchers, the rain stopped. It wasn't until they'd finished supper in Tanya's kitchen that his phone played his latest tune from Tchaikovsky's *Nutcracker Suite*. It was Sergei, and Dylan put him on speaker.

"Men are watching apartment," said the Russian. "Look out window."

Dylan had checked only an hour ago. He parted the blinds and peered down. A large utility van was parked across the street. Three shadowy figures leaned under the awning of the opposite building. A cigarette glowed in the dark. "I see them. There must be at least three."

"Six in front. Two in back alley."

Dylan's heart raced. How were they going to escape from eight men, probably all professional killers? "What do we do?"

"You have backpacks, da?"

"Yes."

"Put all you need in backpacks now. No roller bags. Be ready to run. You have gun, da?"

"Yes."

"Bring it. In exactly twenty—no, thirty—minutes, go into back alley. Hold gun in hand so men see it. Walk toward them. Slow. Do not hurry. I am on other side. No worries. No matter what happens, do not stop walking." Then he hung up.

Dylan stared at the phone, not believing what he'd just heard. The Russian was crazy. When he explained the plan to Margot, she raised her eyebrows in disbelief.

"What's he planning?" she asked.

"I don't know, but he's all we have. He must know what he's doing."

He and Margot repacked what they could from their roller bags into their backpacks. When the time came, they stood before Tanya. "I guess this is goodbye."

"Let me know what you find over there. I've never been to Italy, but now isn't the time for a European tour. And I can't leave Nika." Her face wrinkling, she hugged Margot then Dylan. "You are good people. Take care and text me your new numbers."

They said goodbye then descended the stairs to the back door. On the far side of the barred window, the alley appeared empty. Toward the right, the corridor ended in a high security fence. Dylan took a hesitant step outside and glanced left, the only way out. Just as Sergei had warned, two men lounged at the corner.

Between them and the street were the backsides of four apartment buildings lined with dumpsters and racks of locked bicycles. The smell of rotting garbage fouled the air.

"They see us." Margot's voice was tense. "They're heading our way."

"No matter what, Sergei said to keep going." His heart was pumping faster now, his forehead beaded with sweat. His right hand gripped the gun. As instructed, he held the pistol so they could see it. But what was the Russian up to? Dylan wasn't prepared to shoot anyone.

He kept walking, slowly, toward the street corner, toward the men.

"You, there, halt!" His face in shadows, the first man was tall. Short blond hair was pasted to his forehead. He waved a stubby rifle.

Dylan kept walking.

"He said to stop." The second man, shorter, stockier, swarthier, dropped a cigarette and lifted a handgun.

Both men strode deeper into the alley.

"Did you hear me?" The first spoke again. "I said halt."

Behind the men, a shadow appeared, hugging the wall, silent, moving faster than they. It was Sergei, but how was he going to stop them? These men weren't going to listen to—

A shot cracked the night, and the man with the machine gun crumpled to the ground. Even as the second man whirled, two more explosions echoed down the passageway, and he, too, fell.

Sergei ran to his opponents, fired again, once into each man's skull, then shouted to Dylan. "Run!"

Stunned by Sergei's unexpected murder of their opponents, but too frightened to do anything else, Dylan grabbed Margot's hand. He broke into a run.

Sergei was already racing ahead of them.

The alley dumped into a side street that intersected with the main avenue where the van was parked. Sergei stopped at the corner.

Dylan came up behind the Russian and peered left.

As Sergei snapped a new clip into his pistol, he turned a fierce look on Dylan. "Run to car. *Now!*"

With Margot close behind, he turned right and ran. Behind him, a flurry of shots echoed down the street. He glanced back.

Two men from the van had appeared around the corner, and Sergei had shot them both. The bodies lay unmoving on the concrete. As Dylan watched, Sergei ran to catch up.

He pointed Dylan on, and Dylan broke into a sprint. After the recent rain, the night was cool and humid on his face. Their feet splashed through puddles. Their backpacks jumped up and down against their backs.

At the intersection, he turned right. Margot's feet slapped the pavement beside him. Another look back showed Sergei crouched at the corner, again changing clips, sending an occasional glance at their pursuers.

Dylan ran to the end of the block. He turned left as more shots rang out behind. When he turned the next corner, even more shots split the night.

One more left turn at the intersection brought him to his rental car. They threw their packs in the back seat, and he and Margot slid into the front. He turned the key, and the car started. Just before he pulled away, Sergei emerged from the side street and waved them to a stop.

"In back seat"—he sucked in breath—"are passports, phones, tickets. Go and good luck!"

Dylan shot a glance at the plastic bag he'd missed before. How Sergei had placed it inside a locked car was a mystery.

"What about you?" He faced the Russian.

"No worries." He gestured to the vehicle behind them. "My car."

"Thanks, Sergei. How can we ever repay you?"

His face broke into a smile. "Next time—two bottles, da?"

"Da."

Sergei headed for his vehicle, and Dylan squealed away. He didn't slow down until he was certain no one had followed. On the streets behind them, Sergei had left a trail of the dead. But these days, the police were so decimated by the defunding, retirements, and massive attrition, people hardly bothered to call them anymore. The National Guard was only concerned with the gangs. For those inhabitants remaining, a few gun battles at night in the city of Chicago were hardly worth mentioning.

At the airport, Dylan returned the rental car. Inside the terminal, he and Margot found seats outside Security. To the prattle of announcements over the loudspeaker, he examined Sergei's package. Their tickets were for flights leaving tomorrow afternoon.

The Russian had also left a handwritten note, poorly spelled, advising how to transfer their contact lists to the new phones. He also left Dylan the name, address, and phone number of a man in Paris. "René LeClerc does what I do, only better. He owes me. Reach him in emergency only."

Following instructions, Dylan found a stall in the restroom, removed the SIM cards from their old phones and crushed them, and wiped his fingerprints from the phones and the gun. Then he wrapped everything in paper towels and threw the electronics and the gun into a trash bin.

He handed Margot her new passport. "You are now Michelle Taylor. And I'm Dalton Taylor." He grinned. "We are man and wife, and we live in Carpentersville, Illinois."

She looked at her picture then smiled at him. "Pleased to meet you, Dalton Taylor."

"Pleased to meet you, Michelle." Then he leaned over, and they shook hands.

Reasoning it would be safer beyond the checkpoints, they used their new passports and tickets and swept through Security without a problem. Then they found a spot on the carpet where they laid down, side by side, with heads on their packs. To the endless repetition of inane messages warning them not to let someone put something into their bags and a woman announcer's repeated warnings that travelers on the moving walkway were nearing its end, they tried to sleep. Dylan pondered how silly were such announcements when the world was falling apart around them. Somehow, they slept the night.

The next afternoon, they boarded a plane for Amsterdam, where they'd change planes for Florence, Italy.

CHAPTER 56
THE BISHOP'S VILLA

In the Tuscan Countryside

No sooner had Dylan parked the rental car in the villa's lot and they started carrying their backpacks toward the house than white-haired Bettino ran out waving his hands. "Signore Dylan, it's no longer safe here. Men came asking for you. I didn't like their looks."

"When?" asked Dylan.

"Yesterday." Bettino shot a glance at his watch. "About this time."

"Did any of them have a tattoo on their hands?" asked Margot.

"Odd you should mention that." He scratched behind one ear. "I saw a hexagon with a globe on the back of one man's hand."

Fear contorting her face, Margot clutched at Dylan's arm. "Now where can we go?"

"Not to worry." Bettino smiled. "My friend, the bishop, His Most Reverend Excellency Emilio Gallo, arrived after the men for our usual chat. I explained what happened, and he offers you his place. You may stay there for as long as you like. It's only a short walk over the hill, through the vineyards, and across the stream."

"Can't we drive?" Margot loosened her grip on Dylan's arm and gestured to the rental car.

"I would walk, signorina." Bettino nodded toward the long drive. "They said they'd be back."

Dylan agreed. He showed Bettino their new passports, and Bettino recorded their new names and phone numbers.

"But go now into the vineyard." He nodded toward the hill. "I will hide your car in the garage and drive it over later."

Dylan eyed the detached building, fifty meters distant from the house. "What if they notice there's a new vehicle in there?"

"It's not registered in your real name, is it? I'll say it's mine, and yesterday it was in the shop."

While Dylan and Margot climbed the slope through the vines, Bettino hid the car in the garage and returned to the house.

The two had barely reached the halfway point when a black sedan raced down the lane, raising a wake of dust. "In here!" With Margot beside him, Dylan laid flat in the dry dirt between rows. He peered over the top.

Four men approached the house. They quizzed Bettino at the front door. Then they pushed inside past the old servant. A long while later, they reemerged, ambled over the grounds, made a quick search of the garage, then left.

"That was close." Margot leaned up against a post. "But if we're to stay at this Emilio's villa, I need my paints, canvases, and easel."

He shot her a questioning glance.

"Ever since we pulled into the lane, I've felt a desire to paint again. I need my supplies."

So Dylan called Bettino with the request. They mounted the trail, topped the hill, and descended. While finches tweeted in the treetops, they crossed a bridge over a stream splitting the Turners' land from Emilio's.

As bishop, Emilio Gallo must have done well, for his villa was as large as Father's. It also topped a hill and overlooked vineyards and orchards. Near the house, they passed two white horses munching on grass in a fenced pasture. With a wide smile and kisses on both cheeks, Emilio welcomed them in English.

"Bettino called, signorina." He led them inside. "He should arrive any minute with your art supplies. While you were gone, he showed me your paintings, and I believe the Holy Spirit has worked a miracle in you."

"Thank you." She brushed aside a lock of hair. "Today, I'm tired from the flight and need sleep. But tomorrow, I must paint again. Whenever the desire comes upon me—I am compelled to paint."

"I would be honored to see what new vision God has given you. But tonight, Bettino promises to cook for us a fine dinner of penne pasta, sausages, salad, and bread. You must also try the wine from our vineyard."

Even as the words left his mouth, Dylan's rental car pulled up to the house, and Bettino emerged, arms full of bags. While Dylan and Margot transferred her easel, blank canvases, and boxes of brushes and paints to a second-floor room overlooking the horse pasture, Bettino commandeered the kitchen.

Later, they ate, drank Emilio's wine, and talked. When the weary travelers retired and Dylan snuggled under a comforter with an open window to the sound of crickets, he wondered how their adversaries knew about the Turner villa. Had the men checked all the properties under his father's name? But the men wouldn't know about their new phones, and his text to Bettino from the airport should have been secure. They should be safe at Emilio's.

Still, it was troubling that these men were so persistent, going to such lengths to stop them.

* * *

WHEN MARGOT WOKE THE NEXT day, the desire to paint gripped her so strongly, Dylan had to beg her to eat breakfast.

Afterward, she set up her easel, placed her canvas, lifted her palette, and began squeezing paint from tubes. Off in the distance, she heard a voice—Dylan's?—but so focused was she on her task that the image rising in her mind overwhelmed all else.

She started on the cavern first, for that's where her two figures were chained—somewhere deep underground. Poking among the tubes of paint, she mused. For the pockmarked earthen walls, rough-hewn from rock and under the glare of electric bulbs, only brown, black, and yellow would do. No surface was smooth, and all along the walls, niches had been carved, as if for beds—maybe tombs? The room was vast, but her canvas today would encompass only one corner of a wall where two men sat, side by side, on a bare floor. Chains bolted in the rock led to iron collars wrapping both men's ankles.

As her brush flew over the canvas, she didn't know who these men were, only that their faces would appear, in their own good time, as the spirit moved her. Always it was thus.

The morning heat rose, and sweat dripped off her forehead.

Time passed, and when next she glanced at the clock, it was noon. Dylan called out that lunch was ready, but she ignored his entreaty.

Sometime later, he called again through the door. But she ignored the voice, dipped her brush in the oil, and concentrated on her task.

* * *

AFTER BEING REBUFFED FOR THE third time that day, Dylan left Margot to her work. He'd never seen her so entranced, so focused she could barely acknowledge him. When five o'clock came and went and she was still locked inside her new studio, he got the hint. He walked to the patio under a trellis covered by overhead vines. The afternoon sun was hot, the shadows beneath the trellis, cool.

Emilio sat at a table, nursing a glass of wine, and Dylan accepted Emilio's offer to pour one for himself.

"She works too hard, I think." The former bishop raised his glass toward the house.

"It's her gift." Dylan sipped. "Once she starts painting, she's so consumed, she can't stop till she's finished."

"I am curious to see her creation. That such a one as her, one upon whom the Holy God has laid his hand, is here in my house—I am indeed humbled. How is it she was not taken with the others? And, if I may ask, the same question for you."

Dylan explained how an archbishop's denunciation made her renounce her faith and how he prayed to be left behind.

"I am ashamed for my colleague, the archbishop, that he so egregiously failed to see what I see in her work. And I honor your selflessness and the love you showed by asking to remain behind. So many of us have been so wrong about so many things. Here I am, a bishop, not taken, though many of my priests and parishioners were."

"You are not alone, signore. The world today is filled with those who now regret what they did or didn't believe."

The muffled sound of wind chimes rose from Dylan's pocket, and he pulled out his phone. It was Chelsea, calling the new number he had texted her earlier. "Excuse me, signore." He walked to the edge of the trellis just short of the hot Tuscan sun. "I'm glad to hear from you, sis." He explained where they were staying now and why. "But what have you learned?"

"I'm working at Veritas headquarters. I'm done for the day, walking home to the apartment Father arranged for me. Their brochures and website say they're a computer, telecom, and security company. But I've seen things, and I suspect they do far more than that. The company's building is huge, a twenty-story tower with offices on every floor. My job is to do detailed research on people they want to hire or people they have their eye on, even current employees. I'm essentially spying on people's lives, Dylan, and I don't like it."

"You need to do whatever they tell you until we discover where they took Caleb."

"Of course." In the background, traffic rumbled, and horns honked. "I tried searching on Caleb's name, but nothing came up. Security is tight here. After a week or so, if I work out, Father says I'll get a higher access level. Who knows if even that will be enough? So just sit tight."

"Margot's working on another painting right now. I don't know what it is, but it's got her mesmerized."

"Let me know if she sees anything important. I'm almost home. But since Father got my apartment through the company, I'm suspicious of it. I won't be calling you from there, and if you want to call me, text first. Then I'll go outside and call you back."

"Okay. But after hearing Sergei's warning, I suggest you buy another phone and use that one only to call me."

"That's pretty paranoid, but okay. I'll do it."

Bettino's car came down the drive, and Dylan hung up.

Emilio rose from his seat. "Our friend has arrived to cook us another fine dinner."

Dylan followed but stopped first at the door to Margot's new studio.

* * *

ARCHING HER BACK, MARGOT STEPPED away from the easel. Her fingers were cramped. Her feet were sore from standing all day. And she needed a shower. But the painting was finished. A knock came at the door, and she opened it.

"Come in." She flashed Dylan a smile. "I won't bite."

"You were rather intense today." He grinned in return.

"Sorry." She shifted the painting on the easel. "This is one of the more important pieces I've ever worked on."

He stepped closer to examine it.

His eyes widened, and then he gaped at her. "It's Caleb. And the mystery man from your other paintings. The two are chained together."

"They're down in some kind of dungeon. So if we find Caleb, we'll also find our mystery man."

"Do you have any idea where this is?"

She frowned. "No."

"Who is this person that keeps appearing in your visions?"

"I wish I knew. But he's important. This is the third time I've painted him."

"Whoever he is, Caleb's fate—and apparently ours—is tied up with his."

CHAPTER 57
VERITAS SYSTEMS

Rome, Italy

Friday morning, Chelsea stopped as usual at Flavio Bellini's desk where her boss handed her a pile of papers.

"These are the latest employee applications," said Flavio, "and we need to know all we can about them. Dig deep."

She scanned the list. Some had addresses in the US. More were from Italy, France, Belgium, Morocco, Australia, and the UK—wherever they spoke Italian, French, or English, the languages in which she was proficient.

Flavio then handed her a second pile. A scan told her they were applicants she'd investigated yesterday. She raised a questioning glance.

"I want you to go deeper with these. I realize this is only your first week, but you failed to cross-check them for religious affiliations—especially Christian connections—and contributions to conservative political parties. I also want to see your analysis of all social media posts for the last two years. Find out all that's relevant about how they think, vote, and believe. We don't want employees on staff with subversive ideas or views antithetical to our cause."

Dutifully taking the two piles, she tucked them to her chest. Then she walked to her cubicle and sat before her terminal.

Why, exactly, was a computer and telecom company concerned about their "cause"? When Flavio talked about it, he made it sound almost political. Once, she even asked the woman across the aisle about it. But she just shrugged and pointed to the wall and its globe depicting Europe and Africa and the motto beneath: "Security and Information For The World". But that didn't explain why Veritas Systems needed a "cause" and why she needed to vet employee applications as though they were joining the FBI or the CIA.

The company had given her the power to dig deeply into peoples' lives. As she'd learned on her first day, Veritas had five levels of clearance, and she was assigned level three. With a frown, Flavio told her that only her father's position allowed her, as a new employee, to skip the usual probationary period and receive a level only two steps from the highest.

She did her job, yes, but she hated it. What made religious and conservative views "antithetical" to the company's beliefs? She always thought of herself as a liberal, but having a person's deeply personal views disqualify them for a job troubled her. And why was the company especially concerned about new Christians?

But hadn't the party in power in the US, the one she'd voted for, removed "one nation under God" from the pledge of allegiance? And according to Dylan, much of their party platform was in direct opposition to the Bible. And after winning an election, the big tech companies and social media oligarchs had begun a purge of all conservative viewpoints. Maybe she shouldn't be surprised Veritas was just like them?

After working until midmorning, she grabbed her empty coffee cup, rose from her chair, and stepped into the aisle. The cubicle beside her belonged to Dino Castiglione, a Sicilian who had never once smiled her way. And every time she passed his office, his sliding plastic door was closed. He always held his phone conversations in a near-whisper.

Turning right, she followed the aisle toward the break room. But as she crossed the wide hallway near the elevators, there stood her father, chatting with Flavio.

"Chelsea!" He motioned for her to join them. "I was just coming for you. I'm so glad you're here at Veritas. Have I told you that?"

"Yes, Dad, many times."

"Flavio tells me you're doing good work with only a few glitches, understandable after just one week on the job."

She nodded.

"May I borrow her for a moment?" he asked her boss.

When Flavio nodded, Father waved her to follow. "Come to my office. There's someone I want you to meet."

Down the long aisle they went. There must be four hundred cubicles on this side of the elevators, separated into quarters by hallways, further separated by aisles. Another big room just like it occupied the elevators' north side. All of them worked for Father. And this was only one of ten floors in his charge. At the end nearest the elevators, real offices with real walls and doors lined the wall for the supervisors. Father led her toward the corner office by the windows. When they reached his door, he punched four buttons on a keypad. It buzzed, and they entered.

He led her past a frosted glass door into an office three times larger than the rest. It boasted oak-paneled walls on three sides, a plush carpet, and four cushioned chairs waiting before a massive mahogany desk, with a smaller computer desk beyond. A counter against one wall tempted the visitor with a basket of fruit and cookies beside bottles of wine, whiskey, brandy, vodka, and amaretto. A half-height refrigerator hummed beneath.

A man now stood at Father's picture window, his back to them. He was looking east toward the park and artificial lake dividing Veritas Systems from Worldnet headquarters.

In the break room, the joke was that the lake was stocked with piranha, waiting to receive employees who had three bad performance reviews. What did that say about company morale?

"Carlo Scutari," said Father, "I would like you to meet my daughter, Chelsea."

When the man whirled and offered his hand, she took it. "Glad to meet you, Signore Scutari." He was middle-aged, of medium height, with short black hair and a hooknose. But his gaze was bereft of emotion, impassive, cold as stone. Involuntarily, she shivered.

"Carlo and I are working on an arrangement with Worldnet." Father beamed. "We're expecting big things from the partnership."

"That we are." Signore Scutari crossed his arms.

"Isn't Worldnet owned by . . . Davato?" Even as she asked the question, she knew the answer.

"It is, signorina." Scutari's glance turned toward Father. "I must be going. I will call you tomorrow."

When they were alone, Father laid a hand on her shoulder. "Davato—can you believe it? And Worldnet. We are lucky to be here—you and I—both working for such an important company as Veritas."

"It's important, yes. But, Father, what does Veritas Systems actually do?"

A frown wrinkled his brows. "As you were told when you were hired, we are a vast computer hardware, software, and telecom company. You are in the Security Division where we are creating the biggest worldwide security monitoring, tracking, and information-gathering system the world has ever seen. As far as the rest of Veritas—that is confidential and not your concern. All will be revealed in good time."

"Then tell me this—why is the company's *cause* so important I have to dig deep into peoples' lives—looking at their politics, religion, social media posts, and personal stuff? You'd think we were screening people for the Secret Service."

"Chelsea"—he squeezed her shoulder—"we cannot allow saboteurs or purveyors of falsehood and lies in our ranks. We must be vigilant to keep out subversives who might later pit themselves against the company's goals once the full range of company activities is revealed. Maybe you've guessed we are far more than a mere computer, telecom, and security company, but for now, keep that to yourself. In any event, it's imperative we ensure the loyalty of all who work here. And whatever our means, know it's all for the greater good."

She took a deep breath. He was her father, but had he been corrupted by wealth, power, and ideals that were the opposite of everything in which she—and Dylan and Caleb—believed?

"Okay, thanks for clarifying." She managed to breathe out the words.

A woman in a business suit with her hair tied back to look like a man knocked, and Father opened the door. After they spoke briefly, he turned back into the room. "Excuse me for a moment." He stepped into the hall, the door clicked shut, and Chelsea was alone in the office.

Her glance fell on the computer desk against a near wall. The screen glowed with the words *Veritas Systems High-Security Actions.* Beneath were spaces for a login and password. On the other side of the frosted glass, Father was still talking.

As she set her coffee cup on the larger desk, her heart beat faster. She slid open the middle drawer. As usual, Father had written his login and password on an index card. She grabbed a yellow sticky from a pad and copied them. Barely had she ripped it away than Father reentered. "Sorry. All day long—it never ends. But that's what it's all about." He frowned at the yellow sticky in her hand. "What are you doing?"

"Oh"—she waved the paper—"just reminding myself to pick up some wine and olive oil for tonight." As the words left her mouth, she realized the desk drawer was still out. She reached across the desk, intentionally sliding the drawer shut with one hip while replacing his pen in its holder.

"How is your apartment?" he asked, apparently oblivious of what she'd done. "They do a good job of arranging everything, don't they?"

"They do, and it's a nice place. I like it." She tried to breathe normally. She started to turn away, nearly forgot her cup, then whirled and retrieved it. "But I'd better get back to work."

"Of course. And I'm glad you're wearing a decent dress today instead of that ripped black leather outfit you used to have. And your hair is back to its normal color. Suits you much better." Smiling, he ushered her out.

On her first day, they'd warned her about the grunge look. That night she'd dyed her hair back to blonde and switched to smart, Italian business attire. This week, she'd even grown to like her new look.

After staggering back to her cubicle, she sat. Father didn't have a clue how she felt or what she'd done. But that was typical of him, wasn't it?

Pulling out the yellow sticky, she entered the information into her terminal's login screen. This only elicited a warning message: "Top-level access programs must be entered from a secure terminal."

She sat back and stared. Some high-security programs must be tied to certain physical connections. She'd have to return to Father's office later and try from his terminal. But she'd need the code to open the keypad on his door. And she could only do that after hours when no one was around.

In the cubicle beside her, Dino Castiglione was now deep in conversation on his phone, speaking much louder than usual. She slid her chair up against the open-topped wall, all the better to hear.

"We need our own offices, I'm telling you. Secure and separate." Deep and commanding, Castiglione's voice rumbled from his cubicle. "Group D cannot continue working under these conditions. I've got a new employee in the cubicle beside me—Turner's daughter, can you believe?—and she doesn't even work for us. This is simply intolerable. She's out now, but the way you've got us mixed in with everybody else—I can't keep everything we talk about secret."

She held her breath. Castiglione thought she was gone.

"Sì, sì, I understand. We're just getting going, we don't yet have our own facilities, and you're working on it. But I warn you—this situation is untenable. You must speak with Turner."

Silence followed as the other party spoke.

"All right, I'll wait. But then there's the other problem of even greater importance—we need to expand the space for the high-profile detainees. There are too many of them down there with more coming in all the time. I know the difficulties, but it's possible, no? The machinery exists somewhere, doesn't it? And the walls are easily dug, are they not?"

More silence.

"Wait, wait, and wait some more—that's all you ever say. I'm not happy about this. You pay me to do this job, but I'm not getting the resources to do it properly." He slammed the phone onto its cradle and swore loud enough to carry across the aisle.

She rose from her chair, carefully slid her door open, and stepped into the aisle. Then she headed in the opposite direction from Castiglione's cubicle. If her neighbor thought his conversation wasn't being heard, she mustn't disabuse him of that thought. Taking the long way around, she strode toward the break room to fill her empty cup.

High-profile detainees? Some kind of underground cell? And Dino Castiglione's Group D was part of Veritas Systems' Security Division, also reporting to Father. This was far more than a security and computer company, and now it seemed possible it was connected with Caleb's disappearance.

Tonight, on her way home, she must relay everything to Dylan.

When she added it all up, this was not the kind of company she would've chosen to work for. More and more, she felt like a spy in an enemy camp. But if they were to free Caleb, she must be the model employee, hiding her disgust and her deep, unrelenting hatred of everything she was doing here.

CHAPTER 58
THE UNITUM IMPERIUM

Brussels, Belgium

Daniel 8:23 (HCSB): *Near the end of their kingdoms, when the rebels have reached the full measure of their sin, an insolent king, skilled in intrigue, will come to the throne.*

As the last dignitary entered the third-floor conference room of Worldnet's Brussels building, Davato motioned to Carlo Scutari. His aide then shut and locked the double doors and, crossing his arms, took a position on the perimeter. Today, he had assigned Carlo the role of guard, the only one allowed inside who wasn't part of the august body gathered here.

Seated around a long rectangular table were the presidents, chancellors, and leading ministers of Italy, Spain, Portugal, France, Germany, Belgium, the Netherlands, Greece, Austria, Hungary, Slovenia, Switzerland, and Serbia. Beside Davato at the table's head was François Desroches, president of the EU Commission. Many of the attendees now glanced around the room with what appeared to be embarrassment mingled with fear. For all but a few, the League had gathered enough compromising details to ruin political careers and even send some to jail.

A glass of ice water waited before each man or woman, and each wore a headset with microphone and headphones for translation. As at previous such gatherings, translators sat in soundproof Plexiglas booths on the room's perimeter. All were members of the League. From now on, he would use no UN translators.

Davato stood, and, before switching to English, he welcomed the group in French, Spanish, Italian, and German. "We meet today in secret conclave to finalize the document that each of you agreed to in private. Tomorrow, I will announce to the world our momentous decision and make public the reality of the Unitum Imperium. Friends"—he leaned forward and placed his hands on the table—"we are on the verge of creating a new nation, an entity far stronger and more powerful than the EU could ever have hoped to become. This great union of countries will be the catalyst for a new world order, leading us to a world of peace, prosperity, and progress, a place where man's inner spirit will be freed from all the restrictive dogma, ideologies, and false ideas of the past."

Briefly, he glanced down at a sheet of paper. "You know Russia has moved troops and tanks to its western border. We fear they are preparing to invade Ukraine, Belarus, Poland, and the Baltic countries. To counter this threat, I have asked each of you to provide men and material for a new defense force. The new army will also secure the viability of the Unitum Imperium as a nation. So I now ask you: Are each of you ready to deliver on your promise as early as tomorrow?"

Then he went around the table, asking each man and woman, one by one, how many troops, tanks, aircraft, and missiles they would contribute. François recorded their answers. When Davato didn't receive the numbers he was expecting, he quizzed that leader in his own language until they agreed that, yes, they would provide what was needed. Afterward, he sat back.

"Good. With our new force, we will establish a forward base in eastern Germany. We will place a second in eastern Hungary, another in southern Italy, and a fourth in northern France. When the forces are in place, all former national forces will be disbanded or merged with troops of the Unitum Imperium. At the same time, agents of my new Central Security Agency will set up offices in every village, town, and city. Any questions?"

Most around the table nodded, but the leaders of Germany and Serbia raised their hands.

"What will the Central Security Agency do?" asked Chancellor Conrad Weber.

"They will be my eyes and ears, the means by which I ensure the populace does not stray from our founding principles."

"I see." The chancellor rubbed his chin. "In that case, I would like to keep a reserve force accountable only to Deutschland. A small army composed of German nationals, ready to defend German interests."

"I agree," added President Vlado Cerović of Serbia. "Serbia, too, must have a force composed only of Serbs. For contingencies."

Davato pressed his fingers together. "If we are to become one nation, united in purpose and without division, we must abolish former national allegiances. For any of you to keep a national army would be to cling to nationalism and foment division among the rest. This is not what you agreed to earlier. When the time comes, if you do not join your forces with those of the Unitum Imperium, everything we have worked for will be at risk."

Murmurs of agreement rose from others around the table. Then Davato flipped to the end of a sheaf of papers, took a thick pen from François Desroches, and, while a photographer snapped, he signed his name. François Desroches signed for the EU.

"François and I have signed, and now I ask each of you to sign this treaty as it comes around. This is the formal document declaring that, as of noon tomorrow, each of you will dissolve your parliaments, courts, and executive branches of government, commit your armed forces as discussed, and place command of your nations under my sole and complete authority. This, my friends, is the true beginning of the Unitum Imperium. It is"—he patted the document—"truly the start of a new world order. Any questions?"

Chancellor Weber sat back, pursed his lips, and crossed his arms. "Mr. President, I am having second thoughts."

Silence swept the table as startled eyes focused on the German leader.

"In what . . . possible . . . regard?" Like a chill breeze off an ice shelf, Davato's voice slowed and deepened.

"How are we to trust that your leadership will be in the best interests of Deutschland? And this Central Security Agency—it sounds to me like a secret police organization. You ask a great deal, I think. After all, we have only your word."

Davato pushed away from the table and rose. He strolled around the backs of the seated ministers, chancellors, and presidents until he stood directly behind Weber. "What we are doing here, Conrad, is greater than any one man or country." His hands gripped the back of the chancellor's seat, and his voice now carried all the air of authority and power he could muster.

"The enterprise upon which we embark is greater than you, greater than me, greater than any of us. It's certainly greater than any one nation. We cannot stop it. It is destined to go forward. Indeed, anyone who stands in its way is placing himself in the path of inexorable, unstoppable history. And that is dangerous for Europe, dangerous for the world. No one here today, if he believes in the truth of what we are doing, can let that kind of rebellion against the common good go unchallenged. History will not be derailed by one man's prideful obstructionism, no matter how well-intentioned."

As Davato stepped beside him, Conrad Weber sat rigid, his face pale, his eyes fixed straight ahead. Beads of sweat dripped from his forehead.

"Those individuals who think they know better"—Davato's gaze lowered, and his voice deepened with power and veiled threat—"will find themselves trampled under the steamroller of a destiny greater than any one man's existence. Is not every sapling that stands alone before the hurricane ripped from its roots and washed to the sea? What is one man's life except a handful of sand slipping away onto an endless seashore? So I ask you, Chancellor Weber, what is the sacrifice of a single life when balanced against the greater good of a new, united Europe? The answer to that question is obvious, is it not? So will you not be the first to sign?" Davato motioned to François Desroches who brought the pen and the document.

With François on one side and Davato on the other, Davato slid the papers before the chancellor and, with an arched eyebrow, held out the pen.

Sweat dripping off his forehead, Weber stared at the pen. Shaking fingers took it and signed. As he did, a photographer snapped his picture.

As François followed, Davato took the papers next to the Serbian leader. His face pale, Vlado Cerović also signed as the photographer snapped again. Then he passed the treaty along as one after another leader affixed their signatures and were photographed. When the document made its way back to Davato at table's head, he beamed and held it aloft.

"My friends, what a great day for the world! Here is the beginning of our recovery from the Great Calamity and the start of world peace, prosperity, and progress. I now invite everyone for cocktails and hors d'oeuvres in the Blue Room. As you leave the conference room, I will present each of you with the gift of a gold medallion symbolizing our great union. Display it proudly during my speech at EU headquarters tomorrow."

With those words, the meeting was adjourned. A smiling Davato stood at the exit handing out medallions as more photographs were taken.

But in the Blue Room, the celebration seemed muted, not deserving of his great achievement. It was as if, having seen the full raw power of their leader revealed, the delegates were either awed, cowed, or struck dumb. But any of those reactions were acceptable. What mattered was that everyone had acquiesced to his reign. He was the secret head of the League of Abaddon, the one chosen by the Master himself to rule, and soon he would sit on the throne of the world.

Later, as the chauffeur drove Davato and Carlo back to the hotel, Davato turned to his aide. "Have we a replacement in mind for our friend from Germany?" His reflection bounced off the thick soundproof Plexiglas separating them from the driver in front. "And another for the Serbian leader?"

"We do, sir—men who are totally committed to our cause, men who are next in line for leadership."

"Then see to it that our special agent in Marseilles gets the word. Heart attack, stroke, accident—whatever is required. But it must appear natural and untraceable."

"Of course."

"Good." Davato poured a tumbler of whiskey from the car's portable bar. He poured another for Carlo then raised his glass in a toast. "To the Unitum Imperium and the Master's rule on earth."

Their glasses clinked. Davato smiled. And they drank.

CHAPTER 59

THE RECEPTION

Rome, Italy

At her father's urging and using one of his credit cards, Chelsea had bought an expensive evening dress for the grand reception tonight. Black and sleeveless, with a ruffled *V* front cut well below her breasts, it revealed almost too much skin. Below her hips, the dress tapered, and a side slit starting at her right waist ran to her ankles. Black high-heeled shoes and a black leather purse completed the outfit.

When she exited the elevator, exchanged her invitation for her plastic name card, and entered Worldnet's grand ballroom, each step revealed bare leg. And as she sauntered in, heads turned, exactly the effect she counted on. All the better for the daughter of the great Adam Turner to uncover the mysteries swirling about her.

"Everyone will be there Saturday night," her father had said. "The heads of most European countries, the CEOs of major companies, and bigwigs from Veritas Systems and Worldnet—with their wives, husbands, and mistresses. Davato himself is hosting it."

All this ran through her head as she forced a smile and stepped between the well-dressed men in tuxedos, women in the latest Italian and French fashions, and fawning, bowing waiters uniformed in red tuxedos.

After Davato's speech on Thursday, the entire office floor had been abuzz, and she saw this gathering as the after-game party. In a single day, the EU and the governments of its strongest member countries had been disbanded, replaced by the Unitum Imperium, a new country with a new army and a new leader—Davato, himself. As she'd listened to his words of inspiration, she believed he could fulfill all the high ideals and promises he'd made.

On the evening news, there'd been a few rumblings of complaint, some questions raised. But in the days that followed, the dissenting voices were stripped of media access, then drowned out by overwhelming praise for this new, mesmerizing leader. Everyone was agog over the man, filled with hope and wishing him well. Everyone was also a bit stunned by the speed of the changes.

It was only when she spoke with Dylan after the speech that a chilling fear replaced her initial admiration. "Don't be taken in," her brother had warned. "The number of his name is 666. He is, without question, the Antichrist."

His words were a bucket of ice water thrown at her face.

Tonight, she sought to lay bare the truth of Veritas Systems—

Because someone related to a group of demon worshipers, renting a building owned by Veritas, had kidnapped her brother.

Because a man in the cubicle beside her, working for Group D, was holding "high-profile detainees" in underground cells.

And because Veritas was only a hundred meters across the park from Worldnet, a company owned by a man Dylan had said was the Antichrist.

And now both companies were working hand in hand.

But as she walked among the most powerful people on the planet, some of whom were surely part of Davato's power cohort, a quiver of fear raced across her bare shoulders.

What in the world am I doing? Am I lamb-bait blundering into the lions' den?

"Mademoiselle." An older man, graying but handsome with a Gallic nose, stepped from the crowd and bowed. She recognized his face but couldn't place him. "What lucky young man accompanies you this evening?" He spoke French with a smile.

She presented her hand, and he grazed it with his lips.

"Tonight, monsieur, only my father." She read the white plastic name card pinned to his jacket—François Desroches. Vice President, Unitum Imperium.

"You are her?" He leaned forward to read the card pinned to her dress. "The daughter of Adam Turner?"

"I am." But how had her father's name spread so far as to be known by a man so high up in the new government?

"Truly enchanted." He bowed again as her father appeared.

"I see you've met my daughter, François." Father placed a familiar hand on the vice president.

"I have, and I was about to ask her to dinner tomorrow night." He winked. "But I would not think of doing so without her father's permission."

"With your reputation, François, perhaps I should take a father's prerogative and decline." Removing his hand, Father bowed.

"Oui, of course." François winked again, excused himself, and moved on.

Father planted hands on hips and examined her from head to foot. "When I said to buy something really nice, I had no idea you'd do *this*." He waved at her. "With that outfit, you should be under lock and key."

"Just doing my part as the daughter of the apparently famous Adam Turner." She flashed the extra-long lashes she'd put on.

"Come with me, Chelsea. You must meet the man himself." She followed as he led her in François Desroches's wake. They passed men she recognized from internet news articles, rich men heading the world's biggest companies, and powerful men in high office from every country of Europe. They passed famous movie actors and actresses, a best-selling English novelist, and well-known glitterati.

They stopped before two men whom François Desroches had just joined. In the center, the man who had mesmerized and startled the world dominated. He was speaking with a shorter man, his face pale and colorless, his green eyes hidden behind thick wire-rim spectacles perched on a nose too wide.

As they waited for an opening, Father whispered. "The man Davato is speaking with—they call him the Prophet."

She nodded.

"You are right, Sebastien," said Davato in Italian, his voice smooth, authoritative, "the world's religions should absolutely play a role in our future. We *should* convene the great conclave you suggest. And you *should* present their leaders with this idea of merging Buddhism, Hinduism, Taoism, Islam, and the animistic beliefs into one universal teaching. There are many ways to salvation, and surely they will see the advantages of leaving behind all the tired old dogmas by exploring what unites, not what divides us."

"What do we do about the new Christians?"

"There are so few of them." Davato frowned. "But of course, we will include them. Who can object to a free, fair, and universal salvation open to all?" Apparently just noticing Father, he stepped forward with his hand out. "Welcome, Adam Turner."

"Thank you, sir." Father bowed. "I would like to present my daughter, Chelsea."

As Davato's eyes swept her body, they widened, and a smile crossed his lips. "Enchanted, signorina. Most enchanted."

She drew in a sharp breath, curtsied, and as he reached for her hand, she presented it. His lips grazed her skin, and while they did, she had difficulty understanding how this man, so attractive and full of grace, could be what Dylan said he was. Then he released her and turned to the green-eyed man. "Adam and Chelsea, may I present Minister Sebastien Rey. He will head our new Ministry of Virtue." He cocked his head toward Father. "Adam heads the Security Division of Veritas Systems."

With his skin so pale, did Sebastien Rey ever see the sun? When he grasped her hand, she fought the urge to jerk it away. And when his cat-like eyes focused on hers, she suppressed a desire to shiver.

"The Ministry of Virtue?" She repossessed her hand. "What might such a ministry do?"

"Decency, sobriety, and worship—that is my charge, signorina, ideals sorely lacking in today's world." But as the words left his mouth, the lechery in his eyes left her feeling as if she'd just been undressed.

"How . . . interesting," was all she could think to respond. But she'd never heard of any government, anywhere, focusing on such things. "If I may ask, what is involved in promoting decency?"

"We will root out all the indecent ideas and attitudes that might inhibit mankind from our goals."

"Our goal is personal freedom, signorina," added Davato. "Unhindered freedom in the pursuit of action, thought, expression, and pleasure. We seek to free each person's heart and conscience so they may go wherever their greatest desires lead them."

"So you will remove all restrictions on the pursuit of pleasure?" she asked, trying not to gasp.

"In a sense, yes." Sebastien grinned, and again X-ray eyes seemed to bore through her clothes.

Her head was spinning. Was she to understand that the Ministry of Virtue was charged with promoting the exact opposite of what its name implied?

"Now you will excuse us, Adam, as we attend our other guests." Davato laid a hand on Adam's shoulder and winked. "We must talk a bit later, just you and I, hey?"

Father nodded. Then he, too, excused himself to mingle with the powerful, the wealthy, and the privileged—the new elite of Davato's outer circle.

Stunned by the candid revelations from the Unitum Imperium's leaders, she grabbed a champagne cocktail and nursed it by herself on one of the cushions at the side of the room.

Then, despite her trying to avoid eye contact, one after another of the unattached men approached and attempted to engage her in conversation.

She humored them, letting them think she was interested, and even danced with a few. But through all the small talk, she learned little. Later, she stood with one of the women from her floor, also the daughter of a Veritas executive. But the woman's conversation was shallow, and at the first opportunity, Chelsea excused herself and found the restroom.

As she was returning down the hallway toward the ballroom, she paused at a window overlooking the park. Beyond was the Veritas building, only a short walk around the pond. Her badge was in her purse, she could use some air, and what better opportunity to use her father's terminal than now when the building was empty?

Checking the hallway to ensure no one was looking, she headed for the back stairs.

CHAPTER 60

A REVELATION

Rome, Italy

A winding cement walkway bordered with fading blue and white lilies led from Worldnet headquarters to Chelsea's goal. Rome traffic roared in the distance. A chill in the air carried a hint of fall.

She walked briskly under palm trees that circled the pond, home of the mythical piranhas. The park was empty save for a couple kissing on a bench on the opposite side. She approached the Veritas building's main entrance and pushed through revolving doors into the lobby.

At the front, a guard raised a questioning glance as her badge slipped into the reader. The light turned green, and she flashed him a smile. "Some party over there," she said, "but I forgot to send in my report. It's due Monday."

A nod and a hungry gaze followed her. She yanked on the dress, but she couldn't cover more of her breasts than its design allowed. Only as she neared the corner did his eyes return to the screen and the sounds of a football match.

She exited the elevator on her floor and pushed through into the dark cavern of cubicles now lit only by a few red ceiling lights. She turned left off the first hallway and stopped at the end before her father's office. Pulling up her dress, she knelt and shone a penlight from her purse on the keypad. He'd punched four numbers, but what password would he have used?

His birth month and year didn't work. She tried day and year, but still no go. She entered the same numbers backward and other combinations of his and Mother's, but none would open the lock. Below the numbers, the keypad also displayed letters. When she punched *K, A, T, E*, the lock buzzed. Smiling, she pushed through. She was in.

She sat at the chair before his computer terminal and switched on the monitor. A screen appeared for Veritas Systems High-Security Actions. After entering Father's login and password, she was in.

Another screen popped up with a menu of icons. Reading through them, she stopped at Departments. Clicking on that brought up more icons for Hardware, Telecommunications, Software Services, Security Systems, Broadcasting and Entertainment, and Group D.

Though tempted to learn all she could about each, she clicked on the last one.

This displayed a new screen with six items: Mission Statement, Truth Squads, Truth Camps, High-Profile Detention, Tolerance Courts, and Termination Chamber.

Her heart pounding in her chest, she stared. They were right. This was no ordinary company. Her finger shook as she reached for Mission Statement, clicked, and read.

When duly served with a warrant from any authorized Ministry Division, Group D is charged with carrying out the arrest, detention, trial, incarceration, and execution of miscreants.

Her breath caught in her throat, and she froze. Was Group D some kind of secret police unit? What did any of this have to do with a computer and security company?

Backing out, she stared again at the screen full of icons. The implications of each were sinister, and her heart was racing. But she must stick to her goal.

She clicked on the High-Profile Detention icon then read the introductory statement.

Facilities listed are for administration use or high-profile internment. Note that internment facilities listed below are dedicated to prisoners of some importance, either because of unfortunate family ties, the possession of critical information, or for leaders of seditious groups whose presence in the camps might be inflammatory and for whom further interrogation is planned. Only individuals in the above categories are to be detained in the special facilities. Such individuals are *not* to be sent to the camps. They may be held there indefinitely or scheduled for later termination.

Below that was a list of six addresses, one each in Brussels, Paris, and Berlin and three in Rome. Beside each address was an alphabetic code.

She grabbed a yellow sticky from the main desk and began writing down everything for Rome. But before her pen started on Brussels, the main room's entrance door slammed shut, and she heard voices.

Lights flicked on all over the cubicles, and her heart nearly stopped.

She switched off the terminal, placed the computer chair back against its desk, and shot a frantic glance around the room. Nowhere to hide except under the big desk.

Voices—one of them Father's!—were heading her way.

"My office is the best place to talk." Father's voice moved closer. "I can offer you brandy, whiskey. . . whatever you like."

Bunching up her dress, she bent into a pretzel and kicked off her heels. She slipped under the desk and pulled the chair in after her. She tried to control her wild breathing as the office door buzzed, the door opened, and footsteps entered. The lights flicked on. But one shoe lay still on the rug beyond the chair. She reached out an arm out and snatched it back.

"Whiskey, if you please," said the visitor, and Chelsea almost gasped aloud. It was the voice of Davato himself, and she was trapped under the desk.

Then came the sounds of glasses clinking, the refrigerator door opening, ice dropping, and whiskey sloshing.

"I wanted to speak with you alone, Signore Turner," came the voice of authority. "In the morning, I'm leaving for Brussels, and you, of all people, need to know what will happen a week from Monday. I'm needed back at the reception, so this must be brief."

"Of course."

"To come to the point, ten days from now, I am announcing to the world the four ministries making up the Unitum Imperium government, the four great pillars that will remake society. We'll announce it that Monday, but for security reasons, I won't reveal the actual mechanics of implementation or where the ministries are located until then. One of those pillars is the Ministry of Truth. And at the proper time, we will reveal that Veritas Systems is, in reality, the Ministry of Truth, of which your Security Division is an integral part. Conventus Romanus is, of course, the Unitum Imperium."

A silence ensued, during which Chelsea feared they could hear her heart beating wildly. She scrunched her legs closer against her chest as if, by force of will, she could make herself invisible.

How could this be? All this time, had she been working for the Antichrist's government? Didn't the name for the Ministry of Truth come from the novel *1984*? How brazen was that? Or did they expect that, in today's world, so few people had read the past's great literature they could get away with it? Or were people supposed to recognize the allusion and realize they could do nothing about it? If it was supposed to strike fear and resignation into her heart, it succeeded. She shivered.

But Father was speaking. ". . . guessed as much, sir. We'll be ready to fulfill whatever role the Unitum Imperium presents us with."

"Good. I knew we'd chosen the right man for the job. But one more thing—it's come to my attention that your division is in need of more personnel, facilities, and resources."

"We are expanding and hiring so fast, it's hard to keep up. So yes, we could use more of everything."

"As I suspected. We'll move four floors of this building unrelated to your division to new quarters elsewhere in Rome. Those floors will then be assigned to you. You will also have funds to hire another three thousand employees."

"Thank you, sir. We'll put them to good use."

"And about Group D . . ."

"Yes?"

"Give them their own three floors. With separate badge access. They need tighter security than the rest."

"Certainly. I fully embrace the concept of Group D and its importance. No one who pits themselves against the company—er, the ministry—either in thought, word, or deed, should be allowed to roam free."

Chelsea gasped, but slapped a hand over her mouth. Had they heard?

"Good. Now we should return to the reception." Then his voice softened. "If her father permits, I propose to take a turn with your daughter around the dance floor?"

Her mouth opened, received the fingers of one hand, and she stifled a scream.

"Of course. I'm sure she'd be delighted."

"Charming creature, your Chelsea."

Glasses hit the drink stand, footsteps crossed the floor, and the door opened. The lights went out, first in the office, later in the main room. Then they were gone.

Extricating herself from the desk, she hurried to the computer terminal, logged on again, and navigated back to the list of detainee sites. After she'd copied down the addresses of the Brussels, Paris, and Berlin locations, she looked at her watch. No time to poke into the rest of the secrets here. She had to get back before Davato noticed she was gone.

Leaving her father's office, she hurried down the hall and took the elevator. On the main floor, she made certain the two men had left the building before crossing the entryway.

His eyes now wide, the man at the desk waved at her. "Did you see who just left?"

"No."

"It was Davato himself. He even said hello and shook my hand."

"Wow!" was all she could think to say. "Sorry I missed him."

Then she hurried out of the building and across the park. The two lovers were gone. At the ballroom, she flashed her white badge. Barely had she entered when the president of the Unitum Imperium approached, a wide smile on his lips, a hand outstretched. "Ah, there you are. Chelsea Turner, may I have the pleasure of the next dance?"

Hoping her face wasn't as pale and drained of blood as she felt, she flashed her extra-long lashes and nodded.

Then, as her heart hammered in her chest and she tried to slow her breathing, strong hands whirled her about the room, and she danced with the Antichrist. Hundreds of eyes followed their progress, and a photographer even snapped their picture. When it was over and she'd used up her store of fake smiles, her heart was beating so fast, she feared she would be sick.

After melting into the crowd, she backed out of the ballroom, slunk toward the elevator, and staggered along the sidewalk toward the Metro entrance. For one night, she'd had all the adventure she could take.

CHAPTER 61
THE HOUSE ON THE HILL

From Tuscany to Rome

Dylan was asleep when his phone imitated London's Big Ben tolling in the fog. Fumbling toward the screen's warm glow, he answered. It was Chelsea, and she sounded worried.

"Where are you?" Rubbing his eyes with one hand, he sat up in bed. From the other end of the call came the roar of traffic.

"Sitting on a bench in the dark only a block from my apartment. I'm calling on my second phone like you suggested. Dylan, I attended the reception I was telling you about, and you won't believe what I discovered. I'm scared."

She related all that happened from her evening, and when she'd finished, his heart was pounding.

"You danced with Davato? And Veritas Systems is part of the Antichrist's new government?" He'd just heard it, but as stunned as he was, he had to repeat it.

"Yes, and Father is one hundred and fifty percent with them. Group D *must* be the entity that took Caleb. I wrote down three addresses for what they call 'High-Profile Detention' here in Rome. They also have locations in Brussels, Paris, and Berlin."

"So you think Caleb is at one of them?"

"It would make sense. He's the son of the man charged with overseeing an important division that itself oversees Group D. That would qualify Caleb as a High-Profile Detainee. But I doubt if anyone has told Father they're holding his son prisoner."

"What if we told him? It's his son we're talking about. Maybe Father could get him released?" But the moment he said it, he doubted his own words.

"You didn't hear him like I did. Dylan, they've got their hooks in him—deep. He's on top of the world, with more power, managing more people than he ever had at Turner Enterprises. He'll never give that up. If he knew about Caleb, he might just let him rot in prison, claiming it was his own fault for being so stupid. He also expressed full support for the concept of Group D and what they do." Taking a deep breath, she then let it out. When she resumed, her voice slowed and deepened. "Dylan, I don't know who he is anymore. We can't risk it."

"All right." He glanced at the clock on the nightstand. It was after midnight. "Give me the addresses. Margot and I will catch a train for Rome tomorrow. We'll start there."

She read them off, and after he wrote them down, she asked, "What are you going to do?"

"Check them out, one by one. Somehow, we're going to get him out."

"Okay, just be careful."

* * *

THE NEXT MORNING, A SUNDAY, Dylan and Margot caught a train for Rome, arriving at one o'clock in the afternoon. He had reserved a modest room at the Albergo Colosseo where they dropped their luggage. It was mid-November on a warm day, and they ate lunch at an outdoor café.

They walked to the first location. But it was a construction site on a small plot of land where demolition machines sat idle, waiting for Monday.

They caught a taxi to the next place. The address revealed a small one-story office building, closed now, and when Dylan peered through the windows, it was dark inside. A sign painted above the door announced, "Amministrazione di Gruppo."

On this street as on most others, each house abutted its neighbor. "Let's walk around back." He led her down the block, turned left on a connecting street, then left again. He counted the houses until they came to what should be the building's backside. It was some kind of garage or warehouse. A sliding metal door filled the front with Amministrazione di Gruppo written on a smaller side door.

Turning the knob opened the side door. He stepped inside, and Margot followed.

316

A black van without windows was parked on the concrete floor. He walked past it. The sounds of a hammer hitting metal echoed from the room's far end, and Margot laid a hand on his shoulder. "Let's leave," she whispered. "They're not keeping him here."

"Not yet. Wait for me outside. I'll be out in a minute."

Frowning, she cocked her head then left.

He walked on, nearing a man hammering on something as he lay beneath a second black van. Tiptoeing past, Dylan reached rows of stacked boxes marked "Razioni Militari". Following a path between them, he stopped at a door. When he pulled, it opened. Then he found himself inside the main office, but all was dark. After flipping on his pocket penlight, he found four desks filling the room, but their drawers were locked as were the file cabinets lining one wall. He searched the room's perimeter but found no stairwell leading to a cellar.

They kept no prisoners here.

Quietly, he retraced his steps, passing the man still pounding beneath the car. He hadn't gone two meters when a voice called out from behind in Italian. "You, there!"

He spun and said in Italian, "I guess this isn't an auto repair shop?"

"No. And you shouldn't be here." The man shot to his feet and, with an irritated expression, waved toward the exit. "Get out! Get out!"

"Sì, I am sorry. I had the wrong address."

The man shooed him all the way to the door. Then, after Dylan stepped into the street, the door slammed, and the lock clicked shut.

"You were right," he said to Margot. "There are no detainees here. But I found stacks of boxes filled with military rations. Let's try the last address."

They hailed a taxi, gave the driver the address, and the car wove through traffic, much lighter on a Sunday. The Citroen labored up a narrow lane, climbing a hill in a run-down section of the city. Graffiti decorated the bricks, and weeds sprouted from cracks in the steps. Just before reaching the address, they passed tumbled-down ruins in a yard filled with tall, dry weeds. Rafters, broken bricks, and a tangle of wood attested to a building collapse on a property long abandoned.

But as the car neared the next house and their goal, Margot gasped, and Dylan's heart raced.

The building was an ancient structure with a short, unkempt yard, and as soon as Dylan saw it, he ordered the driver to slow down. Lounging on the steps outside, two men smoked cigarettes.

"That's it!" Margot whispered beside him. "The house I painted."

"Yes, and look through the windows." He caught the shadow of a man carrying an automatic weapon. To the driver, he said, "Keep driving, but slowly."

They crept up the hill, and Dylan sat back, wondering how they would ever get past all those men with guns.

The cab passed six more houses, all constructed of ancient stone, some probably a hundred years old or more. But where the seventh house should have been, the lot had been excavated, replaced by a low one-story metal office building at the lot's far edge. Asphalt parking spaces filled the front. Above the building, a sign announced in bold letters: "Tour Delle Catacombe. 12:00, 13:30, 15:00, e 16:30. Lunedi al Sabato."

"Catacomb tours!" Even as the words escaped his lips, a plan formed in his mind.

"Are you thinking what I'm thinking?"

Putting a finger to his lips, he nodded. "It appears that after the vanishing, they're down to two tours a day. We need to come back tomorrow."

But he kept the rest of his thoughts to himself until the taxi driver dropped them off and they were walking back to their hotel. Then he faced Margot. "Could the painting with Caleb chained to the mystery man have been in the catacombs?"

"Yes! But that tour starts well over a hundred meters from the house."

"Catacombs stretch everywhere beneath the outlying sections of Rome. Who knows how far they extend? We're going back tomorrow, and we're taking that tour. Let's see if the catacombs head north toward our mystery house."

"Then what?"

"Then we're going exploring."

CHAPTER 62
THE CATACOMB TOUR

Rome, Italy

Atter the cab dropped Dylan and Margot, they were twenty minutes early for the one-thirty tour. Passing a bus occupying much of the parking lot, they entered the tour office, a worked-over metal construction shed. The two entrance doors had no deadbolts, only knob locks. Another door led to the back of the building, also without a deadbolt. In a roped-off area, he stood in line behind a crowd of students and paid a frowning middle-aged woman for two tickets. They waited with the students, all between twelve and fifteen, as they chatted loudly, and a teacher tried unsuccessfully to keep the noise down.

Eventually, a young woman wearing a black uniform rose from underground steps. But when she saw the crowd lined up, she threw up her hands and approached the older employee. For a time, the two argued before the young one gave up.

Bearing a forced smile, she faced her charges. "We normally don't lead so many down at once. Some passages are narrow, and with so many, it's hard to hear. Can anyone take the next tour in an hour and a half?"

When no one volunteered, she shrugged. "Then follow me. Please watch your step and use the handrails. It's fifty meters down, and some steps are slippery."

Dylan held Margot back until they were last. Then they descended stone steps carved from brown rock. As they stepped lower, the air cooled. Trickles of water seeped from cracks in the walls and dripped down the stairs. Electric lights strung along the walls lit the way.

At the bottom, they arrived in a large cavern, and the woman began her spiel. "Back in the second century when Rome was much smaller"— her voice echoed back from the stone—"the Senate ordered that no graves be dug within the city proper. They were worried about sanitation and the scarcity of land. In and around Rome, there are some forty different catacombs, with more being discovered all the time. Although their purpose was originally for burial, we find many underground chapels used for later worship, especially as Christian persecution spread. We'll now move to one of these. On the way, notice the many chambers dug into the aisles where they placed the dead. We think we took out all of the skeletons, but if any sit up to watch us pass, please let me know."

Laughter followed, and the group swarmed deeper into the tunnel. They crossed other passages, and Dylan pulled out the compass he'd bought this morning. They were heading west. He needed to find a tunnel heading north.

The guide stopped them in a large chamber where a chipped, faded painting of Adam and Eve in the garden decorated one wall. Stone benches were arrayed before an altar bearing a cross, and the guide asked those in front to sit. "The reason the Romans dug their tombs down here was because of the soft rock called tufa, a volcanic rock that's easy to dig, which hardens after excavation. On our tour today, you will see a variety of Christian art, such as this depiction of . . ."

As she talked, Dylan checked his compass. From this chamber, tunnels led off in three directions. The east-west tunnels were open, strung with lights for the tour. But the dark tunnel to the north was roped off and bore a sign saying, "Ingresso Vietato." He touched Margot's arm and whispered. "I'm going to explore that passage. You stay with the tour. I'll catch up with you later."

After she nodded, he slipped to the back of the room behind students crowding the edge. When no one was looking, he stepped over the rope into darkness. The woman's spiel echoed from the tunnel behind, fainter with each step. When he could barely see, he flicked on the flashlight he'd bought this morning.

Walking faster now, he made sure the tunnel still headed north and started counting steps. He estimated it was about one hundred and fifty meters to the house, which translated into about one hundred and eighty steps.

The passage was damp, and other tunnels occasionally branched off. At eighty steps, he entered another large room, this one lined with shadowy crypts halfway to the ceiling. Two tunnels led away, and he took the one heading northwest. Thirty steps later, the passage bent slightly east.

A light appeared at the end, and he switched off the flashlight.

With the light came voices, and he slowed. He turned a corner, and vertical iron bars blocked the way. Five meters beyond stood a second, similar barrier. And beyond that—a huge cavern, illuminated by electric lights.

As the room came into view, he gasped.

Prisoners occupied the entire cavern. Each was chained to an iron ring bolted to the floor or the wall. Near each prisoner was a bucket—for waste? Even here, a foul smell wafted occasionally past him. Then one of the prisoners slid into view from the right and rested his back against the iron grate.

Dylan moved from one side of the bars to another, but he could see only the room's center. Was Caleb even here? On the opposite wall, two guards with machine guns sat on chairs, looking bored, reading their phones. Behind those two, another set of vertical bars blocked steps leading to the surface. Its gate stood open.

Looking at the scene, it was as if he'd expanded Margot's painting of Caleb to reveal the floor around him. Only without Caleb.

Focusing now on the iron rods, he slid one hand up and down its slimy metal. They were set in concrete-filled holes drilled into the rock, above and below. A gate on hinges occupied the middle half of the barrier. Rusty chains, secured by a heavy padlock, wrapped the frame to the gate. The second barrier was the same.

He hoped the padlocks weren't so rusty they would open with some taps of a hammer. But once inside the cavern, how would he free the men? And the moment he entered, what about the guards with guns?

The man leaning his back against the far set of bars was only five meters away. That gave him an idea.

"Psst!" he whispered. "Can you hear me?" He spoke in Italian, hoping the man would understand.

Twice more, he called, and on the third time, the man shifted in his seat and glanced behind him. "Who are you?" he asked in French.

"A friend. I want to free all of you," Dylan responded. "Can you answer some questions?"

Though the man's face was in shadow, he nodded.

"How many guards are in there? And when do they change shifts?"

"Two, monsieur. They change at eight in the morning, sixteen hundred, and midnight. When they change, the guards here always go up top. There is always a delay before the next ones come down."

"How long a delay?"

"No more than five minutes."

"That's good. I think I can open these gates, but what about your chains?"

"Behind the guard post are two sets of keys on hooks. They leave them there untended. They must believe no one can get anywhere close to their post. Twice a day, one of them comes around to empty our waste buckets and feed us."

"Good. But you'd better turn around. One of them is looking this way." Since Dylan was in shadows, the guard wouldn't be able to see him.

The man shifted position.

"All right," Dylan called to his back. "I'll try to come tomorrow night. But keep it to yourself."

The man twisted around again. "No. It must be tonight." His tone was urgent. "Tomorrow, they're moving us." Then he faced forward once more. But one of the guards was making his way through the prisoners toward the man.

"Then tonight it must be. At midnight."

Dylan hurried back through the passage, switching on his flashlight after he rounded the corner. He entered the first chapel room then jogged to the place where he'd left the group, but everyone had gone on.

Hurrying now, he followed the trail of lights on the ceiling, hoping it wouldn't branch off. When he turned a corner, he met the young woman leading the entire group back toward him.

"Signore," she scolded, "you must stay with the group."

"Sorry." He waited until the students passed and he met up with Margot. Smiling, he whispered in her ear. "I found them. We're coming back tonight."

She returned a broad smile, and they followed the tour to its end.

Outside, taxis were waiting. He ordered their driver to go up and over the hill instead of returning how they'd come. Once back in the city, they stopped at a hardware store. Inside, he whispered his plan to a startled Margot. She expressed reservations, but agreed it was the best they could come up with. After purchasing what he needed, they returned to their hotel.

"There's one more piece to my plan," he said, "but it must wait for Chelsea to get off work."

"What do you want her for?"

He smiled. "A diversion."

CHAPTER 63
THE MAN OF SORROWS

Rome, Italy

Caleb held out his bowl, and the guard scooped into it a portion of beans then dropped a hunk of bread on top. As the second guard stood watch, the first would always make the rounds then return with pitchers to fill cups with water. The sounds of wooden spoons scraping bowls—no metal allowed—filled the room.

Beside him, Baruch Abramovich finished first and sat back against the wall with a contented sigh. "It is good, my friend," said Baruch. "There could be more, but God provides, even here."

Caleb gave his new friend a wry glance. "But it's the same, morning and evening—beans and bread, beans and bread."

"Two days ago, they gave us a bit of cheese. Are you forgetting that?"

"No." Caleb smiled. With his curly black hair, thick eyebrows, wide nose, and friendly smile, Baruch had become a welcome companion in chains. "How is it you see the good in this slop while the rest of us are crying out for some variety, any variety."

"Caleb, you are like the Israelites who complained to Moses about the manna as he led them through the desert."

"Touché." Caleb shifted on the stone floor, rattling the chain on his ankle. "Still, if I ever get out of here, I'm not eating another bean the rest of my life."

"A bit of butter for the bread would be nice."

He threw a glance at a smiling Baruch. "You're putting me on, aren't you? Did I just hear a complaint?"

"Just a mild one. For your benefit." Then he slapped Caleb's knee and laughed.

Caleb grinned as the guard's footsteps climbed the steps to the guard station. The man would soon return with water.

He faced his friend again. "But have you heard the rumor? Tomorrow, they're moving us to a different part of the catacombs. We're going to be cramped for weeks, packed into narrow passages while they expand this place."

"Which means they'll be bringing more prisoners down here. Let us pray they stop after that—not for our sakes, but for the new ones they plan to bring down."

"Why are you here, Baruch? You've never said."

"Neither have you. As for me, I am not exactly sure. I am a nobody. Just a man who leads others in prayer, who listens to their troubles, guides them, and teaches them."

"But the others you lead—they're all Jewish?"

"Of course."

"How many?"

"My flock was a small group of twelve, but no"—he rubbed his forehead—"if you count the other group, twenty-three in all. They sent me warnings to stop what I was doing. But that I could not do. Then one day, they took me. My followers and I were close, very close, and my mission with them was not complete. They took me much too soon. That, I can complain about." A frown knit his thick eyebrows together. "But what about you, Caleb? Why are you here?"

"I started a blog that had a lot of followers. Thousands of hits a day. I was telling folks the truth about the vanishing—that it wasn't because of aliens. It was because Jesus came to earth to take his people up to Heaven at the end of this age. It's called the Christian Rapture, and I came to faith too late. They also warned me. But before the thugs took me away, they sent a demon to warn me."

"A demon?" Baruch's eyes widened. "Seriously?"

"Yes, and that encounter left me injured for weeks. Later, I started my blog again. Then one day, men broke into my apartment. They drugged me, and I woke up here in Italy. My blog was focused on the truth. And I assume that's why I'm here. They don't want to hear the truth."

"Most interesting." He rubbed his chin. "If the men doing this could send a demon to stop you, then . . ."

"Then this is a spiritual battle. And what I was telling folks was the truth."

"I see you believe this with all your heart—that the prophet Jesus took his people out of this life? I know of this 'Rapture' theory but have never encountered anyone who believed it as you do."

"Then what do you think happened on V-Day?"

"V-Day—that's what you Americans call the vanishing?"

"Yes."

"I–I never decided, one way or another. Somehow, it is part of God's plan, but what . . . I don't know. It is a mystery."

"Can I ask you a personal question?" Caleb stretched out his feet, again rattling the ankle chain.

"There is nothing you cannot ask me, my friend."

"Why don't you believe Jesus is the Son of God?"

Baruch peered across the cavern. "Ah, there is *that*, isn't there? The Jewish people believe the Christ has yet to come. We do not believe your Jesus was the one."

"But there is a passage in Isaiah—fifty-three, I think—that describes him. And it perfectly fits the Jesus who died on the cross. I don't have a Bible here, or I'd show it to you."

"Ah, but I do." Baruch glanced around then pulled from his shirt's inner pocket a miniature book. "I have always carried this with me, and they never found it. It's our Tanakh, what you Christians call the Old Testament." He flipped through pages of minuscule print. Then he read:

My servant grew up in the LORD's presence like a tender green shoot, like a root in dry ground. There was nothing beautiful or majestic about his appearance, nothing to attract us to him. He was despised and rejected—a man of sorrows, acquainted with deepest grief. We turned our backs on him and looked the other way. He was despised, and we did not care.

Yet it was our weaknesses he carried; it was our sorrows that weighed him down. And we thought his troubles were a punishment from God, a punishment for his own sins! But he was pierced for our rebellion, crushed for our sins. He was beaten so we could be whole. He was whipped so we could be healed.

All of us, like sheep, have strayed away. We have left God's paths to follow our own. Yet the LORD laid on him the sins of us all. He was oppressed and treated harshly, yet he never said a word. He was led like a lamb to the slaughter. And as a sheep is silent before the shearers, he did not open his mouth. Unjustly condemned, he was led away. No one cared that he died without descendants, that his life was cut short in midstream.

But he was struck down for the rebellion of my people. He had done no wrong and had never deceived anyone. But he was buried like a criminal; he was put in a rich man's grave. But it was the LORD's good plan to crush him and cause him grief.

Yet when his life is made an offering for sin, he will have many descendants. He will enjoy a long life, and the LORD's good plan will prosper in his hands. When he sees all that is accomplished by his anguish, he will be satisfied. And because of his experience, my righteous servant will make it possible for many to be counted righteous, for he will bear all their sins. I will give him the honors of a victorious soldier, because he exposed himself to death. He was counted among the rebels. He bore the sins of many and interceded for rebels.

After Baruch finished reading, he raised unfocused eyes across the room.

"So what do you think?" asked Caleb. "Does that not describe, in perfect detail, the Jesus that Christians believe in?"

"I have read this many times and never associated the man of sorrows with the Messiah. That is what the rabbis teach. But you make an interesting point. And if a demon tried to stop you from putting out your blog . . ." Baruch shook his head. "I will have to meditate on this. And pray."

Footsteps approached, a shadow loomed above them, and Caleb's heart skipped a beat.

"What's that in your hand?" The guard holding two water pitchers nodded down at Baruch's book.

"It is a Tanakh." Baruch lifted a kindly gaze. "The Word of God."

"Give it to me." Setting one pitcher on the ground, the guard reached down.

Baruch handed him the book, and the guard flipped through its pages. "This is forbidden."

"It will refresh your soul, my friend. I suggest you read it."

The guard knelt and unchained Baruch's ankle bracelet. "Get up." A baton slapped Baruch's leg, and he winced. "Now!"

Baruch stood, and the guard led him away, poking him with the baton as he walked.

Caleb feared for him. Anyone breaking the rules was beaten, often severely. Sometimes they staggered back days later, ugly welts all over their bodies. He shuddered.

It was his request that had brought out Baruch's Old Testament, and he felt responsible for this. In all the time they'd been chained together, Caleb had never seen him read it. But, of course, when they were supposed to be sleeping—under the ever-present electric lights—Baruch could have read the book unseen.

The man was a saint, the godliest person Caleb had ever met, and nothing must happen to him. He closed his eyes, squeezing out a tear, and prayed for his friend.

CHAPTER 64
OUT OF THE CATACOMBS

Rome, Italy

After Chelsea got off work that evening, she met Dylan in a park. They sat before a fountain where a stone nymph burbled water from her mouth into a pool of algae and water lilies. But when he outlined his plan to free their brother, a shiver started in her shoulders and spread to her arms. "I've already taken a lot of chances, but this is riskier yet."

"Should we let Caleb rot down there instead?"

"Of course not." She couldn't imagine being chained in a cave underground. She covered her mouth with her hands. "All right. I'll do what you ask."

"Timing is crucial. You must create your diversion exactly at midnight. Not a minute earlier or later. That's when the guards change. That's when we'll break in from below."

"Okay."

"I suggest you drive by the place now to see what you're facing."

"I will." Breathing slowly, she released the tension she felt after hearing Dylan's crazy plan. "If I have to break the law to free my brother"— she smiled—"I should start my criminal career by casing the joint." She hugged him, and they parted.

* * *

At eleven ten, Dylan parked the first rental van in the tour company's parking lot. They'd already checked out of the hotel. Margot now pulled a second van in beside the first. She would leave the keys in the ignition. He would take the keys to his van with him. Their backpacks were in a third rented vehicle parked near the train station.

As expected, the lot, the tour building, and the nearby houses were dark. In the valley below, city lights cast a glow onto the clouds. Traffic, punctuated by an occasional horn, rumbled in the distance.

From the back of the van, he lifted a duffel bag with the afternoon's purchases—a dozen flashlights, two sets of pliers, a length of chain, a crowbar, bolt cutters, sledgehammer, claw hammer, screwdriver, padlock, and, just in case, a hacksaw.

Holding one of the flashlights, Margot followed him to the back of the building, out of sight of the road. He rammed the crowbar into the frame beside the doorknob and leaned into it. On the third try, the corrugated metal wall bent, and the latch popped out of the strike plate. They were in.

Inside, he headed to the stairwell, but a padlocked wooden door blocked his way to the stairs. He wedged the screwdriver beneath the lock plate. A few raps with the sledgehammer ripped screws from old wood.

He found the light switch, and glistening steps led down. They descended the long passage, their feet echoing to the bottom. There he switched on the next set of lights, and they followed the tour route. Where it met the underground chapel, they entered the roped-off tunnel. Flashlights now lit their way to the next large room, after which they traversed the passage to the iron barriers and the prison cave. They switched off their lights.

"It's eleven thirty." Dylan silently lowered the bag of tools and slumped to a seat. "We're early."

"Let's hope Chelsea creates a good diversion." Margot nestled against his shoulder.

"If she strikes at midnight when all the guards are up top, we'll have enough time."

She leaned closer. "We don't even know he's here, do we?"

"We can only trust that he is."

"Dylan?" She laid a hand on his knee. "There's something I want to say to you."

"What?"

"I never expected to be here with you, doing this. I could never have imagined what we're doing here tonight. But"—her eyes searched his—"I can't think of another person in all the world I'd rather be with right now."

He took her hands in his and squeezed. "You mean—you never imagined being down in the Roman catacombs at midnight, about to break into a prison to free a kidnapped brother you've never met, facing armed guards working for the Antichrist, after having been assaulted by a demon?" He grinned. "You mean, you'd rather be down here, doing this with me, than, say, lying on a beach somewhere with a glass of wine in your hand?"

"Well, when you put it that way . . ." A lopsided smile crossed her face. "No, really. The answer is yes! I have come to think a great deal of you."

He looked at his hands holding hers. Her words brought a rush of heat to his face. On impulse, he leaned over, gazed into her eyes, then pressed his lips to hers. When they parted, he was breathing fast. "I—I'm sorry." He glanced ahead. "I shouldn't have."

"No, don't apologize."

But as they parted, he happened to glance through the bars. Where the guards sat, he detected movement. The instant they left their posts was the signal to begin, and one of them was now standing, looking up the steps behind him, listening to someone. Turning back to the room, the man spoke briefly with the second guard then disappeared up the stairs.

"Oh no." Dylan stood and faced the bars. "This is not according to schedule."

"What is it?" Margot rose beside him.

"Something is happening, and it's too early for our diversion." He checked his watch again—eleven forty.

They both watched the steps where the first guard had gone. Minutes passed before he reappeared, leading down a chained man. But the prisoner limped and had to be helped along.

Dylan breathed his relief. "They're only bringing down another prisoner."

"But look—it's him!" Her voice rising, Margot pointed, and Dylan winced.

"Not so loud. Who?"

"The man in the painting. The one chained beside your brother."

Dylan squinted. "You're right! So Caleb must also be here. Somewhere."

The guard led the man into the main room then turned to Dylan's left, out of the line of sight. Then came the clinking of chains, the snapping of a lock, and the guard returned to his post.

It was now eleven forty-five, Caleb must be here, and everything depended on their sister.

* * *

CHELSEA PARKED HER RENTAL CAR some distance from her target. Eleven fifty according to her watch. The car was facing downhill, all the better for a quick getaway. She tried to slow her racing heart.

How strange to be here now, doing this, worrying about her "getaway". She was helping free her brother, yes, but it was far more than that, wasn't it? Her entire life had been one crusade after another—lately campaigning against racism, police brutality, minority injustice. Also marching for the climate and women's rights. But tonight, she found herself fighting against the worst enemy she could ever have imagined—the Antichrist and an evil worldwide regime.

On rare occasions, she'd gone to church but hardly listened to the messages. Most of the time, Pastor Freya's sermons focused on some issue Chelsea was already familiar with, like racism or LGBTQ rights. She knew little about the Bible or the Christ with whom Davato was surely a mortal enemy. What she'd learned of Christianity came from movies, and who could trust them? What she knew for sure had jumped out at her from her father's terminal: detention camps, truth squads, truth camps, tolerance courts, and, scariest of all, termination chambers. Just thinking about the activities of Veritas Systems—now the Ministry of Truth—sent a shiver across her shoulders.

She was helping free Caleb, and that was good. But more than that, being here now, fighting against the Antichrist, was the right thing to do.

Dylan had said how important her timing would be tonight. For the hundredth time, she glanced at her watch. Eleven fifty-five. It was time.

Taking a deep breath, she grabbed the two cans of gasoline from the floor and left the vehicle. She threw a nervous glance down the narrow lane. Only one house had a light on.

Her heart beat wildly. She was about to become a criminal. Breathing deeply, she lugged the cans up the lane toward the empty lot beside the house where Caleb was supposedly being kept.

Before sunset, she'd driven by the place, so she knew the layout. But now the only light came from the city glow bouncing off the clouds. It was enough. At the vacant lot, she waded through weeds and began splashing the contents of the first can onto the broken, tumbled timbers and dry grass. She emptied the second can, wiped her fingerprints from both, and wedged the cans between the now wet timbers. The smell of gasoline saturated the air.

She was now breathing so fast, spots burst before her eyes. She checked her watch. Five after twelve. Oh no. Behind schedule.

Shaking fingers pulled the throwaway phone from her pocket. She dialed the *Vigili del Fuoco*, the Rome fire department. In imitation of a male voice, she reported a blaze.

She laid the phone atop a timber, smashed it with her foot, then grabbed the lighter from her pocket. Stepping back, she flicked it. Nothing happened. She flicked again—still nothing. On the third try, it lit. Carefully, she lowered the flame to the edge.

A whoosh of blaze engulfed her work, singeing the hem of her blouse. She lurched backward.

The sheet of fire bursting from the gasoline was unexpected and frightening. She hadn't meant to create such a conflagration. It would certainly cause a diversion. With the inferno already spreading, engulfing the abandoned ruins and the entire lot, the fire department better come soon.

Whirling, she ran toward the car.

She was still running when the windows in the house beside her lit up, and a woman peered out. Chelsea slipped into the seat. She'd left the key in the ignition. Taking a deep breath, hoping the car would start, she turned the key. The car wouldn't start.

Oh no. This was just like in the movies. The getaway car never started, did it?

Again, she turned the ignition.

But it started. She rammed it into drive, and her foot slammed on the accelerator.

People were now running into the road.

The car squealed around them and down the hill.

Dylan had told her to cover the license plate before she climbed the hill, and now she was glad she'd listened. When she was out of sight down the lane, she stopped and ripped away the cloth. But her heart nearly stopped when she saw the car's clock—twelve o'clock. No! She looked again at her wristwatch, disagreeing with the car at twelve ten. Which was right? Well, at least the deed was done.

Trying to slow her breathing, she drove at a normal pace. Tonight, she would drop off the rental. Tomorrow, she'd return to work as if nothing had happened, as if she hadn't committed arson.

Even if her diversion might not have come at the right time, she hoped the rest of Dylan's plan worked. She'd done what she could, striking a blow for her brother and against the Antichrist.

* * *

AT 11:54, ONE OF THE guards went to the stairs and looked up as if someone was calling down. The guard exchanged words with whoever was at the top of the steps. Then he ran to the second guard to confer.

Dylan gripped the bars, his heart beating faster. This was not part of their routine.

The same guard then ascended the stairs, leaving the other man at his post.

It was 11:58.

Had Chelsea lit her fire too early? Would this throw them off their schedule?

Two long minutes passed while Dylan stood, peering across the room, hoping they would keep to their schedule.

The remaining guard began to pace. Occasionally he glanced up the stairs. At midnight, he leaned into the stairwell and called to someone above. Apparently, he received no answer, as he cupped his hands over his mouth and called again—repeatedly. The man looked again at his watch. At 12:04, he swept his gaze around the cavern, hesitated, then bounded up the steps.

Dylan sprang into action. As he'd done at the Italian hat company, he extended the padlock's shackle and began tapping the hammer on the side of the lock. But the locking pins wouldn't release.

It was 12:06.

His plan was falling apart.

"You're here!" The man Dylan had spoken with earlier had heard the hammering.

"Yes, and we must hurry. The guards have abandoned their schedule."

He tapped several more times. But the lock wouldn't release. He threw down the hammer and grabbed the bolt cutters.

Spreading the handles wide, he fastened the jaws around the chain—and squeezed with all his might. Nothing happened. The chain was thick.

It was 12:07.

Any second, the guards should return to their stations.

He found a different link, fastened the jaws, and squeezed. The chain snapped. With the pliers, he pulled the links further apart, and the chain released. He yanked the first gate open.

Sweating profusely, he moved to the second set of bars. He tried three different links, but none would snap.

"Dylan, look!" Margot pointed toward the guard station.

One of the guards had returned and was scanning the cavern.

Dylan flattened himself against the wall. He was in shadows. Hopefully, the man couldn't see him.

But after a quick look around, the guard again retreated up the stairs.

Dylan returned to his work. It wasn't until he'd tried the seventh link that the bolt cutters snapped the chain.

He and Margot rushed into the room.

It was 12:08.

The prisoners had heard the snapping of metal and the creaking of rusty gates. As the two rescuers raced across the floor, the men stood, and with them spread a growing murmur of hope.

As planned, Margot raced for the guards' station with the new chain and padlock while Dylan scanned the room to his left.

"Dylan?" He'd know that voice anywhere, and he spun toward it.

Caleb was standing beside the prisoner from the painting. Bruises now covered the mystery man's forehead and arms. One eye was almost swollen shut, as were his lips.

"Caleb, we're getting you out of here."

"I don't know how you did it." His brother grinned. "But you are a most welcome sight, indeed."

A glance at the guard station revealed that Margot had chained the gate. And she had both sets of keys in her hands.

He breathed out his relief.

She threw him one set, and he knelt to his brother's lock. The key clicked, and the manacles clanked to the floor. Beside him, Margot began freeing prisoners.

All through the cavern now rose questions and entreaties.

"Will you free us all?"

"How will we get out?"

"We're so glad you're here!"

Dylan unlocked the mystery man beside Caleb and passed the keys to a third prisoner. Then Dylan stood and shouted so everyone in the cavern could hear. "Free yourselves. I'll explain in a moment."

"Don't worry," answered one of the men. "We won't leave anyone behind."

Nodding, Caleb laid a hand on Dylan's shoulder. "This is Baruch. He's coming with us."

"We knew about him, but not his name. Glad to meet you, Baruch." Dylan shook his hand. Then he waved to Margot, kneeling a few meters away and freeing prisoners. "That is Margot Durand."

"The Belgian woman? You found her?"

"Yes, and we flew to Chicago together to free you. But let's get to the gate before it gets crowded."

The other three followed him to the exit. At the gate, Dylan scanned the cavern then cupped his hands around his mouth and shouted across the room. "We've got two vans outside. Not enough for everyone, but they'll take as many as will fit. This passage leads to a catacomb tour office about a hundred fifty meters away. Once you're on top, if you can't fit in one of the vans, head up the hill on foot. Down the street, you'll see fire engines and police where we've arranged a diversion. Now follow us."

The murmuring now mixed with the clanking of chains as the keys were passed along and men stood and headed for the exit.

At the guard station, the warders were rattling the locked gate. They'd been discovered.

"Let's go!" he said. Then he led the others through the gate. A handful had already stumbled into the dark passage before stopping. Kneeling, he distributed flashlights from the duffel bag, turned the rest on, and laid them on the ground for those who came after. There would soon be a steady stream of refugees out of the cavern. Hopefully, by the time the guards broke the chain and padlock, the prisoners would be gone.

With Caleb helping Baruch, the four led the others through the tunnels. The way behind was already crowded.

Out through the first cavern they went. Down the next passage. Along the electric-lit tunnel. Then to the steps. And up to the tour office.

He, Margot, Caleb, and Baruch were first into van number one. In moments, prisoners filled every seat, some even crammed, cross-legged, in back. He started the engine. As more men poured out of the building and found seats in the second van, he turned right onto the lane.

Downhill, whirling lights of fire engines and police cars flashed beside a blazing inferno. He floored the accelerator, but with everyone inside, the vehicle was sluggish.

As they climbed the hill, he kept peeking in the rearview mirror. Only the second van followed. Good. He'd planned an escape route, and his GPS led him up backstreets to the hilltop then down the other side.

A half-hour later, he parked outside Roma Termini, the central train station. He poked his head back inside. "The four of us are getting off here. The van is yours."

The men gushed their thanks, and they drove away. He hoped they could escape. Some would surely have contacts to help them, if not here in Rome, then somewhere in Italy. Amid all the confusion of the fire, those who couldn't take the second van should be able to slip away in the dark on foot.

They'd rented three vehicles using his Dalton Taylor passport and credit card. When the two vans weren't returned, the rental company would think them stolen. He'd never be able to use that ID again.

At one twenty in the morning, the station was open but deserted. While the others waited, he ran around the corner and drove their third rental, a Citroen, to the curb. From the back seat, he pulled out two pairs of trousers, shirts, socks, and sneakers and handed them to Caleb and Baruch. "I didn't know your sizes, but I guessed them from Margot's paintings."

"She drew us?" Caleb's eyes were wide. "Both of us?"

"Yes," said Margot. "That's how we found the house where they kept you and how we knew Baruch was somehow connected with you. After Dylan took me to your family's villa, my visions returned."

Caleb shook his head and exchanged a startled glance with Baruch.

"You must explain these visions." Baruch's voice was strong and pleasant, belying his swollen right eye and the bruises covering his face and arms.

"Later. Right now, you should wash, change, and dispose of those prison clothes." Dylan waved toward a nearby WC. "Then we're driving north."

Caleb looked at the clothes in his hand and at Baruch. Then he hugged his brother. "I don't know how you did all this, but it's amazing."

"It was God, Caleb. He led us to you."

Baruch smiled. "Didn't I tell you, Caleb, that we should trust in God?"

"You did."

Caleb and Baruch headed for the WC to change.

CHAPTER 65

THE HAND OF GOD

In the Tuscan Countryside

It was one forty-five in the morning when Dylan drove the rental car onto the E35 toward Firenze, and at this hour, traffic was light. Margot sat in front while Caleb and Baruch took the back seat.

When they were underway, Baruch leaned forward. "Dylan and Margot, I cannot thank you enough for what you have done. But can you please explain how you knew I was with my friend Caleb in the catacombs?"

Margot then described her gift of prophecy through art, how she turned from God after the archbishop's condemnation, how Dylan prayed to be left behind, and how her paintings showed not only precise details of the Rapture but also led them to the catacombs.

After she'd finished, Baruch sat back. "You have given me much to think about. When we arrive at this villa, I must see these paintings of yours. From what you have said, it is clear the hand of God is upon you."

"Yes," she answered. "Without divine guidance, we would never have found you. And God did this despite my turning away from him. I was so . . . stupid."

"But no, you returned to him, and the Lord is full of mercy. At one time or another, we have all had doubts. His love will never leave those who are his own."

"Thank you, Baruch. Your words are comforting."

"But there's one problem we haven't addressed," said Caleb. "I imagine I smell pizza. And I'm starving."

Dylan laughed. "You're not imagining it. I came prepared."

"Wonderful!" Caleb called out his happiness. "Food that's not beans!"

Margot pulled a box of pizza from under the front seat. It was cold, but the two former prisoners devoured it thankfully, with pieces left over. She also opened a bottle of wine and passed it over the seat.

For a time, the car sped on in a contented silence.

"Caleb," Dylan finally said, "tonight, we're going to Emilio Gallo's villa over the hill from our place. Men came looking for us at Father's villa, and Emilio graciously offered to hide us." Then Dylan told them all that had happened since Caleb had been captured, including how Father was now high up in Davato's government, how Chelsea was working there as a spy, and how their sister found the prison address and created the diversion that helped them escape.

"This is our Chelsea you're talking about?"

"Yes." Dylan smiled at his brother's disbelief. "She's not a Christian yet. But she's seen what the other side is doing, and she's against them."

"Excuse me, my friends," said Baruch, "but yesterday's beating and tonight's escape has taken a toll on me. I feel the need to sleep. "

"How badly did they beat you?" asked Dylan.

"I am sore all over, but I will recover. Later, I must read this Christian Bible of yours and learn how it is that God has done such miracles through you, Dylan, and especially you, Margot."

"Wait." Margot reached into her backpack and handed Luc's Bible over the seat to him. "I brought this along for you. Keep it as a gift. Read it when you're better."

He thanked her, and as the car ate up the kilometers, Baruch and Caleb slept.

While Dylan drove, he thought about what Baruch had said. In freeing Caleb, Baruch, and the others, he and Margot had performed a nearly impossible feat. Could they have done this without divine help? No. God had guided them through Margot's paintings and led them to the cavern. But who, exactly, was this Baruch? And why was his fate entwined with theirs?

As the sun broke over verdant vine-covered hills, he pulled into the lot below the bishop's villa. It was seven thirty in the morning, and the bishop, an early riser, left his coffee on the patio to greet them.

"Dylan and Margot, I am so glad you have returned." Emilio clapped and beamed. "And here is Caleb and a friend—so your venture succeeded! Come in. Come in. My house is your house."

But when Emilio saw how badly Baruch had been injured, he winced. "But what has happened to your friend? What can I do for you?"

"Breakfast!" said Caleb. "We'll tell you all about it over breakfast."

* * *

WHILE EMILIO SERVED THEM BREAD, butter, jam, hard-boiled eggs, and coffee, Dylan told him everything. Afterward, there were showers, and the bishop's mansion provided each with their own room, clean sheets, and soft pillows.

An exhausted Dylan slept until late afternoon. When he woke and met the others also coming downstairs, he found Baruch already there. But his face—indeed, his whole being—was different.

Dylan rubbed his eyes and stared at the man. In some profound way, he had changed.

"He never slept." In the corner, Emilio waved toward Baruch. "He spent all day sitting here, immersed in that Bible. You should have seen what happened to him earlier. Look closely. My friends, it is a miracle!"

Dylan gazed and realization hit him. Where was the ugly bruise on Baruch's forehead? And the welts on his arms? And his swollen lip and eye? His skin was also clear, and his eyes were bright. "You're better . . ."

"I have never felt better in my life." Beaming, Baruch spread his arms wide.

"What happened?" Caleb and Margot spoke almost at once.

"My friends"—a smile was in his voice—"I could not sleep. Instead, I asked Emilio to show me Margot's paintings. When I saw them, I was astonished, amazed, overwhelmed. And I realized how powerfully God's hand has touched her. Since yesterday, after Caleb pointed it out, I have also been reflecting on Isaiah chapter fifty-three. Then I opened your Christian Bible. I read Matthew and John, and the person of Jesus came alive for me. Then I read First and Second Thessalonians. Then Revelation. I read other chapters, and then I prayed." His fingertips caressed Luc's book.

"What I did not understand before has now been made clear. I have been wrong, oh, so wrong. We have all been wrong. The Jesus of this book is the true Christ, the only Christ. He, alone, was God's Son sent to earth, and to our shame, we Jews did not recognize him."

The silence in the room was broken only by the song of a thrush that had settled on the windowsill, now cocking its head toward them.

For a moment, a cloud passed over Baruch's forehead. Then his eyes again lit up.

"The knowledge of that truth roared through me like a mighty wind, and in that instant, Christ, who is truly Lord, healed me." Again, he raised his arms. "You see, don't you?"

From somewhere down the hall, a grandfather clock began tolling. The thrush flapped its wings, but then, as if it, too, were listening, remained at the sill.

"Then a second realization hit me. It is clear that the great God of Hosts, the one who created the world, has chosen you, Margot, and you, Dylan, and even you, Caleb, to fulfill certain tasks in this, the time of the end. He has also chosen your sister, Chelsea, though you say she does not yet know him. He has also chosen you, Emilio, for you gave us sanctuary. Each of you were given a part. And he has also chosen me."

Dylan sucked in air, his heart beating faster. This was what he had pondered on the drive from Rome, but now this man Baruch, the one to whom God had linked their destinies, was stating the conclusion with far more clarity.

"What I did not tell you earlier, Caleb, was that I belong to a secret organization of Jews called the Great Assembly. We started it some years ago after God spoke to me. He commanded me to prepare for some great task. We knew not what it was, only that it was important.

"I mentioned before that I led a group of twenty-three. That's not the entire truth, for we are loath to reveal our real nature. I do lead eleven other men—that part is true. But they, in turn, each head a group from one of the twelve tribes of Israel. I, myself, lead men from the tribe of Judah. Within my tribe and under me are twelve more leaders. And under each of them, if you count all the subordinate leaders, are approximately one thousand souls."

Dylan gasped, realizing where this was going.

"Last year," continued Baruch, "we conducted a census. To our great surprise, the number from the tribe of Judah came to exactly twelve thousand, as did the count of each of the other tribes. The total number of the Great Assembly thus came to exactly one hundred forty-four thousand men. We thought it odd that the counts would arrive at such exact, biblical numbers, for we had not planned it that way. But today, as I read your Christian Bible, it became clear God has planned this all along." He smiled at each of them in turn.

"Yes, my friends, he has set before us a great mission, and it is to bring the truth of Jesus, the One who is the true Christ, to all the world in the coming time of great trial. Just this morning, even as the Holy Spirit healed me, he clarified the reason I was chosen—to reach all of the Great Assembly with the truth of Jesus and prepare them for our true task. When the time comes, God will seal and protect us. Our time is near, but not yet. It will come only after God's judgment of wars, famines, and plagues falls upon the earth. Until then, we must prepare, hide, and make ready."

He stepped forward and kissed Margot's, Caleb's, and finally, Dylan's hands.

"No, no, you mustn't," Dylan protested.

"But don't you see? You, too, are chosen instruments, meant to be here, doing what you are doing in this time of the end. My goal and yours is to bring the truth and the salvation of Christ to willing and open hearts. We are now at war with Satan and the Antichrist, and our task is to deny those dark powers all the perishing souls we can." Beaming, Baruch spread his arms wide. "Believe it, for you, too, are an integral part of God's plan."

Dylan's heart soared. Hope for the future, like morning sunlight bursting through clear mountain air, spread out from Baruch, filling every corner of the room.

Dylan raised hands to his mouth, and tears filled his eyes. He'd asked to stay behind to save a mere handful—his brother, his sister, and maybe Margot. He'd also wanted to serve God, to make his life mean something. And now it appeared that—along with Margot and Caleb and even Chelsea—he had unwittingly played a far greater part in God's plan. The Holy Spirit had spoken to them through Margot's paintings, and they had listened. Even though they hadn't understood where it would lead, they were helping to bring future salvation to millions of lost souls.

Beside him, Margot, this woman to whom his destiny was also inextricably linked, beamed and glowed. Tears of happiness also filled her eyes.

Her happiness completed his. Yes, his life was now complete.

Unless . . . did God have more plans for them?

* * *

REVELATION 7:1–8 (HCSB): *AFTER THIS I saw four angels standing at the four corners of the earth, restraining the four winds of the earth so that no wind could blow on the earth or on the sea or on any tree. Then I saw another angel, who had the seal of the living God rise up from the east. He cried out in a loud voice to the four angels who were empowered to harm the earth and the sea: "Don't harm the earth or the sea or the trees until we seal the slaves of our God on their foreheads." And I heard the number of those who were sealed: 144,000 sealed from every tribe of the Israelites:*

12,000 sealed from the tribe of Judah,
12,000 from the tribe of Reuben,
12,000 from the tribe of Gad,
12,000 from the tribe of Asher,
12,000 from the tribe of Naphtali,
12,000 from the tribe of Manasseh,
12,000 from the tribe of Simeon,
12,000 from the tribe of Levi,
12,000 from the tribe of Issachar,
12,000 from the tribe of Zebulun,
12,000 from the tribe of Joseph,
12,000 sealed from the tribe of Benjamin.

AUTHOR'S NOTES

Would God Ever Leave Anyone Behind?

In this novel, after the archbishop sees Margot Durand's paintings, he declares them works of Satan, after which she apparently rejects God and is left behind. Later, she returns to belief. Dylan Turner also prays to be left behind. Some might now argue that all in the body of Christ are one, and that, come the Rapture, all will be taken up to Heaven, leaving none behind. The question is whether God would allow this if it serves his purposes. Using literary license, I have assumed the answer to that question is yes.

Would the Rapture Take the Children of Unbelievers?

The first view on this subject is that only the children of believers below the age of decision will be raptured. When one considers that God placed the responsibility for children in the hands of their parents, this makes sense. After the age when a child can decide for himself whether or not to follow Jesus, the responsibility rests upon the individual.

The second view is that all children before the age of decision—even the children of unbelievers—will be raptured. We see some support for this in Matthew 24:15a, 19 (NLT) where Jesus says: "The day is coming when you will see what Daniel the prophet spoke about . . . How terrible it will be for pregnant women and for nursing mothers in those days."

We know that God is a God of mercy and justice and that Jesus loves the little children. So it also makes sense that, since God is a God of mercy, he would spare those not yet capable of making a decision, even if they came from a family of unbelievers. And that is the choice I have made in this book.

How Do We Prepare For The End?

No one knows the day or the hour, but given that the major signs have been fulfilled, I believe we are rapidly approaching the end of this age.

If you are not a believer, how do you prepare? My advice is the same as Uri Baranov's: Get a Bible, start reading in Matthew and pray for your unbelief. And then—and this is crucial—find a Bible-based local church that believes in Jesus as the only way to salvation and join it.

For those who are believers, consider this: One way or another, our time on this earth will end. Either it will come through the Rapture of the Church. Or it will come through death. But it *will* come.

Either way, our preparation is the same. Once we leave this life, we will live for all eternity in the blessed presence of Jesus and among those making up his Church in the here and now. What is his Church? It's our brothers and sisters in Christ, those we see on Sundays, during the week in small group meetings, and in Bible studies. I hope you are taking part. It also includes every person who has ever lived who, before Christ, put their trust in God's promises and, after Jesus's coming, who believed in and followed him.

Think about it. We will be together for all eternity. We will all be glorified, of course—given new, youthful bodies incapable of sin. We will have put behind us all death and crying and sorrow and pain. You and I and every other Christian brother and sister will live together in Heaven through "time without end".

If that's the case, we must prepare now. If it's the church body with whom we will spend forever, then we need to engage with that body today.

We should attend church regularly, taking part in both large and small group gatherings. We should tithe and even go beyond the tithe. We should serve in small ways and large, but most importantly we should *engage*. For when we leave this life, we will take with us only what we have sent on ahead—whatever we have done for or given to the Kingdom of God. The rest stays behind. The rest is burned up.

We also need to know Jesus, and to do that, we need to read the Bible regularly and discuss what we find with fellow believers. The Bible is God's revelation to mankind, and within its pages, we find his will for our lives and his plan for the world. There, too, is revealed the nature of God, manifested so clearly in the person of Christ. There also do we discover Jesus's incredible love for us.

We are also charged with taking the message of Jesus's life, death, and resurrection to our neighborhoods, workplaces, and through our support of missions, to the ends of the earth. For how can we rest knowing the fate that awaits unbelievers?

Staying Strong In An Increasingly Evil Culture

To stay strong in our faith, strong in the face of trial, we also need to strengthen the family. God gave us the family—one man and one woman, united in marriage—as the bedrock institution of civilization. It is our refuge in a storm of culture run amuck, our base of resistance against the twisted, immoral ideologies of the world. Indeed, the Church is a family of families. And because of that, those allied with evil seek to marginalize and destroy it.

So how do we live in the world outside the church, in a world increasingly embracing insanity, declaring that evil is good and good is evil? In Colossians 2:8, the apostle Paul warns us: "Be careful that no one takes you captive through philosophy and empty deceit based on human tradition, based on the elemental forces of the world, and not based on Christ."

In today's era, woke ideology—political correctness run amuck—is sweeping the world. But that humanistic philosophy—or pseudo-theology?—is based on atheist Marxism. It's opposed in every way to the teachings of Christ and the apostles. The final goal of the woke is one-party rule, followed by a totalitarian socialist state. But totalitarianism must, of necessity, control the thoughts and minds of its subjects. It cannot tolerate any opposing views. It must crush all opposition. We see this in the cancel culture.

As a survivor of the Soviet Union, the great novelist Alexander Solzhenitsyn neatly summarized Paul's warning, and in the process, he gave us a command for living under the coming woke totalitarianism. "Live not by lies," he said. Hold onto the truth, never agreeing to the lies of evil ideologies. For those who give in—who, knowing they are false, mouth the words that good is evil and evil is good—will be changed. Little by little, they will shave off pieces of their integrity, losing their convictions of what is right and wrong.

In the end, they will lose their souls. Instead, we must hold fast to the truth of the Bible, to the words of Jesus and the apostles. Never give assent to the egregious falsehoods espoused by a perverse, twisted, and atheistic culture.

Whether we die next week, whether the Rapture comes today, tomorrow, or ten years from now, this, then, is how we prepare for the end—engaging with the church, focusing on Jesus, and looking ahead to the life to come. And by taking refuge in the family and holding fast to biblical truth, no matter what insanity the culture tries to make us believe.

FURTHER INFORMATION

For further information on spiritual, cultural, and specific topics addressed by this book, please follow this link: www.MarkFisherAuthor.com/Notes

RECOMMENDED READING

To learn more about the end times, the book of Revelation, Near-Death Experiences, and some food for thought, I recommend the following books:

REVELATION AND THE END TIMES

- *101 Answers to The Most Asked Questions About the End Times*, by Mark Hitchcock
- *101 Answers to Questions About the Book of Revelation*, by Mark Hitchcock
- *Because the Time Is Near* (John MacArthur Explains the Book of Revelation), by John MacArthur

NEAR-DEATH EXPERIENCES

- *Imagine Heaven*: Near-Death Experiences, God's Promises, and the Exhilarating Future That Awaits You, by John Burke
- *One Minute After You Die*, by Erwin W. Lutzer

BOOKS ADDRESSING TODAY'S ENVIRONMENT OF WOKEISM

- *Live Not By Lies:* A Manual for Christian Dissidents, by Rod Dreher
- *When A Nation Forgets God*, by Erwin W. Lutzer
- *Canceling Christianity:* How the Left Silences Churches, Dismantles the Constitution, and Divides Our Culture, by David Fiorazo

POWERFUL ARGUMENTS FOR CHRISTIANITY

- *I Don't Have Enough Faith To Be An Atheist*, by Norman Geisler & Frank Turek
- *Mere Christianity*, by C.S. Lewis

SCRIPTURE REFERENCES

- Chapter 1: The coming of the man of lawlessness—2 Thessalonians 2:3 (NLT)
- Chapter 2: The end will be a time of visions and prophecies—Joel 2:28, 31 (HCSB)
- Chapter 3: Living a life that follows Christ, without the greed and the sins of unbelievers—Ephesians 5:1–8 (NLT)
- Chapter 5: Beware of worldly human philosophy—Colossians 2:8 (HCSB)
- Chapter 7: God's wrath can come via earthquakes—Nahum 1:5–6 (NLT)
- Chapter 8: As we approach the end, knowledge of the end times will increase—Daniel 12:4 (NLT)
- Chapter 9: In the last days, people will love themselves and their money, not God—2 Timothy 3:1–2 (NLT)
- Chapter 11: In the end times, lawlessness will multiply—Matthew 24:12 (HCSB)
- Chapter 12:
  - In the end times, some will follow the teachings of demons—1 Timothy 4:1 (HCSB)
  - Transvestism and transgenderism are detestable to God—Deuteronomy 22:5 (HCSB)
  - Those whose lifestyles center on homosexuality and lustful pleasures will not inherit the Kingdom of God—1 Corinthians 6:9–10 (NLT)
- Chapter 13: Before the end there will be famines, wars, and earthquakes—Matthew 24:6–7 (NLT)
- Chapter 14:
  - Thousands are waiting for the day of decision—Joel 3:14 (NLT)
  - A description of the throne room—Isaiah 6:1–6; Ezekiel 1

- Chapter 15: Creating works on earth that will last into eternity—1 Corinthians 3:11–15 (HCSB)
- Chapter 18: The first trumpet call bringing on the Rapture of the Church—1 Thessalonians 4:16–17 (NLT)
- Chapter 19: The Rapture of the Church—1 Corinthians 15:51–52 (HCSB)
- Chapter 20: When the end comes, it will come without warning. Only some will be taken—Matthew 24:37–41 (HCSB)
- Chapter 21:
  - In the last days, people will listen to whatever their itching ears want to hear—2 Timothy 4:3
  - When those who know the truth about God make up foolish ideas about who he is, he abandons them to their sins, especially sexual sin—Romans 1:24–32 (NLT)
- Chapter 22: Woe to those calling evil good and good evil—Isaiah 5:20 (HCSB)
- Chapter 25: At the trumpet sound, the living will be transformed at the Rapture—1 Corinthians 15:54b (HCSB)
- Chapter 30: The wonders awaiting us in Heaven—1 Corinthians 2:9 (NLT)
- Chapter 31: For those who love God, all things work together for good—Romans 8:28 (HCSB)
- Chapter 35: The opening of the first seal and the coming of the Antichrist—Revelation 6:1–2 (HCSB)
- Chapter 36: When the restrainer is removed, the man of lawlessness will be revealed—2 Thessalonians 2:6–8 (HCSB)
- Chapter 37: The Antichrist will make a peace treaty with Israel but break it after three and one-half years—Daniel 9:27 (NLT)
- Chapter 40: Believers will cast out demons in Jesus's name—Mark 16:17 (NLT)
- Chapter 41: True worship must be in spirit and in truth—John 4:24 (NLT)
- Chapter 42: The number of the Antichrist's name is 666—Revelation 13:18 (NLT)

- Chapter 44: During his reign, the Antichrist will magnify himself above all others and be successful. He will reward his followers—Daniel 11:36, 39b (HCSB)
- Chapter 48: When the Third Temple is built, the Jewish Messiah will come—Jeremiah 33:14–18 (NLT)
- Chapter 51: Regarding demon worship—Deuteronomy 32:17 (NLT)
- Chapter 54: The tools for fighting spiritual warfare—Ephesians 6:10–17 (NLT)
- Chapter 58: With intrigue and insolence, the Antichrist will rise to power—Daniel 8:23 (HCSB)
- Chapter 63: In the seventh or eighth century BC, the prophet Isaiah describes the coming of Christ, the man of sorrows—Isaiah 53.
- Chapter 65: The role of the 144,000 in bringing many to Christ during the Tribulation—Revelation 7:1–8 (HCSB)

MARK'S BOOKS

Christian Historical Fiction:

- *The Bonfires Of Beltane*: Following St. Patrick Across Ancient, Celtic Ireland
- *The Medallion*: An Epic Quest In A.D. 486
- *The Slaves Of Autumn*: A Tale Of Stolen Love In Ancient, Celtic Ireland

General Market Historical Fiction:

- *Death Of The Master Builder*: Love, Envy, and the Struggle to Raise the Greatest Cathedral of the Italian Renaissance
- *The Sun Shines Even In Winter*: A Novel of Invasion and Espionage in World War I (coming soon)

Days of the Apocalypse, a series of Christian end-times thrillers:

- Book 1: *The Day the End Began*
- Book 2: *Days of War and Famine* (planned)
- Book 3: *Last Days of the End* (planned)

To learn more about Mark's books, including his young adult fantasy trilogy, please visit: www.MarkFisherAuthor.com

Made in United States
Troutdale, OR
08/04/2023

11824795R00204